. . . made a slight but mocking bow. *So deep emotions still stir within you. Fret not, for soon you will be reunited with your precious master. It is the least I can do for one who has served me so excellently.*

Idaria struggled to move, but again to no avail. Her fury at herself surged; she had unwittingly helped manipulate Golgren for that beast. If not for her—

If not for you, there would have been other ways, my Idaria. You were simply the most desired tool, and your manipulation was merely the culmination of a lifetime— his lifetime! You still do not understand it, do you?

More and more of the ghastly, living corpses collected around the shrouded figure. They clearly hung on his every word, as if those words were what gave them their mockery of existence.

He gestured at the vision, which revealed only the empty mountainside. *There is nothing about the half-breed that is not the result of my manipulation!* the shadowed form declared with more vehemence and triumph. *From even before birth, from before his very conception, he was mine! How many elf and ogre breedings do you know of, my Idaria? How many?*

She knew of only one, of course, only Golgren.

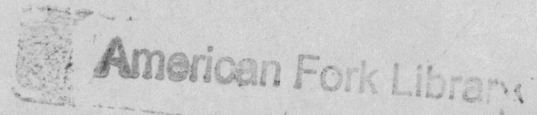

THE GARGOYLE KING

OGRE TITANS

The ambitious Golgren leads the ogre race,
by the gift of a pact with the Ogre Titans,
but they, led by their ruling council, the Black Talon,
have plans of their own.

The Black Talon

The Fire Rose

The Gargoyle King

THE MINOTAUR WARS

The legitimate heir to the stolen throne must overcome his own demons and lead an army of outcasts
into the heart of the empire, and at stake is only the
most expansionist empire Krynn has ever seen.

Night of Blood

Tides of Blood

Empire of Blood

THE GARGOYLE KING

OGRE TITANS ◆ VOLUME THREE

RICHARD A. KNAAK

The Ogre Titans, Volume Three

THE GARGOYLE KING

©2009 Wizards of the Coast LLC

Published by Wizards of the Coast LLC

DRAGONLANCE, DUNGEONS & DRAGONS, WIZARDS OF THE COAST, and their respective logos are trademarks of Wizards of the Coast LLC in the U.S.A. and other countries.

Printed in the U.S.A.

Cover art by Duane O. Myers
First Printing: December 2009

9 8 7 6 5 4 3 2 1

ISBN: 978-0-7869-5238-0
620-24200000-001-EN

U.S., CANADA,
ASIA, PACIFIC, & LATIN AMERICA
Wizards of the Coast LLC
P.O. Box 707
Renton, WA 98057-0707
+1-800-324-6496

EUROPEAN HEADQUARTERS
Hasbro UK Ltd
Caswell Way
Newport, Gwent NP9 0YH
GREAT BRITAIN
Save this address for your records.

Visit our web site at www.wizards.com

With many thanks to the readers everywhere for making 25 great years of adventuring around Krynn possible!

Here's to hoping for many more adventures to come!

Prologue

THE GOLDEN CITY

The sprawling city set in the midst of the ogre kingdom of Kern glistened in the burning sun. The surrounding wall was seamless, perfect, and from a distance appeared made of pure gold. Jagged battlements shaped like upturned claws topped the wall. Great towers rose from the wall's four corners, gleaming spears that thrust ten stories high. On every floor of each tower, all four sides of the building had windows shaped like half moons.

Etched into every edge of the vast wall and its accompanying towers was a repeating pattern, a single symbol: the talons of some great raptor.

At the gates of the city, fabulous, golden doors loomed over all who would enter. On them was emblazoned not the talons, but a handsome, majestic countenance that made the beauty of the elf races pale in comparison. The strong, perfect jaw; the flowing, dark hair; the proud nose; and commanding gaze . . . they appeared to be the markings of a great king. Yet the face was not that of any ogre, as the people of the continent of Ansalon knew them; for that matter, not any race on the face of all the world of Krynn would have recognized the bestial people. Furthermore, the perfection of the face was marred by two things: the great eyes without pupils and the arrogance of the expression. It was a being who knew itself to be a god.

For all the splendor of the wall and towers, they gave but a hint of the opulence within. Vast, elegant buildings with high-arched doors and rounded roofs lined the shining, immaculate streets. It was as if it were a city of princes—nay, *emperors.* No edifice was exactly alike any other, yet all spoke of riches, of power, of glory. Intricate patterns representing the stars and the landscape decorated some; mystic runes, others. Great statues of fantastic beasts, especially griffons, dotted the city, all so lifelike they appeared ready to pounce upon those who might pass by. Massive fountains with elaborate scrollwork unleashed torrents of water in a place known for its harsh, dry surroundings. Magnificent gems of every color artfully decorated most buildings, fountains, and statuary, a king's ransom's worth on each.

All was perfection and above many of the tallest structures rose the symbol of those responsible for creating that perfection. The raptor's talons filled the center of hundreds of huge, fluttering banners—also golden, save for the talon itself, which was utterly black. That was the symbol of the Titans, the gargantuan ogre sorcerers who stood some fifteen feet tall . . . half again the height of most regular ogres. It was the face of their leader that covered the gates. He had been foremost among those responsible for the transformation of what

2

had once been a half-crumbling, ancient ruin of a once-mighty capital, creating something new and even more glorious than its founders had imagined.

And lest any forget that Safrag was not only leader of the Titans, but the one who commanded the power that had resurrected the capital, one had only to gaze upon the focal point of his great achievement: the grand palace. Not in the least did the palace resemble the old marble-and-stone edifice from which the rulers of the current inhabitants' ancestors—the High Ogres—had surveyed their domain. Nay, what stood there was a gargantuan place of sharp, glittering angles and five magnificent towers topped by arched roofs. Though it was in width and depth equal to its predecessor, that was the only similarity. Indeed, the new structure stood twice the height and was not made of marble, but rather of some sleek material that shone brighter than a legion of newly armored warriors at high sun. It was also unique for being the only building not golden in color. Instead, the palace was of a tint best and yet poorly described as greenish blue, a rare, peculiar hue, as if such a mix had been created by the hand of a god.

Rising up at the front were six awesome columns, each shaped into the semblance of the Titan leader. No single column was like another, for in the first pose Safrag stood as a warrior with a sword; in the second, a learned teacher holding a staff, and so on. Though whether stern or wise, the Titan's demeanor resembled that of a father tending his small children.

Two massive bronze doors, also unique in the city of gold, marked the entrance. The talon symbol was etched upon each. Though the Titans had their own sanctum far from the capital, that had been the place from which they ruled back when the city was known as Garantha. Henceforth it would be called, in the musical tongue of the Titans, Dai Ushran, and as explained in Safrag's proclamation, the phrase literally meant "the Golden City."

Only three days had passed since the Titan leader had renamed Garantha. And only three days had gone by since he had used the power of the magical Fire Rose to completely transform the city in less than a single minute's time.

The inhabitants of Dai Ushran still marveled at the astounding feat. The excitement was palpable, more so because they had been promised something else even more spectacular than what Safrag had achieved: the transformation of the ogre race itself.

The moment was imminent. The ogres breathlessly awaited the word to gather. The Titans presented power and beauty on a scale that the grotesque, tusked giants had never dreamed would be theirs to possess or behold. Since the downfall of their ancestors, the ogres had lived in squalor, sometimes pretending to aspire to their former greatness, but always looking more comical than noble. Even those of the upper castes, who regularly donned robes stolen from the elves or copied by the best ogre weavers, looked more like animals dressed for sport.

For a time there had come one among them, a singular half-breed, who had offered some hope, some imitation of their former greatness, by learning lessons from their enemies and training the ogres to be proper soldiers who could win in battle. Golgren of the Severed Hand had been slighter than his fellows but agile and clever of wit. No one remembered such an ogre-elf mix before

Golgren, and most would have assumed, rightly, that such a creature could not exist, much less survive in the wastes of Kern and Blöde. But survive Golgren had, rising up to become Grand Khan of both ogre realms, which he renamed Golthuu, after himself.

But he had made enemies of the Titans, and even those among the population who had been his most ardent followers found it difficult to wish for his return when the sorcerers promised so much more for the future. Yet why did the Titans delay the moment of ecstasy that had been promised? If they could create a new city in a flicker of time, why had they not already begun to lavish the same transformational magic on their people?

It was a question to which several of the Titans themselves desired an answer.

◦━◦◯◦━◦

Three of the Titans approached Morgada first, for they knew that she had Safrag's ear as his apprentice and as perhaps much more. The male Titans were of a kind—tall, handsome, and with the bearing of the gods, some thought. Their flawless skin was of a brilliant blue, and their upswept golden orbs glowed bright. Their ears were long and gracefully pointed, and all three wore their lengthy, midnight-black hair bound in a tail.

They were clad identically in flowing silken robes of dark blue with shimmering hints of crimson. The robes gave the impression of gliding rather than walking. From the right shoulder down to the left side of the waist ran a red sash that ended beneath a golden belt. The left shoulder of each was covered by a decorative armor plate.

5

It was the only piece of armor; the arms themselves were unclad save for a silver band on the right wrist and a crimson one made out of silk on the left.

"He said he would come, and yet again he has not!" snapped the middle of the trio in the musical tongue. As his mouth opened, much of the perfection of his face was lost due to the savage rows of sharklike teeth.

Morgada smiled back at him; the female Titan's teeth were less pronounced but still very sharp. She was as beautiful as they were handsome . . . more so. The most wondrous elf maiden paled before her dark glory. Her raven hair flowed unbound nearly to her waist, and although her garments were almost identical to those worn by the males, they were shaped to fit her lush form well.

"The master delves into the myriad intricacies of the Fire Rose, Kulgrath," she replied with half-veiled eyes in the same tongue. "Time is immaterial where the study of the artifact is involved. You would be wise to be patient."

Kulgrath spread his hands in frustration, displaying the long, ebony nails at the ends of his fingers from which the Titan inner circle, the Black Talon, took its name. Like those of his comrades, they were strong and deadly nails capable of ripping open a throat or disemboweling a foe. Farther back, at the elbow, small, jagged hooks sprouted out of his skin. They, too, were sharp, though of a more ornamental nature. "What does the master need to study? He transformed an entire city with but a whim! He turned Falstoch from an abomination into a Titan again! Surely, he needs no further research into these—"

Though her smile remained, Morgada's voice evidenced a slight chill. "And you would dictate this message to the master?"

6

The pair with Kulgrath drew back a step from him. Sensing their withdrawal, he bowed his head slightly and smiled back at Morgada. "I would never question the wisdom of the master! It's just that we are in the dark; we only seek enlightenment."

"And the Fire Rose to use as *you* desire, yes?"

"I don't deny that I wish to take my turn at commanding it, as Safrag did promise us, but of course when he has deemed the moment proper! We are also concerned for him as well, for we all know the legends of the Fire Rose and its dangers. Even the master should beware of those, Morgada."

"The master—"

The ground trembled. Kulgrath and his companions instinctively reached for support. Only Morgada stood in place, oddly amused. The ogre lands were known for their tremors, some of which had tortured and ripped apart the capital in ancient times. Yet she only smiled in the face of potential destruction.

The walls suddenly rushed away from one another. Great, fluted columns shot from the floor, rising to meet a ceiling abruptly three stories high. The floor itself, once white marble, bore a bluish tint akin to the outside walls.

Striding along as if all was still and not in chaos, Morgada moved toward a rounded window that had just opened in the wall near to her. The male Titans stumbled after, clutching at whatever was available to them, including each other's arms.

And through the window, they saw that not only had their surroundings changed again, not only had the palace once more shifted form, but all of Dai Ushran had been transformed anew. The outer wall had blocky, square projections thrusting outward at the top. The towers were taller and broader and three points crowned each, with the face of Safrag molded into the sides.

A great, golden hill arose in the north quarter, and atop it stood a triangular temple with shining columns that arched skyward. Like the towers, it had a three-pointed roof. The temple was nearly the height of the palace and had a winding path composed of something like glittering diamonds running down the new hill.

As the city quieted, ogres poured from their dwellings into the streets. There was panic, for even their own homes had not gone unchanged. They sported designs akin to the towers and the temple, and the face of Safrag could be found peering out from hundreds of citizens' walls.

"What—what is he doing?" Kulgrath gasped, eyes wide in awe.

"It would seem that he's changed his mind about some of his earlier designs," Morgada sang.

" 'Changed' . . . this is the third time now in days . . . and the most extravagant!" Kulgrath peered at one nearby visage, and his golden orbs could not hide their jealousy. "Most extravagant . . ."

"I was about to return to the master when I sensed your call. If you like, I shall extend your concerns to him."

The male Titan anxiously shook his head. "There's no need, Morgada, no need."

Bowing to them—displaying well some of the physical attributes that Kulgrath and others believed the true reason for her trusted place beside the master—Morgada purred, "As you like."

Ebony flames burst up from the floor and engulfed

her. The female sorcerer vanished, her satisfied smile somehow lingering a moment longer.

"This was a foolish act," one of the other Titans muttered. "She will tell Safrag of our complaints, and he will use the Fire Rose on *us* next!"

"He dares not," retorted Kulgrath. "The Titans are one! It's that female who causes any problems among us. Safrag will see that once we speak with him! He will listen to reason."

"Yes," returned the other, not sounding at all convinced. "We must keep telling ourselves that, mustn't we?"

Kulgrath did not answer, saying no more, instead looking out the window again at the nearest of the huge, decorative faces and frowning.

❦

Slowly—ever so slowly—the panic of the ogres of Dai Ushran was replaced first with calm then with renewed anticipation. The latest transformation of their city was surely a sign that the Titan leader was merely readying things for the race's own fantastic change. He was merely making the capital worthy of their future. Soon, so very soon, he would no doubt appear at the palace steps and begin their metamorphosis from tusked, hairy brutes to beings more powerful than even their ancestors had been.

The many ogres milled around for some time, waiting. However, as more time passed and nothing happened, gradually the crowds filtered back into their altered dwellings. Safrag would summon them when it was time. Surely, he would.

But a shrouded figure flanked by four gargoyles had observed all that from the mountains beyond the capital and did not share their belief. With long, white, oval orbs—the only part of the face not hidden by either the deep gray and black hood atop his head or the tight, golden cloth wrapped across everything below those deathly eyes—the figure had avidly surveyed the new transformation. It chuckled, giving a hint of a masculine identity but nothing more than a hint.

The gargoyles reacted to the chuckle with low, staccato grunts that were their kind's sign of amusement. Nearly as tall as a human when standing straight, they were twice as wide and all muscle. Their musky scent was strong but went unnoticed by their master. They were gray of varying shades, with huge, leathery wings that opened and closed at times as they sought to disperse some of the heat constantly building up due to the oppressive sun.

Their master loomed over them, taller than a human, shorter than an ogre. His shadowy form was thin, and the hands that suddenly stretched out from the voluminous folds of the sleeves were utterly white and all but fleshless. The dark garment in which the gargoyles' lord was clad hung to the ground and almost seemed to cloak nothing but air.

So very perfect . . . came a rasping voice that was not audible, but rather reverberated in the heads of the winged creatures. *All the puppets play their roles. Soon, very soon, the long wait will be over.*

With another chuckle, the shrouded figure simply faded away. The gargoyles bent their heads low then took to the air.

And far below, Dai Ushran suddenly trembled again. The great wall shimmered. The towers spread wide, and their crowns grew rounded.

Through the power of the Fire Rose, the Titan leader, Safrag, molded the capital to his *latest* whim.

I

In the Shadow of the Gargoyle King

Golgren clutched at the harsh, black rock with his lone hand, climbing as nimbly as most others would with two appendages. The re-creation of his right hand through the power of the Fire Rose had not lasted long enough for him to forget the training he had gone through to survive with just the left. The half-breed still had questions regarding Sarth's reasons for removing the new limb, the ancient ogre shaman having uttered that "to possess is not to own" and that "the gifts of gods must always be questioned . . . to see if they are gifts at all."

He had even more questions concerning the withered figure. They included not only Sarth's unexpected appearance in the middle of those forsaken mountains near the Vale of Vipers—far southeast of the capital—but also his equally mysterious vanishing after freeing Golgren and the healing of the half-breed's foul stab wound.

There was far more to the shaman than Golgren had ever suspected, but Sarth was not a worry. Thus far, he had shown himself to be an ally.

The half-ogre bared his teeth at the thought of the fate intended for him by Safrag. After their struggle for the Fire Rose, the Titan leader had left him encased in some crystalline substance so Golgren would become a monument to his own failure. If not for Sarth, again, it was likely that Golgren would have fulfilled that role quite permanently.

Shadows from a greater mountain covered Golgren as he reached the top of the low peak he had been ascending for most of the day. The relative coolness the shadows offered did not soothe the half-breed. His efforts thus far had yielded too little. Golgren bared his teeth, an act that evoked the brutish side of his background even more than usual, despite the fact that he had long before honed his tusks down to nearly invisible nubs.

Still, no one would have mistaken him for a true ogre, not when he stood only seven feet tall as compared to the average nine feet, and also, he was far slimmer of build. Golgren looked more like the elves of Silvanost, from which his mother had sprung. Yet despite a rough handsomeness and features that also inclined toward that other race, no elf would have accepted him as one of their own, especially as he was one of those most instrumental in the fall of the elven realm.

Golgren impatiently brushed back the thick, sweat-drenched mane of dark hair that he generally kept washed and brushed to conform with the elf side of his lineage. With almond-shaped eyes of a penetrating emerald-green, the deposed Grand Khan peered down into the valley ahead, surveying the dark rock, the few withered weeds, the parched landscape. A slight grunt was the only sound that gave hint to his frustrations.

He had seen that valley before. He had traversed it only the day before.

Golgren was not merely traveling in circles; some magical force was purposely turning him away from his ultimate goal.

He stood there, considering his choices. A bedraggled ruler, he was. Gone was his shiny armor. Only the dusty kilt with the metal tips remained. His sandals were worn, almost useless. He was naked from the waist up, the remnants of his garments long discarded. For weapons, he had only his hand and his wits. They had served him well in the past, and they would serve him well again if he ever managed to reach his destination.

Exactly what his destination was, Golgren could not say. He knew only two things. The gargoyles had descended to that place ahead of him, the gargoyles who had watched and harassed him for months. Their mysterious master was surely there, waiting. Even more than the Titans, Golgren desired a confrontation with the shadowy figure.

And the second thing he knew and knew well was that Idaria would also be there.

She was an elf slave, his personal slave. She obeyed his commands and served him as no other could or would. Yet she was an elf and, thus, expendable. There had been others before her. They had proven expendable. Idaria Oakborn was no different.

Yet she was as much the reason for his determination as anything else.

With nightfall less than two hours away—and the shadows of the higher peaks bringing darkness long before that—Golgren began his descent into the valley. He had survived thus far on small lizards and rodents that he had caught and eaten raw—the trappings of civilization easily tossed aside under the circumstances—but he was almost dying of thirst. He had had only a small trickle of water since the night before. However, if it was the same valley, he knew where he could at least locate *that* water source.

Sure enough, just as the growing shadows enshrouded his surroundings, the half-breed found the tiny spring. Even then, Golgren did not stumble madly toward it. Instead, he approached it with the caution of the predator stalking his prey while wary of other threats as well. He sniffed the air but found only the fresh scent of the spring.

The trickle of water sounded like a rushing river to him. Golgren bent low to drink, his gaze ever searching elsewhere.

The ji-baraki rose up from the ground as if blossoming there. Its rough-hewn, scaly back had enabled it, when lying flat, to blend into the rocky, uneven ridge. The reptile stood on two hind legs designed to enable it to run at swift speeds; the forelegs were wielded as weapons, a pair of paws with long, sharp claws. The long muzzle was also full of daggerlike teeth designed to rip into the tough hides of tasty meals. Ji-baraki ate just about anything that had flesh to it, including carrion.

No ji-baraki was going to pass up the sort of sumptuous meal Golgren offered. Standing nearly as tall as the half-breed, the reptile slashed out with its claws. The attack was a feint, though, designed to distract Golgren from the true threat.

The second ji-baraki lunged from behind the half-breed, snapping at his neck. However, as the toothy maw shot forward, Golgren turned halfway. His right arm wrapped around the long neck of the beast as his left seized the head of his attacker. The fetid breath of the carnivore filled his nostrils.

With a strength that his lithe form belied, he gave the head a twist. The snapping of the ji-baraki's neck echoed through the valley. Saliva and blood dripped over the half-breed's chest.

Golgren threw the already dead reptile forward, using it as a shield against the first. Born battling to survive, the deposed Grand Khan had made a thorough study of his potential enemies, be they beasts or otherwise. There was little that Golgren could thank his ogre father for, but learning the treacherous behavior of the ji-baraki many years past was one of them. There was never just one of the monsters around; they hunted either in mated pairs or in packs, and one always distracted the prey for the other.

Fortunately for Golgren, he faced only a mated pair. In those dank environs, he had calculated that would be the case. The area could not support packs of the ji-baraki, especially with such a large flock of gargoyles also hovering nearby.

The surviving reptile hissed furiously at him as it struggled past its dead mate. Golgren was aware that he could not outrun a ji-baraki. However, escape was not what he had in mind.

He scooped up a rock. The piece was just small enough to fit into his palm. As a weapon, it looked highly inadequate for bashing against the hard skull of a ji-baraki, but that, too, was not what Golgren had in mind.

The second reptile dived for the half-breed. Its mouth opened wide.

Golgren turned on the savage beast and thrust his fingers forward. His timing had to be precise, otherwise he would be without *both* hands.

He jammed the stone into the ji-baraki's maw then pulled his spittle-soaked hand away. The startled reptile shut its yap but too late. Still, the close call left jagged, red cuts along Golgren's wrist and hand.

The ji-baraki hacked and coughed, seeking desperately to dislodge the stone. However, its prey had shoved hard, and the stone was deep in its throat. The reptile rocked back and forth furiously.

Golgren was not willing to rely on the stone alone, though. He observed the ji-baraki for a moment then maneuvered around toward the struggling beast's back.

The half-breed leaped onto the reptile, wrapping his maimed arm just under the ji-baraki's jaw. His lone hand locked onto the ruined limb. Golgren pulled back as hard as he could, using his full weight.

The monstrous reptile's head bent back. It was not enough to break the neck, but the angle made impossible the ji-baraki's attempts to shake loose the stone.

The scaly hunter spun in a circle as it reacted to the new threat. It staggered, the obstruction in its windpipe at last taking its toll.

Claws sought to scrape at Golgren but to no avail. The ji-baraki's upper limbs were not designed to reach that far back.

The toothy beast fell forward. As it landed, it rolled onto its side.

Golgren released his grip. The ji-baraki, too weak to rise, flailed around on the ground, its wild throes almost succeeding in knocking the half-breed over.

Finally exhausted, the reptile could do nothing more

than hack pitiably. Golgren came up behind the head of the creature and quickly grasped it and snapped the neck.

Taking a deep breath, Golgren returned to the water. Without a glance back at the two dead predators, he drank his fill. The presence of the ji-baraki precluded any other fearsome beasts nearby, save perhaps gargoyles.

His thirst finally sated, Golgren stepped back from the spring.

Despite the dark, something caused a glittering reflection in the tiny stream of water.

Golgren looked behind him and saw nothing. Yet the silver glimmer had to have some source. With renewed wariness, the deposed Grand Khan studied the surrounding area again. At the same time, he returned to the nearest of the scaly corpses.

Crouching next to the dead creature, Golgren seized one of the upper limbs. With his gaze kept on his surroundings, the half-breed dug with his one hand at the base of the claws. He ripped and twisted at it, ignoring the blood and flesh on his fingers and the stench of stomach gases escaping from the limp body. Ogres survived in their harsh environs by being willing to stoop to whatever was necessary, and Golgren was no exception.

With one last rip, the talon came free. It was not much of a weapon, but it *was* a weapon.

There was still no hint of the glimmer's source, but Golgren did not assume for a moment that it had been a figment of his imagination. The half-breed was not prone to false imaginings.

With the bloody nail gripped tightly, Golgren moved toward where his instincts impelled him. He sensed nothing but if ji-baraki could blend so well into the shadowed landscape, so, too, could other things, especially those wielding magic.

It could not be one of the Titans. Golgren was fairly certain they still thought he was a living statue. However, it could very well be that the figure he sought—the mysterious lord of the gargoyles—had come hunting for him. Golgren was eager for a confrontation with the lord of the gargoyles on his own terms.

A second silver gleam at the corner of his right eye made him whirl in that direction.

Again, there was nothing and yet . . .

The half-breed frowned. He felt as if he had almost but not quite glimpsed a familiar figure, the Knight of Solamnia named Stefan Rennert.

Golgren clutched his makeshift weapon tighter. Stefan Rennert, assuming that he was alive, would not play games of hide and seek with him. The Solamnic was a man of unshakable honor who had first come to the half-breed as a prisoner; his own party, infiltrating the ogre lands, had met with disaster. If he were there, he would have stood in the open and faced Golgren.

Yet the former Grand Khan could not shake the feeling that it had been the knight whom he had glimpsed. He stepped toward the spot then, still seeing nothing, looked left and right.

And as he turned to the right, he saw a crooked gap between the mountains that he could not recall having seen before.

The half-breed bared his teeth in a humorless smile then strode forward. The gap seemed to spread wider as he entered it, and ahead he saw the darkened outline of a vast, jagged mountain. The mountain spread to each side as Golgren continued forward until it filled his gaze as nothing else had.

Yet it was not the mountain itself that seized his attention as much as something high above on the slope facing him. At first, Golgren was not entirely certain that what he saw was real. It was so much a part of the high, murky peak that he had to focus hard to make out the barest details.

Then he realized he had stumbled upon the sanctum of the gargoyles' master.

The sinister citadel appeared to have been carved from the very rock. Its outward walls still bore the roughness of the mountain's skin. There were two extremely narrow towers, one on each side. The towers were topped by long points that reminded Golgren of great teeth. Something had once been carved across much of the structure, but time had eroded it, and it was no longer legible. As he squinted, the half-breed also noted a lone triangular window on each tower and two side-by-side on the main body.

However, there was no sign of any normal entrance. In fact, Golgren could see no route by which to ascend to the mysterious edifice, which was what he greatly desired.

With renewed anticipation, Golgren wended his way toward the mountain castle. He was not averse to climbing a great height to reach his goal, even with only the one hand. He had conquered far worse. That his adversary likely watched and waited also did not bother the half-breed; the overconfidence of his enemies had more than once played well into Golgren's plans.

A chill wind howled through the area. The only other sound was that of occasional falling rocks. Golgren paid great attention to the latter; avalanches were not uncommon in such places. He had already witnessed one. Golgren also noted that the wind had brought with it a heavy, musky scent that matched that of the gargoyles. If there had been any doubt that that was where they lurked, it was forgotten.

The citadel seemed to rise higher as he drew near the mountain. The slope was harsh, almost completely vertical. It would be possible to climb but at tremendous risk.

There came a long, mournful wail. Golgren glanced up but it was only the wind again. Otherwise, all was still quiet. The citadel remained as dark as the shadows swallowing it. To the naked eye it looked abandoned.

He thrust the claw into his tunic and started to climb.

Despite only one hand, Golgren pulled himself up at a steady pace. Sharp eyes sought out the best handholds and places where he would have good footing. The elf part of his blood made him more nimble, more capable of locating a way up, than a much bulkier ogre could have done.

At one point, his footing faltered. Golgren clutched the rock tightly, certain he was going to drop.

Something seemed to stop and hold him, though, enabling him to readjust. He felt as if strong arms had kept him safe. He also felt as if metal pressed against his body, metal such as the armor a warrior might wear.

Yet the sensation quickly passed, and though Golgren looked over his shoulder, he was not at all surprised to find nothing there. A creature would have needed wings to be close behind him, and there was no sign whatsoever of a single gargoyle.

That in itself was significant. There should have been many, many of the leathery beasts about. Their odor was strong.

The citadel drew within range, though the windows still remained well out of reach. Golgren found a slight ledge and paused to take a breath.

Suddenly he no longer stood alone. A golden-maned figure in dark brown robes and hood materialized next to him. Although human in appearance, the figure stood nearly as tall as the half-breed, and his shoulders were much broader. Indeed, though obviously a spellcaster, the newcomer had the build of a powerful warrior. His features had a leonine touch to them, and at that moment, they were set in an expression of utter frustration.

"Hold tight!" Tyranos immediately roared.

No sooner had he spoken than from above came familiar cries. Gargoyles by the scores shot out of the windows. The shadowed forms were nearly as big as either of the two clinging to the ledge. They beat their leathery wings hard and opened wide their beaked maws as they descended toward the duo.

Tyranos thrust out his hand, in which he held a short staff whose head was a five-sided crystal the size of a fist. There were runes etched on the wood. The crystal glowed silver. The spellcaster muttered.

"No," Golgren whispered.

But it was too late. The pair vanished from the ledge only to reappear at the base of the mountain a moment later.

"What by the Kraken?" Tyranos snorted angrily. "This isn't where I wanted to bring us!"

"Return me to the ledge," Golgren commanded.

The gargoyles, gathered in greater number, were nearly upon them. Tyranos's leonine face turned angrier yet.

"We'll just see if you know all my tricks!" he growled in the direction of the citadel. He quickly drew a circle before the two of them.

A hole opened up. Golgren sought to step away, but a terrible suction seized hold of him. He saw the same was happening to his companion.

Grinning, the wizard roared, "Ha! Here we go!"

A cry rose from just above Golgren. The first of the gargoyles was nearly upon them, its taloned paws grasping for the half-breed.

Golgren stretched his hand toward the gargoyle . . . and was sucked into the hole.

❧❧❧❧❧

Idaria Oakborn witnessed Golgren's vanishing, although she had neither watched from outside the dire citadel nor peered from one of its gaping windows. Instead, the elf slave had stood frozen deep within the confines of the citadel in what had once possibly been a throne room. All around there were cracked and ruined statues of a race whose ancient beauty made her feel shabby and as grotesque as her ogre captors. A crumbling spiral staircase led to one of the twin towers. Ancient reliefs worn away by time or covered with immense webs adorned the walls.

The pungent stench of generations of gargoyles made the dusty air even more stifling.

Then there was the throne itself, a high-backed, stone chair with three jutting points at the top, in which the master of the gargoyle legions that roosted there sat, gazing, like her, at where Golgren had stood before he vanished.

The sphere floating before them stood as tall as an ogre. In it, Idaria watched the gargoyles that had been sent to seize the half-breed, at the very moment that the wizard Tyranos had materialized next to him. The creatures looked both furious and fearful; they knew their master might punish them for their failures and they rightfully dreaded his wrath.

But instead of anger, amusement seemed to fill the gargoyle king's mood, despite the loss of his prey. The low laugh coming from him sent chills through Idaria but not merely for herself. She worried for Golgren; she was an elf fearing for the life of an ogre—or, at least, a half-ogre. She was also concerned for Tyranos—despite the distrust between them—and for his faithful servant, Chasm, a prisoner there like herself.

There had been another prisoner among them, the Solamnic Knight Stefan Rennert, but for him Idaria could only mourn. He lay dead in the citadel, slain foully as he had come to her defense; and then he had been disposed of like so much refuse.

Moving like a wisp of wind, the gaunt figure rose from the time-scarred throne. He appeared more ghost than living, his gray and black robes drifting as if the lower half of his form were nonexistent. A deep hood covered most of his head, and a golden cloth was wrapped tightly across the face, obscuring all but the two long, oval eyes as white as ice . . . or death.

My Idaria . . . came his words in her mind, his tone mocking, as he aped the endearment of Golgren. *Have you enjoyed the little spectacle? Do you draw any conclusions from it?*

She did not reply. During the short time of her captivity, the elf had already seen that her captor had a propensity for twisting matters to satisfy his desires. Whatever her words, they would come back to haunt her somehow.

The hooded form drifted nearer. A pale, almost fleshless hand stretched out to stroke her long, silver tresses. Idaria looked as if she had only recently come into womanhood, but looks deceived where elves were concerned. She was much older in mortal terms, being more than twice the age of the Grand Lord Golgren. That had made her think herself the wiser one when she had entered his life. What a fool she was, Idaria had discovered.

He is thoroughly under your spell . . . continued the gargoyles' master. *And perhaps you a bit under his.*

She said nothing, continuing to stare at the scene of many winged forms desperately scouring the area for the half-breed. However, knowing Tyranos as she did, Idaria was certain that they were far from the vicinity.

And far away from her.

The hand moved from her hair to cup her chin.

So well I chose, finding the perfect ivory skin, the slight nose and red lips and crystalline blue eyes to mask the blind obsession within.

Idaria wanted to pull away, but could only stand there, frozen in the remnants of her low-cut green gown—Golgren's favored garment for his slave—as though she were one of the statues or worse. She had only the ability to speak and move her eyes.

Yet while Idaria had nothing to say to her captor, she spoke volumes to herself, silently berating herself. She had truly been that creature's pawn, falling prey to his guise as a Nerakan officer, a leader among the black knights whose hostile domain bordered part of the ogre realms. So determined had the elf been to free her people, no matter what the cost might be to her, that she had agreed to volunteer for slavery and degradation. In return for acting as a spy for Neraka, she had been promised that the knights would guide the elf slaves to freedom once they gained the advantage to seize the ogre capital.

In retrospect, Idaria had recognized many flaws in the plan, flaws that from the very beginning she should have understood. But the elf knew in hindsight that she had been played, just as Golgren had been played. She had been chosen to make the half-breed malleable for the fiend's plots, and she had performed exactly as her puppet master wished.

She sensed other forms shuffling behind her. One crept into the edge of her vision. The ghoulish figure stood taller than she, though not quite as tall as Golgren. It was clad in the time-ravaged remnants of a once-regal robe whose original color could not be identified because it was so faded. Bits of decorative and possibly magical jewelry still adorned the skeletal hands and the barely shrouded chest. Straggled pieces of hair hung limply from the skull. There was only a veneer of parchment skin covering the face. The scent of death was well upon the cadaverous creature.

Yet it was *not* dead.

Idaria had believed otherwise when she, Stefan Rennert, and Tyranos's gargoyle servant had been attacked. The knight's sword had shattered some, even; but the bones merely pulled back together, as had happened with the army of skeletons—*f'hanos*—that had attacked the ogre capital some time back. She had looked into the eye sockets of those who seized her and realized the awful truth. Those beings did indeed live, if by a definition of that term that Idaria had never before imagined.

Their presence nearby chilled her, although it was not as bad as that of their leader. She had suspicions concerning exactly *what* the strange creatures were, yet she could not fathom how they could have come to such a monstrous state. Clearly, though, her captor had been deeply involved in their creation.

And there were plenty of genuine undead around her too. Several rotting gargoyles kept watch on her from a staircase nearby. Even in death, the creatures were subservient to the masked form. The undead who had attacked Garantha likewise must have been part of the plot of the gargoyles' lord.

Only recently had Idaria come to understand what he was after. Like the Titans and Golgren, he sought the glistening crystalline artifact whose shape and burning energies gave it the name of Fire Rose. He had told the macabre throng of living corpses that, with the help of that artifact, he would "set the world right." What he might do with the Fire Rose, the elf could only guess, and those guesses filled her with great fear. She had witnessed the Fire Rose transform landscapes, change the shapes of creatures, play tricks with time, and much more.

That it had such abilities was not so surprising, though. It was the creation of Sirrion, god of fire and alchemy, and the artifact embodied attributes of both those elements. Legend said that the Fire Rose had been given to the last of the High Ogres when they had pleaded for something to help them save their kind from its descent into the beasts that they were. Yet in the end, its magic had done far more harm than good, and the powerful artifact had been hidden away by a few stalwart survivors, keepers of its secrets but no longer.

As the icy eyes of her worst nightmare stared unblinkingly at her, suddenly Idaria wondered if her captor had been reading every thought she had just formed. The elf forced her gaze away, which only brought another chuckle from the shadowy figure.

The pale hand pulled back into the recesses of his robe. The gargoyles' master looked to the image again, where his pets continued to seek Golgren, continued seeking in vain.

Return, he commanded and the gargoyles suddenly swooped upward. As many as were manifest in the vision, Idaria knew that countless more awaited the master's every command.

But she took heart in the fact that, despite so many weapons at his command, her captor had failed to capture Golgren. There was hope yet.

Do you think so? the hooded form suddenly asked in her head, verifying that he *did* share her thoughts. *All goes as it should, my Idaria.*

He chuckled again, clearly enjoying her distaste at those two words. *My Idaria.* Each time he called her so, it sounded exactly like Golgren. The Grand Khan always spoke of her possessively, but he also gave those words a rare devotion.

The gargoyle king made a slight but mocking bow. *So deep emotions still stir within you. Fret not, for soon you will be reunited with your precious master. It is the least I can do for one who has served me so excellently.*

Idaria struggled to move, but again to no avail. Her fury at herself surged; she had unwittingly helped manipulate Golgren for that beast. If not for her—

If not for you, there would have been other ways, my Idaria. You were simply the most desired tool, and your manipulation was merely the culmination of a lifetime— his lifetime! You still do not understand it, do you?

More and more of the ghastly, living corpses collected around the shrouded figure. They clearly hung on his every word, as if those words were what gave them their mockery of existence.

He gestured at the vision, which revealed only the empty mountainside. *There is nothing about the half-breed that is not the result of my manipulation!* the shadowed form declared with more vehemence and triumph. *From even before birth, from before his very conception, he was mine! How many elf and ogre breedings do you know of, my Idaria? How many?*

She knew of only one, of course, only Golgren.

At that moment, if Idaria could have gasped, she would have shown her amazement.

He chuckled again to hear her thoughts, and even worse, she could sense amusement flowing through his monstrous entourage. There was surely little that gave those strange beings pleasure, but her sudden realization of what should have been obvious, of what she should have guessed long before, did amuse them.

Yes, my Idaria, the gargoyle king verified in her head. *He is mine even more than yours. He has been mine since before his birth. There would be no Grand Khan Golgren but for me, for it is I who made possible the impossible.*

II

PUPPETS OF THE TITANS

Wargroch was having second thoughts. The brawny warrior from the dry hill region of Blöde, the southernmost of the two ogre realms, had journeyed from his distant village to Garantha, capital of the half-breed's land of Kern, to serve the same master attended by his two brothers in times past.

But those two brothers, Nagroch and Belgroch, had died for their loyalty. One, Wargroch had discovered, because he had failed to sufficiently serve his master in a certain task. Golgren himself had struck the blow that killed Nagroch. Belgroch had also perished under mysterious circumstances that had convinced the youngest brother that he, too, had been wronged by his master.

Much of that he had learned from the Titan Safrag, who had come to report to him personally. Safrag had not been leader of the sorcerers then; he was merely second apprentice to the Titans' founder, Dauroth. He spoke of his visit to the Blödian as part of Dauroth's campaign to see justice done—and justice in ogre terms meant the death of the guilty party. Wargroch had easily fallen into line and, being clever for an ogre, had proven himself in the eventual downfall of the half-breed.

Looking back, Wargroch was not so certain that had been the right course.

The grim ogre marched through the palace with anxiety. He was concerned that Safrag might follow another whim and transform the great edifice yet again. Such wholesale alterations strained the courage of even the most hardy warriors.

With a toadlike face and a round, stocky form, Wargroch did not resemble the Kernian ogre guards, who were taller by a few inches, had flatter features, and were more gaunt. For generation upon generation, the two realms had been at war, but the larger guards stood at attention as though Wargroch were Grand Khan himself. Indeed, for a short time, he had been master of Garantha—or rather Dai Ushran—in the name of the Titans and their puppet warlord, Atolgus.

Wargroch could not hold back a disturbed grunt. Like him, Atolgus—once a young nomadic chieftain who had been an ardent supporter of Golgren's—had participated in the half-breed's downfall. However, where Wargroch had harbored a desire for vengeance from the beginning, Atolgus had been seduced into his traitorousness by the female Titan, Morgada. She could make him do anything she desired, including slaughter his unsuspecting family and followers in their sleep as proof of his adoration for her.

For his reward, Atolgus not only served as the sorcerers' hound, but he had already become kindred to them. He did not wield spells yet, but he had grown taller and more handsome in the manner of the Titans. His skin even had a hint of blue to it. All that was part of a gradual change that Safrag appeared to be causing as part of a personal experiment meant more to amuse the Titan leader than because it bore any ultimate purpose.

Such a transformation should not have bothered Wargroch since the Titans had promised that all ogres would become part of the new, beautiful, and powerful race, yet seeing Atolgus and what he was becoming made the Blödian question whether such a future was desirable. Atolgus was a fanatical servant of those who considered themselves above the rest of their kind. Not for a moment did Wargroch believe that would change, ever. The Titans would always be the supreme masters, and with the artifact they wielded, those like Wargroch would exist only to obey.

A savage hiss and a burst of hot breath stirred him from his darkening thoughts. A chained meredrake snapped at the ogre commander as he passed. The brooding guard who controlled the huge lizard eyed Wargroch with less respect than his predecessors.

Wargroch realized he had reached his destination, the throne room. He straightened and stared the guard in the eyes.

After a moment, the other ogre tugged hard on the chain, forcing the massive beast back. The meredrake was sandy brown with hints of green here and there, and the creature was approximately the height of a newborn foal. The adult reptiles tended to grow to the size of a mature horse. Ogres used the beasts for guard duty and battle.

Despite being brought under tight control, the meredrake still made one half-hearted snap at Wargroch.

With teeth already as long as his small finger and claws three times that size, the creature could have ripped him apart with ease. Wargroch was thankful that neither the Titans nor their puppet knew of his ruminations.

He hesitated. Perhaps *that* was why he had been summoned to the warlord.

His expression revealing nothing as he stepped up to the two golden doors that, after the latest transformation, led to the throne room. On each of the arched doors was posed a magnificent, robed figure with arms upraised, wearing an expression like that of some beatific god. It was a Titan, naturally, and Safrag in particular. That was the one constant thus far in the series of unsettling renovations of the capital. Safrag always reminded his people that *he* was the hand that actually held the power. Even the other sorcerers bowed to him.

The guard with the meredrake made no move to open the way for him. With a grunt, Wargroch reached for one of the doors.

Both swung inward with no sign of anyone pulling them from the other side.

The Blödian paused again. Despite all the magic and sorcery he had witnessed, as an ogre, he had an inherent distrust of even minor spells. The fact that such forces were bestowed on a lone guard was an intimidating reminder of the power of the new masters.

Wargroch's misgivings mounted but there was no turning back. During the final takeover of Garantha, he had betrayed and assassinated Khleeg, Golgren's second-in-command, and that alone meant he was bound to the Titans. Khleeg's stunned face, resembling his own since both were Blödians, haunted Wargroch at night.

The chamber was lined by curling columns that

resembled flowing water. The room itself was golden, with crimson accents at the edges. An unearthly glow illuminated Wargroch's surroundings, yet one with no discernible source. Rather than the smell of sweating ogres and hungry meredrakes, the soft scent of some herb wafted through the air. Titans did not tolerate the inherent odors of their people.

Five guards flanked the chamber. The colors and illumination played off their shining breastplates, giving the armed ogres a supernatural aura.

"Welcome, Wargroch," said a voice speaking not Ogre, but perfect Common, the language used among the other, more "civilized" races for most dealings.

He went down on one knee. "Atolgus summons! Wargroch comes!"

Intent as he had been on other things, including the protection of his own hide, the Blödian had not yet looked directly at Atolgus. It was far more important to show homage by gazing at the floor as he bent down onto his knee.

Wargroch looked and gasped.

Atolgus was taller yet, a good foot taller than just the other day. Moreover, his features had become less ogre and more Titan. However, that was not the most startling development.

His eyes were not only gold, but they were without pupils.

There was no trace of the old Atolgus anymore. His face looked like that of some unique elf. He did not yet resemble a Titan, but surely that was only a matter of time.

The Titans' warlord sat upon a throne that resembled a great, taloned hand thrusting out from the floor. The "fingers" were spread out as if grasping at the occupant.

Atolgus grinned. When he did so, his resemblance to an elf faded and the Titan in him grew pronounced, for his teeth were nearly as sharp as those of the sorcerers.

"I am growing more like her every day!" he declared gleefully to the Blödian. "Soon we will be equals."

The former chieftain's obsession with Morgada had grown with his constant physical change. Atolgus, though, could not see what was obvious to Wargroch: that he would never be more than a pawn to her.

So the Blödian said nothing. He desired to keep his head on his shoulders at all costs, and saying anything unpleasant to Atolgus or disagreeing with the warlord would not be prudent.

"The gifts of the Titans are truly astounding," Wargroch finally uttered, for he knew that Atolgus expected his agreement. He knew Common as well as Atolgus did, for both had been granted that ability by the sorcerers. However, in Wargroch's case, the Blödian had already achieved a fair grasp of the language before Safrag's rise to power because it was widely known that Golgren favored those who could better speak the language. Safrag had merely enhanced the warrior's skill.

Common was used instead of Ogre for a different reason than the one initially decreed by the half-breed, however. The Titans cared even less for the barking, grunting language of their people, a poor shade of the elegant communication skills of ancient times. Better to hear Common than that babble. Besides, when all were transformed into the new race, it would be the glorious tongue of the Titans they spoke . . . or rather sang.

Wargroch grunted. Perhaps that was why he had been summoned. Perhaps the time was finally approaching.

Instead, Atolgus said, "The *Shok G'Ran*. The Titans would know of them."

It was all that the Blödian could do to maintain an indifferent expression. "What would they know from Wargroch?"

Atolgus rose. He still wore the cloth, metal-tipped kilt of a warrior, but he had disposed of the shining breastplate first given to him in service to Golgren. It simply no longer fit. Wargroch wore his full uniform plus a helmet clamped on his squat head.

The warlord reached to his left side and drew a long, well-crafted sword with gems in the hilt. The weapon had once belonged to Golgren, who had gifted it to Wargroch after the warrior had proven his loyalty to the half-breed. Wargroch, in turn, had given it to Atolgus upon the triumph of the capital's takeover. In fact, the blade that the Blödian wore at his side had been awarded to him in exchange by the imposing Atolgus.

"They would know from the general of my armies if he would choose to be warlord of Solamnia."

The suggestion was so unexpected that Wargroch could only gape. Warlord of Solamnia?

Golgren's sword was extended upward in Atolgus's hands. Wargroch slowly moved forward. Yet it was not death that Atolgus offered to him; it was a role as astounding to Wargroch as the power Safrag wielded in the crystalline artifact.

"We are to eclipse our ancestors, the High Ogres, Wargroch. We are to offer the golden age not to merely our own kind, but to also the lesser races."

"To *all?*" Wargroch managed to gasp as he knelt again, that time under the raised weapon.

The warlord cut the air just above the Blödian's head

then brought the tip to Wargroch's left cheek, touching just enough to draw a single drop of blood from the flesh. It was an ancient ogre anointing ritual. Wargroch had just been promoted, his loyalty to Atolgus and the Titans marked by the drop of blood.

"It will be offered to all—humans, dwarves, Uruv Suurt, and even elves. They will know the great wonder of Titan rule."

Titan rule. Not *ogre* or High Ogre rule. Wargroch noted that distinction.

"And they will all be made new?"

"As she and Safrag see fit." Atolgus lowered the tip of the crimson-touched blade to Wargroch's mouth.

Wargroch kissed the bloodied area, the traditional gesture of acceptance and gratitude for the tremendous honor his superior had granted him. Atolgus then sheathed the sword. He reached out and seized the other ogre by the shoulders, raising Wargroch up again.

And as Atolgus's fingers clutched him, the Blödian felt the coarse fur on his body tremble and spark as though some terrible lightning storm swept through the chamber.

"This is the first of many rewards, loyal Wargroch. She promises that."

Atolgus's Titan eyes glowed.

To his credit, Wargroch did not flinch, buth rather steeled himself. When Atolgus released him, the Blödian did not even exhale in relief. He pounded his fist against his chest in formal salute.

"How soon?" he rumbled, referring to the action he was supposed to take against Solamnia.

"Very soon," was all Atolgus would reply.

The future warlord nodded. Keeping his head low

and his fist on his chest, he backed out of the chamber. Under his thick brow, his gaze remained on Atolgus. The warlord had once more seated himself with a gaze of longing and devotion. If there was nothing physically left of the chieftain he once knew, Wargroch saw that there was also very little remaining of that which had been Atolgus's old spirit. What sat on the throne was entirely subservient to the desires of the female Titan.

The doors shut of their own accord again. Wargroch straightened. He gave the guard handling the meredrake a sharp look, and the other ogre showed more respect. With the doors open, the guard had heard of Wargroch's impending glory. Like Atolgus, Wargroch was clearly favored by the Titans.

Paying the guard no further mind, the Blödian strode on as if headed to another important meeting. Instead, though, his mind raced. Two things bothered Wargroch, indeed warred within him. One was the honor the sorcerers had bestowed upon him through the changed and changing Atolgus. He was to be ruler of all Solamnia. He was to have a rank almost as great as Atolgus himself.

The hardened warrior finally shivered. An image of himself as Atolgus, as Atolgus had become, disturbed him and would not leave his thoughts.

But while the possible promise of his own transformation set Wargroch ill at ease, it was further compounded by a second concern, concern over a pouch delivered by messenger to Golgren just prior to the seizure of Garantha. Golgren had been absent, so Wargroch, left to guard the capital, had naturally taken the message from the ogre courier.

And though it would have made sense for Wargroch to turn the pouch over to Atolgus or the Titans, he had, for some inexplicable reason, kept it to himself, burying it in a safe place just beyond the city walls. Considering the Titans' constant alteration of the capital, that choice was fortunate.

The only other soul who knew of its existence—the original courier—would not betray him. Wargroch had taken it upon himself to kill that ogre. He had decided to keep the pouch's existence a secret. At the time, he had not known why he had acted so out of character, merely that he felt impelled.

It was a decision that, if discovered, would mean an awful fate for him. Wargroch had fought bravely in many a battle and slain many a foe, but he had placed his fate in the contents of a pouch that had, though he had not realized it immediately, planted the first seed of the doubts that assailed him constantly.

It was a pouch with Solamnic markings.

III

MESSAGE FROM THE DEAD

The moment that he felt solid ground beneath his feet, Golgren tore himself free from Tyranos.

"Return me to the citadel," he demanded of the wizard in a low growl.

"That doesn't seem like a good idea to me just now," Tyranos returned with equal vehemence. He glanced around, also furious, but for another reason. "We're still in the damned mountains! We should be beyond them!"

"Good."

The brawny spellcaster snorted. "Oh, not good at all! His power's strong here, and if he seizes you, he'll be stronger yet!"

His comment briefly distracted Golgren from his own ire. "Speak more plainly . . . if you can."

Tyranos did not look at all willing to give explanations. "First we leave; then we talk."

The crystal on the staff glowed. Tyranos reached for the half-breed.

Golgren dodged him. The deposed Grand Khan

41

readied himself to fight hand to hand with the human, aware that Tyranos was one person who might be wily and strong enough to defeat him.

"This is hardly the place for this foolery!" the hooded wizard snapped. He pointed the crystal at Golgren.

The half-breed started to move but halted as he caught sight of a figure who had materialized beyond Tyranos. The armor alone, with its silver sheen and intricate sword symbol on the breastplate, would have been enough to identify the newcomer even if the face of the figure were not somehow visible despite the gloom. The proud face with the short beard running around the chin and jaws was uncommon among Solamnics, who tended toward thick mustaches. There was only one Knight of Solamnia whom Golgren knew who wore his facial hair in that fashion.

"Sir Stefan Rennert?" he whispered.

Tyranos faltered. He spun around and looked where his reluctant companion was staring. "Rennert?"

But there was no one standing there. Golgren's eyes narrowed.

"That was a juvenile trick, well beneath you, oh Grand Khan," the wizard began as he slowly turned back. However, upon noting Golgren's bewildered expression, Tyranos paused. "Or was it?"

Golgren stepped past Tyranos to better see where the knight had supposedly been standing. However, it was exceedingly obvious that no one was there.

"You're not one to imagine things," the spellcaster went on. "And that cleric does have a tendency to pop up when least expected."

"Cleric?"

"Ah, that's right! You don't know. Our friend became

42

a cleric of the bison-headed one."

That made Golgren's eyes narrow further. "Kiri-Jolith?"

The robed figure chuckled. "I see we share one thing in common, a particular distaste for meddling gods." Tyranos paused. "Speaking of which, have you come across a more fiery one of late?"

"I have."

The bluntness of the statement caused Tyranos to grimace. "Then it more than ever behooves us to leave this wretched place—"

"No."

"Golgren—"

Suddenly the half-breed darted past the wizard. Golgren recognized enough shadowy landmarks to know in which direction the citadel lay.

Tyranos materialized in front of him. The spellcaster sounded exhausted but determined. "We *are* leaving."

The two grappled.

The staff flared.

"What by the Kraken?" Tyranos barked, involuntarily letting Golgren know that it was no action of his.

The pair vanished again and materialized a breath later in a place that the half-breed had never expected to see again.

The eight desiccated figures sat around the long, wide table in the exact same poses in which Golgren had last observed them. Standing, each would have been about the height of the half-breed. They were evenly divided between male and female, not that the differences mattered much anymore, not after so many centuries dead. All were clad in dust-covered rags merely hinting at the rich green and blue that they once were.

But the faded color of the ancients' robes meant little in comparison to the obvious glint of gold remaining on the dried skin still wrapped tightly about their skulls. Golgren already knew who the eight were—what they had been long past—but for Tyranos their appearance was a shocking revelation.

"High Ogres!" the wizard gasped, forgetting the half-breed. He pushed past Golgren to approach two of the corpses. Placing one hand on the iridescent pearl table, he leaned close to a male figure whose face still bore the remnants of a star tattoo under its right eye. "The lost nine."

"Except there are eight," Golgren pointed out.

"There should be nine," the leonine Tyranos insisted. He studied the parchment skin, stared into the empty sockets. "The writing said thc nine who fled . . ."

Golgren momentarily lost interest in the citadel. He knew that place, that sanctum buried deep in a mountain of the chain that led to the Vale of Vipers. With Idaria, he had discovered it through an artifact— a signet ring—that Tyranos himself had bequeathed to the Grand Khan through the elf. The ring had led them along a trail through the mountains and beyond more than one magical portal to that very spot. Unfortunately at the time, they had also been pursued by dripping monstrosities and Safrag.

"The signet brought me to this place once," Golgren informed his companion without recounting the rest of the events involved.

Tyranos looked up at him. "Did it now?" He frowned. "I brought it from the tomb of another of these."

"The ninth, perhaps?"

"No. The death of that one came before then, but of

course they must be bound in some manner to the tomb's occupant. I remember an image of a beautiful female."

The wizard quickly glanced at the other corpse closest to him. After a moment, he impatiently shook his head and went to the next.

At the long end of the table, Tyranos came to a halt. He stared at a withered figure. It was a female, and it still had long, flowing hair that when viewed close seemed to fluctuate between gold and silver. The long tresses draped well over her shoulders. Even after centuries, there was enough of her small nose, the curve of her cheekbones, to give some hint of what had once been an astoundingly beautiful face.

"This was her. I know it though I could never recall her beauty perfectly. Yet this was her. She was their leader."

The half-breed's brow furrowed. He indicated the male seated at the other end. Seven of the figures, including the female of whom Tyranos had been speaking, sat almost peaceably, as though they had simply passed away in their sleep.

The same could not be said of the male, however. His expression was contorted, enraged, and a bit fearful.

"What of him? Is he not the leader?"

"Ogre prejudices against female rulers aside, while he was likely second among them, she would have been first." Tyranos gazed off into the empty air. "I know her. I've seen her."

That information only slightly clouded Golgren's previously conceived notions about the eight bodies. "It's obvious he suffered his death differently than the others."

"And he's also facing the direction from which I

would guess someone might enter this place. Am I correct?" When Golgren nodded, Tyranos explained, "He saw their doom coming. The others perished utterly ignorant of it. A simple reasoning."

"Yet he knew who it was who brought their deaths," the half-ogre added.

"Hmm? How do you mean?"

"It is in his face. He knew who was coming to slay and the betrayal involved."

Tyranos moved over to the High Ogre and peered at the macabre expression on the dead one's face. "Be damned if I can see that, but it makes some sense, I suppose." He rubbed his square jaw. "The ninth, perhaps?"

While the wizard's suggestion also made sense, Golgren shook his head. "I do not think so."

"Oh? And what makes you say that?"

Golgren only shrugged, not as fascinated by the subject as Tyranos. He surveyed the chamber, eyeing the runes upon the wall, the arched ceiling. All was the same as he had last left it.

Circling the table of the dead to reach Golgren, the wizard remarked, "I've never been here, but you have. Therefore, this has to do with you, as so much else does."

"You speak in many riddles, wizard," Golgren returned. "So much else, you say? Enlighten me, please."

The sound of movement made both suddenly turn back to the table. The pair eyed the sinister tableau, but the cause of the sound did not reveal itself.

Pointing the staff in the general direction of the table, the spellcaster growled, "I'll say again, oh Grand Khan, that it's by your doing somehow that we're here! You may not be cognizant of how you are involved, but it's true, nevertheless!"

"I do not disagree about that." Golgren frowned slightly. Something was different about the eight figures, he realized. Some very minor—yet it must be *major*—change.

He focused on the male at the one end. When Golgren had last been there, that figure was wearing a talisman adorned by the griffon symbol. Golgren had removed the talisman, putting the object in Idaria's care. He had not been certain if the piece was valuable but thought it best not to leave it behind. When he removed the talisman, the corpse had pitched forward, the top half of its broken body sprawling on the table.

Only moments later, however, when Golgren had happened to look back at it, the figure had returned to its upright position.

It remained that way, unchanged since that incident. Yet something about it burned in Golgren's memory.

"Just what are you doing now?"

Ignoring the wizard, Golgren took a step closer to the male corpse, studying it intently.

He realized what was different. One hand was pointing toward the opposite end of the table. That had not been the case before.

And at that end sat the female whom Tyranos had spoken of as the true leader of that desperate pack of ancient spellcasters.

There was something different in her pose, too, Golgren noticed as he stared at her. But he could not place it. He wended his way over to the second corpse, while Tyranos impatiently but silently watched.

Golgren had not paid as much mind to the female

corpse as he had the male, and so it was more difficult to decide what had altered. As the wizard offered no advice or comment, Golgren knew that Tyranos had not noticed anything amiss.

He leaned with his one hand on the shimmering table as he peered closely at the face. He could see that she had been outwardly beautiful, far more so than an ogre and, yes, even Idaria.

Then something flickered in the High Ogre's eyes.

A startled grunt escaped Golgren before he realized that he had imagined it. The eye sockets were as empty as those of her companions. Only darkness stared out from them. Only—

A beautiful pair of eyes the color of the sun met his own. They were different than those of the Titans, for in them there resided life, love, and hope, not utter arrogance and domination.

It happened so quickly and without warning that the half-breed instinctively pulled back—or tried to. Something secured his hand to the table, anchoring it there no matter how hard he tried to pull it free.

A hand barely covered in cracking skin clutched his own—her hand.

Golgren looked back into the dead one's eyes only to discover that the sockets were dark and lifeless again.

The pressure on his hand ceased. He glanced down and discovered that the High Ogre's hand again rested on the table, where it had been earlier.

"What happened?" Tyranos broke in from behind him. "Did you see something?"

The questions clearly indicated that the wizard had not experienced the same startling thing. Golgren bared his teeth at the mysterious corpse, and only then did he notice that there was something beneath his palm. He scooped it up.

It was a signet ring. The very same signet ring that the half-breed had last witnessed sinking into the earth during his struggles with Safrag over the Fire Rose, in the chamber where the dead High Ogres had secreted it.

There could be no mistaking the artifact. It was circular, with a rune resembling a double-bladed sword with the point down at the center. Above the weapon arced a half-circle, and below the sharp point lay a symbol that reminded Golgren of flames. However, the design alone did not tell him that was the very same signet. No, that was a sense, a feeling, that coursed through him as he gripped it. Yes, to be sure, it was the lost artifact returned to him.

To *him*. As Golgren savored that thought, he sensed the spellcaster approaching.

With great dexterity, Golgren manipulated the ring onto his finger just as Tyranos reached for it.

"You've no need of that, anymore."

Golgren nodded toward the female High Ogre. *"She* believes otherwise, wizard."

Tyranos snorted. "That thing nearly cost you your life before!"

"And saved it many times over." The half-breed pretended to admire the artifact's beauty. "It is a gift I will accept."

The two stood frozen at the edge of struggle. Tyranos had the staff pointed at his supposed ally. Golgren kept the signet facing the robed figure.

With another snort, Tyranos lowered his staff. "Who am I to argue with the ancient dead and a comrade as well?" He bared his teeth in what might have passed for a grin or possibly a grimace. "And so we seem to at least find why we were drawn to here." He studied the chamber. "And while I would cheerfully spend some time investigating what else is here, I believe we are better off leaving for somewhere far, far away, just as I planned."

Once again, though, they were at odds. Stepping away from the spellcaster, Golgren replied, "We part here, wizard. I am going back."

The crystal glowed brightly. "We'll just see about that."

The signet also abruptly glowed, the runes ablaze.

"Oh, damn—" Tyranos began.

A great, fiery light surrounded both, and they vanished once more.

∾≪☽≫∾

She was alone; alone save for a single gargoyle watching over her. The gray-scaled creature perched in front of her, more interested in scratching its long, toothy beak with one paw than in keeping an eye on a prisoner who had no way of escaping.

The shrouded figure and its horrific companions had departed soon after the other gargoyles. Where they had gone off to, Idaria would like to know, but more important was that it was her first opportunity to gain her freedom.

She had been released from her frozen position only to be carried off by her current guard to a chamber deeper in the mountain citadel. There she had been locked in a darkened place that, to her discerning eye, had possibly once been something so simple and yet so grand as a great bedchamber. A few shreds of what appeared to have been fine draperies still hung on the edges of the windows, but

50

that was the only definitive clue. The blackened rubble that lay collapsed in one corner no longer resembled any identifiable piece of furniture, so long had been the passage of time.

The citadel's shadowy lord had said nothing more to her, not even when banishing the elf to that place. Whether he had thought to make her more or less comfortable was a matter of debate. She had only a few rotting furs upon which to sit, and the only light came from a small, glowing, white stone set in the ceiling. The light was just strong enough to let Idaria see that, aside from the still-useful iron door, there was no other exit. The windows overlooked the mountain heights. Stone met her gaze everywhere else.

The gargoyle in charge of her captivity was not the most powerful of the vast flock. Indeed, it was one of the least, a sign of its master's confidence that Idaria was at his mercy. The creature began gnawing on an old amalok bone—the fearsome herd animals being the winged creatures' most common prey—and looked extremely bored. And why not? What hope could the prisoner have of escaping?

But there *was* hope. Dangling just out of sight under her garments was the pendant with the griffon symbol that Golgren had placed on her. At the time, Idaria had shown none of the deep revulsion she had felt instinctively, when Golgren had taken it from the ancient corpse and hung it around her neck.

Her hair hid the chain. There had been moments at the very beginning when she had feared that her captor might notice the upper edge of the pendant peeking out, but he had not.

Idaria might have given little thought to the pendant,

if not for the gentle warmth radiating from it since her capture. She recalled some of Golgren's experiences with the signet and wondered whether his chance decision to give the pendant to her had been mere chance after all.

With casual movements, she tried to draw the pendant out without the gargoyle noticing. But despite her attempts to do so, the winged creature noticed her activity almost immediately. With a warning grunt, it half hopped, half walked to her.

So close, the carnivore's breath, enhanced by bits of rotting meat between its yellowed teeth, was potent. One paw grasped the hand holding the pendant. The artifact came loose, falling against her breast. As it touched her skin, the warmth increased, and to Idaria's surprise, a faint, blue glow radiated from the griffon symbol.

However, instead of growing suspicious, the gargoyle cocked its head and stared in fascination at the pendant.

Idaria quickly seized on its reaction. "Is it not pretty? Do you like it?"

The gargoyle nodded.

"What is your name?"

The creature leaned back, looking not so much angry as frustrated. "No name."

The voice was deep, definitely male. Often, because of their similar builds, it was impossible to tell if some gargoyles were male or female. The only sure way in such cases was to get much too close or listen to the timbre of the voice.

With the identification of the gargoyle's gender, *it* became a *he.* That was to Idaria's advantage.

"No name?" she innocently asked, aware of why a gargoyle would not have a name. It showed that one had a very low rank in the flock. Gargoyles were limited in their use of names. Only when one of the elder ones passed away was a name made available to those existing without one.

"No name."

She thought for a moment. Somewhere far in the past, the creatures had learned enough Common to take upon themselves names that reflected their primitive civilization. Chasm was an example, though in his case he had likely been named by Tyranos, who had raised him. Gargoyles that lived in the mountains most often chose names that indicated stone or geological features.

"I shall call you Stratum," the elf slave finally decided. "It is what we call a layer of rock." It was the first word that she could think of that might work for the gargoyle and that also was likely not to be already used among his kind.

"Sssstratumm . . . Stratum . . ."

She did not have to see how his eyes widened in pleasure, for his voice alone readily revealed how he felt about his christening. The gargoyle began to hop up and down, repeatedly calling out his new identity. Dust clouds rose with each hop as he crowed, "Stratum! Stratum is me! Me is Stratum!"

Before Idaria could prepare herself, the gargoyle wrapped her in his thick arms and hugged her. The elf struggled to breathe, pretending she felt no pain.

Stratum finally released her. Only then did Idaria realize that she had given him far more than she had even intended. It had been her hope that finding a name for the gargoyle would make him feel somewhat more friendly toward her. The elf saw that the thing almost felt like her slave, so grateful was he.

And all that for a single word, a marking of self, she thought.

Yet there was one threshold that Stratum might not cross. With as much delicacy as she could put into the question, Idaria asked, "Stratum, will you help me?"

His answer was without hesitation. The crooked beak bobbed up and down. "Stratum help friend!"

While his enthusiasm was encouraging, that did not necessarily mean he would betray his master for her. Idaria had to be cautious. She had always had an affinity for animals, even more so than many other elves. Some said she was favored by the Fisher King, known to the Solamnics as the god Habbakuk.

The pendant continued to glow slightly. She noted Stratum's gaze constantly flicker back to it. "Would you like to touch it?"

Again, the beak bobbed up and down. There seemed no reason it would not be safe to let the gargoyle examine it closer. Idaria held it forth.

Stratum put two tentative digits on the face. A low sound that resembled the cooing of a dove escaped the brutish creature. It was like a purring of a child.

As the gargoyle marveled at the artifact, Idaria delicately murmured, "Would you help me see my other friend?"

He did not pull away, but his gaze narrowed. "Other is chained above. Master command so."

Feeling somewhat guilty for tricking the simple creature—even if he did serve such a vile lord—Idaria implored, "Please. He is my friend too. I would just see him. Stratum . . ."

Cocking his head, the gargoyle mulled it over. "Come," he finally said, turning toward the door.

For Idaria, the way out was locked by some magic spell, but for Stratum, that was apparently not the case. He swung open the ancient door, which stirred up more dust and squealed much too loudly for the elf's tastes, then hopped out into the passage beyond.

Nearly unable to believe her quick success, Idaria followed.

The corridors through which they passed had all been carved from the mountain and still retained the rough texture of it. They were wide enough for two gargoyles to move with wings half extended. The halls were also lit, albeit just barely, by blue crystals embedded at even intervals in each wall.

They also passed other closed chambers, none of which concerned Idaria other than the potential threat behind their doors. However, despite the low grunting Stratum made as he hurried along, no one emerged from any of them to investigate.

At the end of the third corridor, they came to a spiral staircase that had at some point in the past collapsed. As a frustrated Idaria peered up, Stratum suddenly seized her with one arm and, revealing the astounding strength of which even the least of gargoyles was capable, easily bore her aloft.

They passed one level then another and another. Idaria, who had caught only glimpses of the outside from the vision the gargoyle's lord had summoned, wondered if they were in one of the towers.

At the next level, Stratum suddenly veered to where a railed landing still precariously tipped over the fallen staircase. The winged creature landed on a solid area, where the blackened floor of another corridor gave them firmer footing.

The end of the corridor lay just ahead, its short length further indicating that they were likely in one of the towers. Idaria looked around for any guard but spied nothing.

Stratum hopped down the neglected path. The elf followed. At the other end, they came upon a rusted door akin to the one from her own cell. The faint and ironic outline of a rising sun etched into the door still remained.

With an almost casual show of strength, the gargoyle ripped open the door.

Immediately, a frustrated roar erupted from within. There came the rattling of chains, many chains, and the sounds of struggle.

Idaria's companion let out a frustrated hiss and urged her inside. As she obeyed, she saw the source of all the unwelcome noise.

Chasm was larger and broader of shoulder than Stratum. He was nearly the size of a tall human and broader of build than either Golgren or Tyranos. His maw was less pronounced than Stratum's, and he was a duskier gray. Under a thick brow ridge, blazing eyes that bespoke of intelligence stared at the newcomers. If the gargoyle beside Idaria was among the least of his kind, then surely Chasm was among the most powerful.

But as powerful as Tyranos's servant and the elf's friend might be, even Chasm could do nothing against the many chains in which he had been bound. The gargoyle was wrapped tightly from head to foot, with his legs folded into his torso and his arms tucked behind him to further add to his torture. His wings were folded around his shoulders and limbs. Increasing his misery, he hung from a single chain emerging from the ceiling, which kept the gargoyle roughly three feet off the ground. In such a state, Chasm could not even roll back and forth, seeking leverage.

The chamber was otherwise empty save for decaying refuse that indicated that some of the monstrous flock had in the past used it for living purposes. Arched windows well above were the only reason that it did not stink more than it already did.

Stratum hissed something to Chasm, who growled back as best as his bound jaws could manage. Idaria moved past the smaller gargoyle to let Chasm see her.

He quieted instantly. She sensed the hope and trust in his eyes. Idaria stroked Chasm's head to soothe him then made certain not to forget Stratum. If she hoped to escape, she needed the smaller gargoyle's help.

"Stratum, I thank you for bringing me to him, but please, can you not help me let him down?"

Stratum hissed uneasily. He scratched at his beaklike muzzle, his mind clearly conflicted. "Master not like," he finally began. "But you give Stratum name, make Stratum be Stratum."

The gargoyle suddenly took off, fluttering upward. As Idaria watched, Stratum seized the chain. With a heavy grunt, he tore at one of the thick, oval links.

The link tore. Before Chasm could strike the floor, Stratum held tight to the lower portion of the chain. With amazing care, he lowered the larger gargoyle safely down.

Idaria rushed to Chasm. As she fought with the chains, Stratum rejoined her. He slipped his jaws around one part and bit down.

The chain snapped in two. With a tremendous growl, Chasm flexed.

Other chains flew away, one barely missing Idaria.

She fell back as Tyranos's servant finished freeing himself.

The two gargoyles faced one another over the elf. The tension and distrust was palpable. Idaria moved to defuse the situation by stepping between them. "Chasm, Stratum helped you. Stratum, Chasm is also my friend and, therefore, your friend too."

Neither appeared completely convinced, but they calmed. Idaria exhaled. She stood at the threshold of freedom.

There came from elsewhere within the citadel the cries of many angry gargoyles.

Hissing, Stratum hopped toward the door. He peered into the gloom beyond.

"Coming," he warned her.

Chasm seized the elf and indicated the windows. "We go!"

She looked to the smaller gargoyle. "Come, Stratum! Come with!"

He started to hop toward her then paused. She could read by his actions what he planned to do, all for her having given him a name.

"No, Stratum! Come with!"Chasm gripped her tightly then lifted her from the floor. However, he did not leave but hovered, awaiting the smaller gargoyle.

Stratum hissed. "Go!"

With a grunt, Chasm took off with his struggling charge. The flapping of wings and the shrieking of animalistic voices encroached from the corridor.

Chasm carried Idaria to one of the open windows. As they neared, a lone gargoyle landed there. However, Chasm barreled into the other creature, releasing the hold of one paw long enough to use his claws on the throat of the would-be attacker. Blood spattered Idaria, who was staring at the lone figure standing below.

Gargoyles poured into the chamber. Stratum let out a hiss and threw himself at them.

The rending sounds that came as Chasm flew into the dark, open sky echoed monstrously in Idaria's ears. The wind blew away her tears.

Chasm carried her away from the mountain citadel with more than a score of gargoyles already in hot pursuit.

∞•◊•∞

The gray and black figure materialized in the chamber where Chasm had been held, causing the gargoyles there, including the ones that had ripped apart the hapless Stratum, to pause in their blood-soaked efforts. The leathery beasts bowed their heads low.

The white orbs surveyed the slaughtered Stratum, the bodies of the two larger gargoyles he had managed to slay, then the chains that had held Chasm prisoner. The eyes then looked up to the window through which the two escapees had flown.

Yes . . . came the amused voice in the heads of the assembled beasts. *Go . . . go and serve me well again, my Idaria.*

IV

SAFRAG'S SUGGESTION

The power of the Fire Rose surged to life again, the crystalline artifact filling Safrag's sanctum with a glorious gold and crimson light. The leader of the Titans stood in the center of the wide, stone chamber, all his other long-collected artifacts shunted aside earlier by a single, indifferent spell. Nothing mattered more than the wondrous creation held tightly in his right hand, not even the fact that it *burned* his flesh as if truly made of flame.

The Fire Rose was just more than a foot in height and had earned its name in part due to its design. It had a thick base that halfway up suddenly broke into a dozen different-sized projections jutting at various angles though always aiming upward. There was a definite resemblance to a flower and, because of its fiery hue, it was a more stunning rose than any other.

Legend—and truth, so Safrag believed—said it had been created by the god Sirrion. The High Ogres had fallen out of favor with the gods, for their hubris had caused them to believe they were the greatest of all creatures on the face of the world called Krynn. They had gone from the creators of art, magical miracles, and high learning to sadistic, decadent overlords of all the younger races. Yet not all had fallen so far, and some thought that, if one god granted their appeal, the end might be prevented.

And Sirrion, the last deity they had expected, had answered. He was one of the neutral gods, those who let time and chance be the deciding factor of lives and souls. Neither good nor evil, but often choosing to ally with the former for the sake of saving the world from destruction, Sirrion and his kind generally had little personal contact with mortals, save for those who acted as their clerics.

But the god of fire and alchemy found much of interest in the words of the High Ogres. They sought something to reshape their terrible destiny and insisted they were worthy of retaking control over their existence. Give them the means by which to restore what they had once been, and they would prove that they were worthy of being Krynn's first and most beloved people.

Sirrion did just that. He forged the Fire Rose from the deepest, most primitive energies, those with which the world and all beyond it had been created. Into his gift he poured the pure notion of alchemy, of ultimate change at the very root of existence and reality, and of the unique ability that would enable one person to wield that power.

The sorcerers to whom Sirrion had presented the Fire Rose were grateful bordering on tears. They immediately saw the potential of the artifact and how it could not only save their kind, but make them even greater.

However, Sirrion left them with one last message. Almost cheerfully, he said, "The choice is always yours as to how my gift is used—good or ill or doing nothing. What becomes of you and yours through it will be your decision."

The High Ogres paid that message scant mind, for each was certain that he or she knew the right thing to do, and therein lay the foundation of their failure. None could agree which of them was the best candidate to set hand on the artifact and make their desires come to fruition. They began to war over Sirrion's gift.

The Titan knew only fragments of what had occurred after that. Tales said that one hand or another briefly commanded the Fire Rose, only to have some treachery cause another to grab it. The original hope, to bring the race back to its glory, was lost. The degradation of the ogres ensued. From the most beautiful and intelligent, they had become the most horrific and brutal race.

And somewhere along the way, a pitiful handful of survivors had made the foolish decision to hide away the Fire Rose from all who came after.

However, Safrag held the precious artifact. He wielded it, for the sake of the Titan dream, naturally.

The Fire Rose continued to glow brightly. Safrag could not help but keep gazing in wonder, reflecting on all the betrayal it had caused, all the slaying by his hand. When he had first come into the ranks of the Titans, he had not thought to strive to be Dauroth's apprentice, much less his eventual successor. Only a chance reading of an ancient scroll he had found among his master's collection had stirred those desires. It had shocked him that Dauroth could know that such a miraculous thing existed and not want to find it. It had stunned him further to discover, when told by his master, that Dauroth possessed a tiny *fragment* of the Fire Rose and still resisted its glory.

That had been when the change had come over Safrag. Dauroth could not see the future as it was meant to be; he was blind to what had to be done. He was, therefore, lacking in the vital qualities that the Titans needed in a true leader.

And so Safrag had found the manner by which to destroy his fault-ridden master and his one rival to his cause, Dauroth's senior apprentice, Hundjal. It had proven simple to trick Dauroth into believing that Hundjal was the one seeking the Fire Rose, a quest punishable by death. Once Dauroth had slain the other apprentice, the Titans' founder had ensured his own demise. Dauroth had realized that in the end, but too late to prevent it.

But all was as should be. Safrag controlled the Fire Rose. The ogre race was his to shape, with the world to follow. The mongrel who had dared sit upon the throne and who played at being Grand Khan was presently a frozen monument to both his folly and Safrag's inevitable victory.

Caught up in the artifact's splendor, Safrag paid little mind to subtle changes taking place around him. The thick stone walls bubbled and breathed, changed shade and texture, sometimes seeming as if turning to flesh. Scrolls and tomes on the shelves shivered and flared bright red. A few of the former uncurled as if alive and possibly hungry. Other arcane artifacts shifted position or looked to be melting. A vial transformed into a glowing, green crystal. Small creatures of light—literal fireflies—formed in the air, danced, then burned away.

All that was lost on Safrag. His eyes grew wider and more pale with hints of snow. His skin also paled, remaining blue but with a touch of gold. His features shifted slightly, as if he were becoming another person, one with more ursine traits. Even his garments did not remain untouched, for they flowed as if living.

Also lost on him was the fact that, despite having sealed his sanctum from even those most in his favor, Safrag was no longer alone. Behind him, several of the fiery lights suddenly swirled together. They coalesced into a tall, blazing form—a figure of flame. The flames then stilled for the most part, revealing a watcher who stood not quite as tall as the Titan yet loomed over him like a giant. There was in his face a semblance of elf, human, ogre, dwarf, even kender, and yet in no manner was he related to any of those races. His face was long and angular, and his skin was the color of ash left by a terrible blaze. He wore a mane of rich, red-orange hair that flickered and danced as if wild fire.

But most arresting were his eyes, burning orbs that were long and narrow like those of Safrag, but ever changing of color. They were gold like the sun, red like the deepest blood, brilliant blue, and finally utter white. They were all the colors of flame and shifted from one to the other as rapidly as fire burned.

The god Sirrion watched with amusement as Safrag continued to be mesmerized by his creation. The fiery figure casually stretched his hand to the side. A yellowed scroll flew into his palm. As it landed, it burst into flame. Within less than a heartbeat, there were not even any ashes remaining.

Sirrion's expression mirrored that of someone who had just devoured a tasty meal. He gave one last cheerful glance at Safrag then became a scattering of tiny fiery forms that dissipated a moment later.

Only at that point did Safrag stir. The Fire Rose

dimmed. Most but not all of the transformations faded away with it. Here and there, including on Safrag himself, there were still slight alterations, but only the discerning eye would have noted them.

The lead Titan glanced around as if expecting to see something or someone. When that did not happen, he returned his attention to the care of the artifact. With a gesture, the chamber around him shifted, the walls moving here and there and a doorway suddenly appearing on one part of the sanctum.

All that surrounded Safrag had once belonged to his master. Safrag had worked long and hard to know all the secret chambers hidden by Dauroth's sorcery. Before him lay the most important, for it was where he kept the Fire Rose when forced to part from it.

As the iron door swung open, a chill wind flowed from the other side. Ignoring it, Safrag stepped through. He stood in a frost- and snow-covered room. Safrag thought of it as the Chamber of Ice. It was the one place where he could be certain that the Fire Rose would be not only safe, but subdued.

More than twenty tall mounds resembling stalagmites dotted the floor of the unsettling room. Safrag eyed the first of the snowy piles, each rising more than ten feet in height. As he approached, one hand rose in anticipation.

And at that moment, the nearest mounds shook from within. Snow and ice broke away. A set of grasping, flesh-less fingers burst from one then another. The mounds shattered.

Four skeletal ogre warriors stood with weapons ready. Bits of armor and skin still clung to the yellowed bones. The eyes were nothing but black sockets that fixed upon the Titan.

One of the undead raised its rusted but still serviceable axe.

"*Asymnopti isidiu*," sang Safrag.

But the skeletal guards did not return to their mounds as commanded. Instead, the first took a menacing step forward, its actions immediately mimicked by the other four. A fifth and sixth mound shook.

"*Asymnopti isidiu*," the lead Titan repeated more sternly.

The undead had the audacity to continue to menace him. The two new warriors followed the example of the four. In the background, other mounds began quivering.

Safrag started to gesture then thought better of it. Instead he grinned and held up the Fire Rose.

His desire alone stirred it to raging life. Awash in its glorious light, the skeletal guards hesitated.

The Titan made his wish be known to the artifact.

The Fire Rose blazed.

As one, the skeletons curled into themselves. Their bones became fluid, wrapping around and around until each was bound by itself. The tightening of the bodies forced the skulls to gaze up.

A thick, white substance secreted from the bones, spilling over the undead guardians. It caked the bones until nothing remained but a smooth, white column of ivory the size of each warrior.

Safrag found himself panting not from exertion, but more from excitement. Not only had the skeletons converging on him been altered, but so had those not yet stirring. The Fire Rose had been very thorough in carrying out his wishes.

Why the guardians had not obeyed the original spell only then occurred to Safrag. They had been created to heed only the voice of Dauroth. Safrag had always used his power to perfectly imitate his former master, but in the afterglow of using the Fire Rose in his sanctum, he had forgotten.

The mistake was no longer important. The guards were not needed anyway. Safrag had installed other safety measures far more insidious.

The Titan leader turned back to the doorway then recalled that he had entered to put the artifact *away*. With great reluctance, Safrag wound his way around the hard mounds to where a black, iron chest lay half buried in the ice. With a wave of one hand, he opened the chest. Within, a clear, thick liquid untouched by the cold slowly rippled.

Safrag bent down, holding the Fire Rose just above the surface. Dauroth had created that liquid to subdue the primal forces of a fragment of the Fire Rose, and Safrag used it with the same goal in mind. However, he hesitated, thinking that perhaps he might wield the crystalline structure one last time, just to be certain that he understood its functioning.

At last, fighting the temptation, Safrag set the artifact in the chest. As he reluctantly pulled his hand free, not one hint of moisture remained on him.

His return from the pocket realm to his main sanctum was greeted by a slight red shift in the outer chamber's illumination. It was a silent signal cast by Safrag to inform him when someone sought entrance to his lair.

He had no doubt exactly what the visitation concerned. His expression masked, Safrag had the door open before him.

There were six of them, six of the more persistent

objectors, including three from the inner circle. Kulgrath was among those and most likely the instigator of the confrontation. Safrag noted that for later.

"Great Master," the instigator sang with a low bow. Behind Kulgrath, the others followed suit.

"Kulgrath. Gadjul." Safrag acknowledged the names of the other four as well. His pointed naming of each made two of the lesser sorcerers visibly shrink. None wanted to earn Safrag's wrath.

Kulgrath eyed him oddly. "Master, you are well?"

"Should I not be?"

Kulgrath quickly abandoned whatever stray notion had caused him to ask the impertinent question. "The Fire Rose . . . we felt its majesty. We felt it call out."

"I made some tests of its abilities," Safrag said with a slight nod. "That's what you felt."

"And all was in order?"

The lead Titan's eyes did not betray his impatience. "Of course. It was to be expected."

Kulgrath steeled himself. "Then it is now our chance to wield it? Under your guidance, naturally?"

"Not yet."

His answer came so quickly and with such finality that the other sorcerers visibly started. Kulgrath's eyes flared ever so briefly before the other Titan recalled himself. Bowing low, he replied, "But surely very, very soon. The artifact is straightforward in its use."

Safrag turned from him; the lead Titan was bored with the conversation. "There are intricacies. You must all learn patience."

"The populace is growing restive, Master," interjected Gadjul. "They await their great ascension."

"And they, too, must learn patience," the Titan

leader replied without looking back. "They, too, must learn patience."

He continued down the corridor as if they no longer stood there. The other Titans glanced at Kulgrath, who did not hide his mounting frustration from them.

"We must learn patience," he muttered. "First from Morgada, now him. Patience . . ."

Kulgrath glanced at Gadjul then made a brief gesture for the others to follow. Kulgrath and the group journeyed down the corridor in the direction that Safrag had gone.

All, that was, save Gadjul.

With one last look at his disappearing companions, the lone Titan quickly drew a circular pattern in front of the door to Safrag's sanctum. The pattern was a complicated one with smaller, curved figures within the main body that represented a mirror image of the larger. Gadjul drew the pattern with ease, clearly having practiced it for some time.

Once finished, he stepped back. There was no hint in his expression of concern that he might be caught. Rather, Gadjul exuded confidence.

Under his breath, he sang a single word, the key to the pattern's function. The pattern shimmered then drifted to the door.

A blue haze surrounded the entrance. The blue shifted to green, then red, then finally white.

The sorcerer smiled. The hidden protections had been temporarily nullified.

Gadjul gestured at the door.

Iron tentacles shot forth from the door, seizing the startled Titan. They wrapped around his limbs and torso, even his throat. Gone from his expression was the arrogant confidence; only utter fear was on Gadjul's face.

Titans were powerful not only in sorcery, but also in physical strength. Gadjul gripped the metallic tentacles around his throat and right arm and pulled with all his might. Yet his efforts barely slowed the attack.

He blurted out a short spell. Moisture suddenly drenched the monstrous limbs. They began to rust. The change was accompanied by creaking.

But just as quickly, a gray aura spread over the tentacles. In its wake, the aura left the tentacles pristine again.

Gadjul let out a gagging sound that was as much due to his astonishment as it was to the tightening around his throat.

The tentacles dragged him toward the door. In desperation, the Titan dug his heels into the floor, but Safrag's sinister guardian relentlessly pulled him closer.

Gadjul desperately thrust a hand against the door.

The hand plunged in. Worse, when the sorcerer attempted to pull it free, it would not come out.

One foot also sank in, followed by the rest of the one arm. Gadjul's nose touched the door.

With one final, almost indifferent tug, the tentacles shoved the hapless Titan *into* the door. Gadjul was able to let out only a desperate murmur before he vanished.

The door resumed its original appearance. Silence reigned.

A moment later, Gadjul went flying out as if spewed from a giant mouth. He collided with the opposing wall and fell to the floor.

The door once more stilled.

A thick, iron-gray sap caked the shivering, wide-eyed sorcerer. Gadjul managed to stumble to his feet. Half mad, he stared first at the door then down the corridor where Kulgrath and the others had long vanished.

Mouth agape and still shivering, Gadjul fled in the opposite direction, grateful merely to be alive.

He had not escaped. Gadjul knew that he had been *released*. He had survived only at the mercy of Safrag, who had hidden that spell-protected magical minion in the door for just such intrusions.

But the departing Gadjul knew one other thing: The next time someone sought uninvited entrance to the master's lair, they would *not* be as fortunate as he.

V

REUNION

Golgren and Tyranos landed with a heavy thud. The half-breed made a grab for the wizard's staff but failed to grasp it as the wizard bounced in the opposite direction.

"This is your doing!" the robed figure growled as he came to a halt next to a large outcropping.

"No," was all Golgren answered. He rolled to his feet and was not surprised when Tyranos stood up almost as quickly. The wizard was very agile, very athletic for one of his calling.

And that again reinforced suspicions that Golgren had always had concerning his "ally."

The deposed Grand Khan looked around. While the mountains bore a similar appearance, he was sure those that surrounded him were not all that far from the citadel. They had the same bleak, skeletal look to them and radiated a familiar sense of despair. Whatever had caused the pair to be transported there did not seem to want to send him very far from his objective.

He glanced down at the signet.

"Don't put too much stock in that bauble, oh great one," Tyranos sneered. "Against the Fire Rose, it is worth nothing."

"And so I should hand it over to you, perhaps?"

The wizard snorted. "Keep it if you like."

Golgren turned from Tyranos, more interested in determining just where he was. He considered demanding that the spellcaster bring him to the top of one of the peaks so he could orient himself, but there was always the chance that the wizard might just leave him there.

Something glittered in the gloom surrounding them. That should not have been possible, but when Golgren focused on the teasing flicker, it appeared to be Sir Stefan Rennert.

Coinciding with that, the signet glowed brighter.

"What—?" Tyranos began, but the half-breed was already moving toward the distant, much-too-bright figure. Golgren thought the knight stared back at him. Certainly the knight's hand rose as if to greet Golgren.

He tried not to blink as he increased his pace. Golgren was certain what would happen if he did.

But in the end, he could not help himself, and though it was perhaps no more than a second at most that his vision faltered, that was long enough. The Solamnic was no longer there.

However, there was something *else* descending from above. The size and the wings spoke of one creature: a gargoyle.

Though the ring still glowed, Golgren did not trust it to protect him. Teeth bared, he snatched up a rock and crouched, ready to throw it with practiced accuracy at the head of the beast.

Tyranos clutched his shoulder. "Hold on! That's not one of his! It's Chasm! I can sense that!"

Aware of the wizard's link to his gargoyle servant, Golgren lowered the rock. He eyed the nearing creature and finally noticed that Chasm carried a slighter form in his grip.

"Idaria," the half-breed whispered.

The duo descended. With a rumble, Chasm gently lowered the elf in front of Golgren. She moved with some unsteadiness toward him. Her hair was disheveled, almost completely covering her face. Her gown, already well worn, was closer to tatters.

"My lord," the slave murmured, bowing her head. Her face was even more pale than normal.

"Do not look down when you speak with me," Golgren commanded. "You, my Idaria, must always look me in the eye."

As she did as he bade, Tyranos interjected himself into the situation. "And where's the cleric? Where's the Solamnic?"

Idaria's gaze fell to the ground again. "Sir Stefan . . . he is dead."

Golgren raised her chin so she again looked at him. For a brief moment, the glow of the signet revealed her surprise that it once more graced his hand. "Speak of this! When and where?"

She told them, leaving out none of the terrible details. The knight had been trying to rescue her when the macabre creatures serving the gargoyle king had surrounded them. They had seized Stefan, and one of them had slain him with his own sword. His body had been tossed to a corner where the gargoyles deposited their refuse.

Chasm nodded vigorously in support of her story. They also gave an account of their escape. In the telling, though, the tale expanded to reveal more about the dread master of the citadel and his desires. Golgren and Tyranos did not interrupt, both keenly aware that to do so might cause some memories to lapse and, thus, vital knowledge to be lost.

"He claims utter ownership of you," she told Golgren. "From before your very birth! He says that you would not even exist if not for his desire."

"There is some sense in that," Tyranos muttered, despite a glare from the half-breed. "Ogres and elves . . . the mix is not a workable one."

"No less so than a human and an Uruv Suurt," Golgren returned.

The wizard opened his mouth to retort then clamped it shut. His eyes blazed.

"So," continued Golgren, "I am to be his hound so that he might have the Fire Rose. I—"

Chasm suddenly began hopping up and down. "They come. They come!"

Screeches filled the air.

"Brace yourselves—" the wizard began.

But as he spoke, the signet flared brighter. Light crackled around them, light that shaped itself. The foursome was abruptly surrounded by shining silver shields stacked one upon the other, so they were covered from all sides and overhead.

The cries of the great flock drew closer.

"I had thought we lost them," Idaria muttered. "Forgive me! I should have warned you—"

Golgren silenced her with a wave of his hand. He listened to the thunder of flapping wings. The minions of their foe were upon them.

Then the cries grew more distant. The thunder lessened. As the four waited, the noise became less and less audible.

It became quiet again.

"Now how could they possibly miss a mound of glowing shields?" Tyranos asked with a snort. He touched the nearest shield with the crystal. "How could they—?"

The wall of shields dissipated. Golgren and the others stood in the open.

"The ring is perhaps of a bit more use than you believed?" the half-breed mocked.

Tyranos angrily shook his head. "You still can't win with that! Not when Safrag has Sirrion's gift!"

"Safrag, yes . . ." Golgren thought about the Titan leader. Whatever matter awaited resolution between the half-breed and the master of the gargoyles, it was Safrag who possessed the Fire Rose. "It is a mistake I've made. Safrag has the key."

"So now you intend to go after him?"

"Yes."

The robed figure was not convinced. "I desire the Fire Rose, too, oh Grand Khan, but consider your choices carefully and ask a few questions." Tyranos eyed Idaria. "Ask a lot of questions, like how she so easily managed to escape someone willing to plot for lifetimes to gain the Fire Rose?"

"There was nothing simple about my escape!" Idaria insisted.

"No? He left you alone with one pathetic guard easily swayed by your beauty and the giving of a name? He left Chasm chained but otherwise unguarded? I think your escape was anticipated! He wanted you to find your way back to Golgren here."

"That is not true!"

Tyranos rubbed his jaw. "And for some reason, I feel as if you've left out something important about what happened, maybe why he bothered to keep you alive in the first place, as if you have been and still are of some use to him."

The elf looked in desperation at Golgren. "I would never serve that creature!"

The half-breed's face betrayed little of his true emotions as he answered, "I would never serve him either." Golgren looked again to Tyranos. "And nothing matters now except to march upon Safrag, yes? To wrest the Fire Rose from him."

" 'March upon' him?" The spellcaster let loose a humorless laugh. He gestured at the four of them. " 'Tis a sorry legion you'll march at the head of!"

"The legions I will need, they will be ready to serve my purpose very soon if I beckon them . . . and you will help me, wizard."

"I?" Tyranos looked genuinely puzzled. "And what legions are these that you speak of?"

The half-breed looked over his shoulder to the south.

The robed figure bared his teeth. "You *are* mad."

Golgren nodded with the hint of a grim smile. "Yes, I am."

Tyranos hefted the staff. "Well, we're going nowhere for the moment. This thing has limited powers, and I've used it for a great many things today. I suggest temporary shelter."

With reluctance, Golgren nodded.

The wizard turned to Chasm. "Find somewhere."

A voice behind the half-breed commented, "To the west you'll find what you seek."

He turned.

There was no one there, but the voice had been that of the Solamnic.

"Something?" asked the wizard, gripping the staff like a weapon. Idaria and the gargoyle looked expectantly at Golgren.

"You heard nothing?" the half-breed asked.

"Only that damned, persistent wind," Tyranos retorted. The elf and Chasm shook their heads.

"We go west," Golgren declared, already starting off.

Idaria followed without comment. Chasm looked to his master, who shrugged. "As good a direction as any, I warrant." Then with a frown, he looked back to where the citadel lay. "Better than some, actually."

They walked for nearly an hour, wary for any sound of the return of the flock. However, though once they heard them far in the distance, the cries were headed away from them.

A smaller peak arose before the foursome. At first glance, the mountain appeared of no more interest than the rest, save that they would likely have to climb some part of it if they wished to continue in their current direction. Tyranos looked ready to say something, but Idaria suddenly cut him off.

"There! We must go there!"

Golgren eyed her, but the elf revealed no hint as to her reasoning. Yet he nodded and turned as she indicated.

And sure enough, in an obscure bend shadowed by the peak itself, they came across a narrow hole. For Idaria, there was no trouble slipping through, while the others needed to squeeze a bit.

Inside, though, they found themselves in a very serviceable cave that allowed the four to stretch out. The cave ended in a jagged wall with no passages. Some dried bones indicated it had been used at one point by some predator, but the bones were so old that it was unlikely the creature still lived there.

But in some ways more amazing than finding the cave was the discovery of a small stream of water dribbling out of the back wall. It coursed along for a few yards then spilled through a crack in the floor. Flanking the edges of the stream were more mushrooms of the edible type that Golgren and Idaria had seen elsewhere in the chain of mountains during their hunt for the Fire Rose, only they were the largest yet. There was more than enough for them to share, so the four ate greedily.

Slumber overtook them shortly after, despite even Golgren's desire to stay awake. His last conscious glimpse was that of Idaria, whose mouth was pinched in what seemed some inner discomfort.

Thus, it was not surprising when he stirred to feel her next to him, her lips by his ear.

"My lord, I must speak."

"Yes," he whispered back as he gazed warily at the darkened forms of Tyranos and Chasm. "You must."

"My lord, I said much, more even than I had intended, but still I withheld some knowledge from the wizard."

Golgren silently nodded for her to go on.

"My lord, the shadowed one's plotting goes even deeper. He hinted at one point that even your ascension to the throne could not have taken place without his covert actions."

"He underestimates me. I do not underestimate him. That will be his downfall."

"But there—there is more—about me."

"Yes and it is not for now." Golgren eyed Tyranos.

"But—"

He finally met her gaze. In the dark, her eyes were almost luminescent. "We will speak of spies when this is done."

Idaria shut her mouth. She stared unblinking at the half-breed for several telling seconds then turned her face away from him. The slave adjusted her position to lie at his side, as always.

"A promise has been made," he whispered as he closed his eyes. "A promise will be kept."

The elf's body momentarily stiffened then relaxed. Idaria did not thank him, but her gratitude was obvious in her easier breathing.

Golgren briefly bared his teeth before resuming his sleep. To achieve the promise of which he had spoken, first he would have to regain his empire.

And that meant seeking an alliance with those who despised him even more than Safrag did.

❧❧❧❧❧

"You are mad!" Tyranos growled under his breath. "I won't be a part of such a scheme."

Again, Golgren did not deny it: he might very well be mad. He had long before accepted that he probably was. Yet that madness also gave him advantage over his rivals. They would not always try to do what he would do.

And surely not even the gargoyles' lord would expect such a move.

"You will take me there as I have requested," he replied to the reluctant wizard. "You know you must."

He held out his hand. "Unless you would be willing to give me the staff?"

"Not even in trade for the signet. And if it wants to help you so much, why doesn't *it* transport you?"

He did not know that Golgren had already attempted that feat. However, for whatever reason, the signet had not obliged. So Golgren needed the staff—and Tyranos, since the wizard would not part with it.

"It must be done now," he told the spellcaster. "You cannot fear our destination that much, can you?"

They stood just outside the cave entrance. Day had not yet come, not that it would have made much difference in visibility, given the heavy shadows and clouds. Still, they had awakened early, well aware they would be better served making haste before even the slightest light appeared.

The signet continued to glow, so Golgren believed that it still hid him to some degree from the master of the citadel. However, whether or not that was the case, the half-breed was determined to make his decisions as was necessary. No matter what the lord of the gargoyles had told Idaria, Golgren was no one's puppet.

"I can't take all of us, not for such a distance," Tyranos muttered, the first sign that he might give in to Golgren's demand. "It must be you and me alone. Chasm can take her to safety. He'll do that."

The gargoyle nodded eagerly. Idaria, on the other hand, did not like the suggestion in the least. "I won't leave you!"

"You will," Golgren stated simply. "You have a journey of importance yourself." He told her what he desired.

Both Idaria and Tyranos shook their heads upon hearing his plan, the wizard with a grin.

"You are audacious, oh Grand Khan."

Golgren did not wait for Idaria to accept or refuse his command. To the wizard, he said, "She goes now."

Tyranos gestured to his servant. "Chasm."

Idaria reached for Golgren, but the gargoyle caught her first. She let out a gasp of protest, but to her credit, she did not cry out. Chasm spread his wings and carried her aloft.

Her eyes met the half-breed's as she ascended. Golgren turned away.

"Such a touching scene," Tyranos commented once Idaria was merely a speck in the sky.

"Take me there," Golgren coldly commanded, not needing to explain just exactly where he had decided to go.

"Now that we're alone, I'd like to suggest again what a dangerous folly you are tempting."

The half-ogre waited.

Tyranos glared. "Oh, very well! On your head be it, then. Grab my arm and hold tight! This will take much effort." With a last growl, the wizard added, "Picture the one you want to reach; it'll help."

Golgren nodded.

The two vanished from the mountains—

And a moment later, they materialized in a great, marble chamber worthy of any Grand Khan. However, in contrast to Golgren's palace in Garantha, there were no signs of patching or half-hearted reconstruction there. Everything was pristine. The floor was of the finest white marble, and great, fluted columns with elaborate crowns lined the walls on each side of the pair. A massive banner hung above an artfully carved throne, made to resemble two warriors raising their axes above the head of the current occupant. Another, almost identical throne stood next to the first; it, too, was occupied.

The symbol on the banner immediately evoked a low epithet from Tyranos. That sound, as slight as it was, alerted the armored guards standing at attention against the walls to the sudden and improbable presence of the two intruders materializing in the far corner. Axes and swords raised, they leaped to cut off the pair from those seated on the thrones. With perfect precision, they advanced on the intruders. Their shining breastplates bore the same menacing design as the great banner: a stylized condor.

Never one to cringe before his enemies, Golgren stepped away from the more-cautious Tyranos and presented himself with arms open. Although he was clearly without weapons—and missing one hand—the guards were scarcely reassured.

One of the two seated figures, the male, rose up and reached for a long sword at his side. However, rather than draw it, the figure stepped down from the stone dais upon which the thrones stood. The guards parted before him. It was easy for him to meet the half-breed's gaze levelly, for Uruv Suurt—minotaurs—were generally the same size and height as the deposed Grand Khan, though much broader of shoulder.

"Golgren," the figure snarled, his eyes darting from the half-ogre's face to his missing hand and then back again.

Golgren bowed, a diplomatic smile spreading. *"Emperor* Faros."

Chasm flew toward the direction of Garantha, but that was not his and Idaria's destination. The gargoyle followed a ragged route to avoid those of his kind that served other masters. Chasm was determined to carry the elf where he had been commanded, even at the cost of his own life.

Idaria hung helplessly, still bitter over being sent away. Yet there was that part of her that was aware that Tyranos had spoken some truth, that her flight from the citadel *had* been too simple. Try as she might deny that, the slave could not.

Therefore, Idaria slowly reconciled herself to the role that had been handed to her by Golgren. If there was any way that she might help his mad plan succeed, she would do it.

But would they, of all people, listen to her? Idaria eyed the fast-changing landscape below and wondered if she would even get the chance to ask them what Golgren hoped. Chasm had to carry her far past the capital, beyond the very borders of the ogre realm. It was not merely a question of whether or not he had the strength; she felt comfortable on that score. The question was whether there would be any obstacles in their path.

Assuming they did reach their destination, Idaria knew that it would be hard to convince those whose assistance she sought to join the cause of the deposed Grand Khan. They had no love for him, although one among them had come to respect the half-breed.

But while Stefan Rennert had been willing to sacrifice himself for Golgren, could she convince his leaders, his fellow Solamnics, to possibly risk doing the same?

VI

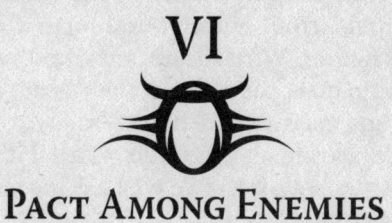

PACT AMONG ENEMIES

The angry throng carried few weapons—a handful of clubs, a sword here and there—but ogres by themselves were a threat, even to their own kind. The mob looked unkempt and even more ragged and wild of hair than usual, as if they had poured out into the streets of Dai Ushran from their slumber.

Indeed, they had done just that. Barely an hour before Golgren and his companions had risen, the capital had been shaken by what most initially had believed was an earthquake. Only when their very homes had begun to change form did they understand they were once again at the mercy of Safrag's whims.

By then, Dai Ushran had become a city of giant spherical structures. Even the towers were topped with rounded crowns. And though it was by mainly torchlight that the mob was able to see, the visibility was sufficient to reveal that the one constant with each transformation was the placing of the lead Titan's visage everywhere.

As the furious crowd reached the outskirts of the palace grounds, from within burst forth a ready force of armored figures. With spears, axes, and swords, they charged out to meet the mob. At their head, astride one of the rare and massive ogre horses, rode Atolgus. In the darkness, he looked as if he were a full Titan himself. However, it was not sorcery he wielded, but a sharp blade and a savage intent.

Matters had been building up to that confrontation for another reason. Many in the throng shouted anger at being continually shaken by the unexpected changes, but they also complained that they themselves had not yet become like the Titans, as promised.

And though Atolgus heard and understood the angry cries, he paid the complaints no heed. He had one intention: to keep order for *her* and her master. If the ogres could not be grateful for their current conditions, they were undeserving.

The armored ranks crashed into the disorganized mob with deadly force. A line of spears at the front slew more than two dozen protesters and kept others at bay. Warriors wielding swords then cut into the second line of protesters, quickly butchering them as well. The smell of fresh blood further stirred the warriors, and they pressed forward without mercy.

The mob did not retreat immediately; ogres were always stubborn, even in the face of certain doom. Thus, Atolgus's forces slaughtered more and more, with only the occasional careless warrior cut down by the disorganized mob.

Atolgus raised his sword, signaling for a new assault. From behind his foot soldiers, archers fired into the air. They did not need even their best aim and limited proficiency for their arrows to find many marks among their targets. Scores fell wounded or dead, many of the former then either trampled by their fellows or subsequently cut down by the advancing warriors.

Finally, the mob broke. Ogres fled in every direction. Even then, Atolgus did not order an end to his troops' efforts. They hunted down all those too slow in flight, slaying dozens more. The bloodbath stained the area crimson.

It was Wargroch who finally managed to stem the frenzy by riding up close to the eager Atolgus and shouting, "All is ended! There should be no more blood!"

Atolgus nearly turned on him, but at the last moment, Morgada's puppet calmed. Without any word to Wargroch, he gestured with his sword to a trumpeter. Raising a curled goat horn, the ogre warrior blew loudly.

Hearing the signal, Atolgus's warriors pulled back. Bodies lay sprawled everywhere; some were hacked apart so badly that they were nearly unrecognizable as ogres.

At last, the warlord spoke to Wargroch. "I leave to you the clearing of the streets!" With that, the former chieftain turned his great mount around and led his warriors back to the palace.

Wargroch was left with the handful of ogres who had followed him out. None of them looked eager to be there.

The Blödian surveyed the massacre. Hardened as he was by his own past, including his own betrayals, Wargroch was nonetheless shaken by the sight.

But there was nothing he could do about it. With a grunt, he called a subordinate to his side. "A wagon. This will need a wagon . . . two."

The ogre saluted then rushed off to find the wagons.

Wargroch signaled the other warriors to dismount and begin the grisly task.

The wagons arrived but a few moments later, no doubt appropriated from some side street. With the situation under control, Wargroch found himself glancing toward one of the outer walls and thinking of the buried pouch. The Blödian considered how just a matter of a few days had altered the situation greatly. Golgren would have given a Grand Khan's ransom for the contents. They represented the possibility of one of his greatest hopes coming to fruition.

But all that mattered not. Golgren had departed before the pouch had arrived; then, according to Atolgus, the Grand Khan had been slain by Safrag's sorcery. The most valuable treasure in the world could have been in the pouch, and it would not change the fact that the Titans ruled the ogre realm and would soon leave their mark on all Krynn.

Nor could an offer of negotiations by the Solamnics concerning a cessation of hostilities and a potential pact against the Uruv Suurt change that reality either.

⋙⋘

As tall as Golgren, which made them roughly two feet shorter than full-blooded ogres, the Uruv Suurt greatly resembled him in the design of their bodies, save that instead of the coarse, ogre hair they had fine coats of varying shades of brown, black, and on the rare occasion red or white. However, their coats were not the most startling factor to outsiders. No, that had to do with their heads.

Whether male or female, Uruv Suurt—minotaurs—had

heads very akin to those of bulls.

Faros was, by the standards of his people, handsome. His muzzle was sleek, and his eyes penetrating . . . so penetrating, in fact, that it looked as if they desired to literally skewer the half-breed.

Golgren reached toward the minotaur emperor.

"Betrayal!" roared one of the nearest guards. He and a companion thrust themselves ahead of Faros and attacked the two intruders.

The wizard used his staff to stop his foe's attack then struck the Uruv Suurt under the muzzle. At the same time, Golgren let his own adversary's weapon shoot past him. He then drove the stump that was his other arm—considered so little a threat by most of his enemies—into the guard's unprotected throat.

"Stop!" commanded Faros.

The two guards stumbled back; the one Golgren had struck was still clutching his throat and coughing.

"The Grand Khan Golgren . . ." The tall, brown minotaur stepped in front of his soldiers, almost within reach of the half-breed. Although the horned figure also wore a breastplate and kilt like his followers—save that the condor on his breastplate was lined by a pattern of tiny, interlinking axes and swords—his uniform did not completely obscure the many horrific scars the ruler bore from head to foot. Even the muzzle and face had not been left unblemished, though those scars were mostly due to battle. The majority of those on the body were due to slavery, first at the hands of his own people then under the ogres.

"The Grand Khan Golgren . . ." Dark brown eyes narrowed as they surveyed the half-breed. "Or is it the *former* Grand Khan? We've heard much of late."

"And I hear of Uruv Suurt marching north into the province of Blöde." Golgren waved aside the disrespectful comments. "But I come not to discuss these trivial matters."

"You should be discussing what reason there is for letting you keep your head," a female voice added. From behind Faros emerged the occupant of the other throne. Her tone bore even more malice toward Golgren than that of Faros.

"Maritia." The half-breed bowed. "It is a pleasure to be in your fair presence again."

The female Uruv Suurt had a less pronounced muzzle and horns only half as long as the two-foot ones of her mate. Her body was more graceful than that of Faros and very much akin, despite the smooth, brown fur, to that of a human or elf female. However, it was a mistake to think she was not as capable in battle as the emperor. Indeed, for a time, she had led the empire's forces in Ambeon and had even been allied with Golgren against her future mate. But she desired his death more than Faros did, for, at the behest of her mother and eldest sibling, Golgren had imprisoned her and seen to the death of her favored brother, Bastion.

"You'll find the company of a hungry pack of mere-drakes more pleasant if you don't give us a reason to keep you alive," she retorted.

"Speak faster," Tyranos muttered, unusually subdued around the minotaurs. "And wisely."

"You travel with humans now?" Faros asked, studying the wizard. "A spellcaster, of course. Golgren no longer has your mother to protect him, Maritia."

Once Maritia had been devoted to her parents, but in the end, she had learned that the Lady Nephera, high priestess of the Forerunner cult, had not only been instrumental in Bastion's murder, but had used sorcery to cause the death of the Emperor Hotak, Nephera's mate and Maritia's father. Maritia had been there when the god Sargonnas, through Faros, had finally delivered unto Nephera final justice, letting the power of her own patron—Morgion, god of disease and corruption—slowly and horribly slay her.

Tyranos's grip on the staff tightened as the guards stared at him with renewed interest. He said nothing.

"He is of no consequence to you," Golgren replied to the emperor. "Less than nothing, though useful. It is I to whom all responsibility falls, yes? And it is I to whom you must speak for the sake of all Uruv Suurt."

"I never know just where your limits of Common begin and end," Faros muttered. "Nor where the limits of your conniving end either, but this should at least be entertaining. We can always kill you afterward."

"Don't listen!" Maritia urged. "That one's already talked himself out of too many deaths."

"He'll speak true. He knows he has to with me." To emphasize his words, Faros tapped the half-breed's chest with the tip of his sword right where the half-ogre's mummified hand hung. The same hand that Faros himself had removed when still an escaped slave leading a revolt. "Still carrying it, I see."

"Always, Faros Es-Kalin."

"Wise." The emperor waved back the guards. "Resume your places—no—better yet leave us."

"My lord, we should not go," growled one soldier, who bore a helmet and cloak that marked him as an officer.

"Rest easy, dekarian. I know this one's tricks. We'll be fine . . . that is, if we can trust your pet wizard, Golgren."

That infuriated Tyranos. "By the Kraken! I'm nobody's pet or slave."

Faros's brow furrowed. He stared at Tyranos, whose eyes blazed.

"Keep your word and you'll have no trouble from me," the spellcaster finally murmured.

Faros nodded, seeming to take the wizard's word far more readily than Golgren's. To his nemesis, the emperor said, "And now? Will you tell us why you've committed this madness?"

The half-breed grinned coldly. "Your legionaries, they do not appear to obey you very readily."

Faros looked over his shoulder to where the dekarian and other soldiers stood near two high, bronze doors bearing the condor symbol. The emperor did not look pleased with his followers. "I ordered you away!"

"My lord! It is *Golgren!*" the officer persisted. "You yourself have placed a price on his head matched by no other enemy of the state! His description"—the dekarian pointed his sword toward the maimed stump—"has been committed to memory by every legionary! All know his connection to the Lady Nephera and her foul scion, Ardnor—begging your pardon, my lady!"

Maritia wore an expression of distaste, but it was not meant for the officer. There had been little familial care between her and Nephera's eldest. He had been his mother's son—a monstrous creature of the darkness, willing to serve the god Morgion. "No offense taken, dekarian, but do as your emperor commands." Her hand went to her own sword. "We have the situation well in hand."

There was no arguing with the reputations of the imperial pair. The guards retreated from the chamber.

There stood but the four—or perhaps *three* as Tyranos appeared not at all eager to be a part of the conversation.

He stepped to the far corner, never taking his eyes off the trio. One hand loosely held the staff, the other was turned fingers down and open palm toward the minotaurs.

"You know our ancient sign of parley," Maritia noted with a hint of approval. "Even most of our own no longer recall it."

"I have no hidden intentions," the wizard snapped back.

The empress shrugged; her interest returned to Golgren. There had been rumors the grand lord had once been fascinated by her, despite their great differences. The female Uruv Suurt had never returned his affection; her loathing for her former ally was well-displayed in her narrowing eyes and slightly flaring nostrils. "Well, Golgren? What is it you want this time? The removal of our legions from your southern lands?"

"In time, yes, but they are convenient where they are. The quicker to send them to where I desire."

Faros laughed. "Where *you* desire? Are you now emperor?"

"No," responded the half-breed with a slight bow, "but I will save your empire."

Both minotaurs glared. Faros exchanged glances with his mate then rumbled, "And in what manner will you save us? This should be entertaining."

"Why, I will save you from the Titans, naturally."

Despite attempting to appear otherwise, the mention of the sorcerers clearly disturbed the imperial couple. Nostrils flaring, Faros rubbed the underside of his muzzle. "And of what concern are the Titans to us?"

"The emperor is no fool," Golgren baldly stated, absently touching his severed hand, "and should not treat me so. The Uruv Suurt, they deal with a warlord who is the puppet of the Titans. You know this, of course?"

"We had some gleaning of that just recently," Faros admitted. "We have just learned of this Atolgus."

At mention of Atolgus's name, Golgren's eyes narrowed imperceptibly. There was no saving the young chieftain; Golgren considered him only another enemy.

"What does it matter?" Maritia snapped. "Better to let the ogres feud among themselves, and in the end there will be less of them!"

The emperor shook his head at his mate. "You know that you don't believe what you are saying. You know that we were discussing this . . . situation . . . only yesterday."

Maritia's expression indicated that what they chose to discuss in private was hardly a matter to be brought up before the hated half-breed.

"Your *spies,*" Golgren corrected, "were misled. The Titans are very good at misleading."

"It seems a common ogre trait," Maritia countered.

In response, the deposed Grand Khan went down on one knee. He bent his head low and extended his hand and the maimed limb to the sides.

"My life is my bond in this," he stated solemnly. "All I speak will be truth, and all which I agree to will stand, or my spirit will walk with both hands severed."

Faros gripped the hilt of his weapon. "I know that oath. There were ogres who followed me from Sahd's work camp who uttered that oath, although not with such flair of words." Again, he rubbed the underside of his muzzle. "Sargonnas take me for a fool, but I'll grant you at least the chance to speak."

Maritia reluctantly nodded. She respected Faros's opinion on that point, even if the giver of the oath was Golgren.

"Atolgus is the puppet of the Titans; he has given the capital to them and, thus, all of Golthuu."

"Golthuu." The emperor chuckled. " 'The Dream of Golgren.' "

Ignoring the mockery, the half-breed went on. "The Uruv Suurt are useful now to the Titans, for they keep my loyal warriors at bay. The offer no doubt was that all southern lands were to be given to the empire, yes?"

"To create a better buffer for Ambeon," Faros answered, referring to the minotaurs' mainland colony and the former elf homeland of Silvanost. The realm had been taken by the forces of Hotak, but Faros had deemed keeping them invaluable to his race.

"But the Titans, once they do not need you, you will follow me to doom. They will take the empire, and they will make the Uruv Suurt once more the slaves of the ogre race."

That last brought a look of intense bitterness to Faros's gaze. The worst fate for his people—even worse than being the slaves of humans—would be a return to enslavement under the ogres. There was no other race that drew such enmity from the horned warriors. The ogres had been the taskmasters of old.

"Never again," growled Maritia. "Never again."

Her mate nodded. "We are speaking of powerful sorcerers, though—"

"And more powerful yet," Golgren interjected. "For they have that which the god Sirrion fashioned, a thing to give them power over all change."

"And we have you, not a very good balance. We'll fight them, though we know we'll lose. We have no spellcasters. There is no honor in such."

Golgren tossed Tyranos a wicked grin. "No."

The wizard glared at them all but otherwise kept silent.

"You don't offer us much," the empress pointed out. "Yourself and this . . . this human. What do you expect in return for that?"

The half-breed's face was all innocence. "I expect the Uruv Suurt to continue to march into Golthuu."

Faros snorted. "When we knowingly face the Titans? You wish us to create a distraction for them while you try to regain your realm! You want legionaries to give their lives all for your sake!"

Golgren replied evenly, "You already make incursions, and soon those legions will be set upon by the Titans and your false ally, Atolgus. Would it not be better for your incursions to remain successful . . . for the sake of Ambeon and the empire?"

"What do you mean?"

"No one knows Golthuu better than Golgren," the half-breed declared with a baring of his teeth. "The legions, they would find that there are better routes, more profitable routes, than those which they use now."

The emperor glanced at Maritia. There was no denying that Golgren was more familiar than any ogre with the terrain of his homeland. He had made it a priority in his rise to power. To know the lay of the land was to know its strengths and weaknesses.

"You interest me," Faros finally returned to him.

"We'll need the latest charts," the empress suggested.

Faros shook his head. "I'll also need to be there . . . and quickly. We'll need the fastest courier ship."

"No," interjected Golgren. "There is a quicker way yet."

He gestured with his stump at a suddenly dismayed Tyranos.

VII

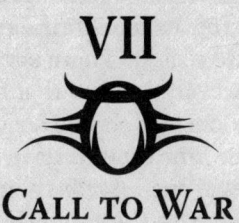

CALL TO WAR

Chasm flew swiftly, eating away at the miles. He was aware of the importance of the mission at hand, and despite the danger, he had every intention of delivering the elf to her destination.

Idaria breathlessly watched the landscape race by hundreds of feet below her. If the gargoyle lost his grip, there would be nothing to prevent her from being dashed on the hard ground, her bones shattered and her body scattered for miles around.

But Chasm seemed to have a sure grip, so Idaria thought about her own mission and what Golgren had demanded of her. For the sake of her people, the slave had to live up to the half-breed's faith in her. Idaria realized she did not want to fail *him,* either, and that raised disturbing questions for her. Because the elf did not want to fail Golgren personally . . .

Before Idaria could follow that trail of thought to its ultimate conclusion, a glint from below caught her eye. She touched a warning hand to Chasm's arm. The gargoyle had veered away from the vicinity of the capital. Below lay the edge of the mountains and, beyond that, a more arid, desolate region. There should have been no village below. However, the glint that the elf had noticed had had a metallic look to it. It was not out of the question that there might be lone scouts out in that direction . . . or a single Titan waiting just for them.

Great wings flapping, the gargoyle adjusted his flight path. Idaria had a better view of the landscape.

What she saw made her gasp. Was that a Solamnic Knight below?

The figure wavered as though it were a heat-induced illusion of the land, so the elf decided that she was only imagining things. However, Chasm suddenly banked then descended toward the metallic glint, the murky figure, the Solamnic Knight. If it were an illusion, then Tyranos's servant shared it with her.

Chasm halted at a level that left Idaria's feet dangling just a couple of inches off the rocky ground. With surprising care, he set her down the rest of the way then alighted himself.

Steadying herself, the elf stared at the figure. It was not merely a knight from Solamnia.

It was Sir Stefan Rennert.

"It cannot be," she blurted. "You are one of *his* creatures!" Idaria insisted, referring to the master of the ancient citadel.

"There is only one to whom I swear an oath now," Stefan solemnly replied. His face and form were utterly devoid of any injury, and his armor gleamed as if freshly polished. He was even clean shaven. "And that is Kiri-Jolith."

Mention of the bison-headed god of just cause

prompted the elf to look around. After the intrigues of Sirrion, she fully expected to see the other deity present. Yet there was no sign.

"He has his tasks, and monumental they are," Stefan commented, as if reading her thoughts. "I've the honor of seeking to help in his place."

"But you—you are *dead*. I saw you die!"

Chasm grunted agreement, the gargoyle partially blocking the ground between the elf and the impossible visitor.

Stefan looked pained. "I don't rightly know if I'm alive or dead or somewhere in between. I only know that as the blade sank into me and I grew cold, then, at the very last moment, Kiri-Jolith came and took hold of me. He kept me safe until I felt strength returning. When I opened my eyes, he and I stood in the midst of what had once been a great castle but which had become merely an arrangement of stones half-buried by time."

Once this was a place of tremendous courage and honor, the god had told him as the human had struggled to rise. *But that was so long ago, when even I was young.*

As was reasonable, Stefan had paid less attention to the god and more to the fact that he was not lying on the floor of the citadel as a cold corpse. He had asked much the same question of Kiri-Jolith as Idaria had directed at him. Was he alive or dead or something else?

That remains to be seen, was all the bison-headed warrior had answered. For the first time, the Solamnic had noticed that Paladine's son looked weary, even somewhat aged.

Things change and yet stay the same, and I wonder whether my place is still here upon Krynn or anywhere, the deity had gone on to say, striding through the ruins.

Stefan had kept pace, aware that he owed everything to the god who had taken him as his cleric, and also aware that he could help Idaria and the others only with Kiri-Jolith's aid.

Finally, Stefan had dared to speak up again, stating that his tasks were unfinished, that if Kiri-Jolith had saved him, it was only because the god must wish him to return to his friends and help them. He also assumed Kiri-Jolith intended to move against either Sirrion or the gargoyle king or both.

But the majestic warrior, looming more than two feet over the human and certainly capable of standing taller should he so desire, had replied that his actions were limited against Sirrion for reasons Stefan would not be able to understand. Kiri-Jolith needed the knight, not the other way around.

"He told me that Krynn is in flux, that the gods are all seeking their proper places in the world," Stefan told Idaria. "Some go by the will of Krynn's people; others attempt to manipulate matters to their own end." The Solamnic frowned. "And others, such as Sirrion, are simply unpredictable."

"But the god of fire is not an evil thing," the elf pointed out. "Not like Takhisis was."

"No, but his nature is mercurial; his decisions are of the moment. He is volatile in the absolute sense. He feels that he has been ignored despite his presence in the aspect of every creature's life. He likes games, too, and though on the surface they veer neither to the light nor darkness, they can by themselves plunge our world into chaos!"

Idaria had already experienced the truth of that statement. "What is your part in this, then?"

The armored figure's expression looked vague. "I've

more than one part, but the one most important as far as you are concerned deals with a grove and your people."

"My people?"

Stefan nodded. "We need to save them now, and for that, you, I, and Chasm here must go into the heart of the Titan realm and their very sanctum."

☙❦❧

General Thandorus had only lately come to Ambeon, but he was determined to make his mark. He had fought as first hekturion in Wyvern Legion during the taking of Silvanost and for his achievements had been granted a promotion to commander of the newly formed Badger Legion, the first such unit assembled entirely in the colony. A stout-muzzled warrior of a dusky brown fur, Thandorus had been in charge for the entirety of three days and had already begun crafting his new command in his own image. He intended for the emperor to hear of Badger Legion's exploits as soon as possible.

The legion was one of those stationed near Sargasanti—the former capital of the elves, renamed for the minotaurs' chief deity—and it was ready to march to the wooden forts located on the western borders. Thandorus would have preferred to march north toward the ogres but hoped that perhaps circumstances west might create an encounter with the Solamnics. What mattered most was raising his legion's reputation as dedicated servants of the emperor.

He sat in his tent, poring over the charts showing the path west. For the first several days of the march, good minotaur roads of stone—carved out of the once-virgin forest—would make the travel swift. Beyond that, serviceable dirt paths continued on to Fort Four, the official designation of his destination.

A guard interrupted. "General! He is here!"

Thandorus looked up. "Who? The governor?" The colonial leader was supposed to meet Thandorus before the morning's march, but that appointment was still hours away. "Why now?"

The legionary, a scarred, hardened soldier whose expression looked uncommonly startled, shook his head. "Nay! Not the governor! The *emperor* himself!"

The commander snorted furiously. Tossing aside a berry-juice-tipped quill he had been using to make notes on the charts, he bellowed, "You dare jest with your general? You—"

"He doesn't jest, Thandorus."

As his commissioning had taken place at a ceremony overseen by the emperor, the general had no trouble recognizing the first figure who stepped into the tent. However, the one who followed Faros inside astounded him, and the third troubled him.

"An ogre? A human?" As Thandorus peered at the pair, he saw the maimed limb of the second newcomer and realized that he was no ogre, but a rare half-breed. He recalled there was only one such with a maimed hand who matched that description.

"Golgren!" Thandorus reached for his gleaming, twin-headed ax, but Faros gestured for him to stand down.

"Matters have changed," the emperor declared. "And Badger has new orders."

Faros stepped to the charts, shoving aside one of the two stools set near the table and leaning over the maps for a better view. Golgren and the human followed his example. Eyes darting between the charts and the infamous half-breed, the general listened as Golgren pointed out several locations in the more vague areas north of the minotaur-ogre border. The more Thandorus drank in the discussion, the more eager he became. The intelligence passed on by Golgren was invaluable; over the past two years, dozens of scouts and spies had unsuccessfully attempted to learn as much.

Eyes afire with anticipation, Faros finally gave Golgren a grim nod. Golgren retreated to where Tyranos waited.

"We are done here," the deposed Grand Khan quietly informed the wizard.

"About damned time!" Tyranos readied the staff.

Before they could vanish, Faros suddenly rejoined them. He paid no mind to Tyranos. With a gaze as strong as the half-breed's, he looked into Golgren's eyes.

"Matters are not settled between us," the minotaur calmly announced.

"A good enemy is more preferable to a terrible one," Golgren replied.

Grimacing, the wizard summoned the power of the staff.

The pair vanished.

And a moment later, Golgren and Tyranos landed in a desolate region. The brown hills led into dank mountains; a harsh wind blew. The silence marked a place barely inhabited by even the most stubborn wildlife. Yes, it was very familiar territory to the former Grand Khan. They were in the midst of ogre country, perhaps but three days' distance from Garantha.

Tyranos all but dropped onto the ground. Gasping, he muttered, "Glad that's over with!"

The half-breed looked around. "Why are we here?

This is not where I dictated we go next."

"Because you may think that with the staff I can send us all over the length and breadth of Krynn, but there are severe limitations and we've reached them!" The brawny wizard held up the staff. The five-sided crystal glowed only faintly. "If I use this right now, we'll likely end up over there." He pointed at a spot perhaps two yards away.

Golgren frowned then sat down beside the robed figure. "You have reservations about where we must go."

"Even more than I did about our previous destination."

"It is essential—"

Tyranos angrily cut him off. "Everything *you* desire is 'essential'! I've gotten little on my end of the bargain! I might be better off on my own, as I was for so long, with only Chasm beside me. And I'd trust that gargoyle a thousand times more any day than I trust you . . . partner."

Golgren opened his mouth to reply then saw a thoughtful look pass over the wizard's face. "What do you sense?"

"Nothing. I'm merely exhausted."

"As well you should be. I did not give the matter proper consideration, how dangerous the meeting with the Uruv Suurt might be for you."

"No more dangerous than for you," Tyranos uneasily countered.

The deposed Grand Khan shook his head. "Untrue. You are to be admired, Tyranos, for all your efforts but especially in this last. This good face you put on, even when likely confronting your own people after so many lonely years—"

The mage stiffened. The color drained from his face. "What by the Kraken do you mean—?"

Golgren snatched the staff from the distracted

Tyranos. Concentrating, he uttered the magical word that he had heard the other use.

The half-breed disappeared. Echoing in his ears was a last-moment epithet from his betrayed companion.

It had been a calculated risk. During the attack by the skeletal army on the capital, Golgren had discovered that he could wield the staff as if born to such powers. It was possible that the signet had something to do with it, but whatever the true reason, it had given Golgren the impetus to dare what he had just done. The pact between Tyranos and him had become strained, and the wizard's actions had given the half-breed reason to believe that he could no longer expect help from Tyranos.

Golgren reappeared elsewhere. However, perhaps because he was not very familiar with the staff, the deposed ruler materialized several feet in the air. He struck the ground hard then tumbled down a hill.

At the bottom, Golgren came to a painful halt. He had lost the staff midway in his descent, but as he raised his head and cleared the dust and tears from his eyes, Golgren spied the staff lying a short distance away. As he had surmised, the staff had retained more power than Tyranos had claimed. It had been the wizard who was weary . . . and untrusting.

Then Golgren noticed a pair of fiery feet clad in sandals of brilliant gold.

The half-breed looked up to meet the amused gaze of Sirrion.

Without hesitation, Golgren moved quickly toward the staff. However, Sirrion raised his right hand, and a furious ring of high, blinding flames surrounded both of them.

"Unpredictable, amoral, mercurial . . . you are more my child than your mother's . . . or his. It will be interesting to see how you are further tempered, should you survive the tempering."

"What do you *want*—?" Golgren started to demand.

Yet Sirrion was already gone. The flames extinguished a breath later. Once more, the half-breed caught sight of the staff.

He also caught sight of several wary riders heading his way, riders who clearly had not seen the god of fire nor his handiwork.

Riders who were Knights of Solamnia.

❦

The time is upon us, the ghostly master of the citadel announced.

The gargoyles shrieked their eagerness. For generations, they had been bred to serve and perish for the master. All their activities, from birth onward, were aimed toward making themselves as fit as possible, readying them for the battle that might achieve his centuries-long objective.

And finally those assembled heard that they were to be so honored.

You know where you must fly. You know what you must do. Go, my pets, and die if need be so that I may obtain that which was so basely stolen from me.

One by one, shrieking all the while, the gargoyles rose from their perches. Vast dust clouds arose as the winged creatures took flight. Spiders and other vermin scurried into the shadows.

The flock leaders roared out orders in their bestial

tongues, summoning the subservient to them. Each lesser flock chose a different avenue of departure from the ancient mountain citadel. Out of the mountainside itself came some, summoned by the voice ingrained in their brutish minds. A veritable airborne army blanketed the already-shrouded sky above the Vale of Vipers.

For a moment, the huge swarm hovered in expectation. Then with a shriek that thundered throughout the dread mountain range, the gargoyles headed toward the ogre capital.

And below, in the macabre chamber where he held court, the gargoyle king summoned his other followers. The dead that were not dead, the unliving that were living—they came to him with a horrid eagerness. Rotted garments clinging to desiccated bodies, the smell of ancient decay clinging to them, they gathered. For so very long, they had been tormented shadows, but that day marked the long-awaited reward for their suffering.

My dear friends, the shrouded figure proclaimed. *My dear, loyal and trusting friends, you who gave so much are soon to breathe, soon to have your hearts pulsing again. You will know love where you only know envy; you will once more feel sated where you know only eternal hunger.*

From out of every dark corner, the shambling forms emerged. Although they in truth numbered only several dozen, their intensity made it feel as if a thousand stood listening. Corpses they might look like, but a hint of the power that they once had yielded was still evident in their ghastly presence.

The gargoyle king had been seated for the departure of his winged subjects, but he stood and *bowed* to those who served him.

I promised you that if you gave me all that you were, we would see our triumph . . . I promised that if you kept me fresh, I would keep you from death long enough . . . I have kept that promise. The Fire Rose will soon be in my grip, and we shall see all that we loved reborn with it.

The rotting figures knelt as one. Although they had no lungs or tongues with which to speak, a wind seemed to rise up from among them; it whispered a single name.

Xiryn, it called. *Xiryn . . .*

Their leader nodded in gratitude. Xiryn reached up to touch the cloth that bound the lower half of his countenance. As he did, he continued speaking.

The decay will be reversed . . . It will be as if these past travesties of life had never been. History itself will be reversed through the Fire Rose.

The skeletal figures clapped their bony hands together, creating a clatter. Over and over, the wind whispered Xiryn's name throughout the ancient edifice.

The traitors will have failed at last, and we shall see our world come alive again and ourselves made whole.

Xiryn pulled down the cloth, revealing his face. The lower half was decaying. There was still enough to recognize individual features, but it was also possible to identify the people to which Xiryn—and, thus, the ghastly throng—belonged.

He no longer had lips, but that did not matter, for when Xiryn spoke, his mouth did not move. Ages past, the decay ever so slowly eating through him had taken his physical voice away. Xiryn spoke through magic and magic alone.

Perfection is returned to us, he called to his loyal court. Raising his arms high, the gargoyle king added, *The day of the High Ogre is upon Krynn again.*

VIII

TEMPEST AMONG THE TITANS

It was an unusual gathering of the Titans, taking place in the chamber where the Black Talon alone always met. Generally, few outside of the Black Talon were summoned there. Yet Safrag had commanded that *all* should attend.

To the rest, that surely meant they were *finally* to have their chance to wield the Fire Rose. It had been a struggle for some to keep their tongues, Kulgrath especially, but it appeared that their patience was at last to be rewarded.

With the exception of Morgada, the rest of the inner circle was already seated and awaiting Safrag. The lone female Titan stood next to the empty, high-backed chair as if awaiting not only her teacher, but her lover as well. Kulgrath shielded his distaste from her view, sharing it instead with a slightly anxious Gadjul and two others among the Talon.

The rest of the assembled Titans stood facing the tall platform upon which the Black Talon members were seated around a table. In the center of the chamber, where the symbol of the inner circle covered the stone floor, sorcerers suddenly fled from a black whirlwind arising among them. Gadjul half rose, stopping only when Kulgrath stilled him with a warning hand.

The whirlwind swiftly grew, its tip touching the ceiling. Yet just as quickly, it diminished, shrinking to nothing in the space of a single breath.

And in its wake it left the fiery figure of Safrag, the Titan leader, holding in his right hand the artifact that was coveted by the gathered sorcerers.

"I am glad to see all of you here," he proclaimed as he gazed at the assembly.

"The master summoned," Morgada replied subserviently. "How could any dare keep away?"

"We've been eager to hear from you," Kulgrath added politely but not at all subserviently.

Safrag nodded then vanished. He reappeared in the chair, the Fire Rose still held reverently in his hand. Morgada smiled in his direction then took her seat next to him.

One of the Titans gathered before the Black Talon dared step forward. Bowing low, his expression humble, Falstoch murmured, "And what wisdom will Safrag impart unto us now? Has he determined how best we should wield the artifact?"

Safrag smiled like a father to Falstoch. "Yes, I have made a final determination."

Silence reigned over the Titans.

The lead sorcerer slowly rose. He held up the Fire Rose, which suddenly glowed brighter. Safrag let its haunting light wash over his companions, who moved toward it almost like moths to the flame.

" 'Sirrion's Blessing,' " he began, using one of the

other names for the artifact, "is a willful and powerful thing. A steady hand and a steady mind are needed at all times to command it. Further, in order to see that the transformations are to the best of our desires, they should be done under considerable guidance."

The rest of the Titans nodded. Safrag's pointed explanation showed how carefully he had studied the Fire Rose's mercurial and dangerous nature. With that knowledge, the sorcerers could surely begin planning its use.

"Therefore," Safrag continued, his smile gracious, "for the foreseeable future, I will continue to retain absolute control over it."

There were gasps of protest. Some of the Titans started forward. Kulgrath rose from his seat and glared, shaking off Gadjul's tugging on his arm.

Ignoring the clear objection to his decree, the lead sorcerer went on. "And in order to facilitate matters most simply, I and the Fire Rose will remain in the capital in the great temple that I have just this day used the artifact to erect. As the one most properly capable of wielding the Fire Rose, I will take each suggestion by all of you under careful consideration and, if judged a fit proposition, will carry it out myself."

"Are we to understand that we're not going to be permitted to use the Fire Rose at all?" Kulgrath blurted.

Although Gadjul shrank back, Draug, one of Kulgrath's other allies in the Talon, added his voice. "It was agreed on from the start that the artifact would belong to the Titans as a whole, with the Black Talon overseeing the situation."

"But that was before I determined how dangerous such a course would be. Already, the avarice is clear in the eyes of too many of you. That is why I must take such actions."

"There is more avarice staring back at us than comes from all our eyes together," Kulgrath angrily retorted.

"We are not the ones so possessed by it," Draug offered.

Morgada pressed back against her seat. Her expression was guarded. Among the Titans watching the spectacle from the floor, Falstoch stepped forward and thrust a taloned finger in Kulgrath's direction.

"Safrag is the wisest among us! If he states that he must keep the Fire Rose to protect us from ourselves, then so be it!"

"Well said," Morgada quietly interjected. Her wary expression did not change.

Gadjul shifted his seat as much as he could to avoid being too close to Kulgrath. The other Titan was too incensed to notice.

"Fawning abomination!" he snapped at Falstoch. "You are unworthy of being one of us!"

The Fire Rose flared, its brilliance blinding all but Safrag, who stared into its flaming depths without fear. As the artifact's glow lessened, he glanced from Draug to Kulgrath.

"I have relied heavily in the past on the advice of both of you, and I appreciate your concerns."

Draug frowned but nodded. Kulgrath remained unmoved.

"You are steadfast in your resolve," the Titan leader commented. "As strong of determination as the very stone of this sanctum."

Draug's eyes flared in sudden horror. Kulgrath's hand

rose toward Safrag as he, too, realized where the master was going.

"It is only right then, that you should be as them."

The Fire Rose burned.

Draug howled and curled into himself. Kulgrath almost managed to complete a spell, but whether it would have done him any good was moot. He, too, suddenly twisted in agony.

For a moment, there was the terrible sound of crunching bones. Then both Titans became thick, gray vapor. That vapor hurtled toward the thick, oppressive walls. Other Titans darted out of the way as if fearing to join the pair's fate.

The two clouds of vapor poured into the cracks. As they did, shrieks rose from both. The stone swelled as if taking heaving breaths.

Then all was silent. No one had to ask what had befallen the duo. The power of the Fire Rose had transformed them into stone.

Morgada rose. "The master has wisely administered justice! The Titans and the Fire Rose are safe from unwise influence now."

"Hail, Safrag!" Falstoch lustily shouted.

The other Titans immediately took up the shout. Safrag nodded benevolently. With his free hand, he then gestured for Falstoch to step forward.

Despite some obvious trepidation, Falstoch held his head high as he walked up to the Talon. Only when he stood directly below Safrag did he then lower his head once more.

"Falstoch, your wisdom is evident to all of us. Therefore, I grant you the seat vacated by Kulgrath."

The other Titans were shrewd enough to immediately

applaud the decision. A stunned Falstoch moved to the seat, where Morgada briefly touched his shoulder in congratulation.

Safrag stared at his audience. "I shall ponder who is worthy of the remaining opening in the Black Talon. As for this gathering, it is ended."

Almost from the moment that he made the pronouncement, the Titans began vanishing in short bursts of black flame. No one wanted to draw Safrag's ire.

Morgada murmured in Falstoch's ear. The newest member of the inner circle nodded then also disappeared. Within moments, only Safrag and his apprentice remained.

"An august choice," the female Titan quietly spoke.

"Falstoch or the removal of Kulgrath and Draug, my dear Morgada?"

She blinked. "Why, both, naturally."

He smiled wider than before, revealing many, many sharp teeth. "And that is why I keep you near me."

The female sorcerer looked as demure as any of her kind could manage. "May I . . . may I merely *touch* the Fire Rose?"

Still smiling, Safrag extended the artifact to her. He did not release his grip, though.

Morgada's long, taloned fingers stroked the flowerlike structure. Her golden eyes blazed bright as she sensed the incredible forces flowing through and radiating from it.

"So much power . . . to remake *anything* or *anyone* . . ."

"To remake even us."

She cocked her head. *"Us?"*

Safrag chuckled. "I have decided that Dauroth's spells were inadequate. I have already begun formulating just what I desire the *new* Titan race to look like."

She gaped, displaying her own sharklike teeth. "You intend to transform all of us, as well as the entire realm?"

"I intend to transform *most* of us. There must be some additional . . . culling."

Morgada bowed. "Whatever service I can render in that regard, I offer."

"Of course." The Titan leader briefly cupped her jaw, then, stepping back, vanished in a burst of black flames.

For a moment longer, Morgada retained her expression; then she, too, disappeared, materializing a breath later in her personal quarters.

The female Titan immediately began concentrating. In her mind, she saw the subtle seals she had learned to put in place. The runes were hidden with deep, ancient spells. Even Safrag would not have been able to sense them.

Satisfied, Morgada turned her thoughts to contacting her true master. She had come there serving another, the shadowy form known as Xiryn.

She had only just become a Titan when he had visited her in a dream. He had sensed her ambition long earlier and, in truth, had manipulated matters so she would be invited to join the sorcerers' ranks. Things had so easily gone her way, and Xiryn had offered her a new future, to help steer the choices of the leader of the Titans until the Fire Rose—Xiryn's ultimate goal—could become his. For her part, Morgada would have a place in his new kingdom that would be second only to his.

With his guidance as well as her own beauty and cunning, Morgada had easily fulfilled his commands to the point where the artifact was nearly in their grasp. Safrag was doing just as Xiryn had predicted; the treacherous leader was playing into their hands.

Especially by seeing Morgada as the only one—save perhaps the fawning Falstoch—whom he could trust near him.

Morgada sensed Xiryn's desire to speak with her. With that in mind, the dark temptress spread her fingers wide and placed both palms over her eyes. A faint, black glow emanated from her, darkening the rest of the stone chamber.

Xiryn, she called in her thoughts.

I have waited for you. There was just a hint of warning or threat in that statement.

I could not reach out to you! Safrag summoned us to dictate his decision concerning the Fire Rose!

Her explanation appeared to soothe him. *And?*

He has acted exactly as you predicted, right down to his intention to transform the Titans too.

Morgada sensed his good humor at that. She relaxed.

Very good . . . The children have been set loose . . . The hand is all that is awaited.

She knew exactly what he meant by "the hand." *Will he come?*

He is as I intended him to be from his birth. He will come because he must come, because it is in his nature to come.

I shall be ready to do my part, Morgada replied.

As you should. The voice faded. *As you should . . .*

Contact was broken. Morgada lowered her hands. A sheen of sweat covered her perfect, azure skin, yet it was caused not by fear, but rather anticipation. Soon all would come together. The only pawn still awaiting was Golgren—Golgren, who had been created through Xiryn's efforts. He was who would wrest the Fire Rose from Safrag, as Xiryn desired.

The female Titan smiled. And once that happened, it would be *Morgada* who took it from Golgren, not Xiryn.

⚬⚬⚬❈⚬⚬⚬

Tyranos let out a growl, not the first. The wizard had to constantly cope with Golgren's arrogance. But at last things were happening as he desired.

Probably the half-ogre was feeling very proud of himself, the wizard thought as he concentrated. *Wonder how he'd feel if he knew that I'd let him take the staff.*

It had been a grueling decision but one that Tyranos had in the end felt necessary. He had a method by which to retrieve the staff—a painful method, granted—but for the moment he needed Golgren's unknowing assistance. Tyranos needed Golgren to act out the plan set in place by the gargoyle's shadowy lord.

The wizard sat near the spot where he had last spoken with the half-breed, drawing new strength from his exhausted body. In very many ways, his concentration was akin to that of a trained warrior mentally preparing himself for battle.

Tyranos had no problem with using Golgren for his personal gain. The half-breed would have done the same.

All that matters is the Fire Rose, he thought. *With the Fire Rose, I can make things right and make me right.*

He suddenly sensed that someone was standing behind him. Tyranos made no move, considering carefully just which of the two possible candidates it must be. The fact that he did not feel any sweltering increase in the temperature helped his guess.

"I thought I'd seen the last of you long ago," he snarled without looking back. "Let us leave it that way."

119

"You know a part of you does not agree with that statement," said the deep, majestic voice.

With an exasperated sigh, Tyranos rose, using only his legs. He made a fluid turn worthy of any fighter, which produced a nod of approval from the other figure.

"You have not let your skills fade," the bison-headed giant remarked.

"For my sake only. No longer to serve the cause of *any* god, even you!"

Kiri-Jolith shook his head. The deity stood more than a foot taller than Tyranos, though the two were alike in the breadth of their great shoulders. "No one serves me, Tyranos. I ask favors of them, and they may choose to grant them or not."

"Semantics. I've seen the proof. I've watched the lives that were sacrificed for you, for Sargas, for all the others. That's why magic became my god, but even there, only the magic itself, not the trio."

"And they've been very patient with you, do you not think?"

Tyranos turned away from the god. "Spare me your philosophical mutterings! We've no more ties between us! Those perished with my uncle, my brother, my sisters, and my friends."

"They gave themselves for what they believed. They saved so many others where your own mentor turned a blind eye."

That last caused the wizard to angrily glance over his shoulder. "I am not him! I wanted only to bring to my people something so many of them feared and yet that could help them!"

The bison-headed god's deep brown eyes blinked once, only once, for the first time. "And then?"

"And then they rejected me as Gragnun's puppet, as dangerous as he turned out to be! Even after I brought him down!"

"They were wrong."

That concession from Kiri-Jolith momentarily pushed Tyranos mentally off balance. The wizard recovered quickly, though. "They were wrong and I was wrong to believe they could understand! I've turned from them, turned from my ancestors! I will become what I should become!"

With determination, Tyranos left. He stalked several steps from where the deity had been standing only to find Kiri-Jolith in front of him again.

"A paltry trick," the wizard muttered.

"You would risk everything to abandon what you were born to be?"

Tyranos sneered. "Yes."

Kiri-Jolith nodded. There was an indecipherable look in his gaze. "Then there is hope for you yet."

The hooded figure was incredulous. "Now what—?"

But the god of just cause had vanished.

"By the Kraken!" Tyranos let out a snort. "So typical."

Then he noticed that something lay on the ground where the deity had been standing.

It was the staff.

Without thinking, he snatched it up. It glowed brightly, apparently completely rejuvenated.

The grin spreading over his leonine face faltered. The last time he had seen that staff was when Golgren had taken it. What did it mean that Kiri-Jolith had returned it to Tyranos?

The staff was the lone item that he had from his past, an artifact once belonging to his mentor, which Tyranos had taken after Gragnun's death, after Tyranos had been forced to kill him. Tyranos had tricked Gragnun into putting it aside, and that had been all the opportunity the younger mage had needed.

Tyranos had regrets about the dishonorable method by which he had slain his former teacher, but not about the actual death. Others had already perished due to Gragnun. Just as Golgren, Idaria, and others were likely to perish at the hands—or magic—of either the Titans or the gargoyles' master.

A low, bestial rumble escaped Tyranos. He suddenly knew exactly what Kiri-Jolith intended. He knew *exactly* what he was supposed to do.

"Well, I won't! You hear me?" Tyranos growled at the sky. "I won't."

The sky was silent.

The spellcaster grimaced.

"Damn all you gods," he muttered under his breath.

Raising the staff, he spoke the command and disappeared.

IX

SIR AUGUSTUS

Golgren awoke as though sleepwalking, with chains binding his arms behind his back, and which kept his legs close together as he walked. At best he could shuffle along slowly.

The Solamnic patrol had treated him rather courteously, considering his ogre heritage. They had not run him through the heart nor had they lopped of his head. They had settled for chaining him and slowly marching him back to their leader through the uneven, hilly terrain far west of his beloved city.

They had not offered him a mount nor did he demand one. Golgren intended to accept whatever trials the humans wished to impose on him. Golgren would not make himself look weak before the knights.

Despite his predicament, there was only one concern on his mind, and that did not immediately have to do with his own welfare. Some time during his capture, Tyranos's staff had vanished. Golgren had not witnessed its disappearance but knew that none of his captors had it in their possession. For one thing, most of them would have looked upon such a magical tool with scorn. While spellcasters were useful at times to the Solamnics, the knights were comfortable with only a few clerics among their number who had been granted powers by their patron gods.

But if the humans did not have the staff, it seemed likely that Sirrion had taken it. Yet Golgren could not fathom why the fiery deity would have first teased the half-breed with its presence, then, without teasing fanfare, removed it from him.

"He's awake," remarked one of the knights.

The others, all seated around a small fire, glanced without interest at Golgren. Even though they knew who he must be, his fate was for their commander to decide, not for them.

"Help him up and give him some food," the leader of the party commanded. His great, brown mustache wiggled as he spoke, almost making it look as if he sported furry tentacles.

Two knights obeyed the order. They set Golgren down carefully then removed the bonds keeping his arms tied. The half-breed cautiously stretched agonized muscles under the watch of his two guards. He then accepted a small bowl of oats that was the same fare upon which his captors had also breakfasted. The faint smell of burned grain wafted under his nose.

Perhaps they expected him to spit out the food, for the guards warily studied each bite he took, as if waiting for him to flaunt his swordsmanship skills. Full-blooded ogres rarely ate such fare, preferring very rare-cooked—even raw—meat and some of the harsh, edible plants of their locale. To most of Golgren's race, the food the knights ate would have seemed fit for only toothless elders almost ready to die. However, Golgren's dual heritage had given him a more egalitarian appetite, although the oats were hardly comparable to the fine dishes his elf slaves had been known to cook for him.

Thought of elf slaves reminded Golgren of what he had hoped Idaria might accomplish. By rights, she should be somewhere far ahead of him, perhaps already meeting with the same human to whom his captors were bringing him. Golgren wondered whether she had made it to her destination or whether the wizard or Chasm had interfered with her mission.

When he was finished with his meal, the guards prepared him for the next stage of their journey. To his surprise, they set him atop a stout, brown mount that they generally used for carrying supplies. They must have discussed their captive and decided that more haste was needed. After all, they had captured the Grand Khan of all ogres. Or, at least, the former Grand Khan.

The journey covered hills that rolled up and down as if they were frozen waves. The monotony of the trip did not end until midway through the day, when Golgren spotted something in the distance that he took to be a large encampment. With each successive hilltop that they reached, it came into better view.

His captors spoke only when necessary, which meant most of the time they rode in silence. Golgren was not certain where he was exactly, although the staff had followed his dictate, bringing him to the edge of Golthuu nearest to Solamnia. It had been fortuitous that a band of riders had come along.

Perhaps too fortuitous. Golgren had not forgotten that Sirrion was involved somehow. It was possible that either he or the gargoyles' master had plans for Golgren and that he was still playing out a role destined for him before his birth.

Finally, they reached the last hill overlooking a large contingent of fighters who had made camp. With a combination of pleasure and irony, Golgren surveyed the full military force. Crisp tents lined the vicinity, all of them in perfect formation. A fine array of horses was tethered to the north. Everywhere, knights in full armor polished their swords, lances, and other weapons. Everyone looked ready to fight at a moment's notice.

He had found what he desired already waiting on his border.

The sentries at the perimeter watched warily as the party approached. An officer of the Order of the Sword stepped up, the great blade emblem filling most of his breastplate.

"Sir Justin! You're back early."

"I've need to see the commander," the lead knight of the party answered. "Is he in the camp today?"

"Just returned—" the other knight halted in midbreath as he registered Golgren's conspicuous presence amid the others. "Paladine preserve us! Is that—?"

"Let us pass," Sir Justin requested, eyes narrowed.

The officer quickly nodded then gestured to the sentries. Sir Justin's riders slowly entered the camp. As they moved through the immense camp, heads turned and voices whispered; the lone prisoner drew everyone's attention. More than one knight stood up and gazed or glared at Golgren, some with wide eyes.

At last, they came to a tall, white tent with a variation of the banner of the Knighthood—a crowned kingfisher bearing a sword and a rose in its talons—fluttering above. Two sharp-eyed sentries stood at the entrance with swords gripped tightly. They did not acknowledge the newcomers. Golgren kept his gaze on the tent flap, certain that, despite the sentries' immobility, whoever dwelled there had been alerted of his coming.

A gauntleted hand thrust through the flap. An elder knight with a long, silver mustache and thinning hair only slightly darker in color peered at the riders from under a shaggy brow. The eyes that studied Golgren were deep blue and shrewd.

"Escort our guest inside," he ordered in a voice that suffered from an unusual rasp.

The half-breed's guards reached to assist him down from his mount, but the chained figure slid off with ease. He did not expect anyone to undo his bonds and, therefore, was not disappointed when the Solamnics immediately marched him forward. The commander turned back into the tent as one of the sentries held open the flap.

The interior was sparsely decorated with two simple wooden stools and a small table. A pair of round-bottomed, bronze oil lamps—unlit—hung from short chains attached to the wooden frame at the center of the ceiling. Over to one side lay a well-worn cotton bedroll that showed that, on duty, even the most prestigious of knights slept on the most simple of mattresses—the ground. Despite the heat, the tent smelled *clean,* for the Knighthood was almost obsessed with orderliness.

A map lay on the wooden table, and although it was rolled up, Golgren sensed that it had been spread out for study only moments before. He was fairly certain it was a map detailing Kern.

The commander drew his long, polished sword and

set it to the side of the table, a safe distance away from Golgren. He then sat on the nearest and largest of the two stools.

"Undo the Grand Khan's limbs."

Golgren hid the slight surprise he felt upon hearing that his arms, too, were to be freed. His prowess in battle, even with only one hand, was surely well known to the Solamnics.

Rubbing his maimed wrist, the half-breed stepped to the stool. However, he waited to sit until invited to do so.

One eyebrow arched, the commander waved permission. At the same time, he reached for a brown flask of wine that had escaped Golgren's notice.

"Not elven fare since that's so rare these days," the human added pointedly, "but some good Solamnic red."

He poured some into a worn, silver mug, which he handed without hesitation to his "guest." At the same time, the guards retreated from the tent. As he sipped his drink, Golgren understood that the commander had given them some unseen sign.

"The Grand Khan Golgren," the Knight of the Rose murmured after taking a sip from his own mug. "Is the wine to your liking?"

"Yes. My thanks. I was parched."

"Not a surprise. And my apologies for the uncivil behavior of Sir Justin's party, but he wasn't warned about you."

Golgren raised an eyebrow slightly, the only hint of his curiosity over that odd statement.

"We also expected your arrival to be a tad bit more . . . straightforward." The commander set down his mug. "But forgive me. I have not introduced myself. I am Sir Augustus Rennert, Knight of the Rose and overall leader of this exploratory expedition."

Golgren ignored the man's titles—even the questionable "exploratory" part referring to the expedition—as Sir Augustus's surname registered. "You are kin to Sir Stefan Rennert?"

"Didn't the lad make that clear? He's my nephew by blood and pretty much one of my sons by pride."

"I see . . ."

"He'd warned us that you would be coming soon, but it would've been more . . . prudent . . . if you'd alerted us yourself. Still, no harm is done as we're yet awaiting word to the missive I sent to Lord Kardon, he to whom I must report."

Sir Augustus's explanations were filled with contradictions and puzzles. He spoke as if he had recently heard from his nephew and as though he expected Golgren to be making something akin to an official visit. Had Idaria reached that place, some of what the commander said might have made sense, but as it was, Golgren grew suspicious.

He kept his face blank, however. "And the details of your missive?"

Pouring both of them a bit more wine, Stefan's uncle answered, "That I took Stefan's recommendations seriously, considered the various aspects of acceptance or rejection several times, and finally gave his ideas my guarded approval."

"So you approve . . ." the half-breed cautiously began.

" 'Guarded approval,' I said, actually." Augustus took another short sip. "An alliance of any sort with a leader of the ogres is one thing, but an alliance with the deposed leader is fraught with questions. Either one, however, presents a complex situation for my superiors."

Golgren understood. The pact that he had still hoped to initiate with the Solamnics had already been submitted, and was, in fact, under consideration. It was a boon to his cause, but how the pact had been initiated still baffled and bothered him. "I am grateful that the Solamnics will consider this and grateful that your nephew speaks so well of it."

"I would've never expected it of him, I admit, but he came here in the middle of night, insisting that I listen and listen quickly. He set out the parameters of what you required and what he felt was necessary for the good of our homeland."

Golgren was still puzzled. "I had hoped . . . I had hoped to cross paths with Sir Stefan on my way here."

"You missed him by two days and a night. He was adamant about the fact that he had another mission to fulfill." The elder knight grew somber. "His brief but poignant farewell leaves me fearful that he believes that he will not survive his other task."

Golgren downed the rest of his own wine. "My respect for Sir Stefan is great. I will honor him always."

"Thank you." Setting down his mug, Sir Augustus rose. "He spoke very well of you, though he gave me some warning, naturally. Give me your oath that you'll behave yourself, and I'll have the shackles taken off permanently."

"It is to my benefit to keep peace with you, Sir Augustus Rennert. I will do nothing to make you regret my presence."

"Spoken as I expected, after how Stefan described you!" The human chuckled. "You are nothing like the stories we've heard in Solamnia."

Setting down his own mug, the half-breed also stood.

"No, you are wrong. I am very much like the stories that you have heard, Sir Augustus Rennert. Very much."

The knight's humor faded. With a curt nod, he indicated the bedroll. "I'll have another of these brought in here. It should go without saying—but I'll say it anyway—that there's only one place you're truly safe in this camp and that's in my presence."

"I understand."

"I hope to have word tomorrow on the final decision. I've sworn to my nephew, though my superiors don't know this, that if the pact is rejected, you'll go free without hindrance. I'll have a horse and two days' rations given to you, and that should suffice."

"Once more, you have my gratitude," Golgren quietly replied.

"Thank me not. Thank Stefan. He insisted that for all of us it was better to do it this way. I don't know why, but you've touched him in a manner I could've never believed possible, and that's also the reason I deem it safe for you to sleep here unbound."

Golgren only bowed his head. His mind raced, reviewing all he had learned and how it would determine his next step. Yet there were two factors that continued to muddy his concentration. The first and most obvious was Stefan Rennert's part in everything.

Stefan Rennert had been dead by the time he had supposedly returned there, through miraculous means of transportation, to convince his uncle of the necessity of the alliance. Not for a moment did Golgren doubt what Idaria had told him concerning the knight's slaying at the hands of the gargoyle king's monstrous followers. Yet . . . the young knight had evidently appeared there.

And that, to Golgren, suggested one thing: Kiri-Jolith.

A guard entered with another bedroll for the half-breed. The fabric was frayed, the material was faded from use, and there was a slight hint of horse smell, but Golgren paid none of that any mind. He was caught up in thinking of the bison-headed deity. What further part the god of just cause intended to play there, Golgren yearned to know. Perhaps Kiri-Jolith desired to gain some prominence over the ogres; either that or the god intended to spread the influence of the Solamnics over Golgren's realm.

If that were the case, the deposed Grand Khan intended to disappoint him.

"I'll be ordering extra guards around the tent," Sir Augustus informed Golgren, interrupting his reverie. "Not to keep you in, but to ensure that others stay out. The men will all be chosen for their trustworthiness."

Golgren smiled slightly, revealing his filed tusks. He knew that doing so lessened the elf part of his appearance. "Are not all knights trustworthy?"

The commander took some slight umbrage. "*All* knights are indeed trustworthy, but not all prisoners are the Grand Khan Golgren."

Golgren bowed as if complimented. He then took to the bedroll. Although the day was not quite over, it behooved him to rest or, at least, to pretend to do so. Besides, he had nowhere else to go and had to wait, good or ill, for Solamnia's response.

"There will be food at sunset," his host informed him. "Something a little better than the meals you received on your way here but still simple fare. In the meantime, is there anything you desire?"

They were treating him very well, considering. Yet it was clear that, if Solamnia chose not to accept the pact, there was a good chance that some eager young knight might take a swipe at Golgren's head before Sir Augustus could guarantee him safe passage away from that place.

"There is nothing. I thank you for your hospitality."

Augustus shook his head. "Again, thank me not. This is all due to Stefan and how dear I hold not only his word, but his life, ogre."

With that, the commander gave Golgren a curt bow and departed the tent. Not for a moment did the half-breed consider rising and inspecting the map or anything else. It was quite likely that eyes were watching him for just that sort of transgression. Any act that hinted at distrustful behavior might ruin what hopes Golgren nurtured for the pact.

He thought again of Sir Stefan Rennert and the young Solamnic's impossible feat. However, thinking of Rennert reminded him of his elf slave.

Stefan, who was dead, had reached his people's encampment. Idaria, whom the half-breed had last seen *alive,* had not, even with the gargoyle Chasm to act as her winged steed and guardian.

Where *was* the elf, then?

Golgren ground his teeth. What could have happened along the way that Chasm had not been able to prevent? Unfortunately, the half-breed could think of many dangers, *two* in particular that were likely. One was the sinister figure who claimed to have been responsible for spawning Golgren himself, who seemed to trail him everywhere. However, it made no sense for the creature who had released her—as Golgren, like Tyranos, believed—to let her go then recapture her so immediately.

That left Safrag, who possessed the Fire Rose and who, very possibly, knew that Golgren was among the living.

Safrag had Idaria. Golgren felt it with certainty.

Safrag had *his* Idaria.

∘₰◌₰∘

Although Safrag did *not* actually have Idaria in his clutches, she was not all that far away from him. Accompanied by Chasm and guided by Stefan, she journeyed into a dark, silent forest. The place unusually frightened her, and it had only a little to do with the lack of any songbirds or insects. No, the very forest itself felt utterly *wrong,* unnatural.

"What have they done to it?" she breathed.

"Made it much like themselves," Stefan replied. He, too, did not seem entirely of the mortal plane, but at least she trusted him. Idaria drew courage and strength from his presence and likely the blessing of his patron deity, Kiri-Jolith. That the god had brought Stefan back from certain death was surely a great miracle. Indeed, it gave her hope they might yet succeed in her quest to save her people.

Even though Stefan himself did not boast of certainty, Idaria had hope. The elf was willing to take whatever risk necessary. If the other slaves were not rescued, they would face a dire fate. At the very least, the Titans desired fresh blood for their spells. They would likely experiment in sinister fashion on those they held captive. Idaria had witnessed the sorcerers' handiwork in the past, and the nightmares remained with her yet.

She clutched her hands to her chest as a chill ran

through her that had nothing to do with the damp, cool air. Early on, the elf had found it odd that the air could be damp and cool while at the same time so stifling. Once more, the oddity could only be the work of the Titans.

And thinking of the Titans, she wondered about Golgren. He had expected her to journey to the Solamnics. Even though Stefan had assured her that he had already taken the proper steps in that direction, Idaria felt guilty. She was absolutely certain that Golgren, assuming he regained his throne, intended to keep his promise to release her people. Yet when the knight had offered her the opportunity to journey with him, the elf had turned away from Golgren's mission with little hesitation. In her heart, she wondered if the Grand Khan was more capable of staying true to his word than she was.

Trying to dispel such thoughts, Idaria shook her head, focusing on her surroundings. The forest was darker than the night should have permitted; indeed, Stefan had informed her from the beginning that it did not matter whether they passed through it in the day or night. The forest would work against them either way. She took that to mean that the shadows would have enshrouded the trio even in the midst of a sun-filled noon.

But the shadows were the least of her concern. Leaning close to Stefan, she murmured, "I could swear that the trees are closing in on us."

"I believe they're trying," he replied in just as subdued a voice.

"You have noticed that too?"

"Shortly after we entered. I think they sense intruders and aren't sure about us."

"Then the Titans must know that we are here!"

Stefan shook his head. "No, I don't think so." He held up the medallion upon which the mark of Kiri-Jolith was engraved. The medallion offered a faint, silver glow that was visible for only a foot or two, yet it gave off warmth. "I would know if that was the case."

Idaria accepted his word, but Chasm, guarding the rear, grunted in distrust. An elemental creature, the gargoyle believed in two things only: his master and his strength, and the former was not accompanying them.

"Should go in front," the winged creature muttered not for the first time. "Protect elf."

Idaria had become the most important person to Chasm other than Tyranos. She treated him as no other did, with a respect that likely even the wizard did not demonstrate. That respect was probably the main reason Chasm had agreed to the change in plans, for which Idaria was grateful. She suspected that Stefan could have taken her from the gargoyle if she had demanded to go with him, but to do so would have made her feel even worse than she did about betraying Golgren.

He is an ogre, whatever his mother was, she tried again to remind herself. Her original reason for willingly becoming his slave had been muddled over time, and she had acted as the pawn of the gargoyle king, it was true. Even more important, though, over her time with the half-breed, Idaria had witnessed enough of Golgren's attempts to raise up his people to see the love and care he had for them and the care he also displayed toward her.

It gave her a headache to try and sort it all out. All that should have mattered was freeing the slaves and yet—

The leaves rustled, yet there was no wind.

Stefan raised his hand, silently calling for a halt.

Something moved in the shadows ahead. It was tall and had an odd gait, as if in part dragging itself along. A scent that evoked images of a moldering grave filled the air. The knight went into a battle stance while Chasm flexed his claws. Idaria prepared to do whatever she could to help them fight.

Then her sharp eyes picked up another figure moving from the right, and behind it was a third and a fourth. The elf quickly looked around.

They were being surrounded.

She tapped Stefan's shoulder. He nodded, understanding her warning.

"Stay between Chasm and myself," Stefan whispered.

The leaves continued to rustle, almost as if urging the newcomers forward with whispers. Idaria counted at least a dozen and knew that there were probably at least twice that number.

The first stepped near enough to enable them to see it better.

Idaria stifled a gasp.

It was an ogre . . . or, rather, the skeleton of an ogre. There was no flesh, no muscle, merely bone. Some tattered garments remained; a few bits of hair clung to the skull. That was all. Its jaw hung slackly, almost as if the monstrosity were trying to speak.

In its bony hand it gripped a rusted but very serviceable axe.

The eyes were empty sockets, yet the skeleton peered around as though searching for something else besides them. Some of the others neared. They were identical to the first, save for their weapons. Some held axes; others, clubs, swords, or spears.

And they all intently scanned the general vicinity in

RICHARD A. KNAAK

which the trio was trapped, which made Idaria suddenly realize that *none* of the undead knew that the three were actually there.

Stefan leaned close. "The medallion is shielding us from their knowledge, but the magic of the forest is strong enough to tell them something is not quite right. We must continue to stand still."

They had little choice. The macabre sentries had them ringed. It was possible that the stealthy Idaria might be able to slip past them, but the other two would not be as fortunate.

One of the ghoulish figures stepped nearer. It passed where Stefan stood and bent forward just before Idaria. The elf sensed Chasm starting to move and ever so slightly shook her head to warn him away.

The movement appeared to catch the skeleton's attention. It tipped its skull to the side and bent closer. The empty eye sockets came within inches of her face. The jaw slowly swung back and forth. So near, Idaria felt an intense cold radiating from the fiend, a cold with which she, as a slave, was well familiar. It was the coldness of death, animating their movements.

Despite the horrific threat the skeleton posed, Idaria felt a moment of sympathy. She doubted that the ogre and his comrades had offered themselves up for such ghastly duty.

To her relief, the skeleton pulled back. It rejoined the others and after tense moments, despite the continued rustling of the leaves, moved on.

Stefan did not signal the other two to continue. The knight remained as still as a statue, and Idaria and Chasm followed suit.

Only the last two skeletons remained in sight.

Watching them as they gradually moved on, Idaria prayed they would not turn back. The trees rustled harder and harder, as if trying to urge the skeletons not to make a mistake, to return.

The final ghoul melted into the darkness. Stefan waited a few breaths longer then pointed ahead. He took a step.

Idaria also took one. As her foot settled, she almost expected the monstrous patrol to come rushing back to slay them. Yet other than the incessant shaking of the tree branches, nothing happened.

Breathing easier, the elf picked up her pace to catch up with Stefan. Behind her, the gargoyle loped along, sometimes on his two legs, sometimes using his other two limbs as well.

Above them, the rustling grew almost thunderous.

Something darted across her path.

Idaria took it for a serpent at first, but it seemed to have no end to its long body. It sprouted from the ground, ran a distance, then bored into the earth again.

She paused to peer at it and finally realized that it was only an upturned root. Thinking no more about it, the elf straightened.

Her sharp eyes noticed that the ground was suddenly filled with twisting, upturned roots.

"Stefan—"

The knight turned to her. As he did, he stepped on one of the roots.

The end of the root shot out of the ground and coiled around his ankle. With a startled grunt, Stefan fell back.

Idaria sought to reach him, only to trip over another root. It wrapped around her foot, sending her down on one knee. In the process, that knee touched another root, which then proceeded to wrap around her upper leg.

"The roots!" she warned. "The forest could not locate us, so it set out snares that would attack when touched!"

Understanding her warning, Chasm immediately took to the air but collided with long, tapering branches that were sweeping down from above. At first, the gargoyle shoved them aside, but then, despite his best efforts, he became entangled. The forest had taken into account the possibility of visitors who could fly. The branches tightened around the struggling gargoyle.

Unable to orient himself, Chasm became more and more enmeshed in the tree limbs. Below, Idaria stretched her arms up in an attempt to keep the roots from seizing them as well.

Stefan hacked with his sword at those that wrapped themselves around him. The blade flashed silver each time it struck, and Idaria could only suppose that Kiri-Jolith had blessed it. The roots fell away from his determined blows.

But the sword was one weapon against a multitude. Stefan held up the medallion and muttered a prayer.

The medallion's light grew so bright, it should have blinded Idaria, but instead she took comfort in the glow. The trees visibly recoiled, however, and both the branches and roots abandoned their harassment of the trio.

Chasm dropped to the ground next to the elf, using his body and wings to shield her from any root or limb that might attack again. Stefan revolved in a circle, making certain the area was safe.

"I had to do it," he explained, "but it likely means that the Titans will detect us and know something is amiss here."

No sooner had he spoken than a bolt of lightning blacker than the shadows struck the ground just beyond his feet. The force of the eruption hurled Stefan into Chasm, who caught the human effortlessly. The knight had been struck, however, and was unconscious. The medallion's glow faded.

Idaria sensed the forest seeking to creep forward again. She rushed over to Stefan, trying to help him.

"You needn't bother. He hasn't very long to live."

Chasm growled. Idaria turned to the source of the foul voice, already aware of just who it was.

The Titan grinned down at her as he raised his hands in spellcasting.

X

MARCH OF THE MINOTAURS

The elf felt helpless. Stefan had been the one who had guided them that far. He had had the patronage of a god to aid him. But it was left to her; for Chasm, too, whatever his great strength, had his hands full.

Had that been the forest of Silvanost, her home, she might have turned to Habbakuk and pleaded with the god. It amazed her that he did not feel the wrongness of the forest.

And even as Idaria pondered that, a transformation came over the vicinity. As if some great hand pulled back the shroud that had draped over the trees and ground, the taint receded. A fresh and wholesome green colored the leaves and bushes, and the scent of spring overwhelmed the dank odors of the accursed forest. The trees took on a fresh, vibrant life; all their wickedness, all the Titan perversion, abruptly was *gone*.

The Titan faltered in his spell. "What—?"

Before he could utter another sound, the transformed area turned on *him*. Branches fell before his gaze, blinding him. More whirled around as if blown by the wind, striking the gargantuan sorcerer like battering rams. The Titan tried to collect his wits but clearly could not concentrate well enough even to muster a vanishing spell.

The very trap that the Titans had created overcame the lone spellcaster. Roots burrowed out of the freshened soil and seized him. He slashed with his talons at them, only to have his savage nails break off.

Idaria watched in awe, aware that somehow she was in part responsible for what was happening but uncertain just how. The Titan was already on his knees, due to not only the roots that coiled around his torso, but the continual rain of blows by the branches.

The blue-skinned sorcerer's knee sank into softening dirt. Both legs plunged under, as if some huge beast below the surface were burrowing a hole.

Despite his obvious panic, the Titan glared. He stretched forth a hand at Idaria. "I'll take you with—"

The ground gave way. With a howl, the fifteen-foot-tall villain dropped from sight.

Tree roots immediately covered the area, churning the dirt like massive worms. In seconds, there was no trace of the Titan even having been in that spot save a slight settling of fresh ground.

Idaria felt her pulse pounding. For the first time, she also sensed a warmth in her palm. Glancing down at it, the elf discovered Stefan's medallion.

"I know this was not your sphere, Kiri-Jolith," she whispered to the air, "but thank you."

"K-Kiri-Jolith," Stefan muttered. His eyes slowly opened. "Kiri—Idaria?"

She gestured for Chasm to gently lower him. The knight balanced himself, found his legs sturdy enough, and nodded. The gargoyle gave a satisfied grunt but stayed nearby.

"This belongs to you," Idaria said, handing him the medallion. "But I thanked your patron for his aid."

Stefan frowned. "I don't think that's possible. At least, not the way you say it. I think that another heard your plea through the medallion, perhaps *through* my patron, and responded."

She looked at the nearby forest, which was still revivified. There was a permanence about it, she noted, that the rest of the tainted realm would not be able to overcome. A place of respite had been created in a land of darkness.

"Praise be to Habbakuk." Like many elves, Idaria had lost much of her faith in the gods who supposedly watched over her people. None of them had stopped the invasions—first that of Mina and the Nerakans, then the sweep of the minotaurs—or had kept the forests from harm.

Yet perhaps she and her kind had been too harsh. Perhaps the gods had had no choice.

"Very curious," Stefan announced, eyeing the path ahead.

Thinking that some other fiend approached, the silver-haired slave followed his gaze. "What is it now?"

"Nothing . . . and that's what's so curious."

Chasm grunted his obvious confusion. Idaria shrugged, unable to clarify what Stefan was referring to.

Stefan gestured at the forest. "Where's the others? Why hasn't anyone come to see what has happened to their comrade? Surely, the rest of the Titans from the sanctum should be confronting us!"

"What do you think it means?" she asked, half expecting more Titans to sprout from the trees.

A slight smile crossed his beaten face. "It could mean that your Golgren has them stirred up elsewhere, especially in the south, since it's too soon for my people." His smile abruptly faded. "Or it could mean that Safrag is already the slave of the Fire Rose, and that bodes great ill."

"Is that so terrible? It will mean dissension among them! They may end up fighting one another for it—"

"And, in the process, destroy others."

Idaria nodded grimly. "But it means something else, too, does it not? It means that my people may be less guarded than we imagined."

The knight frowned slightly. "Yes, it does."

"Then we must take that into consideration, above all."

Stefan eyed her for a moment then turned and led the way. Idaria knew what he thought of her, knew that at that moment she reminded him of Golgren—Golgren, who would drive resolutely toward his ultimate goal even if others might be harmed or threatened. The elf shrugged to herself; she could do nothing about the Titans and the Fire Rose. That was Golgren's problem to deal with. All that mattered was releasing her people.

Yes, I have become like him, Idaria admitted to herself. Very much like him.

And oddly, she found herself wondering if that were such a terrible a thing after all.

❦

The morning saw the southern reaches of Golthuu—the area still called the "province" of Blöde—aswarm with armored soldiers. The distinctive banners of the minotaur legions fluttered high and proud, even more so because the day found them led not by mere generals, but by the emperor himself.

The legionaries were spread over several miles of shrub-filled wilderness. Contact had already been made with those legions who had advanced after the defunct pact with the false warlord Atolgus. Those soldiers were already settled in and served as the advance guard for the new incursion.

The generals knew the truth about the invasion, that it had come at the behest of none other than the Grand Khan Golgren, so in typical minotaur fashion, they had loudly voiced their opinions about that. However, in the end, Faros had convinced all of them of the necessity. The ogre realm was ruled by spell-casters, and spellcasters, especially ogre ones, had no honor. The spellcasters explained why so many patrols already had perished in "accidents" or had just gone missing. Surely, the next step for the Titans would be to conquer Ambeon. It, therefore, behooved the empire to strike first . . .

No matter how many legionaries might perish.

General Thandorus, though one of the newest commanders, had been chosen by Faros to be his executive officer. Badger Legion had the honor of serving as the emperor's personal military force. Thandorus did not mind what some might have taken for a slight demotion; to serve directly under the emperor was, for him, the proudest moment of his career thus far.

Scouts rode ahead of the ground forces, seeking as best they could signs of either sorcerers or the military "hands." Most of the legionaries hoped for a direct confrontation with their ogre equivalents, as death by weapon was far more desirable than perishing in magical flames or some other distasteful spell, but they were prepared to face whatever was necessary. Minotaur soldiers did not back down merely because the enemy used tactics of which they did not approve.

The foremost ranks bore long lances held slightly upward with both hands. The angle was better for wielding them until an enemy actually stood before the line. The legionaries up front also carried at their sides well-honed, freshly cleaned swords and on their backs powerful, double-edged axes. There were daggers in their belts too. The weight of the weapons and the armor the legionaries wore meant little to the minotaurs; trained from birth for combat, they lived for battle. Their eyes held no fear of death, but rather eagerness to prove their mettle and earn honor for both themselves and their clans.

Behind the lancers came several ranks with long swords and axes. The ranks were there to add additional protection for the first lines, should any foe begin to move too close for the long spears to be effective. They were also ready to charge past the lancers if the situation warranted it.

Stationed at various intervals, mounted units with lances, axes, or other hand weapons kept a diligent watch. On a signal, the foot soldiers would break before them, allowing the cavalry free access for a charge of their own. There were hundreds of warriors on horseback, all chosen for their riding skills and ability to engage in battle while in the saddle.

And flanking the cavalry were the archers. With their powerful bows, they could fire well beyond the front lines. Indeed, should an ogre hand march against the legionaries, the first deaths would belong to the archers.

Great weapons rolled behind—catapults, ballistae, and other mechanical wonders that had rejuvenated the empire and worried the rest of Krynn. The steady advance begun under Emperor Hotak and continued under Faros had enabled the latter emperor to start the machine of war and get it running at high capacity, with only a day or two's warning. Whatever his own distrust of Golgren, Faros knew that his rival was correct concerning the threat of the Titans to his people. Better a thousand legionaries and more should pay the sacrifice if it gave Golgren the opportunity he desired to reclaim the throne.

Besides, once ensconced in Blöde, Faros had no intention of turning back. He would not leave Golgren in control of the enemy realm.

Faros, red-plumed helm set over his horned head, surveyed the advance from atop a massive, brown stallion—Thandorus's own steed offered by the general to his lord. Thandorus rode beside him, and a score of officers trailed in their wake. The pair was surrounded by Thandorus's personal guard, who had strict orders to protect the emperor even if it cost the general his life. Such was the intense loyalty that Faros brought out in his subjects. He was seen as the epitome of the storybook hero, rising from battered youth to slavery to rebel leader to emperor. The nephew of the despot Chot the Terrible, he had been an innocent pawn during his uncle's downfall and execution on the Night of Blood. Hotak had tried to ensure that no blood member of the Kalin Clan would remain alive to seek vengeance, yet Faros had persevered through the fiery mining camps of his own people, the brutality of the ogre taskmaster

Sahd, and pursuit by ogres and legionaries alike. To Thandorus and the other officers, he represented the entire brave history of their people.

A bird screeched from high above, drawing the party's attention. One of the officers raised his arm and made a sound akin to the avian creature's cry.

The brown, red-fringed bird alighted. It was a small raptor, used for both hunting and messages. The empire's message network was among the finest in all the known world; the birds were trained to exhibit the same efficiency as their masters.

The officer removed a small note bound to the bird's leg. Without reading it, he handed the message to General Thandorus.

"The scouts report no sign of any hand or any other ogre force for half a day's journey. They have three message birds remaining. The next report comes at sunset."

Faros eyed the rising landscape. "No word of Titans?"

"None."

"We should assume their presence anyway. The damned spellcasters could be miles away; then they can materialize in a heartbeat, right in front of us if they like." The emperor glanced over his shoulder. "Or behind us, even."

"Dishonorable way to fight," growled Thandorus.

"But still a tactic we must watch for. Make sure the guards in the rear are keeping watch on the path we've already taken."

"Yes, my lord." Thandorus snapped his fingers. One of the officers nodded, turned his mount around, and rode off to ensure that the emperor's command was obeyed.

"We're already deep into ogre land," Faros muttered. For a moment, his eyes grew veiled, and Thandorus looked away. The emperor was remembering the harshness of his time as a slave and a fugitive. The general had seen up close the many scars covering Faros's body. Some had come from minotaurs, but most had been delivered by Faros's ogre slavers. "How deep will they permit us?"

Shielding his gaze, Thandorus rose in the saddle. "Perhaps they don't think us worthy of notice, my lord. Perhaps all they care about is the half-br—"

Something swift and sharp burrowed through the general's chest, armor and all. It struck so quickly that Thandorus even had time to glance down at the gap just beginning to grow red before he toppled off the horse.

"Drop!" Faros roared, obeying his own command as he spoke.

The sky filled with hissing darts flying so fast that they were all but invisible until they struck a target. Two more officers fell before the rest could join the emperor. Faros's mount let out a short whinny before tumbling toward him.

He rolled to the side just before the weight would have crushed his legs. Around him, the emperor heard the screams of the wounded and dying and the continued hiss of death from above.

They were not normal weapons. No ogre fired them. Kneeling beside his horse, Faros saw that they had more or less *materialized* above a high ridge to the north.

Scores of legionaries already lay wounded, dead, or dying. At the beginning, someone had been aiming for Faros in particular, but the strike had gone awry. Either the Titan or Titans who had cast the spell—there could be no other source for such an attack—had from a distance mistaken Thandorus for the emperor, or something else had saved Faros.

"I *will* fight my own battles, Sargonnas," the emperor muttered then shook his head at his own mistake. It was not the customary behavior of Sargonnas, though the god of vengeance had saved Faros in the past. Yet what other deity would see favor in his living?

There was only one other, Sargonnas's rival for the minotaurs, Kiri-Jolith.

But one rescue did not mean that Faros was immune to death. Whatever god or circumstance had saved him, it was up to the emperor to prove that he was worthy of living.

The catapults were near but not ready for firing. Faros peered around, squinting as the polished armor of his followers at times blinded him.

He snorted.

Seizing one of the officers, the emperor growled an order. The other minotaur nodded and passed on the word.

Within seconds, legionaries turned to present a frontal angle that at first glance appeared crazy, for it made them more open to the rain of deadly missiles. Yet the deaths of some might be necessary to save the expedition as a whole.

Indeed, more than one soldier slumped as missiles penetrated breastplates and helmets.

Then . . .

The last of the missiles faded in midair. The area stilled; the only sounds were the moans of the grievously wounded.

Faros had judged the light of the sun and the position from which the attack had come and made a desperate play. The many legionaries who had received his orders had turned in such a manner as to shine the light of the sun at the source of the threat. His soldiers had *blinded* the sorcerers with their combined armor.

The reprieve would not last. Still, Faros understood something of spellcasters and had ordered spies to research the Titans for just such a possible confrontation. The spell that had been cast had been a powerful one and indicated more than a single foe. More important, such a spell must be taxing, which meant that the legions had a brief time to prepare for whatever came next.

"Get the catapults ready!" he ordered other officers. "All ballistae too! We don't wait! I want the oil wraps prepared for the catapults! We bombard the high territory!"

As the officers moved to relay his orders, Faros rose. He saw with pride that the legionaries around him quickly were reforming ranks as others helped with the dead and dying.

The first strike of the battle was over. Faros knew the next would follow soon. He had to trust to Golgren's certainty that the Titan leader, one Safrag, would be too caught up in the Fire Rose to reckon the danger of a bunch of minotaurs.

The minotaurs had to survive and trust the deposed Grand Khan. Well aware that Golgren was a hardy survivor, Faros had hope. However, in the end, it did not matter. The empire would have had to invade the ogre realm regardless, sooner or later. If they had waited, the Titans would have been the invaders, and it was always better to take the battle to the enemy.

Faros again surveyed the damage done by the single spell and snorted angrily.

Yes, the emperor thought as he turned to the catapults. It was always best to take the battle to the enemy, even if that meant death and defeat in the end.

XI

Sign of the Kraken

Golgren sensed the arrival of the messenger moments before the rider reached Sir Augustus's tent. The half-breed sat up, certain that a moment of importance was upon him. The clatter of hooves made him briefly bare his teeth, although fortunately there was no one in the tent to see that instinctual reaction.

The voices without muttered too quietly for him to make out what they said. The tone was neutral, which gave him no clue as to the decision of Sir Augustus's superiors. Golgren stepped from the bedroll, taking up a place at the table. He poured himself a slight bit of wine and held the mug close to his lips. He did not drink, though, until he heard the clink of metal and the movement of the flap, marking the commander's presence.

"A reply's arrived, though I expect you know that already, Grand Khan."

Golgren slowly swallowed the sip then turned toward Stefan's uncle. "I had some inkling, yes."

RICHARD A. KNAAK

Augustus chuckled darkly. "You're everything I've heard, especially from my nephew."

Golgren smothered the slight frown that wanted to burst forth at mention of the last. "Your nephew is all I have heard a Knight of Solamnia should be."

"I believe you actually mean that," the elder fighter returned. "Thank you. I think so, too."

"The reply. You have it with you?"

"As you can see." The knight held up his right hand, which gripped a small, leather pouch. Sir Augustus joined Golgren at the table, where he set down the pouch while he poured himself some wine.

Golgren's eyes grazed the pouch. It was of fine, strong leather and had been bound with thin, metal string that would prove much harder to cut quickly than any rope. In addition, there was a great wax seal across the flap. That the seal remained unbroken indicated that the commander had chosen to find out what his superiors had decided, together with Golgren. The pouch had been sent with such haste that the half-breed's sharp nose could still smell a hint of recently melted wax.

"I made a vow of what I would do if they rejected your pact," Augustus reminded him. "I stand by that vow on the life of my nephew."

Golgren said nothing. Taking that as a tacit acknowledgment, the knight broke the seal and removed the contents, a small slip of parchment.

Sir Augustus frowned. "I expected a much longer missive. You'll likely not find this to your taste."

"Please read."

Unfolding it, the commander looked over the answer. He grunted.

156

"Well, it seems we've got an agreement after all."

He handed the brown parchment over to Golgren, who read the response of the high command. The answer was simple enough. The pact was accepted on a temporary basis. Augustus's superiors believed that because of the threat of the Titans, Golgren should be assisted by a military advance into the ogre realm.

That was essentially it. There were some marks at the bottom—scribbles to the uninformed eye— that the knight had not commented on but that the half-breed knew was a coded addendum to what the main message relayed. Augustus had other orders beyond those to which Golgren was to be privy. Like the Uruv Suurt, the Solamnics undoubtedly had plans to expand their interests in Golthuu whether or not Golgren succeeded.

But all that was as he had expected. Not for a minute had Golgren believed the threat of Safrag and the Fire Rose would be enough for either the humans or Faros to endorse the pact. Both sides wanted to deter any potential ogre uprising in the future.

He handed the parchment back to Sir Augustus. With a hint of a smile that emphasized the elf side of his features, Golgren said, "I am very pleased."

"News of the minotaurs' advance in the southern regions was surely a deciding factor," the Solamnic added. "I believe it helped to speed the reply and influenced the outcome."

That was no surprise to Golgren; indeed, he had counted on it. The Uruv Suurt and the knights of Solamnia were longtime rivals on the continent of Ansalon. When one was on the move, the other felt nervous and paid special attention.

Then the commander added something that could only have been cited from part of the missive in code. "My superiors also agree to the free movement of all elf slaves from the ogre lands, though we will not permanently care for them. We'll grant them a short respite, resupply them, and send them on to their exiled brethren, who can care for them more appropriately."

"Of course." No one wanted the added burden of the refugees; in truth, not even some of the exiled elves. That would mean too many extra mouths to feed in an already-turbulent time. Still, the knights would not choose to leave the elves in ogre hands.

Nor in the hands of the Titans.

Augustus put the missive back in the pouch then thrust it into the belt that held his sheath. Finishing the last of his drink, the knight rose. Golgren rose also.

"Your men, they must march soon," the half-breed commented.

"They'll march tomorrow. We've been prepared to move for one reason or another since my nephew came." The knight eyed him. "And you?"

"I must leave now."

"Just as I expected. A horse has already been prepared for you with the rations I mentioned. It's a sturdy animal, one of the largest. Should hold your tall frame just fine."

The horse would have been available whether or not Solamnia had agreed to the pact, but Golgren simply nodded his gratitude. Even with a swift steed, it would take him far longer than he desired to reach Garantha. He had intended to use Tyranos's staff, but that was not possible.

Augustus led him out. The half-breed noted a conspicuous lack of knights nearby. At some point the commander had evidently had the area cleared, with even tents and equipment positioned much farther away. The only other Solamnics nearby were Sir Augustus's own guards and a lone, young Knight of the Crown who held the reins to a dark brown stallion already saddled and packed. The beast eyed Golgren as if it were as distrusting of him as the knights were.

"I've a map you can use—" the commander began.

"I have been here before. I know the land."

Sir Augustus's brow furrowed. *"Do* you?"

Golgren accepted the reins from the younger Solamnic. Although the latter's expression was masked, his eyes reflected both uncertainty and determination. The combination was not contradictory, Golgren thought; Golgren had seen the same thing in the eyes of many a less-experienced warrior. That did not mean, though, that the young knight would not be able to fulfill his role on the field of battle. The better fighters were those who understood their mortality, as Golgren did.

The tall half-breed mounted. Sir Augustus gave him a short nod, which Golgren returned.

The deposed Grand Khan rode off, the dry ground raising a trail of dust in his wake.

His way out of the encampment continued to be devoid of all but a few necessary sentries. Most kept their gazes on the path, but a couple could not help glancing up at the unusual rider in their midst. Golgren acted similarly, all but ignoring them, the half-breed keeping his eyes ahead at most times.

The encampment vanished behind him, and the lost son was returned to the wilds of that part of Golthuu. Golgren urged the mount around a rise, aware of a rough road from years before that would give him a swifter route, at least for the day.

The land was rugged, uneven, and typically arid, but Golgren had no doubts concerning either his or the Knighthood's ability to traverse it. There were worse areas, where only magic might have been capable of covering the distances.

Magic such as the Fire Rose contained . . .

Would that I had the staff, Golgren bitterly thought. But it was not his. A slight intake of breath was all that signaled Golgren's frustration. It must be that it indeed returned to Tyranos.

A warmth touched his hand. He glanced down at the signet ring and frowned to realize that he had forgotten it until that moment. He also wondered why none of the Solamnics had taken it from him. It was not that he thought them thieves at heart, but surely they would have noticed its supernatural qualities.

The ring . . . Golgren gazed at its fiery markings. Could it help him go where he was urgently needed?

He concentrated on the capital, specifically, the palace. He put all of his energy, briefly, into the concentration.

There came a brief moment, oddly, when the wizard's staff formed in his thoughts. Golgren tried to shake off the image, but it was burned into his mind regardless of his desire.

In the vision, the crystal atop the staff flared brightly.

Golgren vanished from the saddle.

❦

Tyranos stood perplexed, clutching his staff, in the place where he had first set foot on Ansalon, not far from where he had discovered young Chasm some years after that time. For him it was the place in all the world of the most solace and peace.

Fearsome waves crashed against the weathered shore as he attempted to refocus his thoughts. Seaweed blanketed much of the shoreline. What he had just experienced surely had to have a cause. But he couldn't explain the staff's odd behavior. After all, Tyranos had not commanded the staff to do anything.

Island-bound Karthay, northeast of the continent, was far from the complicated dangers of Golthuu and had demanded much of Tyranos and the staff, but the wizard had not hesitated. There was something about the place that always soothed him.

Perhaps . . . perhaps because it so reminded him of home.

"Doesn't matter," he rumbled, referring to both the staff's odd behavior and his former homelands. "Doesn't matter."

For all his peace of mind, there was another reason, the most significant reason, he had come there. He would need all the magic that he could muster, and that meant using his other prize. It was the only means by which he could possibly prevent his most important spell from shattering.

From the eastern shore, the wizard cast himself to the midst of the snow-topped Worldscap Mountains. As he regained his mental balance, Tyranos peered down at the jungles far below that particular peak. There was no sign below of any of the local inhabitants, neither those bound to the ground nor the ones who flew the skies. It was safe to open the passage.

He turned to what appeared to be a solid rock face

and drew in yellow light a five-pointed shape. In the center of the rock face, Tyranos then magically etched the crude form of a key.

The key drifted to the very center of the shape then turned on its left side.

The gritty rock face melted away. A slight hint of sulfur rose into the air.

Glancing over his shoulder, the hooded spellcaster quickly entered the portal. He did not plan to remain long on Karthay; the pause by the shore had been necessary, as had been the slumber that preceded it. However, time was of the essence. The empire was surely on the move, and if Tyranos knew Golgren, the Solamnics would within a day be doing the same.

And that meant that the Titans would finally be where Tyranos desired them, the Titans and *Golgren,* naturally.

The glow of the staff illuminated what had obviously once been an inhabited cave. The artwork, crafted with paint made from variously colored berries, indicated winged beings almost like men. A face had been carved out of one side of the cave, again, a mixture of avian and what might have been elf or human features.

But the kyrie had long abandoned that place, sensing its magic and rightly being disturbed by it. Only someone such as Tyranos would find use for the cave, and even then for only brief moments.

He reached the end of the cave. Small stalactites hung from the ceiling, and deep shadows loomed everywhere. What appeared to be a thick mass of webbing covered the back wall so thoroughly that details of what might lurk behind could not be discerned.

"Da ithan!" the wizard called.

The webbing turned a bright, cold blue. It then broke up into tiny crystals that flew away into the air and dissipated before dropping to the stone and earth floor.

Tyranos smiled grimly. Before him stood that which he had sworn he would never use again. The irony was he felt certain it had been created either by some worshiper of Sirrion or the god himself. Perhaps it was, in its crude way, cousin to the Fire Rose.

It was not crystal. Rather, it was made of some liquid that was a blazing orange-red in color. Although the pattern had a beginning and an end, the liquid looked as if it flowed, but to where, Tyranos could not say. He had dubbed the thing the Soul of the Kraken, the latter part of the name coming from the creature he thought its outline most resembled. The kraken appeared to be stretching its tentacles skyward.

Tyranos had discovered its magic by error, as an exhausted outcast collapsed into sleep at the base of the pattern, after cursing his existence and wishing to change not only his life, but his very appearance too. He had awakened the next day to discover that his wish had come true . . . or so he had thought. The moment that Tyranos had started to leave the cave, he had reverted to his original state and his original form.

But upon reentering, the transformation had renewed itself. The wizard had been wily enough to understand the source and had, with magical effort, taken from the kraken symbol a living piece of it. Sure enough, combined with his own spellcasting, that had been enough to maintain the illusion that he was Tyranos, even hundreds of miles from that source. If he truly could not be as he desired, then at least he could *seem* to be.

The wizard touched his chest, and a glow appeared there. It matched the glow of the kraken. Tyranos had discovered long before that the piece he had taken slowly lost its power, but that by returning to that place, he could recharge it. He would need its fullest power if he hoped to succeed with his plans.

Reaching his other hand forward, Tyranos touched the kraken at the center of its "body."

He let out a groan of surprise as his strength drained away from him. His body lurched. Gasping, Tyranos fell face-first against the pattern. He felt the warmth of it against his cheek.

Then the wizard felt nothing but cold rock.

Confused and anxious, a weary Tyranos pulled back.

The pattern seemed as dead as the rock in which it had been set.

"That can't be." Tyranos pressed his hand against the kraken, but there was no transfusion. "You can't do this."

The kraken did not respond.

The wizard banged his fist against it. Still nothing happened.

He finally touched his chest. There, he could feel the familiar warmth. At least the original spell cast upon him was still intact. However, that meant there was no coming back . . . ever. Tyranos either had to work out a new spell that did not rely on the secret source or had to find some other manner by which to make his transformation true and forever.

The Fire Rose could accomplish that, he reminded himself. That was in great part why you wanted it, wasn't it?

The matter was settled then. Tyranos knew what he had to do, and to do it, he had to help Golgren in whatever way possible. Curiously, the wizard did not find the alternative as unpalatable as before. Golgren, he realized, offered a far better a fate for the ogres—and other races—than the Titans.

And other than Chasm, the half-breed was the nearest thing he had to a trusted friend, the wizard realized.

That last realization, though, made him snort loudly as he reached the mouth of the cave. Golgren . . . *a trusted friend.* It would have made his people laugh.

At the edge of the cave, Tyranos went down on one knee. He held the staff tightly and concentrated. What he had never informed Golgren of in the past was that if he exerted his will on the crystal, it was possible to send him directly to a person, not a place. It was how Tyranos had, in the past, come to stand before the half-breed no matter where he was. It was more troublesome than choosing a destination—why that was, the wizard did not exactly know—so the wizard always contrived to conceal the fact that he was slightly exhausted at first.

But as Tyranos imagined Golgren, he found the half-breed's whereabouts harder to sense than they should have been. It was as if either Golgren were in more than one place at the same time or that his location kept changing very rapidly.

"The damned fool!" Tyranos growled, finally suspecting just where the deposed Grand Khan had to be. "The damned—"

The crystal flared, even though the spellcaster had not commanded it to do so.

Mouth agape, Tyranos disappeared.

From just a few steps behind where the wizard had knelt, an obviously pleased Sirrion chuckled. The god then burst into flames, which not only swiftly enveloped him, but spread rapidly into the cave. The entire interior was scorched black, all traces of ancient habitation and—especially—the kraken, banished.

As quickly as they had arisen, the flames died completely. Of Sirrion, naturally, there was no longer any trace.

⊶⊷⊕⊶⊷

The three robed Titans peered down at the approaching legionaries with nothing but contempt in their expressions for the empire's haughty incursion. As far as they were concerned, the matter could have been finished up very quickly, save for settling the question of blame. One way or another, they looked forward to taking out their frustration over their leader's recent decisions on the bull warriors. None of them said anything about it out loud, but all three, watching, understood.

The seniormost, Voran by name, began the groundwork for the next spell. As Faros had surmised, they were pooling their forces as much as possible to avoid draining themselves to the point where they would need to rejuvenate. A few of the other Titans near the southern border were already nearing the point of weakness, though none had dared mention that yet to Safrag. True, it was *assumed* he would help any in need, but everyone wanted someone else to be the first to make that petition.

"No assassination attempt this time," Voran informed the others. "We sweep across their ranks where their fool emperor marches and take him out with hundreds of others quickly and simply."

"The other spell should've worked," sang that plan's creator. "It should've . . ."

Voran and the third Titan present sneered at him. Unable to back up his claim and obviously weaker than the pair, the protester clamped his mouth shut and joined in the spellcasting.

There was a loud crack, like thunder, but it did not come from any spell that they or other Titans in the region had cast. The sound was already familiar to the blue-skinned sorcerers.

A moment later, a heavy, flaming boulder struck a ridge a quarter of a mile from where Voran and his two companions stood. The boulder cracked off a large chunk of rock that spilled back over the ridge.

Voran laughed harshly. "Hezroch and his band are going to have to move again. If anyone needs to beg Safrag for elixir, it'll be them."

"The damned Uruv Suurt have a good eye," the third Titan muttered.

"Which is why we should finish our spell."

The three stood facing one another. At Voran's signal, they clasped hands together. It made for the better melding of their power and enabled Voran to better control the direction and outcome.

Voran sang the words of the spell. To the Titans, singing the spells sounded even more glorious than *speaking* in the Titan tongue. Perhaps it was because, in addition to their richness, the singing words were also filled with magic.

A tremendous cloud of blue energy formed over the trio. Voran uttered the final phrase of the spell.

With a crackle akin to a bolt of lightning, the cloud poured down over the legionaries and their emperor . . . and dissipated.

"What—?" was the only word Voran got out of his mouth before another familiar cracking sound echoed in the ears of all three.

The other two Titans instinctively vanished. Voran, as the focal point of the spellcasting, was still caught up in both the magic and its startling failure for a fatal breath longer.

Clearing his head, he finally noticed the flaming boulder just as it filled the sky above him.

Then he saw nothing more.

❧✦❧

His warriors cheered as the latest boulder reached its mark with perfection that only minotaurs could achieve with their great wooden catapults. However, Faros— again on foot after having lost yet another steed—was not entirely pleased. First, the strike probably hadn't even dusted the sorcerers' elegant robes. The catapults probably had done little except buy the advancing force a few more steps toward their prize.

And although it should have lightened his heart, Faros was also disturbed by the strange dissipation of the Titans' spell. Not for the first time, the sorcerers' handi-work had failed. The legionaries believed the cause was the inefficiency of a dishonorable weapon—magic—but Faros suspected the interference of gods.

"I ask no god to fight my wars for me!" he growled under his breath. "I say again to you, Kiri-Jolith, we win or die on our own merits!"

Even as he spoke, something on the ground ahead glittered. Drawn to the object, the emperor paused to pick it up.

It was a medallion, one he was certain had not been there moments earlier. One of the legionaries would have plucked it up, if not him, because its metal was valuable. It was made of steel.

It was a medallion bearing the likeness of a bison-headed god.

With a snort, Faros tossed it away.

Immediately, there came another glitter from the ground just ahead.

Bending, Faros discovered it a *second* medallion or, just as difficult to credit, the first again. With a defiant shake of his head, the former slave strode past it.

And, for a third time, his gaze was distracted by another glittering object in his path.

In frustration, Faros seized it up again. Although there was no such sign on the god's image, the minotaur felt as if the visage mocked his efforts. He started to throw the medallion away—then, resignedly, finally thrust it beneath his breastplate.

"A shield I'll accept," Faros grudgingly muttered, keeping his voice low as another legionary trudged past him toward the front. "But only a shield. Nothing more."

"Nothing more," the other warrior agreed as he strode past, his back to the emperor.

Faros's eyes widened. He rushed forward to catch up with the legionary, but somehow lost track of him and didn't know who he was, even though there was no place for the other to have gone.

Thunder roiled, thunder without clouds. Faros glanced up, recognizing the start of another Titan attack.

This had better be for the best! he silently warned both the vanished god and the absent half-ogre who had talked him into that mess. This had better be for the best . . .

Letting out a shout, Faros urged his soldiers on.

XII

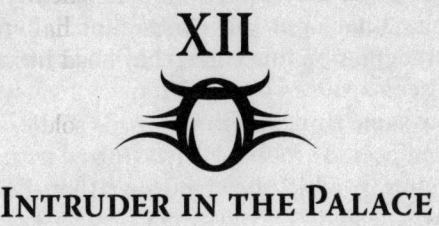

INTRUDER IN THE PALACE

The slavering meredrake hissed, tugging hard on its rusting iron chain and sending spittle flying everywhere as it tried to reach the figure that had suddenly materialized in front of it. The great, green and brown reptile snapped eagerly at the intruder, despite having been recently fed. Meredrakes were always ready to eat, for in the wild, one never knew where one's next meal would come from or whether one would become the next meal of something even *bigger*.

A single gesture silenced the fearsome creature, a gesture only one person could make. Golgren eyed his pet, somewhat interested to see that it was still alive. Nothing remained of the palace that had stood for ages, much less his own brief reign, other than the lone meredrake. He pondered its continued presence in a place that Safrag had clearly remade to his own desires, pondered it and came up with only one answer: Wargroch.

Why his traitorous officer would have kept the meredrake was a question that could wait for later or even forever. If given the opportunity, Golgren would feed his pet the other ogre and Atolgus too. There was no possible redemption for either; they had willingly sided with, or been seduced by, the Titans, which in the end, meant the same thing: betrayal.

Golgren peered around. He recognized nothing about the chamber in which he stood save that the image of the Titan's leader, Safrag's image, was everywhere. His godlike image stretched across the iridescent pearl floor; it stood tall in each perfectly executed statue that doubled as a column. Wall-sized profiles of the sorcerer gazed toward an arched throne that looked as if it had risen out of the floor. It had been designed not for an ogre, though, but clearly a Titan. Atolgus and Wargroch might believe they would gain their own glory for bowing to the sorcerers, but it was clear who would rule from there.

Golgren sniffed the air. Other than the meredrake's heady carnivore scent, there was nothing unusual. No one had been in the chamber for at least a day, assuming that it had even existed that long. It was a wonder that the lizard had not perished during all the many abrupt changes.

Golgren's brow furrowed. He glanced at the beast again then realized his terrible mistake.

The meredrake stood on two legs. Its shape was more that of an ogre. The muzzle was as long and as fearsome as ever, perhaps even more fearsome, with a hint of something slightly ogre.

Safrag had not left the meredrake safe out of any interest in the huge lizard; he had arranged a trap for Golgren just on the off chance that the wily half-breed would escape his eternal prison.

And Golgren had obliged him.

He instinctively reached for a sword that was not there. Sir Augustus had not provided him with any weapons. If Golgren had carried a sword, one of the sentries might have challenged the half-breed before his departure. That meant that Golgren had only a paltry dagger which he knew would not penetrate the mere-drake's scaly hide.

No longer apparently recognizing its master, the transformed meredrake tugged forward. The thick, metal chain easily snapped.

Golgren had no choice but to retreat. He drew the dagger despite its questionable value and kept at least part of his gaze on the creature at all times.

The chain dangling from its throat, the meredrake trudged eagerly toward the smaller figure. Despite having just become half-ogre, the meredrake moved as if perfectly comfortable with its two-legged form.

Brandishing the dagger, Golgren let out a hiss that was one of the commands he had taught the reptile. The meredrake hesitated, its crimson-tinged orbs blinking twice.

Then, tongue darting out, the monster lunged.

Golgren leaped aside as the huge figure dropped. The meredrake crashed into the elaborate marble floor with such force that it cracked part of Safrag's grand image.

The half-breed immediately jumped onto the mere-drake's back. However, before he could attempt to use the dagger, the beast shook him off.

The force of the creature's movement sent Golgren tumbling across the chamber, where he collided with a towering column shaped into a beatific Safrag who seemed to be smiling down smugly on his rival. Golgren had barely time to recover from the collision, for the meredrake was already in pursuit.

The creature came closer to catching him. Golgren rolled under its grasping paws and menacing, long, sharp claws. The meredrake barreled through Safrag's stone effigy, shattering it and sending large chunks flying everywhere.

Rising, Golgren sought the nearest escape. It was not that he feared the transformed reptile so much—although death was likely if he continued to combat it—but rather that the monster was a delay he could ill afford. The longer Golgren was forced to remain in that particular location, the greater the chance that others would come to see what the commotion was.

The half-breed raced toward a side corridor, but the meredrake, rising from the dust, whirled and followed. The corridor was narrow but not enough to truly impede the beast on his tail. Golgren sought to grab something to hurl at or slow his foe, but in creating anew the palace, Safrag had evidently "grown" everything out of the main body. There was nothing unattached. Everything—the statuary, the banners, furniture—was part of the whole structure. It was almost as if he were inside a living thing rather than any building.

The meredrake lunged, but its enthusiasm caused it to slide too far to the right. Its side crashed into the wall, buying Golgren a vital extra breath. He dared not slow his pace, though, for the reptile moved on its two legs and used its new arms.

Then Golgren spotted another passage that was just wide enough to admit two guards side by side. Without hesitation, he dived toward it.

The meredrake mimicked him—only to find the fit was

too snug for its huge form. The beast thrust itself forward as much as it could, but succeeded only in becoming stuck.

Furious, it snapped and hissed at the dwindling figure safely ahead. Golgren paid the meredrake no more attention. His mission was to find his way out of there and locate Safrag.

That he had as yet faced no guards did not surprise him. It was possible that they were too wary of the shifting form of the palace. It was also possible that Safrag had dismissed them and that he was patiently waiting for Golgren to reach him.

The hisses of the mutated meredrake echoed far behind Golgren. But he had to contend with a new threat, which while not immediately dangerous, had even more potential than the beast to turn his plans awry. Safrag's palace had become a veritable maze of corridors, many of them without windows. Golgren had to rely on his innate sense of direction, which was being taxed to its limits. The longer he spent time running around in circles, the more confused and exhausted he was bound to become.

Finally he detected a voice far ahead. What it was saying, Golgren could not tell, but he went in that direction. He gripped the dagger tightly, aware that he was at a clear disadvantage; any guards would be wielding huge axes or long swords.

The voice grew louder and more familiar. For one of the few times in his life, Golgren felt a rage rise up in him that he was barely able to control. He knew that voice, and he had expected to hear it again eventually, but it was too soon.

"Go!" roared the speaker in Common. There was then the clatter of armored figures marching off at a rapid pace.

Golgren peered around the corner, saw that his quarry had his back to him, and thus, he was able to slip up behind the figure.

His dagger's point pressed against the side of Wargroch's thick throat.

"So good to see so loyal a warrior," Golgren whispered, also in Common.

"Grand—" Wargroch's voice halted as the point dug into him, causing a slight dribble of blood that descended onto the officer's armored shoulder.

"A single sound that I do not require will mean your death. Understood?"

Wargroch silently nodded.

Although his prisoner could not see his face, Golgren bared his teeth as he asked, "And Khleeg?"

The Blödian swallowed hard before murmuring, "Dead."

"And it was Wargroch who slew him, yes?"

To his credit, Golgren's traitorous follower did not lie. "Yes."

"There is much blood on Wargroch's hands, dishonored blood. I should slay Wargroch here and now, but there is value in your life . . . if you obey."

"Grand Khan—" Again, the heavier warrior broke off as the dagger dug a little deeper, adding to the tiny, crimson rivulet of blood.

"A whisper only, good Wargroch."

"Grand Khan, I have no honor. I am a traitor, as you say. But I swear on my ancestors to serve you now."

Golgren let the dagger trace a line toward the back of the ogre's neck. "So you did once before. Only one pact now is between us. Wargroch will take me where I wish and I will perhaps not execute him. Yes?"

"Yes."

"Safrag . . . he is here in the palace?"

"No."

Pressing the dagger harder, Golgren repeated his question, only to receive the same answer. What Wargroch did not realize, though, was that the half-breed was reading the officer's composure or lack thereof, a trick he had learned long before.

So at least as to the question of Safrag's whereabouts, he accepted that Wargroch was telling the truth. On the other hand, Wargroch's oath to serve Golgren again had too much bad history behind it to make it trustworthy under any circumstance.

"Where is Safrag?"

"Don't know. Morgada and Falstoch are here. They watch the city for Safrag. There is also Atolgus—"

At mention of the former chieftain, Golgren touched the point to a different part of Wargroch's neck. "Is Atolgus near?"

"No. He waits for the female Titan in his chamber. He always waits."

Aware of the dark enchantments of the lone female sorcerer, Golgren was unsurprised. Atolgus was no more than a hound, then, willing to do whatever she commanded of him and, thus, whatever Safrag desired. Which made him yet another danger.

But Safrag's absence was something Golgren had not expected, and he had to decide what to do. "Morgada is here." Golgren smiled to himself. "Lead us to her, then, good friend."

The Blödian stepped forward, but Golgren pulled him back.

"Betray me and you *will* die even if I forfeit my own

life, Wargroch. Your life is bound to mine."

"As you say," the officer replied. "My sword?"

Golgren had noted that Wargroch carried next to him a sheathed weapon. It was not the one the former Grand Khan had awarded him, but rather another that Golgren was familiar with. The markings on the hilt showed it had once belonged to Atolgus.

"Leave it."

Wargroch said nothing. Golgren lowered the dagger to a place where it could be thrust through a slight separation between the front and back plates of the officer's armor, while remaining hidden from the view of any approaching the pair. He then tapped Wargroch with the blade to let him know to move.

Although shorter and wirier than Wargroch or most other ogres, Golgren had no fear that the other would turn on him. Wargroch knew his former lord well, especially the legendary agility and speed that had enabled the half-breed to bring down foes of even greater might than the Blödian.

"Many guards?" Golgren asked as they walked slowly, close together.

"Few. They are not comfortable here and not needed much."

"But Wargroch is very comfortable here, yes?"

The Blödian dared turn his head slightly toward Golgren. "Grand Khan, you should not come here! You seek Safrag but Safrag also seeks you! We thought you dead, but Morgada told us that Safrag sensed you alive! Since then, he has waited! You and the Fire Rose, the two of you are all he thinks of!"

Golgren's expression remained masked. "This I am aware of. Lead."

With a defeated grunt, Wargroch continued walking. Golgren glanced at the signet. He counted on it to help him against Morgada or any of the other Titans. The risk was great, but Golgren had not risen to Grand Khan without great audacity.

Then the sound of footsteps racing down the hall forced Golgren to drag Wargroch into a side corridor. The oversized, arrogant countenance of Safrag, decorating the wall, mocked the half-breed as he and Wargroch pressed against the opposing side.

Half a dozen well-armed ogres trotted down the main hall. They wore murderous gazes, and Golgren felt certain they were hunting for him.

"You must leave Garantha," whispered Wargroch just after the small band passed.

Golgren did not reply, for more warriors could be heard racing down the hall.

There were nearly a dozen in that group. Unlike the last set, they slowed, as if seeking their quarry in a more methodical fashion. One paused, about to peer down the side corridor, when a harsh voice ordered him to move on ahead.

The Grand Khan bared his teeth as Atolgus stalked past.

The former chieftain was barely recognizable to him. His skin already had a blue tint to it, and his eyes were golden and without pupils. He was also much, much taller than the last time Golgren had seen him, at least two feet taller than the brawniest of his guards.

Atolgus gestured to an unseen follower, revealing in the process that he also sported short but no-less-wicked talons like the Titans. Golgren, who was somewhat familiar with the process that turned an ogre into one of the towering sorcerers, was morbidly fascinated by the unique, gradual transition.

The former chieftain drew his sword—the sword Golgren had originally presented to Wargroch—and followed after his warriors. The half-breed waited for several seconds before deciding that it was safe to continue.

He had no special fear of Atolgus; but Golgren had to keep his concentration on finding Morgada. He felt that she was an essential part of his plan if he hoped to confront Safrag.

"Lead on," he murmured to Wargroch.

The Blödian hesitated. "She may not be where I remember, Grand Khan."

"And it would be foolish for you to see her anyway," remarked another, familiar voice.

"Tyranos," Golgren returned quietly in a low hiss. "Your coming was expected earlier."

Both turned to face the brawny wizard. Although like Golgren, Tyranos was much shorter than Wargroch, there was something in the spellcaster's steely gaze that frightened the traitor.

"Yes, of course you were expecting me," Tyranos countered with more than a hint of sarcasm. "I'm ever at your beck and call." He pointed the head of the staff at Wargroch. "Just like this one used to be."

Wargroch gave an unsettled grunt. "Do I know you, human?"

"Excellent Common. No, but I know you, ogre. I am surprised you didn't slit his throat as soon as you found him, oh great Grand Khan."

"Wargroch still has his uses, as do you."

Tyranos shook his head. "I think you mistake my

reason for locating you. If you want the Fire Rose, the last place you should be looking is here in the palace! All you'll end up with here is your hide decorating one of the walls"—the wizard sneered at the nearest relief of Safrag's face—"with this creature forever leering at your fate."

They were interrupted by the sound of rushing feet and the clatter of weapons and armor; all were coming back from the direction that Atolgus and the guards had taken earlier.

"I can promise you that doom is on the way," the wizard growled low.

"Take us from here," Golgren decided.

"Just like that? I planned for more argument and subterfuge on your part—" Tyranos broke off as the sound of the oncoming ogres neared. "Hold tight!"

Golgren suddenly realized something. "Wargroch comes—"

He and the wizard vanished, appearing elsewhere before the half-breed could finish. Paying attention to nothing else, Golgren immediately pressed his maimed limb to Tyranos's throat.

"Wargroch should have come with us. There was still possible need for him. The Titan Morgada—"

"Welcomes you."

Both males turned. Tyranos scowled. "This was not where I intended us to be!"

They stood in what was clearly some inner chamber in the transformed palace. Safrag's countenance was everywhere, as if spying on them. The chamber was otherwise opulent, with golden walls and glittering crystal lamps and arched wings hovering above the pair. The lamps didn't evidence any link to the ceiling or any other source of light. They resembled starbursts more than anything and burned within as if alive.

The scent of oleander filled the room, the scent of the flower of a plant that was itself very poisonous. A vast, round bed of down with lush cushions and long, silken sheets—all some variation of the same colors as the walls—was the centerpiece of the chamber. Its occupant had an arresting presence. Gracefully sweeping back her long, dark hair, the towering female smiled at the newcomers. Yet her teeth could barely be glimpsed between the full lips, her way of obscuring their sharpness.

"The Grand Khan Golgren," Morgada cooed, "and an unexpected but certainly interesting friend."

Tyranos wielded the staff upright, like a sword or axe. "How you seized control of my spell, I don't know, but you'll find that's the end of your good fortune, Titan!"

"Why, I don't know what you mean. I didn't seize your spell, human."

The wizard snorted but Golgren sensed that, as incredible as it might seem, Morgada sounded as though she spoke the truth. With that surprise in mind, the half-breed recalled the signet.

"No, it was not her; it was this."

"That damned thing plays too many games! It's as bad as that ghoul controlling the gargoyles!"

Golgren eyed the markings. "Small wonder, as both have pasts that intertwine, I think."

"High Ogres, you mean." The spellcaster, his fierce gaze not for a moment leaving the sorceress, shrugged. "I thought as much, but in this case a High Ogre still *alive.*"

Morgada chuckled lightly. "Alive in *some* sense, at least."

The eyes of both males widened in understanding.

"Yes, I know exactly of whom you speak." Morgada suddenly spun, whirling so fast that she immediately became a blue blur. As she spun, she also shrank in size, quickly becoming less than half her height, slightly smaller than they.

"So much better," the female Titan commented. She stepped up to Golgren and the wizard, her every movement enticing.

Tyranos let out a low growl and backed slightly away. Golgren did not budge, not even when Morgada stretched forth a hand that almost but not quite stroked his cheek.

"Watch those delicate nails," the spellcaster murmured, although whether he spoke to her or to the half-breed was not clear.

"I find this height far more to my liking. What about you?" Morgada asked. Despite the fact that she spoke Common instead of the tongue created by Dauroth, her voice was musical. Seductive, deadly music. "He prefers it too. High Ogres were not so tall as Dauroth once led us to believe. In fact, they were about your height, Grand Khan. Certainly, he is."

"You know him very well," Golgren stated bluntly.

"Xiryn? Yes, I know him, and I know what he wishes of both of us."

"Xiryn." Tyranos's eyes narrowed. "I know that name. I read it somewhere . . . in one of the tombs."

"Xiryn is the lord of the gargoyles," Golgren said, staring directly, fiercely, into Morgada's eyes.

Though she still smiled beguilingly, it was she who looked away. "Yes, and so much more. He knows the Fire Rose better than any of us, for it was he who first accepted it as a gift from the god Sirrion."

"How can that be?" Tyranos demanded. "That was long, long ago! Centuries upon centuries! The only things left of the High Ogre race are their tombs and their decadent descendants! No High Ogre could live so long, save perhaps if he wielded the Fire Rose all that time, which he hasn't, it appears."

The temptress laughed at him. "Xiryn is very clever and so very, very determined. Even death fears him."

Golgren suddenly realized something. "He made you. He is why you are a Titan."

"Oh, yes. He manipulated the fool who was already one and used him to gain access for me to Dauroth, who found the notion of finally creating a *female* Titan intriguing, of course. Dauroth had not done so before because he did not want nature to take its course; all Titans were to be his creation, not the cause of a union. That would have lessened his grip on them if they discovered their children would gain from them." She gestured impatiently. "But what really matters is that he accepted me, just as Xiryn intended! Xiryn works to ensure that nothing will keep him from the Fire Rose!"

The deposed Grand Khan bared his teeth. "But he and you are mistaken if you think I will let him have it."

His remark only made Morgada laugh again, louder, but still seductively. "Oh, but you are the one mistaken! I've no intention of letting Xiryn have it . . . not at all!" The sorceress placed one soft palm against Golgren's chest, her talons grazing him so lightly that they almost tickled. "I want to help *you*."

XIII

DARK GUARDIANS

Why do I have difficulty believing you?" Tyranos snarled. "Watch her carefully, oh Grand Khan! Those pretty nails may only be resting on your chest, but you might find them ripping out your heart in the next and last breath!"

"I mean what I say," Morgada insisted, not letting her face show any displeasure. "Safrag is enthralled by the Fire Rose." She looked at Golgren again. "Other than your life, he cares for nothing greater than to use it to remake . . . everything! He even intends to remold the Titans to his own grand dream." The temptress shuddered. "But Safrag constantly changes his mind as to what that grand dream should be, and so I fear that with each fancy of his we will be transformed over and over."

The wizard chuckled darkly. "Now that, on the other hand, is a fear that I can believe you have got! Granted, it takes a powerful mind to keep Sirrion's gift under control."

"A mind more powerful than yours, spellcaster," she replied with a bit of a smirk. "A mind such as the Grand Khan Golgren's."

"So instead of Xiryn's pawn, he'll be your adoring pet! What say you to that, Golgren?"

"That is not what I offer—"

Golgren cut them both off. "And what do you wish from this bargain, Titaness?"

"Without the elixir, Xiryn, or Safrag, there is nothing to keep me from reverting as my power fails. With the Fire Rose, you can make it so that I'll always be alive, like this." Morgada gave him another beguiling smile. "Or you can shape me in some manner that pleases you more . . . even an elf."

"You should turn her into a viper, a much more natural shape for her."

Morgada gave no retort but showed a brief flash of anger.

It was anger that Golgren could exploit. "Keep your word," the half-ogre said to her, "and I will keep mine."

"Splendid!" She was on her feet and almost pressing against him without actually having risen. One moment Morgada was kneeling; the next she was standing.

To the side and out of her view, Tyranos shook his head at Golgren. The half-breed did not acknowledge him; he was more interested in something else. "Where is Safrag?" he asked Morgada. "Can you take me to him now?"

Some of her confidence faded. "To take you to him now would be a mistake. We would all end up like Kulgrath." Morgada paused but did not explain what she meant by that. "He is studying the Fire Rose as we speak. However, even he eventually tires enough that he must sleep. We will wait until then. That was Xiryn's plan, and I believe it to be a good one, Grand Khan."

"There is merit."

Tyranos was not as easily satisfied. "And so what do we do in the meantime? Wait for him to alter this place again?" He grimaced as he studied one of the reliefs. "You sure these wall really *don't* have ears, sorceress?"

"Xiryn showed me how to shield myself from Safrag without him knowing about it. You may trust that we are safe—" But as she spoke, Morgada's eyes suddenly shifted to the ceiling as if hearing something. "Safrag desires my presence! You two must stay here! It's the only truly secure place in the palace!"

Before either could respond, the female Titan vanished.

The wizard did not take her departure well. "I don't plan to wait here and hope that she doesn't bring Safrag back!"

He called upon the staff, but the crystal only dimmed.

"This should work!" Tyranos shook the magical item. "It should!"

Golgren remained quiet, for he had noticed the signet grow warmer. Some force desired them to stay there for the time being, which also suited the half-breed. Morgada could be of more use to Golgren than he had originally intended.

But he was nagged by one concern. There was one other who knew for a fact that the deposed Grand Khan had infiltrated the palace.

"Tyranos, can you summon someone to us?"

"Not Safrag, I assume. You can't be that insane."

"Wargroch."

The spellcaster studied the staff. "No. Not so long as it's behaving like this."

The signet remained warm, which told Golgren that there was nothing else they could do, at least not for the moment. The half-breed surveyed the chamber. "No door in this place."

"Yes, I noticed." Tyranos briefly touched something under his chest, a habit Golgren recognized because he often did the same thing himself. Instinctively, the half-ogre let his hand graze where his mummified appendage hung over his heart.

"So we rest," Golgren declared. Without waiting for any reaction from Tyranos, he slid into a sitting position against one of the many huge faces of Safrag.

The hooded figure glared then joined him. As he settled into some semblance of comfort, Tyranos muttered, "You are going to be the death of me, oh Grand Khan."

Golgren shut his eyes, not trying to sleep, but rather starting to plan and to think anew about a silver-tressed elf slave. "Yes. Likely to be the death of us all, wizard."

❦

Sir Augustus had not said so to Golgren, but his men had actually been ready to march the moment that the half-breed had reached a desired distance away from the encampment. Stefan might have provided the deciding factor in Solamnia's push into the ogre realm, but the senior knight had already been planning for an advance long before. Solamnia saw the instability of the ogres and the seizing of the capital by the Titans as inevitable threats that they could not afford to wait to settle.

Therefore, much of the force under his command was already well into the enemy lands. It was time the world was put in order, and the Knighthood was the only force capable of doing that.

And with the Fire Rose . . . well, perhaps the task would prove even simpler than his superiors had initially imagined. That was in part what the coded message at the bottom of the missive regarding Golgren had concerned. Solamnic codes could relay great amounts of information in seemingly random scratches and not merely the scratches; Sir Rennert had no doubt that Golgren had noticed them when reading the missive anyway. There were other markings set in strategic places and even among the words themselves. Altogether, they painted a detailed picture of just what Sir Augustus's superiors expected to come out of their pact.

The senior knight felt some guilt toward his nephew. Stefan had presented him with a clean, straightforward proposition that should have been to the equal advantage of both sides. However, Stefan was too young to understand the intricacies of matters of state. When it was all said and done, no one would be able to claim that Solamnia had not lived up to its obligations . . . if there were anyone left alive to make any claim. Certainly, Sir Augustus doubted Golgren's chances of survival.

For just the briefest of moments, Sir Augustus's sharp eyes fixed on what appeared to be a figure poised on a high ridge ahead. The knight blinked and when he focused again, he saw nothing.

But Stefan's uncle knew very well what they might face ahead, so he surreptitiously sent a signal to one of his officers. The knight in question slowed his mount, falling back to inform others who needed to spread the word.

As that happened, there came a low rumble that sounded like thunder; but it could not be, for there was no cloud in the sky.

"So it begins already," Sir Augustus muttered. "Well, let's see what you accursed spellcasters are made of when facing Solamnics."

The first of the battle horns blared. The Knight of the Rose adjusted his helmet then drew his sword.

As the clear sky thundered again, the Solamnics charged forward.

⚬⚬⟐⚬⚬

The forest seemed as endless as it was foreboding. Stefan promised her that they were making progress, but more than once, Idaria wondered if they were making *sufficient* progress. They had already been forced to take a long rest—sleep, actually—on the elf's account. That bothered her, for it began to feel to Idaria as if she were entirely to blame for their slowness.

What made it worse was that it was still impossible to tell night from day. By then, one should have followed the other. It was possible that Stefan knew the hour, but the knight never spoke about the passage of time, and for reasons she could not entirely explain to herself, Idaria could not bring herself to ask him what should have been a simple question. All the elf knew was that the Solamnic appeared anxious and beleaguered.

The dark trees continued to rustle ominously, but there had been no repeat of the sinister trap the forest had set for them before. Twice, the trio had avoided skeletal patrols, and once something large and black

190

had leaped among the branches above before moving on. There had been no other Titans yet, but Idaria could not imagine that she and her companions would be fortunate enough to avoid a future confrontation with one or more.

Stefan suddenly waved for a halt. Holding the medallion just ahead of him, he began muttering as if speaking with someone.

A moment later, he glanced back at his two companions, the elf and the gargoyle. "The Titans' sanctum is near."

That simple sentence made Idaria shudder. The culmination of her work, of her suffering, lay just ahead.

Stefan led them on. Chasm sniffed the air, shaking his head. Idaria recalled being told by Chasm that he was sensitive to magic. The nearer they drew to the sanctum, the more the gargoyle appeared bothered by the emanations.

The elf put a comforting hand on Chasm's arm. The winged creature let out a low rumble of pleasure.

Then, through the trees ahead, they sighted a silhouette that grew larger as they neared. It was a tall, massive structure with wide arches and jutting towers. There was a fearsome, fiery tint to its thick, stone walls.

Idaria immediately sensed something wrong about the structure and knew just what it was. "The Fire Rose . . ." she whispered. "This place has been transformed by it."

" 'The more it is used, the more it will demand to be used,' " Stefan replied, clearly quoting someone else. "In that may lie our best hope."

"How so?"

"If it enchants the Titan leader so much, then he may not be very mindful of small things like our task."

The forest finally began to thin out. Stefan made them pause again.

"This ground is accursed even more than the forest," the cleric murmured. "I can't say how, but tread very cautiously and follow closely where I step." As an afterthought, he added, "Pay no attention to any noises you hear. Any distraction could be costly."

He stepped into the more open area, with Idaria behind him and Chasm, as usual, taking up the rear guard. The Titans' sanctum loomed over them.

Idaria stared up. "The building . . . for some reason I can never really focus on it."

"Yes, I noticed that. Keep your eyes on the path I take, my lady. We'll see enough of the sanctum should we reach it."

A sound arose from their left. The area where they walked still featured the occasional crooked tree but otherwise appeared to be a seemingly harmless patch of black soil with small, rounded spots here and there. The elf saw nothing when she looked for the source of the sound, but her action made Chasm growl low in warning, reminding her of the knight's caution.

Nodding to the gargoyle, Idaria kept her eyes trained on Stefan's back. A similar noise rose up from the right, but that time she did not bother to look. There was an odor, too, one that she could not place, but which disturbed her. It reminded her of the musky smell of unbathed ogres and yet not exactly.

From behind her there came a surprised grunt from Chasm. Idaria looked over her shoulder to see what disturbed him.

The gargoyle looked back at her, as if confused by what she was doing.

Only then did Idaria realize that the grunt had not come from him.

She started to turn back, discovering then that she was just slightly off Stefan's trail. It was no more than a step.

Without realizing it, the elf had set a foot down on one of the tiny mounds.

The mound was rumbling. Idaria tried to pull her foot back up, only to find that it stuck to the ground.

Chasm came to her aid, but in the process stepped even farther away from Stefan's path.

"Stand back!" Stefan called, brandishing both his sword and the medallion.

The ground below Idaria exploded. As bits of dirt showered her, a skeletal hand reached up to clutch at her ankle.

Pulling hard, Chasm freed her. The fleshless hand scraped her skin as it lost hold.

Even as the gargoyle helped her to safety, the rest of the monstrous figure rose up from the ground. An undead ogre akin to the forest guards stalked toward them.

Worse, more of the fiends began shooting up to the surface wherever the small mounds were located. All were armed with rusted weapons. Their hollow eye sockets fixed on the trio.

Stefan slashed repeatedly with his blade. With a startling flash, the weapon cut through solid bone. The upper half of the nearest fiend toppled over, crashing to the ground. However, both the bottom and the severed top continued toward the intruders, the top dragging along on bony fingers.

Chasm thrust himself in front of Idaria. The gargoyle seized one of the tall skeletons and, despite the danger of being stabbed, hurled it at the closest other. The two undead ogres collided with a scattering of bone everywhere.

But the bones began to mend and knit together almost as soon as they landed. And the growing ranks of the Titans' horrific guards closed on the threesome.

"Stay between us!" Stefan ordered, making Idaria feel even more useless than before. Yet there was no arguing with his command.

Something struck her foot. The elf gasped as she saw an arm bone sliding past her to join the fragments of one of Chasm's earlier defeated foes. The bone slid and jerked toward its companion pieces as if tugged by an invisible string.

Idaria seized it. The bone fought her, but she gripped it with both hands and gained control. Holding the wriggling bone, the slave watched for a chance to help either of her companions.

Chasm was the ogre undeads' most formidable opponent. With pure, brute strength, he'd rip off an arm of one creature then twisted off the rib cage of another. Whenever he could, the gargoyle would tangle his adversaries together. Chasm laughed as two sought in vain to extricate themselves from each other.

But still the undead came at them, and the only thing that gave Idaria hope was the fact that the Titans were oddly absent. The possibility existed that, from somewhere safe, they were watching the desperate trio, savoring their predicament.

Stefan brandished the medallion, thrusting it toward each monster that came close. The two nearest skeletons reeled away as if burned, but others came at the Solamnic from all sides. The knight tried to fend them off, but they were converging on him.

One monstrous guard raised a chipped axe. Stefan, his back to the creature, did not notice the imminent threat.

Lunging, the elf struck the creature's weapon hand. The sword slipped from its bony grip. The towering undead turned to Idaria.

Slipping under his grasp, she shoved the arm bone between the skeleton's legs, turning it with all her strength. The guard, bending down to grab her, lost its balance. The great skeleton went tumbling.

Idaria immediately lifted her makeshift weapon and crushed in the skeleton's skull. For good measure, she swatted the ruined skull hard enough to send it flying. If she could not stop the fiend, she would at least do what she could to slow it.

Suddenly, Chasm gave a furious roar that made both elf and human look toward him. With furious energy, the gargoyle tore into one skeleton after another and, for a moment, cleared the path.

Pausing in his frenzy, Chasm turned his ferocious eyes to his companions—especially Idaria—and growled one word.

"Go!"

Idaria might have hesitated, but Stefan seized her arm and plunged ahead with her. Behind them, they heard Chasm unleash another tremendous roar, followed by a raucous clatter of bones and weapons.

The entrance to the sanctum awaited the pair. Twin columns shaped to resemble a Titan flanked great doors that appeared to be carved from silver pearl. Emblazoned on each of those doors was the face of the same Titan whose figure made up the columns: Safrag.

"He is well in the thrall of the Fire Rose," Idaria muttered to Stefan.

The knight nodded. "Which means that he is more of a threat than ever to all Krynn."

They strode up the shadowy steps toward the doors. The elf glanced up at the columns. The two Titans that formed columns looked as if they were observing the intruders. Even when she and Stefan reached the doors unhindered, the slave had to peer back at the columns to make certain the figures were not moving.

The Solamnic held the medallion to the doors. With a low creak, they swung inward.

"Don't tread less than an arm's length from me," suggested the cleric. He eyed the arm bone that she still wielded. "We need a better weapon for you. Let me see if he can help us."

Stefan held the side of the medallion that bore Kiri-Jolith's face toward the bone. Momentarily sheathing his sword, the Solamnic then ran his hand along the edge of Idaria's makeshift weapon.

As he did so, the bone glowed lightly and reshaped itself. It became a long, tapering blade, thinner than the knight's sword and with an elegance that was elven in style.

Stepping back to study the results, Stefan suddenly frowned. "I should've asked you first whether a sword was to your liking or even if you can wield one very well."

In response, Idaria tested the sword with a few expert lunges and slashes.

A smile briefly lit the knight's face. "You could train our novices with skill like that."

"Thank you for the blade."

"I was only the conduit. Kiri-Jolith provided the power."

"What does he hope to gain out of all this? What can he do for us?" Idaria asked.

"What he can do for us is as much as what we can do for ourselves. His assistance is limited, though the hope he can give us is not. Krynn is changing and the gods are changing with it . . . and not necessarily of their own volition. My patron's greatest desire, as I see it, is to keep all that change—embodied by the menace of Sirrion more than anything else at the moment—from destroying everything Kiri-Jolith loves."

That said, the Solamnic moved ahead stealthily. Idaria, digesting his words, silently followed.

The corridors were immense; that was no surprise as the chief inhabitants were more than twice Stefan's height. The sanctum was so imbued with magical forces and the elf felt her long hair slightly rise. There was also a tingle in the air, as if lightning had just struck. The same silver pearl material glossed the floor for as far as their eyes could make out.

"Do you know where to look?" she whispered to her companion.

"I've some guidance, but it's limited here. Still, logic would suggest that the slaves would be somewhere down below, assuming . . . ."

He trailed off. Neither dared voice their worst fears; it was possible they were already too late to help her people.

There were no torches or oil lamps, but the corridors seemed perpetually lit. The reddish glow radiated from the crimson walls themselves, which bespoke the tremendous power of the Fire Rose.

"It could restore all Silvanost," Idaria absently murmured.

"Or turn it into something like the forest from which

we just emerged," the cleric reminded her. "Sirrion's creation is not for mortal hands; few, if any, of us have the will to keep its power in check." After a moment's silence, he added, "And that also includes some gods, I suspect."

The elf nodded thoughtfully. Silvanost, if it were ever retaken, would have to be restored through the magic of her people or some other avenue. It was too great of a risk to allow even her ancient race to try to wield the artifact; for all their vaunted glory and superior power, the High Ogres had proven that they were not strong enough. Idaria could only imagine the terrible things that might happen to the elves.

Stefan inspected each side passage as they passed. The Titans appeared not to have laid any traps within their own abode or at least, not so far. There were more than a few wide, massive pearl stairways that led up, but as yet they couldn't find any that led below. Idaria eyed the walls, seeking any hints of a hidden path. Stefan also held the medallion up to the walls, but with as little result as the elf's scrutiny.

Voices arose before them, the first sounds they had heard since entering.

Stefan steered Idaria into a shadowy side passage. The voices grew louder but were unintelligible. From her vantage point, Idaria looked around for the speakers but could not see them.

Without warning, part of the wall to the far left glowed brighter. The twin shapes of two towering figures formed on it.

A pair of Titans melted through the unsettling stone as if it did not exist. They were caught up in preoccupied conversation, a few words of which only then could be understood.

"Hargren has not returned! That leaves only the two of us!" said the first.

"Morgada must've summoned him like the rest! We'll be called before long, mark me!" argued the second. "Sent off to do his bidding like lackeys!"

"What care should we have about a herd of cows tromping through the south or some clanking humans coming from another direction? They are nothing to us! The Fire Rose can sweep them all aside—"

"If Safrag ever decides to act!" the second countered angrily. Then, as if he had just committed some terrible sin, the Titan quickly and anxiously amended, "As I'm sure he will, should he deem it necessary."

"Fool," muttered the other. "Clamp your mouth shut, and let's be done with our task."

Still obviously apprehensive, the two gargantuan spellcasters continued, eventually vanishing down the corridor. Not until they were well out of sight did Stefan and Idaria step out from the shadows. They had escaped notice.

Only then did something strange occur to the slave. "I thought at first they were speaking in that tongue of theirs, but now I realize that I understood everything they said. Why would they be speaking Common here in their sanctum?"

The cleric displayed the medallion for her. "It wasn't that they were speaking Common. Through Kiri-Jolith, we were able to understand whatever language they spoke." He frowned. "Their conversation was interesting. It sounds as if Golgren has managed to get matters moving, as he hoped."

"But they said nothing about my people . . . nothing at all," the elf muttered.

"That may mean very little. Come, let's try the wall from which they emerged."

The knight gingerly stretched his sword to the stone. Rather than sink through, the tip struck the stone with a low clang.

Holding up the medallion, Stefan whispered. The medallion glowed.

Again, the stone did not yield.

Stefan tapped the wall with the sword, frustration mounting in his expression.

"I don't know what else to do, my lady! I expected that the medallion would surely help, but the way is well blocked. I'd need Kiri-Jolith himself to open it, and that is beyond me."

Idaria placed her open palm against the stone. "Perhaps there is a secret switch or—"

The elf toppled through. Behind her, she heard Stefan calling after her.

On the other side, darkness welcomed Idaria.

XIV

SAFRAG PLOTS

A new world existed for Safrag, a world that stretched his imagination beyond mortal bounds. A world where all was possible, merely at his whim . . .

A world where he was a god.

Seated in his otherwise darkened sanctum, his eyes seeing only what lay within the Fire Rose, Safrag thought, *What a blind fool you were, Dauroth! Such power as even you could not dream! Such fear you had of it. Such fear of such a beautiful, wonderful thing.*

Within the artifact, what the treacherous former apprentice imagined were spirits of flame dancing about. In their wild movements, Safrag imagined they danced for the pleasure of he who wielded the Fire Rose, he alone. The whole mortal world would soon dance for Safrag.

Safrag imagined another figure within. He pictured Dauroth alive and privy to all that had been accomplished by Safrag's use of Sirrion's creation. The dream-Dauroth wept for his own ignorance, for all that he might have accomplished had he been as wise or crafty as Safrag.

A voice abruptly broke into his glorious reverie. The Titan leader angrily focused on finding out just who had dared disturb him.

Great Teacher! The intruder was Falstoch, trying by spell to penetrate Safrag's mind. *Great Teacher.*

Only because it was Falstoch—Falstoch who was still new to his role as a Titan and utterly subservient to Safrag—did the master sorcerer forgive him. Even so, it was a tremendous temptation to use the excuse to experiment on Falstoch.

But instead of doing so, Safrag satisfied himself with merely reaching out and communicating with the other Titan. *I hear you, loyal Falstoch. What would you have of your lord?*

The lesser spellcaster was not bothered by Safrag's use of the title. Falstoch knew his place. *My lord,* Falstoch immediately responded. *The Uruv Suurt press harder upon the south, and the Knights of Solamnia have encroached elsewhere! You asked to be informed when either crossed beyond the designated locations and both have, nearly simultaneously!*

Although Falstoch found that upsetting, Safrag did not; it only proved to him that the Fire Rose had granted its wielder infinite wisdom. *So good of them,* he said back to the other Titan. *I will reward their timeliness, but I am less pleased with my children! I expected them to give more of themselves.*

They're growing weak, my lord. Falstoch made it clear that he was not like the rest of them. *But they try. Morgada holds them together as best as any other than your august self could, my lord.*

The flattery was shameless, but Safrag accepted it as

also being the absolute truth. *And the skies? They're clear?*

Of all save our own spells, my lord! There are no storms on the horizon.

Falstoch did not understand what Safrag was waiting for. It was not some mundane augury of weather that interested the lead Titan. No, he was anticipating the third invasion.

He was waiting for the gargoyles.

The palace remains yours to watch, my loyal Falstoch. I know I can entrust it into your hands.

The distant Falstoch radiated gratitude and pleasure.

Safrag cut the spell linking the two. Even that minor of a distraction had left him yearning for the seductive warmth of the Fire Rose.

Command me; use me; let my power be unleashed. Safrag thought the artifact was saying to him repeatedly. They were one, he and the Fire Rose. It amazed him to realize just how incomplete he had been in his previous life, first as an ambitious ogre of a minor but still powerful clan, then as a supplicant seeking the eye of the powerful Dauroth, and last, as the one who removed the Titans' faulty creator from supremacy and took his place. All that time, Safrag had been incomplete.

But no more.

I will remake Krynn as it should be, Safrag eagerly thought. And I will do so with the bodies of all my enemies cast as monuments to my victory.

The Titan leader laughed aloud. In the Fire Rose, he saw many winged shapes, the symbol of the last of those foes. Although they were creations of his own imagination, he was certain the beasts were on their way by then. Their master would be compelled to strike and strike soon.

Safrag stroked the Fire Rose.

But whatever he or the half-breed hope to do, it will not be enough to separate us. No, it will not be enough.

The artifact flared brightly as if in agreement.

❧❀❧

The vast flock descended from the skies, alighting among the gray mountains. They had not settled to rest, however, rather because it was where they had been told to wait. Garantha was not far away, and they waited where the power of their lord could keep them hidden from even the one who wielded the Fire Rose.

The winged furies perched on high precipices, outcroppings, cave mouths; they were everywhere. They stretched long, leathery wings and groomed themselves. Despite their numbers and obvious eagerness, they made little noise as they waited.

After several minutes, a small group of gargoyles rose from their perches and flew off to the south.

Moments later, another batch of the winged beasts rose to the air, but that group headed northwest.

Bred to be swift, neither of the flocks would be long in reaching their goals. The master's plan was taking shape. When the signal came, the main flock would continue to Garantha.

The Fire Rose would again belong to Xiryn.

❧❀❧

Morgada materialized before Safrag, her neutral demeanor revealing nothing of her duplicity. As was the case the last time she had come to the Titan leader—and the time before that—Safrag remained engrossed in the Fire Rose. Behind her facade of loyalty, the sorceress laughed to herself. Safrag acted just as Xiryn had predicted; *everyone* reacted as the High Ogre predicted.

She went down on one knee. "My master, you summoned me?"

Safrag forced his gaze away from the Fire Rose. "Yes, I wished to speak with you about the half-breed."

It was all Morgada could do to keep from showing a flicker of surprise. Of course, Safrag could not know that, at that very moment, Golgren was in the very palace the lead Titan had reconstructed in his own honor. Or could he?

"What of that mongrel, great one?"

Safrag rose and reluctantly turned from the artifact, which bespoke more willpower than Morgada would have expected of him at that point. "I think I should look into his escape from the tomb which I created for him, and I can trust no one more than you to accompany me."

"I am honored."

"As you should be." Without looking at the artifact, Safrag reached for the Fire Rose. It slid across the marble table to his beckoning hand; whether at his command or of its own choice, it was impossible for Morgada to say. "Step to me, my loyal apprentice."

Despite some hidden reservations, Morgada joined Safrag. He gestured.

Their surroundings changed, transforming into the chill, mountainous area where Safrag had said that he had banished Golgren to die. The wind shrieked as they appeared, almost as if decrying their appearance. A dust storm blew. Yet neither disturbed the Titans, who were protected by their magic and stood as if on a calm day.

They peered around, but of the shell that Safrag had described to his fellow Titans, there was no sign, save for a few, half-buried fragments. The rest had either vanished or been destroyed in the mongrel's mysterious escape.

Clutching the Fire Rose close, Safrag bent to examine the area. A black glow radiated from his hand as he ran it over the dry ground.

Symbols briefly reappeared, symbols that Golgren had angrily swept away. They were those that Sarth had inscribed for his reading.

"Tell me, my dear Morgada, do these markings mean anything at all to you?"

She leaned over, curious. "Nothing. What are they?"

"Not drawn by the remaining hand of the mongrel," the Titan leader commented. "And the emanations . . ."

He straightened with such abruptness that Morgada stumbled back in surprise. Safrag looked to the mountains, next at his companion, then once more at where the images were just fading to oblivion again.

"A fourth will not matter," he murmured as though to himself, holding up the Fire Rose to admire. "A thousand enemies may come, but only one matters; only the half-breed matters."

Behind him, Morgada frowned. She quickly erased the frown then, in calm, confident tones, asked, "Have you finished here, great one?"

"Oh, yes, my dear Morgada, I have."

With a casual sweep of the hand that held the Fire Rose, Safrag *seared* the ground, obliterating with black fire the area where he had left Golgren to perish. The sorcerer's eyes blazed as dangerously as the magical flames he had unleashed with the artifact's might.

Then Safrag narrowed his eyes.

"I would speak to you," he demanded.

Thinking Safrag meant her, Morgada opened her mouth to say something then shut it again as the flames darted high, swelling taller than either Titan, for Safrag was speaking to the very fire. The flames turned from black to brilliant red then formed a golden figure clad in long, sweeping robes of crimson: Sirrion.

The fiery deity smiled benevolently at the pair, but his gaze was directed at Safrag. Sirrion extended his own hand.

As if the entire region had been doused with oil, the flames suddenly coursed everywhere. They surrounded the two Titans, enveloping them. Morgada bit back an exclamation. For as far as the eye could see, fire devoured the land.

Sirrion's smile widened. He patted his stomach.

The flames vanished, leaving nothing but charred ground. Anything that could burn, had.

"Your offering made for a tiny appetizer," Sirrion remarked. "I made a better snack of it."

Safrag went down on one knee, holding the Fire Rose toward its creator. "Lord of the Flames, I thank you for your appearance here."

"You stirred my curiosity. You have my gift to Krynn; what more could you possibly want?"

"I have proven myself able to master the Fire Rose, but there are those who would still take it from me if they could." Safrag tried to meet the god's gaze but finally looked to one side. To stare into Sirrion's eyes was akin to staring directly into the burning sun. There was only blindness to be gained by doing do.

Sirrion looked bored with Safrag's statement. The

god shrugged, his wild hair unleashing little flickers of fire that dropped on the blackened land and sizzled for a time. "This is not my concern. The one who proves himself most worthy is the one who in the end has triumphed over the rest. Only that one truly has the chance to master my gift."

"But I have outwitted all of them! The only reason that any of them survive is through trickery, not of mortal means."

"You refer to Kiri-Jolith."

The simple naming of the other god made Safrag stiffen. Morgada, too, could not hide her surprise. "The bison warrior is a part of this?"

Waving her off, the lead Titan growled, "Help me defeat him, and I will raise monuments as high as mountains to you!"

"A pleasing offer," replied Sirrion, "but one which has been made to me before. Others, too, promised to worship me then failed. Besides, I have no quarrel with Kiri-Jolith. We have even fought the dark ones side by side. He only makes the game more amusing."

" 'Game'?" Unlike the god, Safrag did not look amused.

Sirrion spread his arms like a great cleric preaching to his acolytes. "But that is how the true victor will be decided! It's always by the game, and this time, all of Krynn is in play!"

Safrag stood. "I don't understand!"

Morgada watched both in wonder.

"Because you are mortal and you are not me!" Sirrion grinned. "But if it will ease your mind, if you are the victor, the Fire Rose will be yours to shape *all* with!"

"But Kiri-Jolith—?" persisted Safrag.

An abrupt fury spread over the god's countenance. Morgada retreated. "You try my patience, and I am not known for having much, mortal!" As quickly as the fury rose, it settled. "In the end, Kiri-Jolith is only another player, and he must abide by my rules where this is concerned; that is the law between his and mine."

"Kiri-Jolith must abide by the rules," the lead Titan mused. He bowed his head to the god. "Great is Sirrion and great is his wisdom."

"Yes, I am glorious, am I not?" Sirrion patted his stomach. "That was not nearly enough to even come close to satisfying me for a time." He peered around at the ruined landscape. "There looks to be something left to eat here."

Safrag raised his hand to cast a spell. Morgada, recognizing what was coming, seized hold of his arm.

Flames erupted around Sirrion. They spread from the god with ferocious appetite. Even though the area appeared bereft of anything left to burn, burn it did and well.

And burned also would have been the Titans, if not for their swift action. Safrag and Morgada returned to his lair, the scent of scorched ground following them.

Morgada took a deep breath. Safrag stepped away from her, shrugging as though his dramatic encounter with the deity were long forgotten. Once again, all that mattered was the Fire Rose.

"It is mine, Morgada. Did you hear him? He promised it would remain mine, for who else could be victor if even the other god must abide by the same demands as my rivals? It matters not who freed the mongrel or who the master of the gargoyles is. The Fire Rose will remain mine! I will be the winner, and Krynn will be my prize."

"Great is my honor to have witnessed this," Morgada wisely responded, "and greater is my honor to be in your presence."

Safrag gave her words an absent nod as he fixed on the forces dancing within the crystalline structure. "You are dismissed, my dear Morgada."

She did not hesitate. The female Titan bowed low then vanished.

But when she reappeared, it was neither in her chamber in the original sanctum nor in the one in the palace where she kept Golgren and his human companion. Rather, she appeared in the most unlikely place for a Titan.

You were not expected, the figure on the throne coldly rebuked her.

Around the sorceress, figures in the shadows shifted forward. Morgada ignored them, seeing the shambling forms as only extensions of Xiryn.

"I've just come from Safrag," she answered defiantly. "And I think you might wish to listen to my report."

XV

DISCOVERY

Wargroch had informed no one about Golgren's presence. He prayed that his former lord's wizard companion had had the sense enough to take the half-breed far, far away from Garantha. Only death awaited Golgren in the capital.

The Blödian was uncertain how to proceed. His own drive for vengeance had faded with the cold realization that the Titans represented a danger to his people. He had watched Atolgus become more and more monstrous even by ogre standards, and he understood that it was likely to be his fate as well. That went against the fearsome, independent spirit of his kind. Golgren, on the other hand, had always encouraged individual spirit, cultivating the best to become his officers. The Titans desired nothing but puppets, acting as extensions of their will.

If Golgren were slain, there would be no hope of preventing the Titans' desires.

Wargroch owed the deposed Grand Khan a blood debt. That was how the ogre viewed things. For his many betrayals, Wargroch had to make amends, even at the cost of his own life.

There came shouts from one of the lower corridors. Wargroch drew his sword—Atolgus's sword—and rushed toward the noise.

The ogre expected to find Golgren battling the guards, but he beheld a different sight, something he could not have imagined ripping into the hapless ogres trying to fend it off. It was almost an ogre, yet a creature also distinctly reptilian.

And it was quickly disposing of more than half a dozen warriors.

Wargroch plunged into the fray. He saw no reason not to. A beast such as that one could not be part of any ploy by Golgren; it had the stink of Titan spellcasting around it. Safrag was probably experimenting again without regard for his own people.

The fiendish monster had seized an already-wounded guard by the arm and was dragging him close. Great, toothy jaws already dripping with blood opened then snapped shut over the guard's head. There was the gruesome sound of bone cracking and sinew tearing.

With a hiss, the beast pulled back from its prey. The headless body quivered. The powerful jaws crunched down twice. Then, swallowing its grisly morsel, the creature released the body and turned toward the next foe. The headless corpse wobbled a few steps in what was almost a comical dance then collapsed.

Wargroch let out a roar and lunged under the monster's paws. His blade sliced against the scaled torso, leaving a scratch from one side to the other but didn't penetrate.

The reptilian fiend slashed at the ogre, but Wargroch

had been expecting its attack. He literally slid on his belly past the reach of his horrific foe, letting momentum take him out of range of even its long, dangerous tail.

As Wargroch turned, he saw that, from the rear, the creature's resemblance to a meredrake was unmistakable. That verified his suspicion that the sorcerers were to blame for the foul creation. Wargroch added that to his list of failures. More ogres were perishing because he had enabled it to happen.

The transformed meredrake climbed over a lifeless ogre as it lunged toward the remaining guards. As it did, the huge monster slipped on the mangled corpse, momentarily falling forward.

Seeing his chance, Wargroch charged. As he reached the beast, he jumped for its shoulders.

The brawny ogre landed atop the creature's back. With a roar, the meredrake twisted around. Great talons raked the nearby, well-stained walls, but the monster could not quite grab Wargroch.

However, the ogre was faring poorly. Although Wargroch managed to hold on, he could not do much else. The meredrake slammed him against one wall then the other, trying to dislodge or crush him. It was all Wargroch could do to maintain a grip on his sword, much less wield it with any efficacy.

His daring attack had at least drawn attention away from the beleaguered guards. Some withdrew to bind their wounds while others regrouped. Two more guards arrived, axes at the ready.

The newcomers drew the meredrake's attention. The monster ceased battering Wargroch.

The Blödian immediately slashed as best he could at the back of the meredrake's neck. In the old days, before Golgren, it was likely that his sword would have been so rusty that it would have snapped in two upon striking such a hard surface. The meredrake's scales were far thicker than before, however, another of Safrag's "improvements." The polished blade left only a shallow, red line that could not possibly have injured the lizard, but at least Wargroch had recaptured its focus.

The meredrake once more sought to grasp his burden or smash it against a wall. As that happened, the guards moved in again.

"The throat!" Wargroch shouted, staying with the Common tongue even in the midst of the struggle. Other than the inside of the mouth itself—an almost impossible target—the throat was surely the most vulnerable place to strike.

But the meredrake, although taller than the ogres, kept its head bent low as it snapped angrily at its adversaries.

Still, the guards did their best to stab at the creature's face. One dived in eagerly, his axe grazing the lower part of the throat.

The meredrake let loose with a fierce roar. It slashed with its claws across the ogre's chest. More blood splattered the combatants. The warrior's innards spilled out, and the corpse tumbled into the monster, who almost casually shoved it aside.

Wargroch used the distraction to try to climb onto the creature's shoulder. Just as he hoped, the meredrake twisted its head around in an attempt to better see what he was doing.

The ogre officer drove the point of his weapon into the creature's eye. Blood and a yellowish fluid gushed from the ruined orb. A fetid smell filled the ogre's nostrils.

The monster roared in pain. It threw itself against the wall, pinning Wargroch's leg. The ogre let out a howl.

From somewhere beyond the meredrake, a voice boomed a command that, in his agony and struggles, Wargroch could not understand. The meredrake shifted, slamming against the other wall. The Blödian lost his grip. He slipped to the moist floor, his sword flying away.

Wargroch expected his death to come shortly, and he welcomed it. It would be an honorable if gruesome demise and would make some amends for his betrayals.

But the creature paid him no mind, instead focusing on someone ahead. Wargroch raised himself up enough to see.

His eyes widened as he beheld Atolgus. The warlord faced the meredrake alone. Atolgus wore a mad, gleeful expression, a berserker's face that twisted his handsome, Titan features into something awful. He wielded only the sword that had once belonged to Golgren.

Despite Atolgus being nearly as tall as the meredrake, Wargroch still thought the Titans' puppet must have gone insane to try and face such a threat alone. Yet Atolgus laughed as he attacked and feinted, attacked and feinted. It was as if the warlord saw the battle as a game, not a struggle to the death.

Then Atolgus lunged with swiftness that was beyond any ogre naturally born. The blade shimmered as he struck the monster on the chest, and where other weapons had failed to penetrate, his sword performed with only slight hesitation.

The meredrake shivered as Atolgus withdrew his wet blade, again laughing. The creature let out another pained roar as it sought to clamp its great, yellowed teeth on Atolgus's forearm.

Again moving more swiftly than Wargroch thought possible, quicker than even Golgren, Atolgus not only avoided the bite, but turned the scaly monster's lunge into a counterattack of his own. As the jaws sought him, the warlord thrust his sword into it again.

Propelled by a combination of sorcery and Atolgus's enhanced strength, the blade bore through flesh, muscle, and even bone to burst out of the back of the meredrake's skull. Hot ichor drenched Wargroch.

The creature let out a pitiful moan. Atolgus readily removed the blade. Eyes bright with pleasure, he stepped back to admire his handiwork.

The scaled monster dropped in a heap. Its tail swept toward Wargroch. Only a quick jump saved him from an embarrassing fall.

Raising his sword, which flashed one more time, Atolgus let loose with a wild war cry. The surviving guards quickly joined him. Wargroch wisely did the same.

Atolgus's golden eyes fixed on the Blödian. In eloquent Common, Atolgus remarked, "A brave and clever assault, Wargroch! I commend you for softening him up for me!"

Atolgus had never spoken Common so well, not even the last time Wargroch had seen him. Safrag's experiment was continuing even without the lead Titan to guide it.

"But the death blow belongs to Atolgus," Wargroch replied, using his best Common in turn. With his weapon, he saluted the warlord.

However, rather than look pleased, the warlord's face darkened. "He has infiltrated Dai Ushran."

Although at first taken aback by that phrase, Wargroch was able to puzzle out what the sorcerers' puppet was referring to. He hid his dismay, he hoped, at Atolgus's discovery. "You think Golgren is in Gara—Dai Ushran?"

It was still difficult for most ogres to remember that the capital had been renamed.

"The meredrake was his pet!" Atolgus laughed, revealing teeth sharper than Wargroch remembered. "The great one set it as a trap should the mongrel return, which he, of course, dared!"

"Then the beast has killed Golgren?"

The altered ogre's golden eyes blazed. "Do you think him that easily slain?" Before Wargroch could summon a response, Atolgus added, "The mongrel's still here somewhere. Come, let us hunt him down." He chuckled. "I'll give her his head! She'll reward me for that."

Wargroch again hid his churning emotions. He glanced at the small band of guards following them. "We do not need these, Warlord."

Atolgus turned and gave him a sinister grin. "True! We are the Titans' greatest servants! We can do it by ourselves!" He dismissed the other ogres with a wave of his hand, saying, "Clear the corpses! Search the outer levels!"

The guards obeyed. The warlord nodded to Wargroch. "Now! We will find him for her!"

Wargroch nodded agreement. Sword gripped tightly, he followed Atolgus, letting the sorcerers' puppet take the lead.

☞☜✦☞☜

Morgada had not yet returned. Tyranos had reminded Golgren of that fact more than once. The wizard paced back and forth, while the half-breed continued to sit with his eyes closed, his thoughts concealed from his companion.

The wizard's pacing suddenly stopped. Golgren's eyes opened to slits.

Staff held before him and his other hand flat against his chest, Tyranos appeared to be readying a spell. However, the hooded figure hesitated at the last moment, which brought a slight smile of understanding to Golgren's lips. The smile vanished and the eyes closed again before Tyranos turned back to observe him.

"Are you going to just sit there?"

"We cannot leave, so, yes."

Shaking his head, the spellcaster growled, "And yet you insist you must reclaim your realm. Just how will you do that sitting there?"

"I have been . . . considering."

" 'Considering' what?"

Before Golgren could reply, the walls shimmered. Golgren immediately rose to his feet even as Tyranos gripped his staff with both hands.

"Someone other than Morgada seeks entrance," the half-breed murmured.

"Someone who's also a Titan," the wizard added.

One wall suddenly heaved inward, as though it were clay softening. It receded then heaved in again, almost like some great beast breathing.

"I warned you," Tyranos said.

Golgren said nothing, instead striding to the vast bed and ripping off one of the shimmering silken sheets. Expertly, the half-breed used his single hand to twist the sheet around and around until he could readily grip it.

His companion snorted. "Are you planning on trying to strangle someone? Won't you need another set of fingers for that?"

Again, Golgren did not reply. His focus was on the wall.

A black stain suddenly spread through the shifting wall, as if some unseen wound caused it to bleed black blood. The smell of burning ash filled the chamber, causing Tyranos to start coughing. Small tendrils of smoke snaked upward from wherever the inky stain spread.

The wall began to melt, pooling into molten slag on the ground.

A gigantic figure burst through.

Golgren tossed the sheet toward the intruder.

The sheet opened as it flew, just as intended. It spread, immediately enveloping the looming figure of a Titan.

Momentarily distracted, the sorcerer stumbled. He let out a curse that caused the sheet to turn to cinder.

But Tyranos, finally understanding what Golgren had planned, had already charged forward. Swinging the staff like a mace, he struck the Titan in the stomach.

A black flash erupted where the crystal touched the sorcerer. Both he and Tyranos were hurled in opposite directions. The Titan flew against the ruined wall, accompanied by another fearsome black flash. The wizard simply crashed.

The Titan did not immediately move, but Tyranos managed to rise. He touched his chest then stumbled toward Golgren.

"I think—I think I can transport us away now that the wall's breached! Hurry!"

The half-breed leaned into the wizard, helping the latter to maintain his balance. Tyranos concentrated.

The Titan stirred. Golgren recognized the Titan's face, although he had not seen it for a long time. When last he confronted him, years earlier, it had been just before he had vanished, apparently the victim of Dauroth's ire.

"Falstoch," the half-breed muttered.

The crystal flared. Golgren's surroundings grew murky.

And suddenly the half-ogre found himself falling to his knees in a corridor. Tyranos was nowhere to be found. An angry sound from his left warned Golgren that he was not far away from the Titan. He pushed himself up and peered in that direction; the part of the wall that Falstoch had destroyed stood only a yard away.

Falstoch himself had not discovered where Golgren had landed, although surely some spell of his was responsible. The half-breed had no time to concern himself with Tyranos's fate, for the Titan already was turning toward the opening.

Golgren jumped through the hole, crashing into Falstoch before the Titan knew what was happening. Despite the sorcerer's immense size, Golgren was used to fighting larger adversaries. Falstoch landed hard. The Titan let out a grunt and, for the moment, lay still. Taking no chances, Golgren planted his maimed limb across the fallen sorcerer's windpipe.

A rasping sound escaped Falstoch as Golgren pressed. The Titan raised a hand.

A shock ran through the half-breed. He tumbled back, his body quivering from brief but intense pain.

"I knew she couldn't be trusted," Falstoch gasped in Common. "I never truly trusted her, although I pretended to do so! She was always too close to the master, always using her devilries on him! She went so easily from worshiping damned Dauroth to bedding Safrag!"

Golgren tried to rise, but a backhanded gesture from Falstoch sent him slamming to the floor once again.

"Only I can truly be trusted by the master! Safrag

gave me back my glorious self after Dauroth punished me for daring to disobey him by searching for the Fire Rose! My life is Safrag's now, and any who betray it must pay!"

Golgren could move his hand but could not find no weapon. "I was a prisoner of Morgada," he managed.

The sorcerer shook his head, his expression eager. "Oh, no! If that was true, she would've brought you to him right away! That was his command! If one of us found you, we were to bring you, dead or alive, directly to him." A sinister grin spread across the blue countenance. "I choose *dead.*"

Still unable to do anything to help himself, Golgren stalled for time. "And so clever is Falstoch! How did you know that Morgada hid me here?"

Falstoch loomed over him. One glowing palm faced Golgren, continuing to keep him flattened. "Yes, I am clever, so don't try to stall. Abandon all hope. Your wizard friend has gone wherever he planned, and he won't be able to return here! It would require far more power than a mere creature like he has."

"Then tell me of your cleverness and finish me."

The monstrous spellcaster grinned even wider. "I knew she was up to something! Always hovering around Safrag and then vanishing into one of her lairs, either here or in the great sanctum! Even great Safrag could not detect her duplicity!"

Golgren had slowly managed to slide one foot over closer to Falstoch's. The Titan prevented him from rising but not from moving sideways. The half-breed braced himself. It would take all the might he could muster to trip Falstoch or push him off balance.

"Then only a short while ago, I sensed her working subtle spells, seemingly insignificant ones by themselves, but together acting to shield something in her chamber! I knew that the master would not notice, not with the artifact radiating such power around him! I had to take the chance, wait until she was gone from the palace, to discover what was so very important to her that even Safrag must not know. It turns out that she was intent on betrayal, with you as her ally."

The irony was that Falstoch was half right; before that day, all Morgada's secrecy had concerned her service, however treacherous, to the gargoyle king. Golgren bared his teeth in a predator's smile at that knowledge. Falstoch was ignorant, in so many ways.

The Titan hesitated. "You've no reason to grin, mongrel! I've granted you the first part of your wish, and now give you the second! I doubt the master would mind in the least if I brought you to him entirely *flayed* and perhaps, after all, still breathing."

Golgren shoved his foot against the Titan's leg.

The force caused Falstoch to slip forward before he righted himself.

Fury overtaking him, Falstoch snarled, "No more of your pathetic tricks."

The sorcerer shrieked. He stumbled back wildly. As he did, something so bright that it forced Golgren to shield his eyes burst through the Titan's chest from behind.

It was a familiar, five-sided crystal.

Black ichor poured out of Falstoch where the crystal had emerged. The sorcerer continued to shriek. His entire body shook, and as his fingers scraped at the horrific wound, he turned to the side, revealing the true cause of his torment.

"Get . . . moving . . . Grand Khan!" Tyranos blurted, the wizard appearing to be suffering nearly as much as his victim. Sweat covered him and his eyes bulged with strain. Tyranos was surrounded by the same glow that emanated from the crystal.

Golgren turned to go then shook his head. "No, wizard, we go together."

"A fine—a fine time—to turn noble!"

Falstoch clamped his mouth shut. Black, burning tears coursed down his cheeks, the unearthly handsomeness of the Titan completely leaving. He gripped the crystal with both hands and frantically began singing in Dauroth's magical tongue.

Tyranos shrieked. However, the powerfully built mage did not slow his own attack. Like Falstoch, Tyranos clamped his mouth tightly shut and forced his pain into his attack. Energy flowed from his chest into his arms then into the crystal.

Glancing from one to the other, Golgren threw himself at the Titan. The same forces encompassing the two spellcasters surrounded him. Even as searing pain coursed through him, he used his strength and leverage to twist one of Falstoch's hands free.

The effect was immediate. Falstoch's spell faltered. The Titan screamed again. He flung Golgren aside then fell to his knees.

The wizard fell with him. As Golgren stopped his fall, the half-breed witnessed not one, but *two* fantastic transformations.

Of the two, the most grotesque, most terrifying, was that of Falstoch. The Titan first began to shrink. At the same time, his body started to lose cohesion. Parts of Falstoch dripped onto the floor.

With a roar, Tyranos threw more effort into his spell. His own shape had become broader and more animalistic in form. His face stretched forward, as if seeking to leave his skull.

Yet that was still nothing in comparison to the sorcerer's fate. There remained in him little resembling a Titan. Falstoch was an amorphous mass that exuded a nauseating odor like that of a bloated carcass. His fine raiment had faded. The Titan's cry had been reduced to a pathetic, bubbling sound.

Even then, Tyranos pressed on. Unlike Falstoch, his robe had filled out with the changes in his body. Course, dark brown fur covered any visible skin, including his face. The brow ridge had grown thick; the nose and mouth formed a sleek muzzle. Two long ears thrust out of his hood. The wizard was still roughly the same height as before but even more muscular.

And although Tyranos lacked a pair of horns, Golgren could not mistake the realization, which would have been clear to anyone who witnessed the transformation, that the wizard was an Uruv Suurt . . . a *minotaur*.

A terrifying final hiss arose from the blob that had been Falstoch. What remained of the Titan stank even worse than earlier. The flesh had a horrendous green tint to it. As Golgren approached, the last of Falstoch melted to liquid, which spread over the once-immaculate floor and even under the half-breed's very feet.

But Golgren no longer cared about Falstoch. Instead, he stepped over to the mage, who held the dimly lit staff to his own chest. Tyranos's breathing was ragged, but he still managed to look up at Golgren with defiance. The hood slid back slightly, and only then was it revealed that where there should have been a fine pair of yard-long horns thrusting up, only two cauterized nubs remained.

That was the sign of a minotaur marked for dishonorable crimes among his people.

"So now you know the truth," Tyranos rumbled, the timbre of his voice exactly the same as always. "Now you know what I am."

"This was no secret to me for some time."

The Uruv Suurt snorted. "No, of course not! You're Golgren! You know everything and whatever you don't know, you figure out! Of course, you knew what I was all the time."

Golgren shrugged. "What you are does not matter. What use you provide does."

Tyranos finally began to catch his breath. He used that breath to laugh harshly. "And *that* truly is the Golgren I've come to know so very well." The minotaur grimaced from pain. He gazed at the staff. "I think . . . I think I can manage to restore it now."

The crystal glowed slightly brighter. The glow gradually spread to Tyranos, enveloping him.

Once again, his shape began to change. He reverted to the human form so familiar to Golgren.

The effort left Tyranos gasping again. "Hard enough . . . hard enough to use so much power to get back here . . . without having to . . . to do all this!"

Golgren assisted him with standing. "There was no need to use more precious magic to change to this illusion."

The wizard glared. "Yes. There was. There always will be. Now you know one of the main reasons I want the Fire Rose so badly. I refuse to remain what I was born, not if I can help it. Better to die pretending to be human than live as something I curse each day."

The half-breed did not respond except to ask, "Can you take us from this place?"

That question stirred a brief and sardonic grin from Tyranos. "Changed your mind about leaping into the fire with Safrag?"

"No more than you."

The smile faded. "You're right there. I think I need a moment more, but then I should—"

Both were suddenly struck by a fearsome force. Tyranos was slammed against the far wall. He crumpled like a rag doll; whether unconscious or dead, it was impossible to say. Golgren, who at the last moment sensed danger, received less of a blow. However, it was still enough to send him rolling across the chamber.

Through tearing eyes, he saw that the attack had not been instigated by some resurrected Falstoch, but rather another familiar figure.

Atolgus peered through the gap, his expression akin to a mad beast. There was both fury and pleasure in his expression. He wielded Golgren's former sword, only its blade was surrounded by an aura. The warlord's other hand glowed with a similar illumination.

The transformation to whatever variant of Titan Safrag expected of Atolgus was all but complete.

"You taint her chamber!" the sorcerer's puppet declared. "For that alone you should die! I'll bring your head to her! She'll reward me for this!"

He stepped inside. Only then was a second figure revealed standing behind him, one known even better to the half-breed.

Wargroch brandished his own weapon. His look grim, he rumbled, "It is a good time to die, oh Grand Khan, a good time to die."

XVI

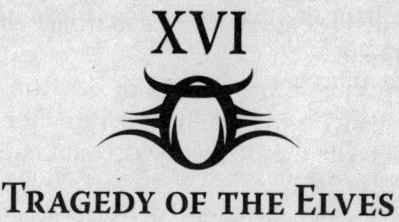

TRAGEDY OF THE ELVES

Idaria opened her eyes only to see darkness so intense that at first the elf believed she had gone blind. Then the darkness grew just a bit fainter, enough for her to tell that she stood in some corridor. That was all, though.

That she could see no better even with her elf-sharp vision instantly told the slave that the darkness was born of Titan sorcery. Idaria turned, seeking Stefan. However, there was no sign of the Solamnic.

She finally dared whisper his name. Her voice did not even echo. Idaria waited, hoping for some reply.

Instead of Stefan, she heard the slight clink of metal from farther down the black corridor. Even though it was only for the briefest of moments, Idaria had no trouble identifying the source:

Chains.

Steeling herself, Idaria followed the sound. Although she did not hear it again, she felt certain she followed the correct trail. Besides, to turn anywhere else in the black abyss would be foolish. The slight sound gave her the only concrete clue she had as to what had happened to her people.

Her own breathing pounded in her ears; the otherwise utter silence made the slight noise a thousand times louder. On and on the elf moved without finding any sign she was any nearer.

Finally frustrated enough, Idaria cleared her throat.

The brief sound was enough to elicit another slight clinking of the chains, and that time the sound was much closer. The elf felt her heart quicken.

At last, daring to take a great chance, she quietly called out, "I am here to help. I am an elf."

There came a bit more clinking but not nearly enough to represent the hundreds that should be there. Idaria swallowed hard, fearful she was too late.

A male voice—an elf voice—murmured something that she could not understand. Idaria moved toward the voice only to nearly walk into an unseen column.

Growing more frustrated, she struck a fist against the column.

A dark blue light illuminated her surroundings.

Idaria let out a gasp at the sudden change then another, much more horrified gasp, at the sight before her.

She stood at the entrance of a vast chamber that appeared little changed in comparison to what Safrag likely had accomplished with the rest of the sanctum. The walls were a deep gray stone, and the floor was a striated marble combining black and crimson. Squat, fluted columns like the one with which the elf had almost collided dotted the immense room. There was no source for the blue illumination.

A number of disturbing smells greeted her. One was that of scorched flesh, something to which she had grown all too familiar. Another was the iron scent of blood. Again, that was a smell she knew too well. The third was less recognizable and, therefore, more frightening. It was the charged air odor that Idaria most associated with lightning during a storm. In such a place, that odor brought to mind terrible images.

But none of what she saw or smelled truly mattered much to Idaria, who had finally found her people . . . or what remained of them.

They stood in positions of fear, pain, and despair. Some were bent as if seeking to turn from their fate, while a few others stood tall and proud like the race Idaria remembered before the fall of Silvanost.

Hundreds of elves stood clustered before her, transformed into statues composed of what seemed to be amber. They ranged from those finally showing the age that only the most ancient of elves revealed to the very young, to those that had barely known the glory of the forested realm before the coming of Mina, the Nerakans, and, later, Golgren and the minotaurs. There was no order to the throng. They had evidently been transformed en masse after being herded into the subterranean lair.

However, not all had suffered that fate. Some chains rattled again, and Idaria discovered the one elf who still retained his fleshly form . . . but little else.

He lay bound and spread-eagled to a stone platform designed with five distinct appendages, one for each limb and a smaller one upon which he rested his head. Above him hung a sinister, spherical device of iron from which sprouted six evil tentacles—leather hoses, in truth—that descended to the captive's wrists, ankles, and attached to both sides of his neck. The tentacles ended in hooked ends that penetrated the veins.

Idaria shivered. The hoses were transparent and revealed that, once, some crimson liquid had flowed through them.

She rushed to the elf's side. Idaria did not know him, but visibly he looked not much older than she. Yet his skin was like parchment, and he was clearly in death's grasp. Her frustration mounted; if she had been able to get there even a few hours earlier, then perhaps she could have saved that one slave.

His eyes had been shut, but they opened to reveal pupils almost white. That was no normal elf trait; Titan sorcery had caused the deviation, likely as part of the foul process that kept the prisoner alive while his blood was drained from him. The Titans desired that blood be as fresh as possible, perhaps in case something went amiss with the Fire Rose. With elf blood, they could still make batches of the insidious elixir that had been used to create or rejuvenate their numbers.

Idaria reached for the hoses attached to his neck, but the elf managed a faint shake of his head.

"The deed . . . is done. I am gone. You must save the rest . . . if you can."

"Save the rest?" Idaria looked around but saw no other survivors. "Where are they?"

"All . . . all around . . ."

He meant the transformed elves. Idaria frowned; imminent death must have stolen the other elf's senses. He did not know the others had suffered a gruesome fate.

His eyes shut as he strained to make his explanation clear. Through cracked lips, the dying prisoner managed to gasp, "They . . . they can be remade. The spell only . . . only is to hold them until ready."

Whirling from him, the silver-tressed slave stared at the legions of macabre statues. "They are alive? They can be brought back?"

The elf did not answer her. When Idaria turned back to him, she saw that he was dead.

"Im corpuris den flau esada," she murmured, using an ancient elf prayer. "May the body give back to the forest as the spirit flies." Idaria touched his cheek. She did not even have a name by which to remember the latest victim of the Titans' foul sorcery.

But the unnamed one had given her some hope. Somehow, there was a way by which all the prisoners could be released.

Abandoning the brave soul, Idaria rushed through the chamber. Any object or symbol that looked of interest to her she marked, but none seemed promising. The scrolls were written in indecipherable Titan script, and the many arcane devices looked so ominous, Idaria feared that, using them, she was more likely to do harm than good. She wished that Stefan were there to use his medallion and divine the best means of proceeding.

"Stefan!" Idaria gasped. She glanced over her shoulder in the direction from which she had come. In her desire to find her people, the Solamnic had momentarily slipped her mind.

Stefan was still on the other side of the wall.

Rushing to the magical entrance, also illuminated, Idaria pressed her hands against the stone barrier. Despite her expectations that she would be able to pass through as she had earlier, Idaria met with resistance from solid stone. Growing more anxious, she pressed harder but with no better result. She had been able to enter easily enough but could not leave.

Then Idaria recalled just what purpose the place served. The Titans had created an entrance suitable for ushering in elf slaves, but with the flow purposely designed for only one direction. That had easily prevented any of the prisoners from trying to escape, however futilely.

She was trapped. Idaria pounded on the wall. "Sir Stefan! Sir Stefan!"

There was no reply.

◆─◆─◆

The Solamnic had thrust himself against the wall the moment Idaria had passed through it, but he could not follow her. Uncertain as to why she had been able to do what even the medallion could not grant to him, he wondered if perhaps the doorway were magical and intended to keep the elves prisoners.

The knight knew he had to find a path to Idaria and help her get her people to safety before his time ran out.

But how? How could he—?

The medallion grew warmer. It was all the warning that he received.

Stefan thrust the medallion into his breastplate then charged. Veering toward one wall, he gritted his teeth and leaped.

The wall gave him enough purchase but just barely. The Solamnic literally raced three steps up the wall. He extended his sword arm, ready.

The Titan materialized almost exactly where the knight calculated he was going to appear. The towering sorcerer's expression turned from menace to utter astonishment.

Stefan swung.

The edge caught the sorcerer across the lower half of his throat. There was a flash of black light then a silver one. Titan sorcery sought to protect the blue-tinted fiend; the just power of Kiri-Jolith sought to cancel that protection.

Gravity and the weight of his armor hurled Stefan to the floor. He landed in a crouching position as the Titan reached toward him.

But the sorcerer merely toppled, his detached head striking the floor first with a disgusting squishing sound before bounding past the Solamnic. Stefan threw himself back against the nearest wall as the huge corpse flopped down where he had just been standing.

The dead Titan was one of the two he and Idaria had observed earlier. Idaria's entrance into the hidden chamber must have alerted them to their presence.

Stefan braced himself against the wall and quickly looked around, wondering when the second Titan would show up.

Something clutched the wrist of his sword arm. Stefan instinctively grabbed the weapon with his other hand.

A three-digited, red paw that had sprouted from the wall held his wrist. The Solamnic chopped it off at the base. The paw released its hold, dropped to the floor, and faded.

But another blossomed near where the wall met the floor, immediately grabbing for his ankle. Stefan dealt with that paw as he had the first, chopping it off, then spun around to cut off yet a third reaching all the way from the opposing wall.

In swelling numbers, clutching paws began sprouting from both sides. Wielding his sword with two hands, the knight moved in a continual spin, chopping off one attacking appendage after another. Each he severed fell to the floor, only to dissolve to nothing.

As he turned toward the other end of the corridor, he caught sight of the second Titan gesturing. Like a puppet master, the sorcerer was coordinating the strange attacks. Stefan tried to charge him, but a flurry of grasping paws created a menacing barrier between him and his adversary. For every one the Solamnic dispatched, it seemed another two sprang into existence.

His armor kept their sharp talons from ripping him apart but also slowed him down. Stefan could not reach his quarry at the far end of the corridor, no matter how hard he tried.

Slash went his sword, again and again. Each time the silver light that bespoke of Kiri-Jolith's blessing overwhelmed the dark sorcery, yet still the attacks multiplied and continued. Stefan summoned every iota of his training, leaping, dodging, and cutting.

But he gained little, and soon the Titan would devise a more lethal stratagem. He had one hope. The Solamnic whirled around one more time, chopping away at another set of grasping paws. Then, switching his grip in mid swing, he *hurtled* the sword like a spear at the sorcerer. At the same time, the cleric uttered a short prayer to his patron.

The Titan gaped as the blade flew fast enough at him to pierce his protective spells, burrowing deep in the right shoulder. The gigantic figure clutched at the blade. "N-not—" was all he managed to stammer before falling back against one wall then dropping to his knees.

The paws dissipated. Stefan wasted no time in racing toward the stricken spellcaster. The Titan was not dead and, thus, still a danger.

Looming over the bleeding giant, Stefan planted both hands on the hilt of his weapon and pushed on it. The Titan cried out. His own talons scraped against the Solamnic's armor, leaving sizzling scratches down one leg.

Easing up on the pressure, Stefan said, "One chance and one chance alone for you to live! Assist me with freeing my friend and her people, and I'll spare your life!"

"Never—*ah!*" The scream came as Stefan pressed on the sword.

His voice filled with revulsion for what he felt forced to do, the Solamnic tried again. "Do as I say! Swear and I'll stop this!"

Despite his agony, something in the Titan's expression briefly shifted. Then he cried, "Yes! I swear to help you!"Stefan nodded but then his expression turned grim. Still leaning hard on the sword to keep the Titan from concentrating enough to cast a spell, the cleric removed the medallion. He slipped it over the stricken sorcerer's head.

As the Titan registered what he was doing, Stefan stepped back and, silently praying to Kiri-Jolith again, plucked the blade free. The Titan let out a brief cry then planted one hand against the wound.

"There's no need to heal it," the Solamnic informed him. "That has already been done."

The blue-skinned giant stared at the wound or, at least, where it once had been. It was truly healed.

"Strong sorcery," he muttered.

"It's not sorcery. It's faith."

The golden eyes flashed at the knight. "Then you had best pray for your god to be ready to receive you now!"

Stefan had already been prepared for such deceit. As the Titan started to cast his dark magic, the medallion glowed. The sorcerer gasped sharply, doubling over in pain.

"Your own power turns against you whenever you choose to use it so," Stefan explained, "and you can't remove the medallion. Only I can do that."

The Titan glared but said nothing.

Stefan stepped farther back and waited. The towering sorcerer seemed to think it over then slowly rose.

"I have no choice but to obey. You spoke of your friend and her people. That would be the elf bitch who beds the mongrel—" At the warning in the Solamnic's face, the Titan quickly went on. "I can take you to her people, yes, but where is she?"

"With them already, I believe."

A brief, knowing smile escaped the sorcerer. Stefan gestured with the point of his sword at the wall. "Take me through there, and remember that I'm the one who can remove the medallion, not you."

Scowling, the Titan strode over to the wall. He raised one hand palm forward.

The wall turned hazy.

"We may pass through," the spellcaster said.

Stefan waved his sword. "Lead."

With a curt nod, the Titan stepped into the wall. As the last of him vanished, Stefan immediately followed. The knight's body tingled as he moved through.

He emerged to find the Titan awaiting him. A deep blue illumination filled the area and revealed that behind the Titan stood an obviously relieved Idaria.

"I feared that something had happened to you!" she blurted, rushing to his side.

The Titan smirked. Catching his look, the Solamnic tapped his own chest. "Remember the medallion and your oath."

The smirk vanished. Somewhat sullen, the towering figure started down the corridor.

Idaria shot a look at Stefan then rushed to catch up with the Titan, daring to grab his arm. "Can you free them?"

He looked down at her with unconcealed contempt. "It seems I have no choice."

Before she could explain to Stefan, they had stepped out into the immense chamber. At first, the Titan's massive form blocked the knight's view. As the sorcerer stepped aside, his face registered shock at the spectacle of the frozen elves.

"Kiri-Jolith protect us!" the knight growled. He brought the blade's tip up to the Titan's chest. "What've you done to them?"

"Preserved them healthier than you would have found them otherwise," retorted the spellcaster.

"Undo this!"

"It will take some doing. There must be patience."

Stefan frowned. "I'll brook no delays, and the medallion will reveal any duplicity on your part."

The Titan did not reply. Instead, he turned to the nearest of the figures. Stretching forth a finger, he let the tip of his talon touch the forehead of the frozen form.

A small, black spot appeared on the head of the elf, a female who likely looked more her true age than prior to her enslavement. Most of the elves had aged as none of their kind normally did until very old. They looked weathered, worn . . . almost human.

The black spot swelled then grew what seemed spidery legs that quickly spread over the elf's still form.

But no sooner had that happened than the spot and its appendages faded away. The Titan swore.

"This will take more effort than I anticipated. Morgada had a hand in the original casting. For the last slave, Vradoc and I worked together to resurrect him. Vradoc is dead, thanks to you, human. I must do the work alone now."

"That will take too long," Idaria countered. "There is no telling what time we have before another Titan returns."

"I can do nothing more than what I said." The sorcerer indicated the medallion, which lay dormant. "And this proves my words true."

Stefan frowned. "It would take days and days to free all of them."

The Titan's expression revealed nothing.

Idaria reached out to the frozen figure. Her hands gently touched the pained face. The transformation was so complete that the elf even cut her finger on the sharpened corner of the chin.

As she pulled the injured finger back, Idaria saw the blood absorbed into the figure. The frozen elf evinced a slightly different hue.

The knight, eyes flashing, stepped up beside her. "What did you do?"

"I don't know. I'm not sure. But there may be a way." Idaria turned to the Titans' last victim. She pointed at the sinister device above the corpse. "That is filled with elf blood."

The sorcerer nodded. "Yes. Even though we have the Fire Rose, elf blood has . . . interesting, valuable properties."

Idaria's hands briefly tightened into fists. Her angry glare was such that even the spellcaster took a step back. "Let us pray those properties remain for a time, even after death."

She exchanged a look with Stefan. Understanding, Stefan grimaced but nodded. The Titan cocked his head in clinical interest.

"Yes," he murmured. "The blood could possibly do it."

"If it does the job and we leave with the elves, you'll have done your part," the knight informed the blue-skinned spellcaster. "I will free you. Our agreement will be over."

"Then let's be done with this, human." The Titan raised his hands, but instead of casting a spell, he removed the hoses from the body. Stefan mumbled a prayer for the dead. Idaria flinched as the sorcerer paid little mind to how his tugging caused the hooks to pull out with bits of flesh.

Twisting the device around, the Titan manipulated it so the appendages faced not the legions of petrified elves, but rather, himself.

Idaria protested. "You should let it pass over them."

He looked at her with some slight contempt for her ignorance. "I know what I do. You want them all freed quickly. I must be the conduit."

Without waiting for her or the knight to reply, the Titan adjusted the hoses. He then began speaking in the singing language.

"Do you understand him?" the elf quietly asked Stefan.

"No, he wears the medallion, and I dare not remove it. Trust in Kiri-Jolith that he'll do as he says. Any subterfuge on his part will be turned back upon him. If he's honest, though, he need fear nothing."

Idaria did not look persuaded. However, there was no real choice but to hope that the Titan would do as commanded.

The sorcerer sang louder. Idaria's hair tingled as it would have if lightning had discharged nearby. The odor that she had associated with that elemental force grew more evident.

A black aura formed around the Titan as he stretched out his taloned hands. He bent his head up, staring at the foul device.

A second aura suddenly surrounded the container housing the elf blood. However, that aura was green, a green reminiscent of the forest of Silvanesti. Idaria felt a tear slip from one eye.

The Titan brought his taloned hands together. The two auras moved toward one another, melding. The black took on an emerald hue as the sorcerer gained control of his spell. The Titan's expression was one of both exhilaration and astonishment.

"So much life! So much energy! Why did not Dauroth or Safrag ever tell us what it would mean to take it into ourselves in such a manner?" He grinned, his sharp teeth giving him a very hungry appearance.

"Recall your task!" Idaria shouted.

The sorcerer sniffed at her then turned to face the hundreds of dread statues. The device continued to feed the green aura into his black one.

He spread his hands toward the enchanted figures and once more sang the magic. Despite the beauty of his singing, there was something that both the human and the elf found ominous in it.

Then from his hands burst the green-black aura. It shot to the foremost of the statues, engulfing it. Almost instantly, twin, like-colored streams dispersed from the first figure to the two nearest. From each of those elves, two more streams shot forth to touch another pair.

Within seconds, the aura had spread through a hundred. From there, it even more quickly doubled its number then quadrupled it. On and on the aura spread until at last, within less than a minute, it had touched *all* of the imprisoned elves.

The Titan raised his hands to the ceiling. His singing reached a grand crescendo.

Great emerald flames rose up around each elf. Yet the flames did not burn the figures; rather, they melted away the enchantment. Hard stone dripped away, revealing flesh. Raised arms lowered and stifled screams erupted, only to die down as the screamers realized they were free. Moans arose everywhere as the slaves sought to recuperate from their horrific ordeals.

The flames rushed through the ranks, adding to the living. Some elves turned and clutched one another in relief. Others crouched in fear, thinking that perhaps some more dire fate awaited them. Most turned to stare at the Titan, expecting that he was lord of their futures.

Then a few noticed Idaria and Stefan—especially the Solamnic's weapon—and the confusion spread. Not even a Titan was haughty enough to permit a prisoner to hold a sword.

Idaria raised her hands for silence. Elves in the front signaled to those in back to quiet.

The last of the slaves had been freed. The Titan

finally dropped his own hands. The aura faded. The sorcerer looked exhausted but still exhilarated.

Seizing the moment, Idaria called out, "We are here to bring you to freedom!"

Some of the prisoners stared suspiciously at the Titan, who sneered back. The elves remained as frozen in place as if they were still statues.

"She means what she says!" Stefan added, brandishing his weapon. "But you must quickly gather those who are weakest and help them follow! We must leave immediately, or we risk losing our chance!"

When, still, the Titan seemed more of interest to the slaves than their calls to freedom, Idaria finally shouted in frustration, "He can do nothing to you anymore! Come!"

With that, the surge of freedom began in earnest. Moving with far more animation than they had perhaps in ages, the slaves converged on the trio. The elves were still cautious enough to veer away from the Titan, who watched in amusement.

Idaria and Stefan were faced with a flood of living beings. The two turned to lead their charges out.

A belated concern touched Idaria. To the sorcerer, she asked, "Will they be able to pass through the wall?"

"The way is open in both directions now."

Trusting to the medallion to keep the Titan true to his word, Idaria called out to the slaves, "Go no farther than the hall directly outside! I will join you once I have made certain that there are no delays here."

"Yes, mistress," replied more than one subserviently.

"I am not your mistress! You are no one's thrall anymore!"

With tentative smiles, the elves moved on, a flow of humanity.

"It's happening!" Idaria breathed. "It's happening! We've a chance to go home—"

"The only place you're going is back to serving *our* needs!" she heard the Titan declare in a loud, gleeful voice.

There were screams near where the giant sorcerer stood. Black flames erupted around the Titan, flames with an emerald tint.

Pressed against the walls by the streaming, suddenly fearful bodies, both Stefan and Idaria could only watch in horror as the Titan betrayed them. With only his own powers, he had been unable to withstand the holy essence of the medallion. However, it was no longer his power alone that the dark sorcerer wielded. He was still linked to the blood-draining device.

The Titan was using an elf's life force to overwhelm the medallion, and neither Idaria nor the Solamnic could stop him.

XVII

REDEMPTION

A very good time to die," agreed Atolgus. "My ascension is nearly complete! I'm a true Titan now! Equal to her and, therefore, worthy of her!" He took a step closer to Golgren. "And with your head as a gift, worthy of her love."

Golgren did not argue with the crazed warlord. Atolgus was too far gone and too much of a threat to the half-breed.

The deposed Grand Khan readied himself for a desperate leap at his adversary. The advantages all belonged to Atolgus.

As if reading Golgren's mind, Atolgus laughed again. "Come to me, mongrel! Come to—"

Atolgus gasped. His back arched, the warlord bending so much that his face looked to the ceiling. The sword fell from his trembling hand, and he whirled in a half circle.

Another sword was buried in his spine.

The sword wielded by Wargroch.

"Flee, Grand Khan!" the Blödian shouted. "Hurry!"

Atolgus tried in vain to reach the blade lodged in his back. Meanwhile, Wargroch desperately fended off Atolgus's other hand. Despite the tremendous wound, Atolgus was still very much alive, his stamina enhanced by the magic within him.

Indeed, Morgada's puppet, with a furious roar, seized Wargroch by the throat with his other hand. The Blödian grappled with him, grabbing Atolgus around the waist and wrestling as best he could with the much larger figure.

But Wargroch had again underestimated the altered Atolgus. Wargroch's powerful grip meant nothing to the larger ogre. Ignoring Wargroch, Atolgus added his sword hand to the Blödian's throat.

With what was almost a casual twist, the warlord broke the other ogre's neck. Wargroch let out a short gurgle then went limp in Atolgus's grip.

But as that happened, Golgren barreled into his back, the half-breed using the force of his jump to shove the sword deeper.

Atolgus grunted. He fell to one knee but still fought. Shaking like a wet amalok, he dislodged his slighter foe. Golgren landed hard but managed to roll to his feet.

The transformed chieftain's hands glowed darkly. The golden orbs burned with menace. "I will—will—"

The severity of his wound momentarily seized the gigantic warrior. He faltered.

As Wargroch had risked himself, so Golgren threw his smaller form into Atolgus's arms. Unprepared, the warlord caught him in an awkward grip. The energies Atolgus had been summoning burned Golgren's skin where his hands touched the other, but the half-breed clutched his larger foe's neck.

A laugh escaped Atolgus. The Titans' puppet seemed undaunted by his punier foe.

But Golgren had no intention of trying to choke Atolgus. He had only one attack, one attempt, left to him.

Opening his mouth as wide as he could, the half-breed *bit* into Atolgus's throat.

Hot blood spurted over Golgren's face, but he continued to sink his teeth in as far as he could. Ogres had much stronger jaws and harder teeth than elves or humans, and even Golgren's mixed parentage had not moderated that one trait.

With effort, Atolgus finally pushed his smaller foe away. However, in doing so, he enabled Golgren to rip away a good portion of the flesh.

A river of blood gushed from the gaping wound. Even more than the sword in his back, the torn throat took a toll on the Titans' puppet. Atolgus staggered. He tried to say something, but only a wheezing sound escaped from him.

The former chieftain fell first to one knee then both. His golden orbs lost their evil radiance.

Atolgus fell dead.

Golgren wiped his mouth as clean as he could. His gaze strayed to Wargroch. He gave a grunt of satisfaction at the Blödian's final honorable actions then turned to Tyranos.

Once again, the wizard had reverted to his true form. Golgren leaned down to check on the minotaur.

Tyranos opened his eyes. Immediately, he saw his own hands. He snorted in anger.

"I won't let this be!" the mage growled.

"What matter is it?" Golgren responded dismissively.

"My kind turned their back on me for my crimes of

'magic,' and so I turned my back on them! Humans are far more adaptable; I will be one of them, and the Fire Rose will see to it."

Their argument went no further, for the sounds of battle had drawn guards to their vicinity. The ogres, obviously fearful of intruding wherever Titans were concerned, tentatively peered inside.

Several gaped at the sight of Wargroch then doubly so upon sighting Atolgus. There was no one to tell them that the former had sacrificed himself to wound the latter, so to their minds came the logical conclusion: Both had perished at the hands of Golgren.

Then they saw Tyranos, and the discovery of an Uruv Suurt in their midst made them forget all else. The first of the guards charged through the hole.

"Can you transform yourself quickly?" Golgren hissed to the wizard.

"Yes." And with that one word, Tyranos became a human again.

Golgren nodded and stepped forward to confront the guards. He did not strike a battle stance; instead he simply stared.

The ogres faltered then stopped.

"Lower your weapons," the half-breed commanded as if still Grand Khan.

The guards hesitated.

Golgren frowned. His eyes narrowed in anger.

One guard obeyed. That was enough to make the rest follow suit.

A light flared behind Golgren. Without glancing back, he said to the guards, "This is no Uruv Suurt. This is a human. A curse made him appear to wear the wretched skin of an Uruv Suurt."

The guards looked perplexed. It was not that they did not understand Common—and Common was what Golgren had chosen to speak to them because it reminded the ogres just who he was—but they were obviously uncertain whether a human in their midst was any better than one of the horned ones.

"I suggest that now is a good time to leave this place," Tyranos whispered in his ear. "If that isn't asking too much, oh Grand Khan."

Giving him a slight nod, Golgren said to the guards, "I leave you now, but I will return shortly to bring order back to Golthuu."

Tyranos cast his spell. The pair vanished before the awestruck eyes of the ogres.

◦◦◦◦◦

Idaria prepared for the worst, but then the Titan's laugh became a howl of rage. He doubled over, stricken.

Despite the elf blood at his command, the Titan had underestimated the power of the medallion . . . or rather, of Kiri-Jolith. The sorcerer clutched his throat and chest as if unable to breathe.

"Reject your evil intention!" Stefan shouted to the Titan. "Reject it and your pain will pass!"

However, either the spellcaster did not hear Stefan's offer or he refused it, still thinking he could overwhelm the medallion. The Titan gritted his teeth and raised one hand as if to cast a spell.

Instead, he let loose with a new, more terrible roar. Unable to endure, the sorcerer collapsed into the frightened and confused throng.

Fearful for her people, Idaria pressed toward where

the Titan had fallen. However, she had taken no more than a step when she noticed a sudden and ominous change over the elves gathered ahead. The fear and confusion had vanished, replaced by an emotion it took her a moment to recognize.

Fury.

Instead of moving toward the entrance, many of the elves suddenly reversed direction. A muffled shout arose. Several slaves raised fists then swung them down.

"No!" Stefan called from the other side. "Don't fall to his level!"

The mass of elves paid him no mind. More and more swarmed to the spot where the Titan had fallen. The sorcerer, already stricken helpless by his own treachery, howled as the slaves pummeled him.

The cleric turned to Idaria. "My lady, make them stop! This isn't right!"

But Idaria instead watched grimly as her people struck out at one of their great tormentors. A part of her—a small part of her—urged her to do as Stefan pleaded, but the rest of Idaria had witnessed too much of the atrocities of slavery.

The other elves were in a frenzy. The Titan managed to raise one hand—whether to plead or seeking to attack, it was impossible to say—but then he sank back in defeat. Elves who had been driven to the brink of starvation and exhaustion found the strength to vent their anger.

And though she might still have been able to stop them, Idaria remained silent and still.

It was over quickly. With bloody hands, the attackers shambled back, giving both the Idaria and the knight a glimpse of what remained of the Titan. There was little recognizable of the once-handsome sorcerer. His face was smashed in; his chest had been crushed. It was an unforgettable sight, and yet it was not the most terrible that Idaria had witnessed since the fall of Silvanost.

Stefan was the only one to express horror. He looked from the other slaves to Idaria. "This was wrong! You're not Titans, not ogres! You're elves!"

Idaria answered for her people. "And you have never been a slave."

The cleric's eyes widened. He looked again at the sea of embittered, beaten elves. His voice mirroring his own exhaustion, he muttered, "Kiri-Jolith forgive us."

"He did not stop us," she responded as harshly as before. Turning to her people, Idaria commanded, "The entrance . . . and hurry!"

The elves flowed on. As promised by the dead Titan, the way was open. By the scores, the slaves vanished from the dread chamber.

Idaria joined the exodus. She did not look back to Stefan. Whatever gulf lay between them, the silver-tressed slave could only think of her fellow prisoners . . .

And think how she more and more acted like Golgren.

Outside, the corridor was filled. The moment Idaria stepped through, eyes turned and fixed with desperate hope on her.

Pushing to the front, she wasted no time. "This way."

Murmurs arose as the elves journeyed through the sanctum. It was not the same structure through which they had been marched. Idaria paused long enough to tell them that it was no concern to them. All that had to happen was for Safrag—or any Titans, for that matter— to return and the escape would fail.

Idaria gave thanks when the exit from the sanctum came into view, even though that meant they had to traverse the sinister forest. However, compared to the evils of the Titans' underground chamber, skeletal ogres and such paled.

That did not mean that the throng could travel blithely through the wooded area. Once outside, Idaria quickly organized the slaves into groups, with those who looked healthiest becoming part of a defensive force. True, they had only their hands, but that would have to do. Older and injured elves were taken within the ranks, where they could be better protected.

Stefan finally caught up with her. He still did not look pleased with what had happened inside, but the medallion was around his own neck. There were no signs of blood upon it.

He nodded satisfaction with her arrangements. "You could be a Knight of Solamnia."

"Or a Nerakan?" she could not help retorting.

He grimaced. "I've no right to put myself above those who've suffered so greatly. Let's now concern ourselves with getting your people to freedom."

A face abruptly filled Idaria's thoughts. "Sir Stefan, I must ask one thing. Do you know where Golgren is? I must know because I realize now that I must stay away from him."

"But why?"

She studied the dark forest, her thoughts on both the past and the future. "Because the gargoyles' master indicated that I still had some role he wished me to play. I will not be his puppet."

"As you wish. The path I intend for us will take your people toward Solamnic-controlled lands and, coincidentally, far away from Garantha. Is that to your satisfaction?"

Idaria stiffened. "Yes. Thank you."

The cleric shrugged and, without another word, walked to the front of the makeshift column. Brandishing his sword, he pointed at the forest. "Stay close to one another, and ignore all sounds and images. The Titans are distracted, but we must get as far as we can from this place! The forest is dangerous, but with our numbers and faith in Kiri-Jolith, we will prevail!"

Some of the slaves looked doubtful, but they nonetheless followed the Solamnic. Idaria took up a place at the back of the column to make certain no one was left behind.

The column proved far more lengthy than Idaria had expected, and yet not nearly so great as the elf had once hoped. So many slaves had died, and more were likely to perish before journey's end. Idaria fought back tears.

There was at first a sinister silence when the refugees entered the dread forest, as if the elves had trespassed upon some realm of the dead. The silence was broken only by the ominous sound of the rustling of leaves. The escaped slaves huddled close to one another. The stronger ones kept a wary watch, although what they would do if the forest attacked was a question no one could answer and all prayed would not be necessary to discover.

Curiously, there were no signs of the skeletal guards. In fact, there was no sign even of those that had sprouted from the sanctum grounds. Nor was there any hint of Chasm's fate. Neither Idaria nor Stefan had spoken of Tyranos's servant when they had stepped out of the Titans' lair. What both believed was that the gargoyle had given up his life for them, and all they could do was prove themselves worthy of the winged creature's sacrifice.

The party moved on for hours. They had no food,

no water. They had not dared stop to look for any inside the sanctum. One benefit of the terrible spell cast upon them had been that they were no thirstier or hungrier than when they had first been made prisoners, but that would not be enough to see them through their ordeal.

So when the column came to a sudden halt, Idaria knew why. She quickly joined Stefan, who looked as pale as the elves and seemed in some unsettling manner even less substantial.

"Are you all right?" the elf asked in concern.

"I'll last," he responded. But then he added, "We need to feed them, and I fear this is as far as they'll be going this night. We made good progress, though not nearly so much as I wished."

Idaria gazed up at the trees. "But what can we do for sustenance here? Or water, even? Anything in this forest would surely be poisoned or worse. Do you have some miracle in mind?"

"If there's a miracle this time, it'll be your doing." He removed the medallion then handed it to her. "You were able to touch some part of the forest the last time you wielded this. Perhaps you can do so again."

"I will certainly try." However, Idaria did not know how to begin. She awaited instruction from the cleric, but Stefan only smiled ruefully. The forest was not the domain of his patron, although Kiri-Jolith had already done much for them.

She walked a short distance away from the column, giving her just enough seclusion to concentrate better.

"Habbakuk," Idaria whispered. "If it is you, please hear me. I do not know if you can help us, but I must ask. You have every right not to listen, but if you could merely show us food and water, or how to acquire them, it would greatly help us."

Her father would have reprimanded her for such an inglorious prayer, lacking in ornate verbiage and so sparse. But both he and that time were long dead.

Nothing happened. Idaria turned to Stefan, but he stood in silence. Focusing again, she repeated her make-shift prayer and waited.

Still, nothing happened.

Frustrated, she walked back to Stefan, the medallion already stretched toward him. "There is no point, it seems. Neither Habbakuk nor any other power heard—"

Idaria stopped as she noticed first the Solamnic's expression then those of the refugees nearest the pair. They were all staring past her.

She looked where they gaped and saw several tiny, gleaming pools of water. Each was the size of a footprint and illuminated their immediate surroundings. That they were the size of a footprint turned out to be the least part of the surprise. For each pool had evidently been created by her returning steps.

But the pools remained so small for only a moment more before gushing up and spilling over toward one another. As they spread, the area around them grew brighter yet, and a loving warmth that Idaria had not felt in ages radiated toward the party. The scent of fresh spring flowers wafted toward them even though none could be spotted.

Before she realized what was happening, elves were streaming past her to reach the glistening water. Idaria started to warn them to be careful then decided that there was no reason to be concerned.

Still, the crowd grew so swiftly that she and Stefan

had to step to the side. The elf even had to press against a nearby tree, something that she would have considered very dangerous before but, in the presence of the swelling pool, bothered her not in the least. All of the nearby trees seemed harmless, as if they, too, had been affected by the miracle.

"We have water, at least," she commented. "Perhaps we'll find food before long—"

"Your hand!" the knight interrupted, indicating the one touching the trunk.

She eyed her hand, expecting to see that it had been infected by some sinister poison in the tree. Yet at first glance Idaria saw nothing wrong.

Then her gaze shifted to the tree itself. There, her hand print radiated a lush green from which began to sprout small stems. As the two stepped back, the stems became full branches. At the same time, the lush green spread over the tree. The other branches took on a healthy appearance akin to the new ones.

And from the branches, small, red fruits began to sprout. At first they were the size of peas, then cherries; then they grew to be on par with the largest apples. They were a type of fruit, though one that no one there could recognize.

Idaria was the first to dare pluck one. Without hesitation, she bit into it. Rich, sweet juices spilled down her chin as she devoured the succulent delight.

With the first swallow, her weariness began to abate. She felt revived, fresh.

"It will nourish us well!" the elf declared to Stefan. To her people, she called, "Everyone! Come and partake of this fruit!"

"Will there be enough?" the knight asked.

In answer, another fruit began blossoming from exactly where Idaria had plucked the first. Within seconds, it was already nearly as large as hers.

"There will be enough," she responded with a smile.

Elves who had been waiting their turn by the expanding pool turned to the tree. Idaria worked to organize the lines so no one suffered too long a wait. Soon all were drinking and eating, in turn.

"All will share fairly," she insisted as she cautioned patience.

Among those who finished drinking and eating, Stefan began choosing the strongest to rebuild the column's defenses. The forest had not attacked them thus far, which was both encouraging and suspicious.

Idaria finally returned the medallion to the cleric. He accepted it gratefully.

"You have used the gift of life, my lady. I had faith in you."

"I am grateful to Habbakuk or whichever god granted me these miracles, and that is all." Seeking to change the subject, she said, "I did not see you eat or drink."

"When matters are settled for the night, I will." He looked around. "We've been very fortunate . . . too fortunate. Either the Titans are extremely distracted by what Golgren sought to put into motion or . . ."

She understood immediately. "Or the gargoyles' master has begun to play his final hand."

"There is a third possibility. Safrag may be choosing his own course of action that goes against what his followers know." Stefan grunted in dissatisfaction. "Forgive me, my lady. Best if I return to the task at hand. With an unoccupied mind comes too much second thought. That's all it is."

Idaria watched him in concern but said nothing. She returned her attention to seeing to her people. Though refreshed in one way, they still needed sleep. There was no thought of continuing onward.

But as the freed slaves began to settle down, thoughts of Golgren rose to the forefront of her mind again. The elf shook her head; she had her people to save. Golgren was no more concern of hers, nor was the fate of the ogre realms.

And yet . . .

Idaria suddenly walked off toward the glistening pool. A few remaining slaves bowed gratefully to her as they finished sipping from the water. Idaria herself was not thirsty; she had come there to contemplate matters that nagged at her mind.

Kneeling by the pool, she peered into it. Despite the darkness surrounding the region, the water itself perfectly illuminated her face. Unfortunately, that meant that it also revealed her worried, almost fearful expression.

Then the pool revealed something else. A winged form that darted among the trees. Smothering a gasp, Idaria carefully turned her gaze skyward.

A hulking form dropped from among the branches, seizing her by the shoulders. It hefted her into the air before she could even make a sound.

The winged fury soared above the forest. By then the elf knew what had her in its clutches. It could only be one creature, a gargoyle.

But it was not just *any* gargoyle; it could be but one: Chasm.

It was difficult to tell, but to Idaria the gargoyle appeared unhurt, despite the desperate struggle with the undead. The gargoyle's wings beat hard as he not only ascended, but headed farther and farther away from Stefan and the refugees.

Finally collecting her wits, Idaria shouted, "What are you doing? Why did you take me?"

His voice sounding even more gruff than usual, the gargoyle answered, "My master . . . he tells me in head that Golgren . . . he needs you."

Idaria struggled with conflicting emotions. "No! I should not get near him! That would be dangerous!"

Chasm did not look down at her. "My master . . . he says Golgren is dying."

The words struck Idaria sharper than a sword. All concern of the possible danger, of falling prey to the sinister machinations of the gargoyle king, all melted away. Golgren was dying.

A ray of hope filled her. "I may . . . I may be able to help." She did not have the medallion, but surely Habbakuk would hear her appeal nonetheless. Surely Habbakuk would help her somehow. "If we do not arrive too late."

"Will not," assured the winged creature.

Idaria spoke no more. Stefan would guide her people to freedom. All that mattered was reaching Golgren . . .

Nothing else.

❧❀❧

"My lady?"

Stefan searched the area of the pool, even though he had already done so twice. The elves with whom he had spoken had insisted they had last seen her in that area. The knight knew Idaria well enough that he did not

259

think that she would go wandering off into the forest, at least not without good reason.

Clutching the medallion in one hand and keeping his sword ready in the other, Stefan finally took a few steps deeper into the dank forest. The refugees did not know that their chief benefactor was missing, and Stefan didn't care to inform them. If they found out she was gone, there might be mass hysteria.

As he walked, Stefan prayed to his patron for guidance. As a Solamnic Knight, he was not one to ask for aid at the slightest inconvenience, only when absolutely necessary. If there was any clue, however remote, to Idaria's disappearance, he needed to find it and know it quickly.

Kiri-Jolith—who Stefan knew had many other battles to fight—responded. The medallion glowed a little brighter as the cleric turned northward. What that meant, he did not know, but he silently thanked the deity and pushed on.

The forest was still wrong there. Stefan could sense that it desired to strike out at the refugees, but something held it back.

The path grew narrower, more treacherous. Although the forest did not attack him, it tried to hinder his progress. Stefan impatiently chopped away at tangling branches and roots. All the while, the medallion indicated he was on the right path.

"May she be unharmed," he prayed. "I'm already fallen; at least let her be unharmed, my lord."

A shape in the darkness caught his searching eyes. At first, it looked as if it were pressed against a tree, but as Stefan neared, it became evident the figure was *snared*, branches wrapped around the body so tightly that only the outline could be discerned. If not for the medallion, the knight would not have noticed it.

"Have no fear, my lady!" The Solamnic moved in, expertly slashing at the branches, thinking of nothing but freeing the elf.

The tangling branches fell in pieces; a moment later, their captive, finally released, also fell. Ragged breathing informed Stefan that he had found the tree's prisoner still in time.

But the one that the knight had rescued was not Idaria.

It was a badly beaten and scratched *Chasm*.

XVIII

Secrets of the Lost

Day had become night, and night began to give way to day, and the battle had not ceased. An exhausted Faros had no idea at all of the struggle of Sir Augustus and the Solamnics, although he would have admired their determination and battle skills just as they would have respected his legionaries.

But such mattered little against the foe both fought. Magic was anathema to the Solamnics and the minotaurs. Faros especially resented that he needed a god's assistance again, yet without it, even his best soldiers would soon all be dead.

Slowly but surely, the minotaurs were being defeated. There was no talk of retreat; it was not the minotaur way, especially against *ogres* of any kind. Kiri-Jolith had granted them what aid he could offer, but the onus was upon Faros's people, and they fell short despite their best efforts.

There were bodies everywhere. The smell of death dominated the senses. A legionary lay sprawled to the side of Faros, his eyes staring blankly and with a terrible, ragged hole in his breastplate and chest. His heart had literally exploded from within. He was just one of many to have perished so.

We will not live out this new day at this rate, the emperor thought. Yet he continued to push his fighters forward. At that point, they did not fight for Golgren—no honorable legionary *would*—but rather because it was evident to all that such power as the Titans possessed must be confronted, or indeed, sooner rather than later, it would crash down on the empire.

And there seemed little that the minotaurs could do about that eventuality save die. Without warning, the ground to Faros's right opened up. At least a dozen legionaries toppled into the newly created ravine. Some might have survived to climb out, but the gap closed as quickly as it had opened.

"Fight like warriors, not cowards!" the emperor growled at his enemies.

But the Titans would fight as they pleased.

An explosion rocked the vicinity, tossing Faros forward. He was not the target; the sound of splintering wood was immediate verification that one of the remaining catapults had been struck. Fragments rained down, some of them from the decimated machine, others, more grisly, from the unfortunate crew. The sharp tingling of the fur that accompanied the aftermath of lightning informed Faros what spell had been used.

The last of their heavy machines was gone. They had no more weapons that could reach the distant sorcerers. Faros grimly corrected his earlier assessment. We'll not live to see midday, much less sunset.

An ominous shadow fell across the emperor. He

looked up, but what he saw was no new spell by the minotaurs' foes.

A vast swarm of winged creatures was heading toward the Titans.

They were gargoyles, more than any minotaur had ever seen. Faros tried to estimate their numbers but failed. That they were no allies of the Titans was quickly made evident by the beasts' fierce cries as they dived toward the area where the sorcerers awaited. However, such primitive creatures couldn't defeat spellcasters, Faros knew. They might buy a momentary reprieve for the legionaries, which Faros would use as best he could, but no more than that.

A blue haze materialized before the gargoyles' initial ranks. The winged attackers dived straight into it.

Faros snorted. The beasts did not even have sense enough to avoid certain death.

But only two of the gargoyles—the ones farthest to each side—fell dead. The rest were suddenly covered with individual golden auras that seemed to protect them.

The emperor's brow wrinkled. Gargoyles with magic?

The flock continued to descend. A few more of their number perished from other spells, but most of the gargoyles were actually going to reach the hidden Titans.

Faros raised his sword and shouted for attention. Legionaries in the area looked to their emperor.

"Regroup!" he commanded. "Form ranks! Let no one lag behind! Sound the call to advance!"

As his soldiers gathered, Faros bared his teeth in a grim smile. He and his army might still die that day, but they had just been given a chance to take a few of their enemies with them, and that was all a minotaur ever asked.

The minotaurs were not the only ones to discover an aerial army coming to their aid. Sir Augustus also witnessed the coming of countless gargoyles, creatures he assumed had to be some part of Golgren's plan. Like Faros, the knight took immediate advantage, coordinating with his subordinates a renewed strike. At the back of his mind, though, he wondered at the power of the half-breed, that he could summon such beasts.

And if he could, why did he really need the Solamnics and the minotaurs anyway?

☙❧✵❧☙

With a shrunken Morgada at his side, the true master of the flocks observed all from his sanctum.

The distractions are in place, the gargoyle king said approvingly. *He will now act.*

"But he's suspicious. He knows of you."

Xiryn gazed at her with his frosty eyes. *And that is why he will act. Because of his suspicions and the belief that since he holds the Fire Rose, he holds all.*

That made Morgada smile. "And like Dauroth, confidence will gain him only death."

You know your part, the ghostly figure continued with a gesture of dismissal. *For you, it should be simple.*

The female Titan bowed. "Yes. It'll be very simple."

She vanished in a bloom of black flames.

The gargoyles' lord chuckled. *Yes, simple and not at all what you think, my treacherous puppet.*

Rising from the throne, Xiryn summoned his monstrous followers. The ghastly figures surrounded him.

We are ready. Your reward is due.

He raised his left hand, and both he and the sinister throng disappeared, leaving only the wind to haunt the ancient citadel.

⟡

The place in which Golgren and Tyranos materialized was not the one that the wizard had chosen. That was made clear to the half-breed by the colorful expletives unleashed by the hooded figure the moment their location came into focus.

Yet if it were not the place of Tyranos's choosing, the question as to why they had appeared there was one that Golgren found intriguing enough to ask his companion.

"Why ask me?" Tyranos snapped back. He gestured. "Ask them since they seem to like your company so much! They probably know better."

"They" were the mummified high ogres seated at the ancient table. The duo had once again returned to the ancient mountain sanctum.

As if intending to do just as the wizard suggested, Golgren stepped near the prime female. She sat exactly as last time, but appearances could be deceiving. The half-breed peered closely at what had once been her eyes, waiting to see if anything would happen.

Behind him, Tyranos let out a sarcastic laugh. "Looks like she's got nothing to say this time! You must've offended her somehow."

The hand nearest Golgren *moved*. Even though the half-breed sensed it happening, he did not shift his own away.

The gnarled fingers wrapped around his wrist.

267

Golgren's mind filled with visions of the past.

They were a pitiful handful, the survivors of the once-great race. The prize they thought would salvage the legacy of their people had instead added the final nail to their coffins. The Fire Rose had turned out not to be salvation, but rather damnation.

As they hurried to secure it from those who had once been their friends, allies, and even family, the small group of spellcasters also had to fight against the Fire Rose's seduction. They all wanted to use it, and some had even suggested, quite convincingly, how it could be still become a force for good for the High Ogre race.

But in the end, overall agreement remained that the Fire Rose had to be not just hidden, but covered with enchantments that would prevent the most corrupted of them from regaining it. Xiryn had become so obsessed with the god's "gift" that he had murdered those who most trusted him and had seduced several others to his terrible cause with dreams of immortality and ultimate power. He was a threat not only to what little remained of the High Ogre race, but to the rest of Krynn as well.

So the small band had made it to that hidden place and set in motion their plan. They secreted the Fire Rose in the hidden chamber deep within the mountains of the Vale of Vipers then made certain with the last of their strength that Xiryn could never place his hands upon it even if he reached the location.

Yet there were those among them who did not trust to even that "absolute" solution. They no longer had the might to destroy Xiryn, and Xiryn would never willingly end his pursuit of the Fire Rose. He would seek a way by which to have it.

Thus, they gathered in that hidden place to formulate

some new plot. Each had some reserves of strength, so they hoped that what she suggested might work. She was their leader. Her mate, who was second among them, sat across from her. Other than their son—who was long absent on orders from her—her mate and the rest of the High Ogres would be giving all that they had left, which likely meant death for the weakest.

But then just as they were beginning, there came the rush of cold wind and the flapping of wings in that place where neither should have been possible. There had been no warning. Her mate had seen death coming, and she had felt it on her back. The rest, thankfully, never felt their doom. Neither did they hear Xiryn's triumphant laugh.

What they also did not feel, nor even did Xiryn sense, was that it was not his spells that sucked their lives from their bodies. It was her work, a last moment's hope that she shared with only her mate. Their power, their life energies, she sent to the one left who could keep watch against Xiryn.

Their son. His handsome face appeared—

Golgren tore away from the skeletal hand. The female corpse shifted slightly then somehow readjusted to the same position from before.

"Answer me, Grand Khan!" Tyranos was shouting. "What, by the Kraken, are you—?"

"Sarth . . ." the half-breed murmured. "Sarth . . ."

"Yes, Sarth," came a familiar, wizened voice.

Both Golgren and Tyranos turned to where the male counterpart to the female sat. There, standing behind the corpse, was the hunched figure of the ogre shaman.

Golgren's eyes narrowed. "But Sarth in the vision was a High Ogre, not a lowly ogre."

The shaman chuckled, a harsh sound without any humor to it. "And this is the true Sarth now. I have changed with time and made time change me as necessary."

"What do you two mean?" snarled the wizard. He gestured with the staff at the shaman. *That* is a High Ogre? He hardly looks like one! He's too tall too! Morgada had it right; they were only our height."

"There are many who look as they are not," Sarth countered, eyes suddenly so piercing that Tyranos had to turn his own gaze away. "And many who are more than they appear," the hunched figure added, looking to Golgren.

Unlike the mage, Golgren stood steadfast, meeting Sarth's eyes. "So I have been told."

In an uncommonly touching gesture, Sarth briefly placed one hand on the male mummy's shoulder. The shaman smiled softly to the body then, with his staff, made his way toward Golgren and the female corpse.

"I've forgotten their names. I've forgotten my own. Sarth I took when I chose to go among the descendants of my misbegotten people. I let the magic shape me as it had them and then buried myself among them, waiting for Xiryn." Sarth spit out the last word. "That name, though, will forever burn in my memory."

Golgren still had questions. "I have known you, Sarth. There was no sign, no hint."

The withered shaman stepped past him to ever so lightly touch the cheek of the female mummy. Sarth's eyes glistened, though no tear fell.

"I made myself forget. Sarth the shaman simply went on from region to region, tribe to tribe. Only Xiryn's actions could awaken the true me . . . or as much as survived the centuries."

The wizard snorted. "You can't be a High Ogre, not even the missing ninth! They lived too long ago! The other one, he's survived, but more as a ghoul than a living creature."

Without looking at Tyranos, Sarth answered, "Xiryn took upon himself a quicker, more powerful spell, but with a slowly degrading fault. He lived but his body *forgot* that. He decayed, even though he walked Krynn. To slow that process, he took from his rabid followers some great measure of their own life forces and magic. They became even less than him, husks, trapping sparks of existence within, living off his obsession."

"But you found a better way, eh?"

It was Sarth's turn to snort. "No. Only one that kept me from becoming as Xiryn. I did not ask for it; my parents thrust it upon me. And if it were my choice, I would be dead."

"You came to my people," Golgren interrupted. "Came to them before I was born."

He had sensed Xiryn's probing presence, Sarth explained. Observing from the citadel that had once been a place of hope for the dwindling High Ogre race, Xiryn had developed, over the recent generations, an avid and inexplicable interest in the degenerate heirs of his kind. Sarth, stirred to action after so many centuries, long sought the reason. After a while, he decided that Xiryn sought any vestigial trace of the race's greatness in the beasts that represented it. But Sarth found little success, and the shaman had again buried himself in his ogre persona, forgetting his true identity for another two or three generations.

"But I slept too deep then. Only shortly before you were conceived did I awaken and discover the truth of

Xiryn's plan! The forced creation of a thing that did not by common nature exist on Krynn—an ogre breeding successfully with an elf!"

There had been several experiments made by Xiryn, but Golgren had finally been deemed the successful candidate. Xiryn indifferently slaughtered the others. He wanted no one to use his very plot against him. Despite having discovered no trace of any of his enemies, his paranoia kept him wary. So wary, in fact, that Sarth had to tread very lightly, lurking in the shadows and continuing to be an ogre shaman in deed as well as appearance.

"What an enchanting story!" rumbled Tyranos, swinging his staff like a club. "Does it go on much longer?"

"No longer than the tale of an Uruv Suurt whose shame makes him desire another skin."

The wizard brandished the staff. "My life is mine and no others, ogre!"

"You have chosen to bind your life to the Fire Rose. Therefore, your life is bound to his," Sarth retorted, indicating Golgren. "To gain the prize, you must help him attain it."

Tyranos grunted. "He's this Xiryn's creation and *you* want him to do exactly what the gargoyle king desires? That makes no sense!"

It was Golgren who understood what Sarth planned or, at least, hoped. "Yes. It is the only way."

"But only if you're strong enough. Against Xiryn, no one has been."

The mage finally comprehended. He gave an evil grin. "You might as well hand it to Xiryn and bid him good luck with it! Besides, haven't you forgotten another problem? The Titans, for instance?"

"The Titans were not planned for by either myself or Xiryn. They were, so I unearthed, one of the many convoluted plots of dread Takhisis—"

"Ha! So I always thought!"

Sarth ignored the outburst. "But though she is no more, another may have chosen them to be his messengers to the world."

"Sirrion," remarked Golgren.

The ancient gestured at their surroundings. "My parents and the others, they beseeched Sirrion to take back his 'gift,' but the god only grew angry, as he, being fire, oft does. In his furious departure, he scorched a part of the cavern, as you have no doubt seen. Sirrion simply answered my people's first prayer; he sets no blame upon himself."

"The gods, they rarely do," the half-breed agreed. "The Titans . . . you think they serve Sirrion's desire?"

Sarth shrugged. "We may all be serving Sirrion's desire. Fire is conflict; we fuel it as if we had put wood to flame. Only peace and understanding can tame the fire, and peace and understanding are things long lost to our people's thinking, Guyvir."

"You have been warned not to call me that."

"If you cannot forgive the hatred of your father, you cannot wield the Fire Rose successfully. If you do not wield it successfully, then whether it is Xiryn, the Titans, or Sirrion himself, the Fire Rose will forever change not merely the ogres, but the rest of Krynn . . . and not for the better. Sirrion wishes to be honored, and constant change is to him the greatest of honors. A Krynn in constant flux would be the most grand of temples dedicated to the fire lord."

Tyranos rubbed the crystal, which flared brighter under his touch. "Sirrion isn't Takhisis. He's not evil."

"No," the half-breed interjected. "He is not good either."

Sarth nodded, seeming like a pleased teacher. "And so you understand *what* about him, Guyvir?"

"That, being neither, he is more dangerous than the dark gods."

"Madness!" growled Tyranos, stalking up to the shaman. "An *indifferent* god threatens the stability of Krynn? You think the others will just let it happen?"

Squatting, Sarth drew a symbol in the floor, his bony finger cutting through rock as if it were sand. The symbol, hidden from the view of the other two, flared bright for a breath then settled.

"In some ways," he said, not looking up from his task. "Sirrion is dominant among them. Change currently envelops not only Krynn, but the gods too. They vie for places they never held before and come into conflict when they should not. If I were as mad as Xiryn, I would almost say that Sirrion stirs all of this . . . and possibly merely for his entertainment."

The wizard turned on Golgren. "Are you hearing this? Do you trust this fool any more than you do the Titans? I wonder now if he really just wants to use you to get the Fire Rose for *him?* Have you considered that?"

The half-breed met Tyranos's angry gaze with a calm, level one. "Yes, and he does *not* wish it."

"And how can you be sure?" Tyranos turned to Sarth. "Tell us truly—"

But Sarth was gone.

The spellcaster swung the staff across the empty space once occupied by the shaman. Tyranos let out an oath that not only honored his minotaur lineage, but also would have burned the ears of some very hardy legionaries.

Golgren let the wizard rant. The half-breed went down on one knee to inspect what Sarth had drawn. There were, in fact, two symbols, not one. The first was a large, graceful wing, which did not in the least resemble those of a gargoyle.

The second was a slim tree that, despite its simplicity, very much resembled one very familiar to Golgren. He had seen it many times on the tapestry that had once hung in his palace.

It was an oak tree . . .

An oak tree and the wing of a large beast.

Golgren rose. He surveyed the chamber, including the gathered dead. His eyes suddenly shifted not to Sarth's mother, but rather his father and something the half-breed recalled he himself had taken from the corpse and let Idaria wear.

A pendant that bore the symbol of the griffon, a creature whose wing was shaped much like that which Sarth had drawn.

"She will be there," Golgren remarked in an almost matter-of-fact tone. "She has no choice."

"What's that?"

The deposed Grand Khan turned back to face Tyranos. "It is not merely Xiryn who desires Idaria to be there when the Titans are confronted, it is the dead who wish it as well."

XIX

GARGOYLES

There was something odd about Chasm, something Idaria felt that she should be able to put her finger on but could not. At times, it almost came to her, but then her mind, suffering much weariness and concern already, always lost hold of the reason.

They had flown most of the night, the gargoyle silent throughout the majority of the journey to conserve his strength. They were drawing nearer to Garantha, though they still had far to go. The gargoyle might be willing to continue, and certainly in spirit the elf desired too, but Idaria needed a drink of water, if nothing else.

She spotted a likely place below. "Chasm, please descend!"

Grunting, the gargoyle shook his head and pushed on. "Please! Only for some water!"

Her winged companion cocked his head. With a curt nod, he banked and began his descent.

There was indeed water below, a small river trickling down from a mountaintop. The elf eyed it gratefully.

The gargoyle set her down a few yards from the stream then fluttered over to a place a bit farther from her. With sudden, eager abandon, Chasm began slurping mouthfuls of cool water.

Idaria knelt by the river and began to sip. She had been slightly chilled throughout the long flight, and her shoulders were sore from the manner by which Chasm had been forced to carry her. The water, though, soothed her enough so that she could at last concentrate. She thought about Golgren, so desperately in need of her aid, but then her thoughts shifted. She wondered why Chasm had insisted that they leave so quickly; Idaria had not even had a moment to alert Sir Stefan.

Swallowing another mouthful, the slave peered at her companion. Idaria watched his movements. Her eyes narrowed in conjecture.

As if sensing the elf's interest, the gargoyle straightened. With a slight flap of his wings, Chasm leaped from his location and descended again next to her.

Staring into the brutish face, Idaria began to register just what was wrong.

Before that could happen, though, a fearsome roar shook the area. Chasm whirled from her, the gargoyle responding to the menacing call with an equally powerful roar.

The elf also turned to the sound. "What is it?"

A muscular, winged beast threw itself at Chasm. Idaria jumped to the side as the pair collided. The gargoyle and his attacker rolled into the water, sending it splattering everywhere.

Idaria stumbled back, wanting to help Chasm but not certain what she could do. Her hand clutched at her breast, as if seeking out the medallion she had returned to Stefan.

To her surprise, she found her fingers gripped around something else. The elf glanced down at her hand.

It was a pendant, one familiar to her. The sign of the griffon peered back at Idaria. Yet despite the fact that it hung around her neck and surely must have been there since Golgren placed it there, Idaria had utterly forgotten about it until that very moment.

A familiar sensation flowed through her, the same sensation that she realized had flowed through her during the two "miracles" to which she had given credit to the medallion and, possibly, Habbakuk.

But both Idaria and the Solamnic had been mistaken. Everything had been the result of the ancient artifact, a High Ogre relic that had shielded itself from even the gargoyle king.

Her discovery of the pendant's properties was momentarily thrust to the back of her mind by another startling revelation. Both Chasm and his foe pushed away from each other, the two creatures dripping from the water from which they had just risen. For the first time, Idaria could identify what had attacked her friend.

It was *Chasm*.

The two identical gargoyles hissed and spit at each other as they slashed at the air between them with their powerful claws. Their backs arched and their wings stretched wide in what was clearly an attempt by each to show dominance. Yet since both were, to all appearances, Chasm, such displays looked futile.

The elf studied each in turn. Only one could truly be Tyranos's servant. The other must be obeying the commands of the monstrous High Ogre.

That the Chasm who had carried her was the false one was obvious, but with the struggle, Idaria could not identify which that was. The illusion was absolutely perfect.

The Chasm on the right lunged. His twin started to rise up but not quickly enough. The first Chasm crashed into the second's torso, and both went rolling out of the water.

The pair fought with tooth and claw, seeking any soft area to rend. Both gargoyles evinced thick, scaled hides, so most of their strikes did little more than leave scratches. However, it was while observing that aspect of the fight that Idaria had her first inkling as to which Chasm might be the true one.

One Chasm was virtually unmarred, greatly resembling how best the elf recalled him. At the moment, he had the advantage. He had forced the other Chasm on his back, pressing down so the latter could not make use of his wings to push himself up.

In addition to his predicament, the second Chasm was far more scarred than his adversary. Those scars covered his body from head to foot. He also appeared more exhausted, as if he had just flown with the greatest of swiftness to catch up to Idaria and her companion.

"You are the true Chasm!" she muttered. Her hand squeezed the pendant, which warmed even more.

A gray energy enveloped the gargoyle that the elf had recognized as her true friend. At first, neither noticed it, but then the real Chasm suddenly shoved hard, tossing his false twin back. Moving as if rejuvenated, Tyranos's servant jumped at his foe before the second one could recover. As he did, Chasm let loose with a cry of challenge—a cry that sounded part gargoyle, but also part another great beast, a griffon.

The false Chasm met the true one head-on. Briefly, they became locked together with no advantage to either. However, the true Chasm slowly but surely started to bear down on his adversary. Again he let loose with the call that was part griffon.

The impostor slashed uselessly with his claws across Chasm's chest. Chasm returned the attack, and his claws tore through the hard scale surface as they had not earlier. Ribbons of skin flew from the other gargoyle; in their wake rivers of blood issued forth. The second Chasm stumbled.

Giving no quarter, Tyranos's servant flung himself atop his staggering enemy. He clawed the second gargoyle again and again. Each time, the previously thick hide gave way easily. Under the onslaught, the bleeding impostor fell to his knees.

Chasm bent back one arm of his foe then bit into it. As the false Chasm shrieked, the true one ripped out a chunk of flesh from the arm and spit it away.

The sorely wounded creature dropped facedown on the ground as weakness and blood loss took its toll. Chasm raised his claws and tore out the back of his twin's neck. For good measure, he also twisted the head nearly to the back, the snapping so loud, it made Idaria shiver. She released the pendant, which dropped back onto her breast.

Chasm paused as if suddenly exhausted again. As he settled back, the dead gargoyle was transformed. Although he retained his general shape, most of his resemblance to Chasm vanished. His muzzle became more pronounced, and his color also altered, turning mud brown.

The dead gargoyle looked much more like those that served the High Ogre.

Panting heavily, Chasm made his way to Idaria. She saw that while he had not suffered much due to the fallen gargoyle, there were indeed many scars on him from an earlier danger. Even though the pendant had clearly aided him, part of its effect had apparently been temporary. Chasm was better than when he had arrived but still diminished from his previous trial.

"Where did you come from?" the elf asked as she tried to help ease his pain. "How did you find me?"

"Came from forest," the winged creature grunted. "Fought skeletons. They fall to Chasm!" He said that last with some pride. "Then hear voice. Elf's voice. Follow you into forest. Lose way."

"You endangered yourself for me?" Chasm belonged to the wizard; he should not have worried himself over her.

"Friend needed me," he reminded Idaria. "Trees attack. Not like first time. Someone waits." He hissed. "Too late, smell my kind."

The story began to make sense. The presence of other gargoyles had meant the presence of their master as well. He had used his power to manipulate the already dark forest to seize Chasm and make him a prisoner.

"But why keep you alive?" Idaria asked, the answer coming to her but a breath later. "Of course. For such a strong illusion spell, he likely had it draw off your life. That kept you weaker, but it also saved you." Something else came to mind. "You did not free yourself, did you? Was it Stefan who did?"

Chasm's head bobbed up and down. In his short, primitive sentences, he conveyed to her what he had learned from the Solamnic about her sudden vanishing. There had been immediate agreement that Chasm was best suited to give chase. Stefan had to remain with the refugees. Chasm, meanwhile, could follow her scent.

"You . . . followed my scent this far?"

Again, he bobbed his head. "Know your scent like master's."

The gargoyle had to push himself to his limits to catch up as quickly as possible. Both he and Stefan had feared the worst.

But what was more upsetting to Idaria was the fact that she had played into the dark one's plots, as though she were a willing accomplice. All it had taken was the fear that Golgren was dying and only she could somehow save him.

"I was a fool!"

Chasm snorted. "No fool."

"Yes, I was and, worse, I may be about to become an even bigger one."

The gargoyle cocked his head in concern.

Idaria's fingers grazed the pendant. It was the true reason for her "miracles" and it had also helped save Chasm. And it had been given to her by Golgren and perhaps also by someone who had been dead for many centuries but still fought against the gargoyle king.

"We continue on, Chasm. We go as this foul creature's even more foul lord intended."

Chasm shook his head, but Idaria remained determined. She stared into the gargoyle's gaze until at last Chasm reluctantly nodded.

"As mistress says."

"As I ask, Chasm. You leave me the moment we reach there. This is my choice, not yours."

"Where mistress goes, Chasm goes and fights for her."

He stared right back at her with determination. Idaria

at last reached out and stroked his cheek. The gargoyle almost purred.

"Very well," she said. "We go together but not to merely fulfill our enemy's intent. We have power of our own, Chasm." The elf indicated the pendant.

That finally brought some cheer to Chasm. He had felt the pendant's power. "Make Chasm so strong, all fall to him!"

"That's right." Idaria let her companion believe that for the moment. "We will defeat them and save Golgren and Tyranos."

The gargoyle let his tongue run over his muzzle as he anticipated their victory. "Chasm thirsty. We go after Chasm drinks."

"Drink your fill." Idaria watched him move off to the water. Her confident expression changed to one more doubtful. She looked down at the pendant. While it had clearly been of much help, it would hardly be sufficient to face the threat of the Titans or the gargoyles' master.

"But it may save Golgren," the elf whispered. "It may save him."

Her eyes widened as what she said—and what she meant by it—became clear to her.

❧❧❦❧❧

The minotaurs had made inroads thanks to the gargoyles' arrival. They had as yet to actually confront any Titans, but the fact that the sorcerers were still being successfully hampered and harassed by the winged creatures was a good sign that the tide had, at least for the moment, turned.

Faros kept to the forefront. He did not trust himself entirely to Kiri-Jolith's medallion, though. In the emperor's experience, a god's protection had a way of disappearing at the most inopportune moments, and according to Golgren, there was more than one god involved.

The sacrifices had been many, and every legionary there expected countless more to come. They also expected one more enemy, so when the last finally revealed itself, the minotaurs reacted not with concern, but with roars of pleasure. They had something upon which to test their swords.

The ogres came rushing down at them in far more order than in generations past. The officers had for months been warning their soldiers of the new generation of foes, but even still, the first row of legionaries suffered greatly as a flight of arrows assailed them.

Faros was among the fortunate few, but he did not thank the bison-headed god for that fact. The emperor gritted his teeth and met the first ogre warrior he came upon. The ogres were clad in the breastplates of Golgren's elite hands. Perhaps once they had been loyal to the half-breed, but to the minotaurs they were only ogres, and as such, they were to be slain on sight.

The ogre he faced was more skilled than any Faros had previously fought, save Golgren himself. It took nearly half a minute to finally slay the larger fighter. Some of the techniques used by the ogre indicated influences from the minotaur race.

"Outcasts," the emperor growled as he dueled with a second warrior. Golgren had employed minotaur traitors to retrain his people.

A legionary near Faros fell prey to an ogre sword. The soldiers were having a more difficult time than most of them had expected. Ogres were half beast and without skill; that was the common belief.

But *Golgren* had succeeded in changing that.

Faros dodged a clever strike by his adversary then used a trick that he had made up himself. The ogre hesitated. That was all the minotaur needed to run him through a seam in his armor.

Given a moment to catch his breath, Faros glared at what Golgren had wrought and the Titans had subverted.

"We survive this and we shall keep coming, Grand Khan," the emperor muttered. "I'll not fight sorcerers just to someday be ruled by you. The banner of the empire'll fly over Garantha, not yours over Nethosak."

Another ogre came at Faros. The minotaur's blade met the ogre's, and the latest duel commenced. Yet as Faros battled the ogre, he pictured a foe more his own size . . .

And with one hand.

XX

THE TEMPLE

Sarth had imparted much information of relevance to Golgren, but before departing, he had failed to say something singularly important.

"The staff still can't transport us from this place," Tyranos explained. "There's some force blocking our way."

Golgren studied the mummified High Ogres. None of them revealed any reason the pair was trapped there, yet there was no other immediate explanation.

At last, the half-breed decided, "Then we will find another way."

"We've looked in either direction and both are—if you'll pardon me for saying so—dead ends."

It was true; the other paths ended in suspicious collapses. Sarth had made no mention of that, and the wizard and Golgren had agreed it was unlikely that he had been the perpetrator.

Yet if not Sarth, who?

Golgren abandoned the uncommunicative mummies

and strode over to a wall that he had not ever studied thoroughly.

The half-breed frowned. "This is different. This has changed."

Tyranos joined him. "What was on it before?"

The deposed Grand Khan shrugged. It had not been important then. "Not this."

This was a vast panorama that filled their view. It was the picture of a glorious city that gleamed gold despite being carved from only rock. The architecture was reminiscent of Garantha, yet more fabulous, perhaps Garantha as it had first looked.

An urge to touch it filled Golgren, yet when he raised his hand toward the wall, the signet fought him for control.

"Look out!" Tyranos roared.

A blinding glare burst from the image, enveloping them.

Instantly the two found themselves standing in the midst of the great city itself.

Everything was made of gold, gold the color of the sun. High, spiraling towers rose around them. A vast, segmented walkway led up to a rounded temple with winged arches.

The half-breed did not have to ask who it was who had brought them there. Only one being could be so audacious.

To the empty air, Golgren said, "Sirrion desires us for something. Will he tell us what it is?"

At the top of the temple's glittering steps, two massive bowls that had themselves not existed a moment prior shot forth high streams of golden flame. The flames arched toward one another, entwining as if vines. The ends descended to a spot exactly between the bowls.

The fire formed into Sirrion.

"Welcome to your kingdom, if you'd have it," the deity proclaimed with a grin.

Shielding their eyes, both stepped back from the fiery god. Yet instead, their actions brought them *closer*.

"Come now! Don't be shy! All of this is yours, elf-ogre, if only you've got the resolve! The moment is coming and the choice could be yours unless you make it *theirs*."

There was no need for Sirrion to say whom he meant, either the Titans or the gargoyle king. It mattered not to Sirrion who seized the Fire Rose. All that mattered was that someone used it.

Tyranos stepped in front of the half-breed. "There's another choice! Let me have your gift! I'll use it as it should be used!"

Sirrion shook his head. The grin was replaced by an angry frown. "If you can take it, it becomes yours, but your fate belongs to another's control."

That brought a curse from the wizard. "Neither Sargonnas nor Kiri-Jolith are masters of my fate!"

"Did I say it was them?" Sirrion blazed with fury. "Are you correcting me?"

"He is impetuous," Golgren interjected. "None would ever correct you."

The grin returned. "No, not if they're wise." The flames subsided to a point. "Will you have my gift, then, elf-ogre?"

Glancing at his severed limb, the half-breed calmly replied. "No. I must leave it to chance."

Sirrion appeared torn between frustration and a temptation to concur. The god rubbed his chin, sending sparks flying. Finally, he grinned again. "Interesting . . . and so very right!"

"What by the Kraken's gotten into you?" muttered an angry Tyranos.

Golgren did not reply. He bowed his head to Sirrion, who accepted his obeisance.

"Chance, as always, is the most fascinating course!" the god cheerfully remarked. "Yes, I was right about you."

Sirrion exploded into flames. Golgren and Tyranos fought for balance as the entire city turned on its head.

The pair reappeared but not back in the chamber of the mummies.

Instead, they stood in an empty area that at first glance to most would have seemed just one more worthless piece of untillable land. There was little life save a few hardy and ugly shrubs with sharp stickers for leaves. The landscape itself consisted of tall, dirt-brown hills and little else.

Tyranos eyed their surroundings with contempt. "Now what backward part of Krynn have we dropped into?"

The half-breed did not answer, for he was racing away from the wizard at breakneck speed, seeking a place that he had not seen since his youth. That it would still exist was a definite possibility, for who would care to seek it out? That would mean risking life and limb, not to mention starvation.

And for what? There was nothing of value there unless you were a half-breed, who had been given at birth the name Guyvir, *the Unborn,* the mongrel who should not exist.

He found the crevasse looking exactly as memory recorded. Golgren pressed against it, discovering that reality was different than memory. He had been slighter, shorter as a youth, so had easier slipped inside. As an adult, he had to squeeze himself against the rock. Golgren ignored the scraping of his flesh and the dust in his lungs. All that mattered was to gain entrance.

At last he did. The cool cave air soothed some of the sting from where his skin had been removed. Still, the half-breed paid little attention to his injuries. All that mattered was *her*.

There was just enough light to see the crumbling temple. The shattered relief of the two battling mastarks remained, the gleam of one creature's furious orb— carved from some brilliant, orange-red stone—greeting him as if welcoming back an old friend . . . or an old adversary. Beyond, other cracked walls and small alcoves stirred other memories, not all of them pleasant.

His foot knocked something. He peered down to see some of the jawbone and other skeletal remains of a large animal. They were the bones of a ji-baraki, an ogre-sized reptilian predator of that land. Golgren knew that, even without seeing the rest of the skull, which was missing. After all, he had killed the beast himself.

Then a rounded shape to his right made the half-breed forget all else. As if mesmerized, Golgren stepped toward a high pile of stones dug from the ruins. They were set in the shape of a six-foot-long mound, and if that caused resemblance to a burial place, it was because that was what it was.

It was where Golgren had buried his mother.

The half-breed went down on one knee to the side of the mound. A few withered plants lay atop the mount, somehow a little bit of their flowery scent still clinging to them. It had taken much effort for a young Golgren to find those plants; they were the best he could do. His mother deserved more than this, the semblance of the lush world she had forsaken when taken prisoner long before.

Words barely discernible to the naked ear spilled from his lips, words in a tongue that Golgren had not spoken since the fatal day he had lost her.

"Didn't even know you knew how to speak Elvish."

Golgren did not turn to the wizard. "Leave me."

"This was where she died?"

"No. She died two days earlier."

The wizard let out a snort that indicated surprise, not ridicule. "And you carried her for that long a time? You didn't tell me that you were part minotaur too!"

Still facing the mound, Golgren bared his teeth. "Leave me!"

"Pay your respects; I can appreciate that. Just recall that there's a living elf you seem interested in, albeit in another way."

The wizard was silent after that, but his words had an effect on the half-breed. Even though he wanted to stay longer, Golgren finally rose. The look in his eyes when he finally turned to his hooded companion was enough to make Tyranos momentarily grip the staff in self-defense.

But just as quickly as he had glanced at the mage, Golgren shifted his attention elsewhere, to the faded image of the battling mastarks, although his thoughts still lingered in a different place.

"So," Tyranos finally dared interject. "Any particular reason why Sirrion or maybe your friend Sarth might've dropped us off here? Surely not merely so you could pay your respects?"

Golgren suspected Tyranos knew the truth. "There was a dagger. With it, I slew the ji-baraki who sought to dine on her body. It remained with me until lost when Garantha was attacked."

The wizard rubbed his chin. "Yes, I was never quite certain about that. What did our friend in the citadel hope to gain from the attack?"

"He stirred the situation." Golgren did not explain further. Instead, he wandered over to where one wall had fallen down due, years before, to his careless leaning against it.

"Ah! He was setting all this into motion! Yes, that sounds right—be careful there!"

The reason for Tyranos's shout had to do with Golgren's suddenly stepping atop what was clearly a loose piece of stone overlooking a deep gap behind the wall. The half-breed stood perched atop the stone for a breath or two then dropped into the pit.

Golgren heard his companion shout something else, but it was lost to the half-breed as he landed. Centuries had not much altered the petrified garbage those who had built the temple had left behind. The first time that Golgren had landed there, he had been concerned only with finding his way back up. At the moment, though, he was hoping to locate something of value, a dagger or other weapon akin to the one he had lost. It was to him the most logical reason he had been sent there.

The pit was the only area that Golgren discovered was larger than memory claimed. The hopes of locating what might not even exist dimmed as he searched without finding anything.

Then, among the refuse, something stirred. Golgren groped around for some kind of weapon. He came up empty. Whatever stirred, the half-breed would have to face it unarmed.

There came a hissing sound, one so familiar, it sent a rare chill up the deposed Grand Khan's spine. He knew the calls of many predators, but it was worse than that; it was as though he recognized the hiss as the voice of someone he knew.

Golgren watched the darkness even as his hand dug around for anything that might be wielded in a fight.

From above came Tyranos's voice. "Are you all right?"

The half-breed did not answer. He was lost in time, remembering when last he had faced that most heinous foe. There were perhaps only a few others he hated as passionately, chief among them his father and the Nerakan who had slain his mother.

Something rose up from the refuse ahead of him. At first, it seemed an indistinct shape. Then as it moved toward him, Golgren made out the long, tapering forelegs and the sleek, sinister skull. The thing hissed again at him.

It was a ji-baraki but not just any ji-baraki. He sensed it was the one that he had killed, built from the missing skull set atop a collection of smaller bones and other fragments. Together, they reconstructed the body of the male beast Golgren had caught scavenging the corpse of his mother.

And in turn, it sought revenge against its killer, just as Golgren had taken revenge on it for desecrating the dead body of the only person who had ever cared for an unwanted infant.

The skeletal ji-baraki opened its toothy maw—the lower jaw composed of other bones and fragments—and hissed a third time. Golgren had tossed that skull into the refuse pit as a final gesture of his victory. He had forgotten about it until that moment.

As the ji-baraki hissed, it changed form. From skeleton, it became something part mist. The ghoulish aspect of its fleshless appearance remained, but it drifted as much as stalked toward him.

"Stand clear!" Tyranos shouted, the wizard abruptly materializing next to Golgren. The crystal crackled and a bolt of arcane energy shot forth to enshroud the ghostly beast.

The ji-baraki shattered.

The wizard raised the staff in triumph. "Ha!"

Then, from wherever some piece had landed, new shapes started to form. They were composed of the ancient refuse, and as they grew, each took on a macabre aspect of the undead monster.

As Tyranos swore, Golgren continued to sift through the rubble.

A sharp edge cut his hand. Despite the pain, he seized the item and drew it up.

It was a dagger identical to the one that he had found so many years past. Golgren hefted the blade just as the nearest of the reanimated fiends struck. That ji-baraki had no true skull, but the ancient bits of refuse had formed one with just as sharp a set of "teeth." Worse, the body was half mist and as much coiled around Golgren as it did strike at him with its "claws."

He parried the claws with his dagger. Emerald light flashed each time the blade touched the phantasm. The ji-baraki recoiled.

Nearby, Tyranos sought to keep two more at bay. He used the staff as a physical weapon, swinging at anything that came near him. The crystal crackled with lightning as it hit the phantasms, but with a lesser intensity that marked a different spell at play. Whenever he struck, the "bones" would fuse together, making it harder and harder for the beasts to move.

The "jaws" of Golgren's foe sought to close on his throat. The half-breed thrust the dagger up through where the creature's jaws met its skull. As the blade sank in, the emerald glow spread.

The spirit beast let out a shriek identical to that of a true ji-baraki in mortal pain. The misty part of the body faded, and the rest fell in a clatter. No new monsters were spawned from the remains.

But there were still many more to be dealt with. Like the cunning predator after whom they were fashioned, the fiends began to organize in packs that surrounded their two targets. Tyranos, who had just finished turning one into a solid mass that could do no more than wriggle, was seized at the legs by another. A second ji-baraki attacked the hand best gripping the staff.

The magical artifact slipped from the mage's grasp.

Golgren, too, found himself in dire straits. Although his blade was useful, it could be wielded against only one at a time, not three. As one lunged, Golgren, instead of meeting it, ducked low. At the same time, he thrust the blade sideways in his mouth, like a brigand getting ready to climb a mast, and used his free hand to seize a larger piece of rubble.

Just before one phantasm's jaws would have bitten off part of his face, the half-breed thrust the chunk into it. Like the real predator, the magical one struggled to free its mouth. Its claws scarred Golgren in several places, but he was able to spit out the dagger into his hand just in time to strike the oncoming second. The blow would not have been fatal to a living creature. However, it proved enough to drive back the one fiend.

Maneuvering the first between himself and a third, the half-breed readjusted his grip on the dagger. He shoved the blade into what passed for the gullet of the shadow creature and grinned in satisfaction as the wound burst open in a blaze of emerald light.

Beside him, Tyranos gripped the throats of his two nearest attackers. They, in turn, sought to ensnare his lower body with their smoky torsos and rip away his face with their jaws.

The wizard muttered a spell under his breath. His foes suddenly flew at one another as if drawn by some intense display of magnetism. Their makeshift bodies became entangled.

Scrambling to his feet, Tyranos stared beyond them. "We've got a lot more trouble coming!"

Peering past his own adversaries, Golgren saw immediately what the spellcaster meant. There were a dozen more of the ghoulish reptiles, each a hodgepodge of whatever refuse could be pulled together from the surrounding garbage.

Golgren considered the dagger, the best he had against the monsters. Without saying anything to the mage, he again set the blade between his teeth and looked to the side, where Tyranos's staff lay. Golgren dived for the staff. Taking it up, he rested it in the crook of his maimed limb. As he seized the dagger once more, the half-breed pointed the staff toward the oncoming pack.

"That might not be the best idea," his companion warned as he braced himself for a lunging creature.

Ignoring him, the half-breed placed the tip of

the dagger on the crystal. An emerald hue spread over the head of the staff.

Golgren shouted out the words he had heard Tyranos use.

Bright green lightning burst from the crystal, shooting out at each of the monstrous attackers. The lightning enveloped them.

The ji-baraki phantasms hissed as one. Then each collapsed into mangled heaps, reverting to the ancient refuse.

Falling to one knee, Golgren eyed his victory with pleasure. Once more, he had slain the beast that had feasted on his mother's corpse.

A powerful hand ripped the staff away from Golgren. "You shouldn't be able to use this so readily! I spent years learning its secrets!"

Golgren did not reply. Rising, he inspected his find. There was indeed no difference between the dagger he held and the one that he had lost, yet he knew somehow with utter certainty that it was a twin, not the same one.

"Imagine you finding that here," the wizard remarked sarcastically. "What pure luck it isn't."

"No, in that we agree." Golgren inspected the ornate hilt of the dagger. There was no mark to indicate any special reason it should have come to him. Yet that in itself made him wonder. "I was meant to have this, to replace the one I was expected to wield at the right time. This was a test of me."

" 'A test'?" the hooded figure snorted. "Oh. Our friend from the citadel?"

"No, that might be true, if he and Sirrion were of one mind." Golgren bared his teeth at Tyranos. "You must look to your own gods, Uruv Suurt, to explain this."

"Kiri-Jolith . . . and never call me that again."

"Kiri-Jolith," the half-breed agreed.

"You're very popular with the gods suddenly. It'll be the death of you." The wizard shrugged. "So. Do I take it that you want to return to Garantha and get this over with, one way or another?"

"I wish to get this over, but Garantha is not going to be our immediate destination."

Tyranos's brow rose. "No? Then where, exactly, if I'm not too bold to ask?"

Golgren told him.

The wizard grimaced. *"There?"*

"Yes. I see now that something lies there that I will also need . . . first."

Though not convinced, Tyranos nonetheless nodded. "As you wish . . . and against my better judgment."

They vanished then appeared where Golgren had hoped they would be. The landscape for some great distance looked as if an astounding upheaval had taken place. Hills had been reduced to rubble. Mountainsides were shattered, leaving vast gaps that looked as if some giant had taken a bite or two out of them. There was no flat ground. Massive rocks jutted up in surprising places, and treacherous ravines were everywhere.

But even more unnerving was what lay among the rocks: *bones,* countless bones. Some were of immense size, bespeaking a beast several times the height of either of the pair. Most, though, were of a more familiar length and form, and though they were scattered, one skull was enough to identify *all* if only because, though it was akin to a human skull, it had powerful tusks.

It was an ogre skull. It was one of the many ogres who had once fought for three warlords determined not to let an impure half-breed become their master. Golgren himself had slain the first among them and taken his head back to the capital as sign of his victory. That had marked the end of internal resistance to the half-breed's ascension to power, at least for a time.

But that ogre and the hundreds more that could be found there had died *far* from that place. A power at that time unknown to Golgren had raised them up and sent them from that distant battlefield to where they stood. It had sent them to attack his precious Garantha, just beyond his sight.

"Our friend did this," the wizard said. "Our friend with all the gargoyles."

Tyranos's eyes widened in understanding. "Ah! I see it! Dauroth wouldn't go hunt the Fire Rose, but our friend knew that if Safrag was leader, then he *would!* This was all to stir Safrag into taking over, wasn't it?"

"Yes. Dauroth's death is Safrag's doing, so I believe."

"Ha! So Safrag owes his rise to the very same creature who saw to it that you were born."

"Yes, it would seem so." There was something in Golgren's tone that warned his companion not to pursue the subject any further.

The hooded spellcaster peered toward where Garantha lay. Although obscured from their view, it was not all that far away. "We should be safe for the moment, unless the Titans are actively observing this area, but I still don't understand what you want from here."

Golgren had edged away from him. "If it is found, you will understand, Uruv Suurt."

"There are things you indicate I'd better not mention; for the last time, calling me *that* is one thing that *you* should not bring up again." He waited for Golgren to reply, but when there was nothing, Tyranos gave an angry snort.

The half-breed was busy searching for something. His foot kicked up a leg bone. A tingle raced through his fingers, one that did not originate with him, but rather emanated from the dagger. Golgren paused. The reaction had been weak but definite. He was close, very close. As he had suspected would happen, the dagger he held was the key.

"You plan to scour this whole area? That could take some time, oh Grand Khan."

The half-breed bent down to touch the ravaged ground. The dagger tugged in his hand.

"It is deep, very deep. But it is here."

Tyranos grimaced. "Oh, come now! Are you trying to tell me that, so quickly, you've not only found the area where it lies, but also you can detect how far down it is hidden?"

Golgren looked up at the mage. "Your staff. Can it break open the way?"

"What do you think this is? A shovel?" Still, despite his protest, Tyranos stepped over to the spot. "Show me exactly where."

Golgren used the tip of the blade to mark the location. That done, the half-breed moved back. Grunting, Tyranos braced himself then muttered a spell.

The crystal glowed.

The ground cracked open. The fissure was only a couple of feet wide at first, but then it spread in both directions. Tyranos shifted to one side as he continued to press his spell.

"How deep?" he asked. When Golgren shrugged, the wizard growled, "Wonderful."

The fissure became some twenty feet long and half again as wide. Tyranos glanced beyond Golgren and him in the direction of Garantha. The risk of discovery increased with each moment that the mage continued his spellcasting.

With a gasp, Tyranos withdrew the staff. The fissure was several yards deep. The wizard eyed it with skepticism. "You've got your hole. Now what? I don't see a damned thing!"

In response, Golgren thrust the dagger between his teeth and jumped into the fissure. Even with only one hand, he expertly gained a hold on the side then continued climbing down. The half-breed moved swiftly and efficiently, well aware that each second was precious.

He was not quite at the bottom of the fissure when he sensed through the dagger that he was near his goal. Golgren paused to study the jagged sides of the crevice.

The rock supporting one of his feet loosened. Golgren managed to shift his foot before the piece broke away. He was still far enough from the bottom to injure or even kill himself if he fell.

Facing the wall upon which he hung, Golgren noticed that the dagger's reaction seemed muted. The half-breed peered over at the opposing side.

The moment he did, the dagger reacted. Golgren braced himself then pushed off.

He caught hold of another rock thrusting out from the other wall. His body slammed against the hard surface, nearly causing him to lose his grip. Golgren bit down. The blade shifted, the edge nicking the side of his mouth.

Ignoring the blood that began to dribble out of his mouth, the deposed Grand Khan inspected the wall.

From the dagger, he sensed that he was very near. Unfortunately, Golgren's single hand became an impediment. He could not hold on with his other limb. However, Golgren made no move to call to Tyranos for help.

Looking down, the half-breed sought out more secure footing. Managing that, he braced himself then reached for where he thought he had to search.

His digging consisted of short scratches and grabs into the dirt and stone then quickly clutching a hold again. Golgren did not give up when the first few attempts yielded nothing. The dagger had led him so close; he was determined to succeed.

His fingers grazed something that felt like metal. Golgren did not feel any hope yet, for in that place there would be a lot of metal buried in the stone and rock—weapons, armor, and such.

On his next grab, he loosened his as-yet-unseen find. Bracing himself better, Golgren thrust his fingers deeper.

The hidden object finally came free. However, it did so with such ease that not only did Golgren almost lose his balance, but the object itself came *flying* out.

He caught it at the last moment then twisted back to the wall. With only his thumb and index finger, he clutched his prize and managed to get just enough of a grip on the rock with the rest of his hand to keep from falling.

Moments later, Golgren returned to the surface.

The wizard cocked his head. "I'd ask if you found what you were looking for, but I know you too well."

Paying no heed to Tyranos, Golgren focused on the direction in which Garantha lay. "We are done here. It is time to go and meet Safrag."

"And the other."

"And the other," the half-breed agreed. "Tell me, Tyranos, how great is your desire for the Fire Rose?"

The hooded form did not answer, which was answer enough for Golgren. The half-breed readied his dagger. "I tell you this, wizard, if you do as I say, you may have the chance to wield it yet. If you seek it on your own, I promise nothing for you."

"Would it surprise you to know I've little faith in your promises right now? It's you, me, maybe Idaria and Chasm against the Titans and the gargoyles' master. Who would you bet on, oh Grand Khan?"

Golgren's answer was immediate. "On myself."

"Naturally."

"Will you listen to what I wish?"

Tyranos smiled grimly. "I really don't have much of a choice at this point." The broad-shouldered spellcaster gestured curtly at the half-breed. "So. What's your great plan?"

Golgren displayed the dagger. "It begins with this."

XXI

Morgada's Betrayal

An ominous stillness hung over the ogre capital, so noticeable that even the most stalwart ogres remained in their domiciles despite the constant threat of their surroundings being wildly altered at Safrag's whim. Something was in the air.

The only ogres visible were the guards on duty, and their grim expressions betrayed their desires to be somewhere far away. Those standing watch by the palace were the most unsettled, for they knew that anything that happened would surely involve the Titans and, thus, the palace.

All could sense the imminent danger, though they did not know in what form it would come. Nor did they know how much time remained of the calm before the storm, which as it turned out, was no time at all.

Morgada materialized in her chamber and let out an uncharacteristic gasp at what she found. Atolgus and Wargroch lay on the floor of the chamber, obviously slain in battle. The female Titan gritted her teeth at the sight then noticed more bodies beyond the hole that someone had blasted in the wall leading to the corridor. There were several guards beyond, all lying as if asleep, yet certainly dead. The smell of blood, generally intoxicating to her, instead repelled the sorceress.

"Falstoch is no more."

She spun to find Safrag standing behind her. "Great one! What do you mean about Falstoch?"

The lead Titan, the Fire Rose nestled in the crook of his arm like a beloved infant, casually pointed to a moist spot on the floor. "That's all that remains of Falstoch, who was most loyal. I learned of his death from the guards who, failing their initial duties out of misplaced loyalty, I killed a moment ago."

Morgada could not refrain from shivering. "But how? What happened here?"

"The mongrel and his pet wizard. How else, dear Morgada?"

"We must avenge Falstoch!" she quickly responded. "Let me be the one to deal the fatal blow."

Safrag shook his head. He looked to the Fire Rose. "Falstoch's death is a minor note. What matters more is that I sense the game has reached its end. He's come for what belongs to me, fool that he is."

"Golgren is here?"

The lead Titan sneered. "I've only just realized that the great mongrel himself is only a tool! No, Morgada, I mean the master of the winged watchers! *He* has come! Shall we go to meet him, you and I?"

She immediately moved to join him, standing on the side where he held the Fire Rose. "I am honored to serve."

"Yes, you should be."

In the blink of an eye, their surroundings changed.

They were still in Dai Ushran yet outside—indeed, *atop*—the palace.

And moreover, so were the rest of the Titans, every *one* of them.

One bowed, an act that the rest quickly imitated. "We have come at your summons, Safrag, though you now leave the realm's borders filled with marching Uruv Suurt, mounted humans, and hundreds of foul gargoyles."

"My lord—" Morgada began, confused.

"Hush," Safrag quietly ordered her. To the other Titans, he said, "Let the fools savor their moment of triumph. They won't have it for long. Besides, we are here on a far more important mission than a matter of a few insects with swords and claws."

He turned to Morgada and, to her surprise, *handed* her the Fire Rose.

The other sorcerers looked at one another in surprise and, for some, consternation. All coveted the artifact for their own purposes, and all had considered ways by which they might convince Safrag to let them use it, if only for a brief time. But he had given it to Morgada as if it were nothing.

Her face lit up. "My lord! I—I am honored! Truly, I didn't think myself worthy of this!"

"No one else is more worthy of *this,* dear Morgada," he replied with a fatherly smile. "Come now! Isn't there something you wanted to do with it?"

Morgada's expression was caught between anticipation and confusion. "What—why, of course—yes!"

"Then do as you please."

With those words, a change came over the female Titan. Gone were all traces of worship for Safrag.

Instead, Morgada leered at him. Those sorcerers who could see her face muttered among themselves and did their best to edge away from Safrag.

A sudden wind whipped up, shoving the reluctant spellcasters back to where they had been standing. Still seemingly ignorant of the change coming over Morgada, Safrag politely commanded, "Remain in your places, all of you."

"Yes," interjected Morgada, both hands tightly holding her prize. "It'll make it easier to get rid of you all!"

Before the other Titans could react to her declaration, Safrag shook his head in mock sadness. "Dear Morgada, you made the wrong choice."

The Fire Rose flared but not as it ever had done previously. A black radiance spread from the artifact to Morgada's fingers. She gasped and tried to let go but could not. The female Titan's face twisted from triumph to fear.

"Did you think me so befuddled by your beauty that I'd stay ignorant of your plans of betrayal?" Safrag grimly asked her. "If there is one thing I'll not tolerate, it's betrayal. I gave you a chance to redeem yourself, but you chose to stay aligned with the master of the gargoyles."

"You—you could not have known!" Morgada's arms and much of her upper torso were bathed in the black radiance. Despite her legs being free, still, she did not move . . . or perhaps could not.

"I am *Safrag*. I always know. Unlike Dauroth, I did not accept the dreams and ambitions suddenly thrust upon me as divine! Every urge, every gift, bears a price. I discovered that price the moment the first of the winged watchers appeared, and I knew then that your unique presence could hardly be a coincidence any more than some of the advantages that came my way."

Morgada could no longer respond, for her entire body was encased in the radiance. Only her frightened, golden eyes remained visible.

The Fire Rose transformed, suddenly becoming a cylindrical tube made of some black, gleaming metal.

Safrag held up his hand. In it materialized yet another Fire Rose. "The true one. Did you think I would ever let someone else even *touch* it?" The lead Titan's eyes blazed. *"Anyone?"*

If that last comment disturbed the other sorcerers, none dared show their true emotions. All had only to gaze at Morgada to see what could befall them.

"The spell was forged with the Fire Rose, so you should be honored for that much, dear Morgada. Set to unleash if you proved your loyalty to any other but me. I am fair, after all."

He held the Fire Rose toward her. The energies within swirled furiously.

The black cylinder crumbled to dust. Morgada's hands followed suit. The female Titan watched in silent horror as her arms also turned to ash. The dread spell overtook her body, her legs, her head.

Morgada managed a faltering gasp just before she collapsed into a pile of black dust. The pile of ash then swirled around, re-forming.

In her place stood a lifelike onyx statue of Safrag.

"You honor me with your presence," he remarked with a chuckle.

But as Safrag laughed at Morgada's folly, a sound like roiling thunder caused the Titans to look up. However, it was not thunder; rather, it was the beating of countless wings.

The third and largest of Xiryn's flocks had been unleashed over the capital.

Grinning, Safrag spread his arms as if welcoming the creatures. The Fire Rose burned brightly.

"It is time to put my empire in order!" he shouted not only to the other sorcerers, but also to the gargoyles, even. "It is time, don't you agree, oh Grand Khan?"

And Golgren, who materialized but a short distance behind him, bared his teeth and responded, "Yes, sorcerer. I agree."

∽⊶⊙⊷∾

Frustration mounting, Stefan urged the elves forward. The refugees were moving as fast as they could, but that was not what piqued the Solamnic.

"I should be there," he muttered to himself as he paused to watch the column progress. "I should be there."

"A battle is won on many fronts," commented someone next to him.

The cleric did not show any surprise. He had become used to Kiri-Jolith's abrupt appearances. "So I understand, my lord, but I yearn to be there to give my all! Rather me than her! What good is Idaria in this situation?"

The bison-headed god went unnoticed by the elves. Like other deities, Kiri-Jolith could choose at whim who did and who did not see or hear him. "She may be doing the most good of all. A battle is won on many fronts, and many of those fronts do not involve swords and axes. Thoughts and emotions are also powerful tools and ones that even the gods cannot ultimately control."

"I don't understand."

310

"Now you know what it is like to be a god of Krynn."

Kiri-Jolith gestured. Ahead of the column, a figure appeared. He was a perfect likeness of Stefan.

"The conjuration will suffice for them at this point," the deity remarked. "The Titans are paying no mind to their sanctum. Their leader has other interests at the moment."

Stefan went down on one knee in homage. "I'm grateful for this last boon, my lord!"

"Do not be. This is the only help that I can grant you, just as I have been able to give the Grand Khan one last hope. From here, you and he must find the path to victory. I already have overstepped my bounds. Because of that, for Sirrion and I, there must be a reckoning of sorts, whatever the outcome."

"I don't understand."

Kiri-Jolith frowned, though it was obvious that his frustration was not with Stefan. "This is the Age of Mortals, Sir Stefan Rennert. However much we gods still interfere and desire to interfere, it is you and yours that ultimately will tip the balance. How you do that will help determine which of us—Sirrion or I—is at the disadvantage when we make our case to the others."

The Solamnic rose, suddenly troubled. "My lord, I fear to ask . . . but Chasm had to fly after Idaria after the medallion would not work to send me to her, and—"

"Because you were needed where you were." The bison-headed god's deep brown eyes stared into Stefan's. "Do you think I would raise up this conjuration of you only to leave you without the means?" When Stefan hesitated, the god chuckled. "Yes, you are wise not to trust even me. My kind has a habit of leaving mortals caught in the midst of things!"

Kiri-Jolith gestured and Stefan vanished. Still invisible to the elf refugees, the god of just cause surveyed the conjuration for a moment longer as it led the refugee column forward. There was an immense exhaustion in Kiri-Jolith's face that had not been evident when he had spoken with the human. The deity had done his best to hide his weary condition.

"May you fare well," he whispered, speaking not merely to the column or the departed Stefan. "May you all fare well . . . if it is still possible."

◦⚬⟡⚬◦

Chasm's powerful wings bore Idaria along at a dizzying pace, but still Garantha looked distant. The elf grew impatient.

"Can we go any faster?" she asked him, feeling guilty for asking.

The gargoyle grunted and exerted himself all the more. Every muscle showed strain. Idaria flushed, a sign of her guilt at making such a demand. Chasm obviously was weary. The gargoyle's breathing was rapid, and sweat dripped from him.

"It is beginning," the elf muttered to herself. She had whispered the same words more than once over the past several minutes. Somehow, Idaria sensed that the confrontation between Golgren, Safrag, and the gargoyles' lord was already starting.

She felt a warmth on her chest: the griffon pendant.

Idaria finally understood. "You are what tells me that? You?"

As if in response, the pendant grew warmer.

Clutching the High Ogre artifact, she stared at the

landscape ahead. "If only you could do something to help me get there swifter."

Nothing happened. No wind suddenly rose up to carry Chasm and her faster toward the capital, nor was the gargoyle's strength rejuvenated.

With some disappointment, Idaria let the warm pendant again settle upon her breast. She stared ahead, trying to draw the distant horizon toward her.

Then a *hole* opened in the sky ahead. A gold radiance framed it. Its width and breadth were just enough to encompass both the gargoyle and his charge.

Chasm instinctively veered. Idaria let out a belated protest.

"No!" she called. "We want to head towards it!"

The gargoyle issued a questioning grunt.

The elf held up the still-warm pendant. "I called it into being with this! It's our path to the capital!"

"Smells not right." Chasm growled.

"What did you say?"

"Smells not right!" The gargoyle veered more to the north, seeking to go around the hole's side.

The magical gap swelled to more than ten times its original proportions. Only barely did Chasm avoid soaring headlong into it.

Despite her companion's wariness, Idaria thought the gargoyle was wrong and struggled in his grip. The abrupt imbalance caused the gargoyle to involuntarily change direction again.

They swung toward the hole. Chasm growled, attempting to regain his balance. He turned from the edge of the astounding gap.

The hole swelled again. This time it grew to too great a size for the gargoyle to avoid.

Idaria smiled but a sudden coldness on her chest made the smile falter. She touched the pendant and found that it was the cause of the chill.

And the nearer the pair got to the hole, the colder the pendant became.

"No!" she cried. "No! Turn back!"

It was too late. Chasm and the elf plunged into the magical gap. Instantly, they were tossed around by powerful energies. The elf's hair rose as if electrified. Idaria bit back a cry of pain as Chasm squeezed tighter to maintain his grip on her. They were surrounded by nothing but the swirling energy of a thousand different and constantly changing colors.

"Bad!" the winged creature roared. "Bad!"

Their surroundings crackled, and once more they were in the air.

But they were not alone.

The moment it became clear where they were, Chasm attempted to veer around and head back into the hole. However, before he could do that, the portal simply dissipated.

Undaunted, the gargoyle tried to rise higher into the air. As he did, however, a wide net fell upon him. Chasm twisted to escape the new danger, but in doing so, the gargoyle lost part of his grip on Idaria. The elf tried to grab onto him yet only succeeded in making Chasm lose the rest of his hold.

Idaria slipped free. She screamed as she plummeted.

A powerful paw grabbed her left wrist while another seized her right ankle. The halt was jarring; for a moment, Idaria lost consciousness.

Recovering, she tried to look around for Chasm. Instead, another gargoyle face, that of a dusky, beaked male, leered down at her.

"Master has need of you," the new gargoyle rumbled.

She struggled, though to no avail. There was no sign of Chasm.

The gargoyle who had spoken took charge of her. He descended with her toward a place among the high rocks. As they neared, Idaria made out Garantha, not all that far away to the west. There was a strange and unsettling orange-red aura rising from the city and, more obviously, a vast swarm of creatures like her captor circling above the capital. The swarm was clearly attacking something within the city.

"Golgren," she murmured.

The gargoyle made a warning sound. Around them, scores of his kind perched on whatever outcroppings were available. Even with so many attacking, their master still had more in reserve.

I have waited long, so very long. And gargoyles breed so quickly. the familiar voice murmured in her head.

The shrouded figure materialized before Idaria just as her guard set her down on the ground. Although she could not see the face behind the cloth, the pale eyes evinced pleasure.

Pleasure was an emotion that Idaria herself knew she would never feel again. "Why?" she all but spit at the horrific spellcaster. "Why bother letting me think I escaped only to play this game?"

She heard his laughter in her head. *My puppet had to hear your earnestness! Even though he knew that you could not have escaped on your own, he still would like to recognize in you a desperate need to help him at all costs! You proved yourself! You proved that he could trust you in the end.*

"And he can!"

And that is what we are counting on. As the gargoyle king spoke, around them formed the ghastly entourage from the citadel. *That is what will restore us to the glorious forms we once wore, as well.*

Idaria stared in shock at the monstrous assembly. She could sense the foul eagerness in the black pits that were their eyes. "You could not have planned for this . . . or for the Titans!"

He gave her a mock bow. *What was not planned was adapted for, and the Titans have been almost as providential as our Golgren.*

The pendant grew warmer again, so much so that the elf expected that the gargoyle king surely sensed or saw the relic. Yet neither he nor his ghoulish companions reacted as might be expected. Idaria was not certain whether to take hope in that or mark it as a sign that the pendant would avail her nothing.

He trusts you utterly, the shrouded figure went on, leaning close. *He knows that you of all would sacrifice whatever necessary. He believes in you, and thus, your lie will be the final stroke that gives control of the Fire Rose over to me.*

Idaria might have tried to deny his words, but her body would not obey her. She could not move. She could only look into his white eyes.

Do not be so crestfallen, elf. A chilling hand stroked her cheek, the sensation like that of icicles scraping her flesh. *I will not kill him. I will be him, and then you will have both of us, and we will have you . . . and all Krynn.*

XXII

WAR OVER GARANTHA

Dagger gripped tightly, Golgren did not look at all shocked to know Safrag had been aware of his existence. Nor did it appear the lead Titan was disappointed by that lack of shock.

And both were not in the least surprised to find the air filled with gargoyles.

"Persistent gnats," Safrag remarked. Casually turning his back on Golgren, he confronted his fellow sorcerers. "I will let you feel the gifts of the Fire Rose and allow each of you to choose exactly how you would prefer to remove these pests!"

The artifact flared. From its petals burst fiery bolts that arrowed out and struck each Titan. However, rather than cause the Titans harm, it instead made each sorcerer raise his fists in what could only be described as utter exultation.

"It—it's so much more than I could have ever imagined!" sang Gadjul in the Titan tongue. "All we were . . . all we are is nothing compared to it!"

He thrust one fist toward a part of the vast swarm just out of reach of the sorcerers. From that fist erupted blazing, black streaks of energy that mirrored the bolts of fire that flowed into him and the others.

His spell spread as it reached the attackers, encompassing dozens. Some of the gargoyles wielded objects that briefly seemed to stave off the Titan's spell, but that defense was short lived.

The gargoyles caught in Gadjul's spell twisted like wet cloths being tightly wrung out. Their cries were enough to disturb even the hardiest ogres hiding below. Not so the Titans, however. Gadjul only laughed and pressed his spell.

From fearsome, winged beasts, the gargoyles were transformed into water drops, but they were water drops that rose skyward. The drops blinded those gargoyles directly behind. Indeed, each drop *burned* like the energies within the Fire Rose itself. From the many he had decimated, Gadjul had created death for scores more.

The other Titans did not stand idle while Gadjul kept busy. Each was casting a spell of his own choosing, using the power of the Fire Rose to terrible effect. The sky filled with monstrous transformations that began to wreak havoc on those gargoyles higher in the formation. The winged attackers perished in droves, some turning into unrecognizable shapes or dispersing into liquids, energies, or clouds of sinister gases.

A grinning Safrag glanced at Golgren, who had not budged. The lead Titan indicated his followers with his free hand. "The smallest of the Fire Rose's gifts and look what they can do with it! The magic of the Titans is a poor thing compared to such power, and the Titans themselves are a poor creation of a failed goddess."

With that, Safrag's eyes grew brighter. The Fire Rose also surged.

The other Titans began to change form even as they continued their assault on the gargoyles. They grew thinner and taller yet, and their skin changed from blue to a blinding gold. Their faces became of one kind—semblances of Safrag's—and long, silver hair cascaded down their backs. Their garments became form-fitting robes of a fire-red color, with a blazing flower symbol etched in their chests.

"So much more appropriate," the lead Titan commented. "Why bother with the false legacy of the High Ogres? Why not create a new order? A race of such perfection that even our ancestors looked like shambling mockeries in comparison?"

Still, Golgren did not move. Safrag's brow briefly furrowed, but the half-breed was too far away physically to attack the sorcerer. However, the sorcerer nevertheless finally raised his hand toward his adversary.

The building beneath Golgren's feet suddenly softened. Before he could react, his feet were sealed up to the ankles.

"You will watch all of this, mongrel," Safrag cheerfully remarked. "You of all people deserve that experience! In fact, I may even let you live when all is said and done, live so that you can savor the rise of the ogre race and the transformation of all Krynn by my hand!" He chuckled. "Of course, you won't necessarily look as you do now . . . or look like *anything* anyone has seen before."

Safrag turned from Golgren.

And the half-breed threw the ancient dagger at the sorcerer's back.

The weapon struck Safrag, but as it did, it, too,

transformed. The blade split open, bending five different ways. The handle became a pair of bright silver gossamer wings. The altered weapon fluttered up, changed into a fantastic flying flower with long, leafy petals of gold.

"In the end, so very predictable," Safrag stated. He gestured and the flower hovered under his nostrils. As if he had no care in the world, the towering sorcerer—himself still unaltered—sniffed his creation then sent it on its way. "Now be good and watch as I do what both you and Dauroth could only dream of doing."

With the other sorcerers keeping the gargoyles at bay, Safrag scanned Garantha. Clutching the Fire Rose with both hands, he held it out over the main part of the capital.

"Come out, my children!" he called in Common, his voice booming like thunder and causing both his followers and foes to momentarily falter. "Come out, my children, and become your future!"Garantha blazed with the crimson-orange light of the Fire Rose. As Golgren silently watched, the light began to settle over the dwellings of the city's inhabitants.

A flat stone roof *peeled* as if it were a piece of fruit. Another followed then another and another until, in moments, all that the eye could see had been opened in that fashion.

And from each building, figures began to rise up into the air. The ogres of Garantha . . . or Safrag's Dai Ushran.

Most were far enough away that their expressions could not be seen, and not one made a sound, likely as Safrag dictated. The few that Golgren could see close up were fearful. Trapped by such powerful magic, their bodily strength was nothing. They were reduced to little more than helpless children.

By the scores then the hundreds, they were gathered up. Whatever caste they were from no longer mattered. In the eyes of the Titan, they were all lacking.

But not for long . . .

"I will not rule over beasts!" Safrag proclaimed. "I will be a god above gods!"

The Fire Rose burned. As it did, so, too, did the captive ogres.

However, before Safrag could fulfill his intentions, a hooded figure suddenly materialized behind him. One hand outstretched toward Golgren, Tyranos thrust the head of the staff into the lead Titan's back just as he had done before, to Falstoch.

Accompanied by violent sparks of magical energy, the crystal bore through Safrag, its head emerging out of his chest. The Titan let out a gasp.

Only then the sorcerer steadied. He seized the crystal with one hand. Fiery forces from Sirrion's gift poured into the crystal.

With a guttural roar, Tyranos went flying back. He would have fallen to his death, but a gargoyle appeared from behind another building to catch him.

Chasm, who had escaped his captors too late to help Idaria, hefted his master back to the roof. The wizard regained his balance just as Safrag began to pull the staff by its head through his torso. He shot Golgren an incredulous look.

"Even death is transformed by the Fire Rose!" Safrag cried as he tugged the last of the staff free. The removal was accompanied by a horrific sucking sound, for the gaping wound swiftly began to seal itself. There was no sign of blood. In fact, what could be glimpsed inside the Titan's wound was not akin to tissue, organs, muscle, or even bone. It was as if Safrag were made of one gray, solid material throughout his body.

Tyranos muttered a spell. The staff vanished from Safrag's hand, returning to his grasp.

The sorcerer remained amused. "Oh, you could have had that back! Once, I might have prized that toy, but now it is nothing, just as you are."

Pain suddenly wracked Tyranos. He tried to move but could not. Crystalline growths spread over his body.

"I shall shape a temple to honor my achievements, with each of you to mark the passing of an age of fools before the rise of the new Golden Era."

Tyranos tried another spell, but his mouth was no longer working. As with Morgada, only his eyes remained untouched by the change. The rest of him had become pure, transparent crystal.

Safrag shook his head at the wizard. "One more alteration! Let us see your shame in all its glory!"

The crystallized mage twisted. The harsh crack of glass accompanied each turn, each alteration. Tyranos's form swelled and his face expanded.

In moments, there stood a statue of a minotaur, a statue whose only sign of life was two glaring eyes.

"Uruv Suurt you were born; Uruv Suurt you shall forever exist!"

Chasm leaped from the shadows, seeking to avenge his master. He got no farther than Tyranos, for the air around him solidified to stone, and the gargoyle was swallowed whole.

"The would-be wizard and his loyal pet. You two act as one; you shall be one."

The captured gargoyle was flung into Tyranos. The wizard shattered but the pieces immediately flew back, attaching themselves to Chasm. Minotaur and gargoyle were fused together, creating a macabre, crystalline figure with wings, two distinct heads, and eight mismatched limbs, the last of those creating an image reminiscent of a strange arachnid.

The lead Titan started to turn back to the task of remaking his race when he noticed the efforts of his fellow sorcerers. Safrag looked displeased.

The Fire Rose brightened. The other Titans became as wet clay. They shrank slightly and grew broader of shoulder. Their hair reshaped into lion's manes of gold; their skin became shining silver. Their eyes were piercing black, and instead of five fingers, each hand boasted four elongated ones ending in nails of pearl. They wore full suits of thin, flexible armor that matched their hair in brilliance and color. The only hint of their previous incarnations was the symbol of the Fire Rose that adorned breastplates.

Yet that did not please Safrag either, as one might have expected. He shook his head, declaring, "Not perfect. It must be perfect. I shall have to start all over again."

At that, a few of the other sorcerers raised their voices in protest. "Great Master," one called carefully and humbly. "These forms are wondrous! There's no need for further change! They cannot be outdone!"

"At least experiment on the populace first," suggested a second. The Titans saw nothing wrong with treating the rest of their race like raw materials to be used however they pleased, but when it came to themselves . . .

Safrag frowned. He held the Fire Rose high, and a ceiling of flame suddenly draped over the capital and drove back the attacking gargoyles. The winged creatures for the moment no longer held much interest for him, however, and he asked of the dissenters, "Are you then questioning my decisions?"

Those who had protested were quick to shake their heads or answer wisely. Yet still the lead Titan did not look satisfied. He fixed his baleful gaze on the first and second who had spoken.

"Perhaps these forms would be more to your liking," Safrag said curtly.

The pair shrieked as their bodies bent and twisted. All the beauty of a Titan vanished in each of the two, and a more familiar—not to mention *grotesque*—shape was theirs.

They had been changed into ordinary ogres. From their expressions, Safrag had left them with all their gained intellect intact, which all the more visibly crushed their spirits.

"Is that more to your liking?" When the pair shook their heads, the lead Titan smiled. The Fire Rose flared, and the two were restored to their previous shapes. Safrag tittered.

Above Garantha, the ceiling of flames faded. The gargoyles immediately resumed their attack, regardless of the great cost to them thus far and the little they had to show for that cost.

"Finish the vermin," Safrag ordered indifferently. "The power of the Fire Rose flows through me into you. Finish them off and, if you please me, I will deign to hear your thoughts on what the final guise of our race ought to look like."

The Titans did not hesitate to obey. Again, gargoyles perished by the scores, in numerous and ghastly ways, as the Titans eagerly vented their frustrations on their enemy.

Safrag had almost forgotten Golgren, but it would have been good for the Titan to glance one last time at his foe. He would have seen, then, that the half-breed was *free,* thanks to Tyranos, who had accomplished that feat—one of two magics he had bestowed on Golgren—before attacking the Titan.

And Golgren stood poised, ready to make use of the *second* of the wizard's gifts, when suddenly a voice whispered in his head.

The moment is now. Rise up and reach forth to the Fire Rose. Now.

Although aware that such a strategy at that moment was probably suicidal, Golgren found his body obeying. Against his will, he raced toward the sorcerer.

Somehow Safrag sensed him coming. The Titan spun around and, giving the half-breed a patronizing smile, beckoned him on.

The roof over Golgren became fluid. A raging river of liquefied stone, it washed Golgren toward the waiting Safrag.

Without warning, the Fire Rose quivered and fought to escape the Titan's grip.

Safrag let out a gasp and held tight his precious prize. The Fire Rose leaned toward Golgren, as if attracted to him.

"No! It's mine! Mine!" Safrag succeeded in maintaining his hold, yet the Fire Rose continued to strain toward Golgren.

Something *broke* from it, a small fragment, the very fragment that Safrag had once used to locate the artifact.

Seize it. Seize it, ordered the voice.

Golgren did what the voice commanded. The fragment flew unerringly into his palm. His fingers tightened around it.

Golgren once more stood on a solid surface. He bared his teeth in a grin and displayed the fragment for Safrag to behold.

All else forgotten, the sorcerer laughed harshly. "That tiny bit will avail you nothing, mongrel! The full Fire Rose is a thousand times stronger!"

Sirrion's creation burned brighter than ever but so, too, suddenly, did the piece that Golgren wielded. A monstrous light erupted around both figures. Heat more scorching than the noonday sun beat down on the two adversaries, yet Golgren and Safrag refused to succumb. A battle of wills took place.

And between the duo materialized a third, terrible being:

Xiryn.

The High Ogre's snowy eyes were wide with triumph.

My two cat's paws, he spoke in their minds, each word taunting Golgren and Safrag. *My perfect puppets.*

Golgren struggled to move. It came as no comfort to him that Safrag, too, was finding it impossible.

Xiryn extended a bony hand toward each of them. The two could do nothing to prevent themselves from joining with the shrouded figure. Safrag was forced to his knees.

The end of the long waiting is at hand! Xiryn proclaimed, his words ringing harshly in their heads. *The centuries upon centuries of striving, of being patient, are at last at end.*

As his two captives closed with him, the gargoyle

king placed a hand on each of their shoulders. Golgren and Safrag both shivered.

One we shall be: the master,—he indicated himself—*the strength,*—he nodded his cowled head to Safrag—*and the impossible vessel*—he gave a last nod to Golgren. *The destiny of the High Ogres—of all ogres—has finally come.*

XXIII

THE GARGOYLE KING ASCENDANT

Sarth sat just beyond the walls of Garantha, drawing images in the dirt. They were not like those of the past—reminders of what he needed to remember or necessarily veiled warnings to Golgren—but rather a final testament to what he had done and what he still needed to do.

"Welcome, Knight," he said in perfect Common, his accent even hinting of Solamnic origins. Of course, Sarth could speak in whatever accent he needed. The spellcasting had taken centuries, but it had proven useful many times.

"Who are you?" Stefan Rennert demanded, coming around to confront the wizened figure. "You wear the guise of an aged ogre, but your voice indicates otherwise!"

Sarth did not look up. "It would have been better if your patron would have told you, but it does not really matter in the end. We face the same enemies, and we hope to save the same people. That is what you need to know."

"Golgren and Idaria! You know where they are?"

Sarth cackled. "Where would Golgren be but in the worst of places seeking to make destiny his? He is inside the city, Knight. As for the elf . . ." Sarth drew a pair of ominous eyes then two long lines where the nose and mouth should have been. "Where do you think?"

"The fiend has her?" Stefan started toward the gates of the city, but Sarth snapped his fingers. The noise was so loud that the human had to look back.

"Think why Kiri-Jolith deposited you near me and not near them. I have considered that fact carefully since your arrival."

"I've no time for your games!" the Solamnic retorted. Yet Stefan did not depart but rather stepped closer to Sarth.

"You have little time," the aged figure agreed. "And I have had far too much of it. We are at opposite ends of the spectrum in that regard, which makes us need one another."

"Make some sense."

"As you wish." Sarth stood and, in doing so, revealed to the knight that he was more than a head taller than the human, despite initial impressions. His fine, patrician features made the ogre look as handsome as an elf. He wore a rich, silken robe of blue, with black stars crossing diagonally over the chest.

Stefan steeled himself. "I know what you are."

"Then you know to listen. You must be prepared to follow exactly as I suggest. Our part to play may be significant; it may be of little value. That depends on what the others do with what we give them to work with, good or ill. Are you prepared to listen, human?"

"I am."

Sarth nodded. "We won't survive this."

The Solamnic's expression did not waver. "I am past that concern."

The High Ogre smiled sadly. "Yes, we both are, aren't we?"

Sarth drew an image in the air between them. The image—a griffon's wing—flared a bright gold.

The pair faded away.

∽∾◯∾∿

Idaria struggled in the clutches of her monstrous captors. Xiryn's horrific entourage stood as though frozen. They clearly were waiting for some silent summons from him, and the reason for that filled her with dread and apprehension, especially for Golgren.

"Set me free!" the elf demanded again. "This is not right! It goes against all aspects of nature! It is an abomination!"

The figures remained silent. Yet in their hollow eyes, it was possible to read their hunger. That hunger had built up greatly over the many centuries, as they had surrendered to Xiryn's cause.

A ragged figure only vaguely identifiable as once being female, judging by the strands of hair on her skull and the slighter shape of her rotting form, suddenly looked up with more animation than any of the other creatures had shown. The others followed suit. They pressed forward eagerly, eyeing the capital.

Yessss . . . came the wind that was not wind but the collective voice of those surrounding Idaria. *Yesss* . . .

She felt their powerful, ancient magic stir. Although what Xiryn intended was awful in and of itself, again all that came to the elf's mind was a single name: "Golgren . . ."

Xiryn had told her what her part in his plan was to be, and that part was about to be played.

She would prove Golgren's downfall, and there was nothing that Idaria could do about it.

◦⌖◦

The Titans did not stay idle upon Xiryn's return. They knew who he must be, and Gadjul was the first to react. The sorcerer used the energies the Fire Rose had fed him through Safrag to strike at the shrouded figure.

But before the spell could be completed, a cold, flesh-less hand seized the Titan at the small of his back. A white, deathly aura passed over Gadjul, and although he remained conscious, his body slumped as though only invisible strings kept it from falling.

The ghastly figure behind him was one of Xiryn's entourage. His appearance startled the other sorcerers, if only briefly. Some quickly recovered and moved to act against the new threat.

Then they, too, were seized from behind.

One of Xiryn's creatures stood next to each Titan and, although they were only roughly half as tall, they clearly commanded the much-larger sorcerers through their hands. As one, they made the Titans straighten. The eyes of the giant sorcerers were filled with confusion and not a little fear.

Atop the surrounding buildings, others of the gargoyle king's followers appeared. They stared not at their comrades, but at the ogres of Garantha, who still hung helpless in the air.

From where Golgren and Safrag also stood frozen, Xiryn chuckled once more. *The rest will have their pick from the populace so neatly gathered by the Titans . . . once matters up here are settled, naturally.*

Safrag found the will to speak, if briefly. "I . . . know you. I know your voice."

Yes, the one in your dreams, the one urging you to take your "rightful" place over your master, he who found the strength to defy my will, even after the goddess Takhisis had abandoned him and his hopes. But you . . . you were so much easier to sway because you thought you knew everything.

Safrag managed a growl but no more.

Xiryn focused on Golgren. *And you, child of my ambitions, your every defiance of my wishes only has served in the end to make you more as I hoped.*

Golgren's gaze was all the half-breed needed to communicate his desires where Xiryn was concerned. The gargoyle king laughed then murmured something.

Both Golgren and Safrag groaned from renewed pain. Each felt as if their skin was slowly being peeled from their body.

The Fire Rose blazed. Its energies surged from the trio to the other Titans and their horrific captors, utterly enveloping both groups.

The sorcerers' bodies grew a translucent blue. The Titans began to shrink. They dwindled to the size of the decaying fiends that kept them frozen. Their mouths gaped like those of fish left to suffocate on land.

And when the Titans were no taller than Xiryn's followers, the ghoulish figures, their skeletal hands still pressing against the Titans' backs, began to *step into* the ogres' diaphanous forms. The Titans' eyes were the only indication that the sorcerers struggled against the act, but they struggled in vain.

The skeletal figures fit into the Titans as one might a garment, letting the sheer outlines drape about their fleshless bodies. Titan and ghoul merged. In doing so, the sorcerers faded while their captors began to take on new sinew over their bones. Veins wrapped over their arms, legs, torsos. Beating organs swelled to life, and skin began to cover what it had not for ages.

Glorious, golden skin wrapped over the skulls, and white strands of hair became lush silver or other grand colors. Death's-head grins became full-lipped smiles. Bodies filled out in both feminine and male fashion. Even the ragged garments mended, once more becoming opulent robes and gowns of black, gold, red, purple, and green.

The last of each Titan melded into their captors, their eyes pleading until the very end. In their place and that of Xiryn's sinister horde stood a legion of handsome and beautiful figures the likes of whom had not been seen in such numbers since the fall of their race all those centuries past.

The assembled High Ogres preened. They touched their perfect faces and graceful bodies, as if seeking to reassure themselves that they were truly, fully restored. Laughter broke among them, moving from one to another, laughter that was filled not only with triumph, but also with a little madness.

The Titans have provided worthy vessels. I thank you for that, Xiryn joked to Safrag. *Just as you two shall provide me with the ultimate vessel.*

He brought them closer yet, so Golgren and Safrag, though they were of different heights even on their knees, stared into one another's eyes. Golgren floated in the air, but Safrag was no less imprisoned than he. The hate the two shared became secondary to that which they felt for the gargoyle king.

The hate feeds me, so continue to dwell on it, the shrouded figure informed them. To Golgren, he added, *You are strong, so very strong, but just strong enough, even in your hate. You have the will needed to resist the temptation that the Titan could not but not enough will to resist me.*

The other High Ogres gathered around the trio. Their beauty was marred by the hunger their eyes still wielded. Their grins were as vicious as those of the sorcerers, even though the High Ogres' mouths did not evidence the same savage shark teeth. The ugliness that marred Xiryn's followers was due to the fact that, like the Titans, they were obsessed with the Fire Rose. They wanted it, needed it.

Above, the surviving gargoyles alighted onto whatever buildings suited their fancy. Once there, they hissed and shrieked their joy at their master's victory. At that moment, there seemed little difference between the savage creatures and their master's people.

My foolish enemies made certain that even if I found their hiding place for it, I could not wield the Fire Rose and that no natural creature of Krynn could do so for me! Xiryn said gleefully. *But in their overconfidence, they provided me with the clue I needed. You, who should not exist, have given me at last my prize!*

Safrag could only stare in bitterness, but Golgren, pressing, finally felt his fingers begin to move. Feeling hope, he threw all his will into his remaining appendage.

It, too, moved. Motion was his again, but for how long was a question. Golgren let the fragment from the Fire Rose slip to the last two fingers then shoved his entire hand up.

His remaining fingers sought Xiryn's throat, but instead he grabbed the gargoyle king by the cloth covering the bottom half of his face.

Startled, Xiryn pulled back. For his effort, Golgren ended up with the cloth itself. He nearly lost his precarious hold on the fragment. Only with the best effort—and the smallest of his fingers—did he manage to keep the piece pressed against his palm.

The desiccated face of the lead High Ogre stood revealed to his followers. His skin was withered and crisp. Although they had seen him like that in the past, some of his restored followers instinctively gasped.

Xiryn glared at them, his white eyes silencing all. He could not physically speak, his jaws barely held together by a few dried, ancient tendons, but his thoughts roared in Golgren's head like a raging thundercloud. *The melding could have been accomplished with little relative agony, a reward for faithful if ignorant service, but I think I will savor every last scream of yours, every last pleading.*

"I . . . do not . . . plead!" Golgren tipped forward, managing to seize Xiryn's robe at the chest.

The gargoyle king did not move back, for to do so would have meant releasing his hold on the pair. He also did not strike out immediately at Golgren, which was what the half-breed had counted on. Xiryn did not dare chance that in his fury he might slay the one being who would give him his precious Fire Rose.

The other High Ogres converged on the trio, hands grasping at he who dared touch their leader. Golgren gritted his teeth, trying not to let them separate him from Xiryn.

The Fire Rose and the fragment flared brightly.

Xiryn's followers were flung far in every direction by an invisible force. A few fell with screams from the palace rooftop, while others had to use their renewed powers to save themselves from a similar fate.

The reaction made Golgren grin darkly at his captor. "The Fire Rose is not all yours yet, Xiryn."

Oh, but it shall be, my child, the phantasm replied with equal confidence. He no longer tried to pull back from Golgren. *Have you not wondered at the wizard's pet being close enough to come to his aid? Do you not recall what last task you gave him and who was with him? He was of no more concern to me, and so when he tried to escape— without his companion—I permitted him. I knew he would come back to die, and she was all that was important . . . to the two of us.*

Xiryn's white eyes looked to the left. Despite himself, Golgren looked that direction. At first, all he saw were some of Xiryn's followers who awaited restoration from the populace. Then they parted, letting others edge to the forefront.

Held tight in the grip of two was *Idaria.*

A strong vessel I sought, Xiryn said. *But one that could also be managed, just in case he thought himself better than he was, a weakness that could be exploited, a weakness tested and retested.*

"Then you should have tested further. This elf is nothing to me. I have had a hundred like her."

A hundred like her? Truly? After all the trouble I went to in order to find just the right one? The one that touched the lonely spirit, the one that would in turn be touched despite her revulsion? The shrouded fiend laughed, his jaws shaking.

Golgren said nothing. His eyes went from Idaria to

337

Xiryn and back to the elf again. He opened his mouth to speak.

Then a voice familiar to him quite calmly said, "A weakness can also become a very powerful strength, Xiryn."

For the first time, Xiryn looked at a loss. The white eyes stared past Golgren and Safrag at a figure that the gargoyles' master seemed to know as well as the half-breed did, even though the newcomer was not exactly as Golgren had last seen him.

I know you, Xiryn finally answered. *I know you . . . and your foul mother.*

Sarth nodded sadly. He stood revealed as another of the handsome High Ogres, save that his face was lined with bitter experience. "Yes, Xiryn. We have known each other for far too long."

In the shaman's hands materialized a long, pointed staff, made of what appeared to be shining ivory. He raised the point toward Xiryn.

The gargoyle king reacted instinctively, his hands pulling back in a spellcasting gesture. In doing so, he released both of his captives.

Golgren and Safrag both turned on the ancient High Ogre. As they did, however, Xiryn struck out at what he evidently considered the greater threat: Sarth.

The shaman made no move to avoid certain death. Indeed, he did not even cast the spell that he had appeared ready to hurl at his rival. Instead, Sarth did nothing but smile with satisfaction as Xiryn's attack overtook him.

There was no subtlety to the shrouded sorcerer's spell. It struck Sarth hard. Pure energy of a gray hue spread over him. Sarth dropped his burning staff as his skin blackened. The shaman made no cry as he died, his burned body collapsing where he had stood.

Yet the distraction aided Golgren. Through the fragment, he used the Fire Rose against the gargoyle king. Xiryn could make no audible sound, but his sudden pain echoed in the heads of all.

However, Safrag also still held the full artifact and, in his own obsession, refused to yield his link to it. Against all reason, the Titan fought Golgren's will. The half-breed's attack faltered as he found himself battling on two mental fronts.

The unexpected opposition bought Xiryn the chance that he needed. Recovering enough to speak, he warned, *Recall your elf, my child! Recall what will happen to her! Accept your fate, and she will live! Do not, and my servants will ensure her death will be one that will give nightmares to you, or the Titan—*

But from the direction where Idaria was being held captive, there came a powerful battle cry. One of the ghouls went plummeting as an armored figure shoved him from the rooftop. A keen blade cut through the torso of another. An armored hand seized a startled Idaria and dragged her from the macabre throng.

Stefan Rennert had come to the rescue.

XXIV

SACRIFICE

We have lost, Idaria had thought as she had watched the spectacle unfold. Golgren was strong of will and wily, but he could not hope to defeat such odds. The evil that wielded the Fire Rose would eventually sweep all the lands, taking with it even her rescued people. *No one* would be able to escape it, no one.

That was before the strange figure had materialized near Golgren and the others. Idaria had not recognized him, but she, like the rest, had heard in her head the gargoyle king's recognition of him, recognition and *uncertainty*. The elf's hopes had been revived only to come crashing down a moment later when the would-be rescuer had perished so easily and without even actually doing anything. It almost seemed as if he had known all along that he would die.

"But why?" Idaria had blurted. "Why?"

The answer had come a moment later in the form of Stefan Rennert. The knight was suddenly among the ancient ghouls, slashing through them with stunning swiftness and expertise. Three of Xiryn's followers had already perished before the rest instinctively pulled back from the danger in their midst.

That gave the Solamnic the chance to act. Seizing Idaria, he pulled her toward the gap made by his charge.

"Hurry, my lady!"

"How can this be?" she shouted as they ran.

His tone was grim. "You may credit my patron in part, but for the most, thank the sacrifice of the one called Sarth!"

"Sarth!" The elf knew that name.

Stefan slashed at one figure trying to waylay them. The creature's bony hand went flying to the side. The ghoul clutched the ruined limb and retreated, but others kept reaching for them. "He was a High Ogre like them, only more . . . whole! His powers were limited from his long watch for their master, and he knew he had no chance against him!"

Idaria ducked grasping fingers. "Then why sacrifice himself?"

"Because he knows what you mean to Golgren . . . if you'll pardon me for saying so!"

His words left her speechless, even though they confirmed her innermost secrets.

Stefan fended off another of Xiryn's followers. He used a combination of his sword and the medallion hanging from his neck. On a hunch, the elf clutched the griffon pendant and held it up. As she hoped, those attackers nearest to her cringed at it.

Yet still their odds of escape dwindled, for the gargoyles were descending toward them from above. In another moment or two, they would be upon the pair.

The Solamnic refused to accept the inevitable, though.

"If we can just make it to the other ledge, Sarth left one spell set there for us! It was all he could do! A brief portal! It'll take us back to the refugees!"

If he thought his explanation would urge her on, the Solamnic was sorely mistaken. Instead, Idaria felt conflicted, and her eyes widened as she quickly peered over her shoulder in the direction of Golgren's continuing struggle.

"It will only bring danger to them!" she suddenly cried, referring to the elves. "Xiryn will hunt them down once he is done here! There will be no escape anywhere!"

She pulled free of Stefan's hold.

The knight faltered. "My lady . . . Idaria . . . what're you doing?"

"Freeing all of us," the elf solemnly responded. "Freeing Golgren."

Idaria ran back the way they had come.

❦⟐❦

Despite Golgren's nearly successful attack, Xiryn laughed out loud as he saw the elf turn back in his direction. Golgren, frowning, also spotted Idaria and wondered why she wasn't escaping when she had the chance. The gargoyle king gestured at the scene, his servants swarming toward the elf and Solamnic.

You see? Even fate and chance are my servants! Remember my warning and my offer, child of my ambition! Her life for your surrender! I expect no more defiance from you, merely acceptance of what I intend to make of you . . . and me.

The half-breed sneered, his gaze darting from the

macabre figure to where Idaria stood, trapped at the edge by the ancient High Ogres. Farther back, the gargoyles harassed Stefan.

I was much weakened by the act of your creation, ensuring that you would be viable, the shrouded figure mocked Golgren. *It added to my ... physical deterioration, and I was forced not only to mostly observe, but to take on fools as my servants, ever dispensable fools like the Titaness Morgada, who did her part and then died for her greed, as to be expected.*

By then Xiryn had recovered from Golgren's attack. He reached again to grab the half-breed and Safrag. Golgren grunted as the ancient sorcerer's power flowed through him and his pain surged.

We will become one, Xiryn proclaimed once more. *The power of the Fire Rose will bloom for me.*

The awful visage of the gargoyle king filled Golgren's view. Golgren managed to tear his gaze from the withered, decaying face, though not out of any fear of Xiryn. Instead, his attention was drawn to a particular rooftop.

And his eyes widened at what was taking place there.

⋙⋘

"Idaria!" Stefan called back. "You can do nothing for him! Make your way back to me!"

The elf ignored the Solamnic. She could see Golgren far below—the conqueror of both ogre realms, the Grand Khan, the master planner in part to be faulted for her people's situation and yet, through fate, their only hope. He was bent in certain defeat.

"May the gods forgive me if I am wrong," Idaria whispered as she reached the edge with the grotesque figures trying to grab her despite the pendant. "And may Golgren forgive me if I am right."

One of the ghouls snagged her shoulder, but a deft twist by the lithe elf enabled her to pull free. Eyes moist, Idaria smiled.

She dived headfirst off the building.

Behind her, Idaria heard Stefan shout out her name. She had a brief glimpse of Golgren's shocked, staring face before the angle of her swift descent turned him from her sight.

A winged form caught up to her. Even without a proper view, the elf knew it was not Chasm. Whether or not it had been, she would have chosen to do what she did, undulating in midair to avoid being seized by the creature at the last minute.

The ground was nearly upon her. Idaria braced herself, murmuring one last word, one last name: "Golgren . . ."

⚬⚬⚬❦⚬⚬⚬

Idaria vanished from Golgren's sight, but the last sight of her remained burned in his mind. He bared his teeth, and his flashing eyes radiated only a hint of the rage building up inside.

That rage, that elemental anger, poured into the Fire Rose. It easily overwhelmed Xiryn's control and even shook Safrag from the Titan's obsession. Wordlessly, Golgren offered the Titan one choice: Join in his rage or be swept up in it.

Safrag wisely chose to join.

But Xiryn was offered no such option. Instead, Golgren ripped away the power that the gargoyle king

345

had already usurped through him and turned it to his advantage. He pressed the shrouded figure with the forces of the Fire Rose and felt for the first time *fright* emanating from his adversary.

However, Xiryn's many servants were not about to let their master be undone, for his defeat would be theirs also. Those who had been resurrected joined with those still decaying to add their own sorcery to the effort to stop Golgren. Moreover, gargoyles swarmed above, ready to pounce if the opportunity arose.

Golgren looked to Safrag. The Titan nodded and made suggestions, and the half-breed welcomed his efforts. Between the pair, the Fire Rose burned as it never had before.

Guided by the pair, its forces swept over Xiryn's minions. They had desired a new Golden Age, so gold was what they were granted . . . or rather, *became*. Whether resurrected or still wearing the semblance of undeath, the High Ogres' doom was the same. Their bodies suddenly gleamed like the sun, the transformation so immediate, few likely had the chance to suffer it.

A searing wind then cut through their ranks, and as it did, the gold that once had been the High Ogres became a storm of dust that blew through Garantha, making the city sparkle as if it had been transformed into the shining city in the vision shared at one time or another by Dauroth, Safrag, and Golgren.

The gargoyles fared no better. Some did try to turn and flee at the sight of the High Ogres' demise, but the Fire Rose's power was great, and its reach was long. Few reached farther than the capital's outer walls. There was no dramatic display for their ends as there had been for Xiryn's fellow sorcerers; Golgren and Safrag turned the gargoyles into pure vapor and let the same wind carry off that vapor to the four corners of Krynn.

Indeed, not only did the gargoyles in Garantha perish thusly, but so did those that hovered over the areas where the minotaurs and Solamnics marched. The Fire Rose knew no boundaries; wherever the creatures who had served Xiryn flew, perched, or hid, the artifact's magic sought them without mercy.

It was an exhaustive feat, and therein lay its only danger. Though he had focused on the Fire Rose for barely the length of a single breath, in that time Golgren had neglected to concentrate on Xiryn. The High Ogre instantly seized upon that moment to regain his hold upon the pair and the Fire Rose.

It is mine! the gargoyle king roared in Golgren's mind. *We are one! It is destined! I will have it no other way!*

Golgren steeled himself. With very little effort, he again tore mastery of the artifact from Xiryn.

"You made me to control what you could not," he reminded the High Ogre. "I am the impossible—and ultimate—wielder of the Fire Rose."

Xiryn's already-hideous countenance contorted horribly. *You were created to make the Fire Rose and me one! You were created to serve no other purpose!*

"Very well," Golgren darkly answered. "You and it shall be one."

At Golgren's mere thought, the petals of the Fire Rose *opened*. From them erupted a terrible golden flame. It shot high then, despite no wind in that direction, twisted toward Xiryn.

Too late did the High Ogre sense what Golgren intended. Xiryn reached for the half-breed, perhaps with some ill spell in mind, only to be engulfed by the golden flame. The shrouded figure silently screamed as his desiccated body easily burned.

Although Xiryn burned well, he was not reduced to ash. Rather, he merely continued to suffer, his face and form blackening.

"So there, the Rose is yours and you are the Rose's," Golgren concluded bitterly. "You are welcome to each other . . . forever."

As Xiryn continued to shriek, the golden flame bore him up. The gargoyle king shrank but not because he was being burned away. He shrank so he could be fitted between the petals. No more than the size of a blade of grass—and then smaller and smaller yet—the High Ogre was dragged into the artifact. Xiryn was plunged deep into its bowels, the ancient sorcerer screaming all the while.

He vanished into the eternal flames within. Golgren willed the petals to seal again, which they did.

Only then could Xiryn's cries no longer be heard on the mortal plane, though at Golgren's command, they did continue and would continue for all time.

"But it is still not enough," the half-breed finally muttered.

Just then an intense force struck him from behind. As he fell, it was all he could do to maintain even a modicum of control over the Fire Rose. An odd pounding in his head began, as though trying to break what remained of his concentration.

As Golgren struggled to regain his senses, the half-breed heard Safrag say, "A fascinating and informative spectacle! One from which I have learned much, mongrel, such as not to underestimate you, anymore! Hence the spell—last moment, I admit—robbing your focus."

Groaning, Golgren clutched himself at the waist as he rolled onto his side and away from Safrag. The Titan, the Fire Rose in his hand, loomed over the stricken half-breed.

"There is only one little thing I need from you, mongrel, and then I gladly will reunite you with your dead slave! I'd like my prize to be whole again. The fragment, if you please." The gigantic sorcerer extended his taloned hand. "With it, I will create of the ogres an entire new race of Titans! I can see the vision clearly now, the golden city with all its golden population! Can you not see it too?"

"I . . . see only . . . your death," Golgren gasped, his face still pressed against the stone.

"You are mistaken. It is your own death that you see. Now give me the fragment if you wish your fate less terrible than the one we granted that fool of a High Ogre."

"I will . . . not."

The Fire Rose flared. Golgren cried out as it sought to remake him, but then, after a moment, the spell abruptly failed. The half-breed lay still, in pain, but alive.

"The fragment cannot save you forever!" growled Safrag. "It only delays the inevitable! Give it to me!"

Golgren managed to turn his head enough to face his rival. "No, Safrag. You . . . must take it from . . . me."

The Titan's sharp teeth clashed together. His golden orbs flared almost as brightly as the Fire Rose.

The towering sorcerer gripped the artifact tightly in both hands. Its sudden increase in radiance presaged his dire intentions. "Very well, have it your way, mongrel. I *will* take it from what little there is left of you."

Safrag muttered. Golgren's hand shook. He struggled

to keep that hand close to his waist, but the effort clearly took its toll.

"Like calls to like, mongrel! I am master of the main artifact! The spell I cast will not give you what you need to keep the fragment yours much longer!" Safrag raised the Fire Rose above his head. "Surrender to the inevitable! You have no choice."

Golgren's hand began to pull away. With a groan, the half-breed made one final effort.

The fragment slipped through his fingers. He made a halfhearted try to retrieve it but was moving too slowly. Instead, his hand slapped against his waist, but without the valuable prize.

The fragment flew to a victorious Safrag.

XXV

THE FIRE ROSE

Eyes gleaming, Safrag reached for the floating shard.

With the swiftness of a ji-baraki, Golgren rolled onto his feet. His hand left his waist, but he held a dagger identical to the one that he had earlier tossed at the Titan.

It was the second dagger, which he had located in his mother's tomb.

The half-breed lunged.

Safrag didn't notice until the last moment, surprise vying with contempt. "You cannot—"

Golgren seized the fragment with his teeth before the Titan could grasp it. The piece flared as he thrust the dagger toward the sorcerer's stomach.

The Fire Rose glowed, but the abrupt shock in Safrag's face revealed that he was no longer the one wielding its power.

"No!" the Titan began. "I hold it! I hold—"

The dagger, with the energies of the Fire Rose surrounding it, sank deep.

"But *I* control it," Golgren returned through clenched teeth.

Safrag howled. No blood spilled from the wound, only the same fiery energy as that which had embraced the dagger. Safrag had no more blood; he had long become like the second hand that Golgren had gained through the artifact: a shell of what was real, a false miracle, the truth of Sirrion's gift.

Keeping his teeth clenched and ignoring the shard's own powerful energies, Golgren twisted the dagger. His will flowed into the Fire Rose and, therefore, into the blade. As he turned the weapon, Safrag, still howling, turned with it.

The half-breed gave the dagger a final twist *back*.

Like a puzzle, Safrag tore into jagged pieces that went flying in all directions. His desperate cry continued for a moment after his dissolution. The still-living shreds flew beyond the walls of Garantha before they at last burned to ash then scattered.

The Fire Rose floated by itself for a few seconds then dropped. Golgren released the dagger before deftly catching Sirrion's creation.

The blade clattered harmlessly, the energies fading. The ancient weapon was blackened from hilt to point, and the smell of melting metal was everywhere.

Breathing raggedly, Golgren stared at the Fire Rose. The blazing forces within churned wildly, enticingly.

"You do me proud!" declared a maddeningly cheerful voice that made the half-breed grit his teeth. "I expected it to be you, but there were enough variables that made the game so very interesting!"

Golgren spit the fragment out. It paused in the air then flew unerringly to the artifact. Like a child clinging to its mother, the piece adhered to the Fire Rose, the two melding together.

The half-breed looked up. Sirrion smiled benevolently at him. Bright flickers of flame constantly escaped his wild mane of hair.

"You expected it to be me?" Golgren rasped.

"Oh, yes, although the others would have made for some interesting outcomes should they have succeeded!" He waved the thought off. "But enough of that! You have earned the honor of gaining my great gift! You will be the herald, the catalyst, of the new age, during which the ogres will look to me as their chief patron!"

Straightening, Golgren looked up at the lord of fire and alchemy. "You . . . our god?"

Sirrion spread his hands. "And what better herald could I ask? The impossible child! You truly are what the Fire Rose—and thus, I—am about! How droll! How very appropriate this is! You will create a most fitting kingdom to honor me, oh yes."

Golgren wordlessly stepped past the god. He went to the edge of the roof. Midway there, the half-breed took note of the still-floating populace.

Expressionless, Golgren held forth the artifact. The Fire Rose flared.

The ogres began drifting safely to the ground.

With a curt nod, Golgren reached the edge, leaned over, and peered down.

Idaria lay sprawled on the stone walkway below. Her arms and legs were bent at angles that made it seem as though the elf were boneless. Her face was turned skyward and she looked as if she were sleeping . . . if one did not immediately notice the pool of blood that was staining her long, silver hair and shredded gown.

A clink of armor foreshadowed the appearance of Stefan Rennert next to her body. Panting from exertion, the human bent over her. He muttered something that sounded like a prayer.

Golgren suddenly looked over his shoulder at Sirrion, who stood smiling at the outcome. "Can this bring her back to life?"

The smile not in the least fading, the deity casually remarked, "The elf has already moved on. No matter, though. You can use the Fire Rose to give another her semblance if you like!"

"It will not be her."

The smile faltered, a hint of impatience arising in Sirrion. "No, her spirit is gone! I've told you that already! What does that matter? You can create a better Idaria."

Turning to face him, Golgren flatly replied, "Yes, if I chose to keep this thing." He stretched the Fire Rose toward its maker. "I want nothing of it. To restore her life is the only use I have for it. If that is beyond its feeble powers, you may take it back and then leave and never return."

"Take . . . it . . . back?" Sirrion burst into flames. He was a living elemental, pure fire. "Take it back?" he repeated, his voice growing more strident, more painful to hear.

YOU REFUSE THE GREATEST GIFT EVER GRANTED A MORTAL?

His voice was as Golgren and Idaria had first heard it, a terrible thundering in one's head that made Xiryn's a pale whisper by comparison. Yet Golgren did not press his hand to his head, nor did he stagger under the mental onslaught. He calmly stood there, the Fire Rose still extended to Sirrion.

Intense heat washed over the half-breed; then it

enveloped the entire city. Below, cries of panic ensued as many ogres who had witnessed the arrival of the god no doubt assumed that he was about to raze Garantha. Sirrion stalked toward Golgren; the deity was taller and more menacing than any Titan.

AND YOU REFUSE TO WORSHIP ME? ME?

Sweat poured down Golgren's body, but none of it due to fright, only the searing heat. Golgren cocked his head. "I do."

More than four times the mortal's height, the being of flame transformed into the faceless golden sentinel.

YOU CANNOT! NOT WITH ALL I OFFER, ALL THAT YOU FEAR I CAN DO.

A circle of flames surrounded Golgren. It would have been simple to deal with them using the Fire Rose, but he was aware that was what Sirrion desired of him. The more the artifact was used, the more the Fire Rose's ability to seduce increased. Even Golgren, molded—not created—to wield it would eventually succumb to its power. Like a moth drawn to flame, he would immerse himself in the Fire Rose until it burned him out.

WITH MY GIFT, YOU CAN RULE ALL.

"No." Golgren took a step toward the ring. As he suspected, the flames shrank from him regardless of whether he was using the Fire Rose. Sirrion desired his servitude too much.

"No," Golgren repeated as he closed on the elemental giant. "This is not how I desire to rule, for, in truth, it would be the Rose that rules, not me." He paused just within reach of Sirrion. "The ogres will always honor and fear you, Lord of Fire, but I—I, Golgren—will foist no god upon my people. Not you. Not Sargonnas. Not Kiri-Jolith. When we fell, no god smiled upon us then.

Through centuries, we were used and used again, and no god came to *truly* help us. We survived without any of you, and therefore, we do not need you now."

YOU WILL HONOR ME MOST—

Golgren shook his head. "We will honor no god above all the others, not even you."

Though mouthless, Sirrion roared. Fire enveloped Golgren and his surroundings.

Then the flames and the agonizing heat withdrew. Golgren, who had briefly had to shield his eyes from the flames, saw that the robed incarnation of the god had reappeared.

"You will do very fine!" Sirrion remarked jovially. "Once you make up your mind properly!" He gestured at the Fire Rose. "For your keeping, while you think about matters and my gift's usefulness! After all, you have minotaurs deep in the south, Solamnics at another gate, and dark knights testing other boundaries! How valuable a prize my flower might look under those circumstances, and how valuable a caring patron you might have in me."

Sirrion chuckled and flames once again surrounded him. They were so sudden that once more the half-breed had to cover his eyes.

When he was able to see again, it was to discover the god was gone and the artifact was still in Golgren's hand.

"No." Golgren turned, seeking Sirrion. However, there was no sign. The half-breed bared his teeth in anger. "No."

With as much strength as he could muster, Golgren slammed the top of the Fire Rose into the building. The impact was accompanied by a loud, booming noise. A long, jagged crack developed along the building.

But the Fire Rose went unmarred.

Brow furrowed, Golgren sought out other assistance. He looked to where Tyranos and Chasm remained a grotesque, mixed statue.

The Fire Rose made short work of Safrag's diabolical spell. Wizard and gargoyle instantly separated then changed back into their true selves.

Chasm let out a hiss of glee, hopping up and down. The scaled creature flapped his wings, testing them. Again, he hissed merrily.

But what escaped Tyranos's mouth was not any sign of gratitude. Where the guise of a human had once covered him, he was fully recognizable as a minotaur clad in wizard's garb. Summoning the staff, he thrust it toward Golgren.

"You should've changed me immediately! Use the Fire Rose!"

"You would not wish it, wizard. You would be changed inside as well as out."

The minotaur snorted. "What do I care if blood flows in my veins or some magic! I am a spellcaster, after all! Give it to me, then, just for my own transformation! I'll give it back right away! You'll see."

Yet there was a growing avarice in Tyranos's voice that was unmistakable, especially as, with each passing moment, Golgren's own desires increased.

"No," replied the half-breed. "I want you only to tell me how to destroy this."

"You want to destroy it? Ha! The hubris of the great Grand Khan! This is the child of a god! You know what happened to the High Ogres who tried to do as you want! They failed! In desperation, they even tried to hide it forever, but that wasn't possible either!"

Despite those words, Golgren raised the Fire Rose

with the intention of trying a second time to smash it. Then something that Sirrion had said returned to him.

"You can't even try again, can you?" mocked Tyranos, mistaking the half-breed's pause. "You want to use it, after all, don't you?"

Slowly, Golgren shook his head. "No . . . but I must . . ."

❦❦❦

Faros had led his legionaries deeper and deeper into ogre territory. The way remained clear, even more after the astounding destruction of the gargoyles. True, they had not done anything but watch after the Titans had vanished, but the emperor had been certain that at some point they intended to attack. Then the creatures had all taken to the air, shrieked, and turned into vapor.

To Faros, who knew him so well, that could only mean that, against all odds, Golgren had done the impossible, as promised.

And that made the Grand Khan all the more dangerous. Faros was determined to see to it that his old enemy did not live to enjoy his return to power.

A tremor shook the legionaries, sending many dropping to their knees. Great clouds of dust rose everywhere. The ogre lands were rife with such violent movements of the ground, but often they passed swiftly. According to their training, the minotaurs kept themselves still to wait it out.

But the tremor only grew worse, and a shadow rose ahead of Faros. The emperor cautiously got to his feet. At first, all he noticed was the dust.

Then Faros saw the *wall*.

It was as tall as the nearest hills and growing by the moment. He looked left and right and saw no end to it. Just as unnerving, it was *moving,* moving toward the invaders.

"Sound retreat!" Faros shouted. There was no honor in standing their ground and being wiped out by . . . whatever was approaching swiftly. It was magic on a scale that even Faros, who had faced Nephera and her son Ardnor had never experienced.

Horns blared. The alert was picked up by those ahead. The proud lines of the empire began a hasty but orderly flight.

The immense wall reached the hills ahead of the invaders and swallowed them whole. The wall's movement was accompanied by a thunderous sound, the grating of unimaginable tons of rock and earth. Faros had called for the retreat just in time, for it was too loud for even the strongest horns to be heard.

The minotaurs began their retreat in a standard trot. But as Faros looked behind him, he saw that the pace was not enough. Cursing, the emperor ran faster, and those around him followed suit.

Within moments, the retreat became an ignominious rout.

Yet at that point, the wall's pace slowed. It kept the legionaries on the run but never quite caught up to them. The minotaurs were pushed southward, always southward.

Would they be chased all the way to Ambeon?

A hekturion running alongside the emperor waved for his attention. The other minotaur pointed back over his shoulder. Faros looked, wondering what new menace pursued them.

It was not a new menace, not exactly. It was, despite

its fantastic appearance, merely confirmation of Faros's suspicions. Shaped into the wall was the huge relief of a face: Golgren's face.

The Grand Khan's visage loomed over the minotaurs. It was repeated at a regular distance for as far as the emperor could make out. The knowing faces stared down at the soldiers.

The wall stopped.

The halt was so abrupt that many of the legionaries continued to run for some distance before realizing they were no longer pursued. The invaders paused then glanced back at the wall.

Faros warily eyed the many faces of Golgren. Belatedly, he realized that the eyes were not exactly staring at his people, but rather at the ground directly in front of the wall.

It was not over yet.

"Keep them moving!" the emperor ordered the nearest officers. "Keep them moving!"

Although they did not understand why, the officers immediately obeyed. Shouts and horns got the bewildered minotaurs on the move.

No sooner had they begun the retreat anew than the ground shook once more. Yet the wall did not move. Rather, a great crack suddenly cut across the landscape, running parallel to the massive barrier. In moments it covered miles, cutting off any hope by the minotaurs of perhaps seeking to climb the high wall.

The crack became a ravine, a deep, deep ravine. As Faros pulled back with his legionaries, he saw that, like the wall had done earlier, the ravine was spreading in their direction.

And the faces of Golgren kept watch over all of it.

THE GARGOYLE KING

Only minutes before, a confident Sir Augustus had urged the Solamnic forces forward, his intentions mirroring those of Emperor Faros. The half-breed had somehow succeeded in his plans, which to the senior knight meant that it was more important than ever to press on. The ogre realm could not be permitted to rise up under Golgren's cunning rule.

Then a sense of unease had come over Augustus. He knew the feeling, knew that it arose not only from years of honed instinct, but also from some subtle warning by the divine powers that watched over the Solamnic orders.

"Sir Bertrum! Sound the halt! Swiftly!"

The other knight looked puzzled but gave the signal. The horns blared as the expedition came to an immediate stop.

"What is it, my lord?" Bertrum, a younger, black-haired fighter asked. Around them, other knights leaned toward their commander, also curious.

Augustus swallowed in sudden anxiety. He had no source for that abrupt concern, but he trusted his instincts as much as he trusted his beloved nephew. "Turn the ranks about! Now!"

It was not a standard order, but it was an order, so Bertrum signaled for the command to be passed on to the men.

There came a thundering sound.

"The sorcerers are back!" someone growled.

Augustus Rennert shook his head. "No. They're defeated. We'd have never come this far if they had not been."

361

The thundering grew more intense. The ground began to quiver.

Ahead, the horizon grew more distant.

The commander squinted. No, the ground was *rising.*

"Get the lines moving!" he roared.

Bertrum and some of the others stood in their saddles, trying to make out what they saw. "My lord, what—?"

"There's a damned wall racing toward us! Get the men moving, or we'll be crushed by it."

Like the minotaur emperor, Sir Augustus also had no doubt as to the one who was behind the astounding conjuration, and the faces appearing later would only serve to verify his beliefs.

❦

"It is done," Golgren announced, a touch of weariness in his otherwise bland tone. Only his eyes gave any hint that, in actuality, he suffered from far more than a touch of weariness. "The spell will finish itself out. Uruv Suurt, Solamnics, Nerakans . . . all will understand what I wish them to understand."

Tyranos bent over the hunched figure. "You need rest. Give the Fire Rose to me."

Golgren shook his head. "No." He straightened. "No, you do not want this, and I will not give it to you."

"So you do plan to keep it for yourself."

The half-breed glared. "No, I wish to destroy it still."

"Something you cannot do," said another, familiar voice.

They both turned around to see Kiri-Jolith standing beside them. However, the god was not alone. Stefan

Rennert was also standing there, the Solamnic looking pale, almost deathly.

The deity bowed his head to Golgren then eyed the Fire Rose. "And before you ask, it is something that I cannot do either."

Golgren thrust the sinister artifact toward him. "Then take it from Krynn. Take it and place it so far in the heavens that it will be no danger to this world."

Kiri-Jolith looked at the half-breed with interest. "The Grand Khan Golgren now fears for the rest of Krynn?"

"Does not the god of just cause fear for it in the hand of the mongrel, of Guyvir?"

The bison-headed deity shook his head, saying, "I came into this situation concerned for the sake of the humans and the minotaurs, two races of particular interest to me. Yet I also was concerned for the ogres, so long bereft of purpose and guidance . . . until the coming of the one who calls himself *Golgren*. Golgren represented the ogre race's best chance in centuries to rise above the brutality to which they had been condemned, for which they have paid too high a price. I am forbidden to act directly, but I did what I could throughout the years to see to it that such a hope could be nurtured."

That caused Tyranos to snort with derision. "Are you telling us that you *also* had a hand in the emergence of our dear Grand Khan? Ha! What a jest! For one who's strived to be his own creature, Golgren, you seem to belong to everyone else!"

"Golgren's ultimate decisions were and are still his, lost one, just as yours are yours."

The wizard scowled. "If that's the case, then give me the Fire Rose! That's my decision! I want it!"

Once again, Tyranos brandished the staff at Golgren,

that time with clear menace. The two stared at one another, gazes battling. The wizard would not back down, yet neither did Golgren.

Only when Kiri-Jolith stepped between them was the battle of wills broken. "The Fire Rose was not the cause of the High Ogres' fall, but it eliminated any hope of redemption by those few who sought to regain their former glory here. Xiryn was the most ardent of its victims, but he was not alone. When those few who had the will to—for the time being—fight the Rose's seduction—managed to steal it, they called to me to help them destroy it. At that time I could not, due to the nature of its making by Sirrion."

"But it *was* damaged," Tyranos pointed out. "The fragment proves it."

"Damaged, not destroyed and with an effort that cost lives and left the fragment in the control of Xiryn. And though he could not wield it, Xiryn used it through the centuries as a lure, drawing unwary and ambitious spellcasters to his cause while he formulated his master plan and sought the artifact—"

"Which you hid oh so well."

The god continued to ignore the mage's arrogant tone. "Yes, I did guide them to what even I thought was a place where it would remain buried forever. Yet I discounted the obsession of some mortals, like yourself."

"Spare me your woes," Tyranos interjected. "Give me the artifact, and no one need ever worry about it again."

"Xiryn said the same thing. Will you be the next Xiryn?"

"It does not matter," Golgren stated. "You will not have it, wizard, despite our agreement." To the god, the half-breed demanded, "Show me a way to be rid of this."

Stefan, who had been silent all that time, stepped up. "That would be my duty."

Tyranos did not take that lightly. "Yours? Why yours?"

"Because it's my choice," the Solamnic answered calmly. His face was more pale than ever. "And it is a way for me to fulfill the oath I took to myself just before I died."

Golgren arched a brow. "The citadel . . ."

The knight bowed his head. "I was on the edge of death when my patron came to me. But he came to me because I demanded it of him. With my last conscious thought, I prayed to him to let me redeem myself for failing"—he swallowed hard—"for failing Lady Idaria, you, and everyone else, myself included."

"For the gods, there is no more powerful demand that a mortal can make of them than such a prayer at such a time." Kiri-Jolith grunted. "Only you can release yourself from this vow, Sir Stefan Rennert, and I ask you to consider that now."

"I'll not change my mind. I'll do as we discussed. You know my time's short on the mortal plane. You stirred the last embers of my life long enough for me to help, even though I failed to help Idaria."

"Very well." The armored deity reached out a hand to Golgren. "I will take the Fire Rose now."

But Golgren would not give it up yet. "What will be done with it?"

"There is another place. A place between places, truly. There, I will hide it."

"And someone will eventually find it again," argued Tyranos, the crystal on his staff flaring.

"Doubtful, but if they do, this time it will be well guarded."

Stefan straightened, looking proud. "Such is my decision. Until it no longer needs be—even unto the end of time—I will guard the Fire Rose from all tempted by its legend!"

Without any further hesitation, Golgren handed the artifact to Kiri-Jolith, who, in turn, gave it over to the Solamnic. As Stefan took hold of the artifact, the Fire Rose's inner energies faded. Only a hint of its terrible power could be sensed.

The god of just cause then did a startling thing; he went down on one knee before Stefan, in clear homage. "You are what my father, my brother, and I sought to believe of the Knighthood, Sir Stefan Rennert. I am honored."

"The honor is mine to serve," the Solamnic replied. His body took on a translucent appearance. Stefan quickly glanced at the half-breed. "My lord Golgren, forgive me for failing her."

Whether Golgren intended to answer him became a moot point, for even as he finished speaking, Stefan Rennert—and the Fire Rose—vanished.

Tyranos let out a frustrated howl as he leaped to the spot where Stefan had stood. Chasm, who had stood quietly in the shadow of his master, reflected the wizard's frustration with a long, angry growl.

Rising, Kiri-Jolith confronted the minotaur. "There is in my power the ability to grant your request to be transformed, but I would like you first to consider the consequences. Recall those that you loved, those you lost, and what you may lose in the future."

"None of that matters! Change me! Make me no longer a minotaur! Change me!"

But the god did not do so readily. "Now is not the

time. You must discover the full truth about yourself before you can demand of me such a thing . . . if you still desire it then."

"Damn all you gods!" Tyranos bitterly shot back. "Damn all your word games and tricks! That knight was a fool who was probably manipulated into sacrificing his eternity, the elf was tricked into killing herself for an ogre, and you . . ." He spit in Golgren's direction. "You are the biggest fool of all!"

Tyranos raised the staff as if to use it. Then the crystal flared brighter and he, too, disappeared.

Chasm hissed at the god and Golgren then took to the air. Ever linked to his master, undoubtedly he would find the mage wherever Tyranos had chosen to go.

"A pity," Kiri-Jolith murmured. "But destiny still has a heavy hand to play where he is concerned . . . a destiny his own choices still shape." To Golgren, the deity added, "The Fire Rose is no more a part of your life, Grand Khan. Sirrion's capricious interest in you should wane. Such is the nature of fire." He shrugged. "Still, I will watch. Times have changed, and perhaps even the predictability of gods has also."

"And will you now demand fealty of ogres for this offer?"

"No. I owe you for Sirrion, though you will never know the full reason why." When Golgren said nothing in return, Kiri-Jolith concluded, "As I owe you much, I will also do one last favor."

Closing his eyes, the god raised his hands to the sky. As he did, a slight tremor shook Garantha. Golgren, just starting to step away, looked around suspiciously.

The maddening alterations made by Safrag on Garantha melted away, and in their place returned the familiar, centuries-old image of the ogre capital. Kiri-Jolith was restoring the city to what it had always been, thereby erasing the mark of Safrag; the Titans; Xiryn; and most of all, the Fire Rose.

Eyes still shut, Kiri-Jolith muttered under his breath then lowered his hands. The god gave a deep sigh and appeared slighter in size, though still overwhelming.

"It is all the same as it was, save for one small thing I chose to do," Kiri-Jolith said as he opened his eyes again. "I thought you might want the one small thing."

But the bison-headed warrior saw that the half-breed was no longer close to him. Instead, Golgren once more was leaning over and peering down at where Idaria still lay dead, sprawled.

Nodding sadly, the god departed.

XXVI

ASHES

Weeks passed on Krynn, weeks of tension and of not a little fear—all of it focused on the ogre realm.

To the south, legions of minotaurs stood battle-ready, their siege machines prepared. Each fortnight, the ranks were expertly shifted to keep the soldiers ever at their peak. Attack might come at any moment. They faced no ordinary foe.

It was the Grand Khan Golgren.

Solamnic Knights also patrolled those lands nearest to the ogres, but Sir Augustus Rennert was no longer in command. He had left after the retreat to confer with his superiors to discuss what had happened and what could be done.

The Nerakans, too, surveyed the new borders of the ogre realm, but with a trepidation more akin to that of the minotaurs. They prepared for a war certain to come.

Golthuu—the name was only just beginning to spread from Solamnics and the minotaurs to other places—was all but entirely cut off from the rest of Ansalon. A great *canyon* surrounded the combined lands of Kern and Blöde, even cutting through the land of Khur. Behind the canyon—and further securing Golthuu—stood the great wall of stone, a veritable mountain chain wrapping around Golgren's domain.

Curiously, the creation of both wall and canyon had happened in such a manner that those in its path had been given enough warning to flee. Of course, no one believed for a moment that the half-breed ruler had spared lives out of any goodness; rather, it was suggested and accepted that he had simply been displaying how perfect his mastery was over the magic he wielded.

Yet no word—no warning—had been issued from Golthuu until the day Solamnic Knights stationed at the one entry point remaining in the west awoke to find a large column heading out from between the lone crack in the vast wall. That column moved unerringly toward a single land bridge made of stone that had been carved out by the same magic as had created the canyon over which it crossed. Not once had the Solamnics dared to use that bridge; they suspected that it existed solely for some reason known to only the Grand Khan. And on that morning, with the winds high and the skies dark, they discovered that purpose.

The elves numbered in the hundreds, even more perhaps. They were weary and hollow-eyed and their garments were tattered. Yet they did not seem frightened, not even as they marched under the gaze of ogre sentries flanking the gap.

The sentries, in turn, watched the flow of refugees as if very pleased to see them go. As soon as the last of the elves had crossed the bridge, the ogre sentries slipped back into the shadows of the crack, disappearing without a word.

The elves carried food and water with them, enough to last two or three days' journey more. Questioning revealed little, save that they had been rescued by one of their own kind who was helped by a brave human Knight of Solamnia named Stefan Rennert. The elf had vanished, but the knight had led them to a place not far from there before he, too, had disappeared. However, he had told the elves to wait. Ogres would be coming who would, at their master's command, lead them the rest of the way.

The Solamnics took the elves in tow. They would soon be united with their kinsmen and fellow exiles.

And once again, Golthuu and its master settled into an ominous silence.

✧◦❂◦✧

But while the other races and realms worried about the terrifying magic the Grand Khan of the ogres was capable of wielding, in Garantha itself there was no sign of impending war. However, the capital was a somber place, even though its inhabitants attempted to go about their daily lives.

Outwardly, the city looked the same as before, but there had been, as Kiri-Jolith had promised, *one* alteration. It stood at the entrance to the palace, where once a prominent statue of Golgren himself had been set. There was a different figure: a slim, female figure with long, flowing hair who looked with kind eyes upon any who stood before her. One hand reached out, as if to give comfort to the ogres, even though she herself was obviously an elf. The figure was astonishingly lifelike and colored exactly as the one after whom it had been modeled. Many ogres swore that, at times, the female statue did move.

The statue stood atop a large, thick structure of marble that to all appearances seemed solid. However, upon his approach, Golgren had found the marble foundation open and waiting.

Waiting for Idaria's body.

Understanding that, the half-breed had deposited the broken and bloody burden that he had carried with him into the waiting tomb. He set her gently in place then arranged the signet atop the griffon pendant that she still wore upon her breast. Golgren had not marveled when the tomb had then sealed itself, the entrance transformed into just another wall. Gods were capable of many miracles . . . but only up to a point, it seemed.

The Grand Khan had not visited the tomb since then, though guards stood watch over it and servants kept it clean of any dust or debris. Indeed, the ogres of Garantha had seen little of their lord since his return. The revolt spurred by the Titans had collapsed without them or their puppet to shore up support. No other ogre desired to face he who had vanquished the sorcerers and reshaped the land. Golgren's rule was restored.

Despite that, though, the Grand Khan did not issue any great edicts preparing his people for conquest of the other races. He did not summon his warriors from around the realm to lead them into battle. He did not even receive the many missives sent to him by the Solamnics and others. Those rested unopened next to his throne, ignored as if they did not even exist. Indeed, all that the half-breed once disparagingly named Guyvir—*unborn*— had conquered was ignored.

Instead, the once-ambitious Golgren sat day after day, staring at a worn, elven tapestry. It had been restored with the rest of the palace by Sirrion's creation, or perhaps it was one of the last gifts of a sympathetic Kiri-Jolith.

A tapestry of an oak tree . . .

TRACY HICKMAN
Presents
The Anvil of Time

The Sellsword
Cam Banks

The Survivors
Dan Willis

Renegade Wizards
Lucien Soulban

The Forest King
Paul B. Thompson

The lost stories of Krynn's history are coming to light.

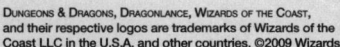

They engulf civilizations.
They thrive on the fallen.
They will cover all trace of your passing.

THE WILDS

THE FANGED CROWN
Jenna Helland

THE RESTLESS SHORE
James P. Davis

THE EDGE OF CHAOS
Jak Koke

WRATH OF THE BLUE LADY
Mel Odom

FORGOTTEN REALMS

The New York Times BEST-SELLING AUTHOR

RICHARD BAKER

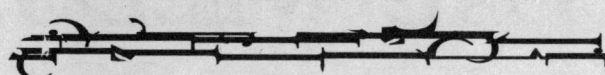

BLADES OF THE MOONSEA

". . . it was so good that the bar has been raised.
Few other fantasy novels will hold up to it, I fear."
—Kevin Mathis, d20zines.com on *Forsaken House*

Book I	Book II	Book III
Swordmage	**Corsair**	**Avenger**
		March 2010

Enter the Year of the Ageless One!

FORGOTTEN REALMS

Ed Greenwood
Presents
Waterdeep

BLACKSTAFF TOWER
STEVEN SCHEND

CITY OF THE DEAD
ROSEMARY JONES

MISTSHORE
JALEIGH JOHNSON

THE GOD CATCHER
ERIN M. EVANS
FEBRUARY 2010

DOWNSHADOW
ERIK SCOTT DE BIE

CIRCLE OF SKULLS
JAMES P. DAVIS
JUNE 2010

Explore the City of Splendors through the eyes of authors
hand-picked by FORGOTTEN REALMS® world creator Ed Greenwood.

OPEN UP A WORLD OF ADVENTURE WITH THE

DUNGEONS & DRAGONS®

ROLEPLAYING GAME STARTER SET

RUN THE GAME
Build your own dungeons and pit your friends against monsters and villains!

PLAY THE GAME
Explore the dungeon with your friends, fight the monsters, and bring back the treasure!

GRAB SOME FRIENDS
AND THE
STARTER SET
AND
START PLAYING TODAY

playdnd.com

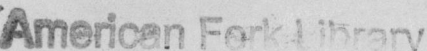